## Monsters

To Lisa,
It is so nice to
finally, meet you! Thank you!
Enjoy!

# Monsters

**Sarah J Dhue**

Sarah J Dhue
2017

First Printing: 2017

ISBN 978-1-365-97089-4

Sarah J Dhue

www.sarahjdhuephotos.com

# Dedication

To my family, Mom and Deborah, for their never-ending support and help with this project.

To my friends, for their support and understanding when I had my nose buried in a notebook, laptop, or one of the many printed drafts.

To Maeva's Coffee, for an environment which fosters creativity, and a very supportive group of employees and fellow customers.

To NaNoWriMo, for challenging me to write 50,000 words in a month. I did it, and then some!


And most of all, to you, my beloved readers.

*To Dad – for always encouraging me to be creative, introducing me to the Universal Monsters and other old movies, and sharing some of your own paranormal fiction with me when I was just a kid. You were one of my first creative role models and I wish you were here to read this; it's your kind of story.*

3

# Introduction

This is a world much like our own. People work day in and day out, bustle about on public transit. Fall in love and raise families. Crimes are committed, heroes serve justice, and tyrants fight for positions of power.

But in this world so much like our own, monsters are not merely legends told around the campfire: vampires lurk in the night, werewolves run under the full moon, shapeshifters hide behind borrowed veneers, and magicians weave fantastic spells – for a price. They are living breathing citizens among the hustle and bustle of everyday life. In this world, sometimes the lines of what a true monster is get blurred; sometimes the true monsters are just everyday folk.

These are their stories: the monsters, everyday people, and most of all, the *true* monsters hiding behind human faces.

# Chapter I

Edward Jekyll sat at a table for two on the sidewalk in front of the café. The wind gently tousled his short brown hair as he reached into his coat pocket and wrapped his fingers around the small box. Despite the brisk weather, he was clammy. Today was the day. He had rehearsed this moment in his mind for years, but now that it was here, he felt both exhilarated and nauseous.

His green eyes surveyed the busy street and sidewalk, searching for her familiar face. Elsa McIntire. He had known she was the one almost instantly. Not only was she physically beautiful, but she had a glimmering beauty within.

While Edward strived to be a good man, he knew deep down that he allowed his hate to control his decisions far too often. His despise for monsters was no secret. Being a journalist that covered mostly the crime scene, his disdain and prejudice rang out loud and clear to all his readers. But overall, he liked to think he was a good man.

In spite of his shortcomings – his hate - Elsa had stuck by his side all of these years. Not only stuck by him, but loved him wholeheartedly. Edward knew that she was too good for him, which was why he had put off this moment for so long. But he could wait no longer. He knew in his heart that this was what he wanted. He was in love with Elsa McIntire, and he wanted to spend the rest of his life with her.

He felt a combination of jubilance and heartache knowing that she would undoubtedly say yes; while he loved her more than anything, he only wanted the best for her. And in his humble opinion, he was not 'the best.' Edward swore to himself that he would try - even harder than he ever had - to be a better man. A better man for himself, but even more so for Elsa.

Ah! There she was, walking down the street toward him, wearing the white denim jacket he had bought her for their one year anniversary. Her blonde hair was pulled back in a ponytail, her bangs falling into her hazel eyes as she walked down the sidewalk looking down at her smartphone.

Edward suddenly felt a wave of nervousness envelope him and clumsily shuffled to his feet, pulling out Elsa's chair for her. She looked up from her phone, brushing her bangs behind her ear. When she saw him, a smile spread across her lips. "Hey."

"Hello dear," he said as she pecked him on the cheek before sitting down. He pushed in her chair, and then sat down across from her.

"So, how was your day?" She rested her elbow on the table, leaning her face against her hand.

"Pretty good. Haven't had a decent case to follow in the past few days... but good, nonetheless." He began bouncing his leg anxiously, trying to work up the nerve to ask her that elusive question. Maybe he should wait until after they'd had their food. "What about you?"

"Oh, same old same old. Better now." She reached across the table, gripping his hand. She felt it drenched in sweat. "Are you okay?" Elsa's tone grew serious.

"Fine. Just trying to decide what to order," Edward half-lied. He actually had been so worked up about popping the question that he had totally forgotten to even glance through the menu. He picked it up, perusing the soup options. Maybe that would kill the queasiness growing in his stomach.

Elsa looked at him suspiciously, her lips forming into a sly smile. "Okay..." She also picked up her menu, even though she was fairly certain she would just order the special.

Edward knew that Elsa wasn't dumb; she knew him better than anyone. She knew something was up. He exhaled heavily. He wanted the moment, when it came, to be a complete surprise. He had to calm himself, act normal, pretend the box in his pocket didn't feel heavier by the second. The waiter came to take their order and then took their menus.

"So at work today there was this super adorable golden retriever that got brought in for a checkup. Cutest thing, and sweet too," Elsa gushed, thinking about the dog. Edward was listening to her, but his mind kept wandering to why he had actually asked her to meet him here. Elsa was a veterinary assistant; she was particularly fond of large friendly dogs. Edward kept telling himself that he was going to get her a dog someday. But a dog was a serious commitment, just like some other things…

"Really Edward, what's wrong?" Elsa reached across the table to grip his hand, her voice breaking through his thoughts.

He looked up at her, his eyes meeting hers. He smiled, taking in every detail of her face: her tightened jaw, the worried look in her eyes. "Nothing's wrong… Elsa, I love you. I… I try to be a good man. Lord knows I try, but I'm jaded. Bitter because of my past." She chuckled exasperatedly, squeezing his hand. "But I am really going to try; to try to be a better man for you. Because there is no room for hate in a life filled with love." He absently put his free hand in his coat pocket, fondling the small box. In all twenty-eight years of his life, he could not recall ever feeling so nervous. "That's all I want for us. A life filled with love, *our* love. Elsa, I-"

"Thief! *Thief!*" a man's voice rang out, and Edward saw a man running out of the retail outlet down the street, ducking through the pedestrians with a large bundle tucked under his arm.

10

The shop owner, a large Chinese man, was yelling after him and pointing. "Stop, thief!"

Edward pulled his hand free from Elsa's and began running down the street after the guy. He had not seen the man's face as he had run out of the store, but he had seen his blue windbreaker. Edward nearly tripped on the bundle, which now sat in the middle of the sidewalk. It would appear the robber had dropped it in his attempt to escape. Edward looked around and noticed a man in a blue jacket standing at the crosswalk waiting to cross. He was no longer running, trying to blend in to the crowd.

"Hey, you!" Edward shouted, grabbing the man's shoulders. He could hear sirens behind him, the police arriving at the retail outlet.

"Let go of me, man!" The thief flailed around, trying to break free, grabbing ahold of Edward's scarf. "You've got the wrong guy, let go of me!"

Edward looked over his shoulder to see the shop owner directing the police to the street corner he and the thief were standing on. "Good, the police are here."

"I'm telling you, I didn't do anything! *Let me go!*" He swung at Edward in an attempt to punch him and narrowly missed. It was then that Edward got a good look at his face.

"Hey, I know you. You're that reporter for *The Southern Bell*. You're Lawrence Talbot, the shapeshifter."

"And I know exactly who *you* are," Lawrence said with disdain. "There isn't a monster out there who doesn't know who you are, Edward Jekyll." He spat the name. "Is that why you're trying to pin something on me? Because I'm a shapeshifter? Because I'm 'abnormal'?" Lawrence was fairly short, with wild brown hair and intense cerulean eyes. His jawline revealed the beginnings of a beard.

The police approached. "No," Edward defended himself, "you're wearing a blue jacket, just like the thief. And besides, now that you mention it, shapeshifting is a handy ability for getting away with theft."

"So what? You're wearing a blue jacket too." Lawrence poked his index finger against Edward's jacket. "That doesn't prove anything."

"Is that him?" one of the officers asked.

"Yes, this is him." Edward released his grip on Lawrence.

"I didn't do anything, this crazy asshole just has a vendetta against my kind." Lawrence irritably readjusted his jacket.

"Thanks Jekyll." The other cop tipped his hat to him. He turned to Lawrence. "What do you mean 'your kind'?"

"You mean you don't know who I am? Well I'll tell you: I'm Lawrence Talbot, undercover reporter for *The Southern Bell*. And I'm going to be straight with you, gentlemen, I *am* a registered shapeshifter."

"Do you have your ID and registration card?" the first officer asked.

"Yes sir." Lawrence reached into his pocket, and the second officer rested his hand on his holster. Lawrence brought out his wallet, smirking at the officer before opening it and taking out a few cards, handing them to the first officer. "Go ahead and check the security footage. You won't see me. Or my jacket." He leered at Edward.

"Let's run these in the system first to make sure everything checks out, and then do that." The first officer looked up from the identification cards at the second officer, who nodded. "Mr. Talbot, would you please come with us?"

"Of course. I have nothing to hide." He went without a fight, and Edward slowly walked back to the café.

"What happened?" Elsa asked worriedly as he sat down across from her.

"A robbery. I think I caught the guy, but we'll see." He was watching the police confirm Lawrence's information over Elsa's shoulder. They put Lawrence in the back of the police car,

13

recovered the stolen goods from the sidewalk, and entered the store. Edward nervously stirred his now-cold soup with his spoon. After what felt like eons, the two exited the shop and let Lawrence out of the cruiser, handing him back his identification cards. The first cop climbed into the driver seat, but the second approached Edward and Elsa's table as Lawrence walked away on down the street.

"Everything checked out in his favor," the officer said, resting his hand on Edward's shoulder. "He wasn't on the footage. Even if he had changed his appearance, it would appear that the thief was wearing a different style of jacket. Thanks for trying though. At least the goods were recovered." He removed his hand and set his jaw. "See ya around, Jekyll." He walked back to the cruiser and climbed in. Edward watched in bewilderment as they drove away.

"Edward?" Elsa said after a few minutes of awkward silence. She saw tears forming along the brim of his eyes.

That perfect moment, that moment he had waited so long for, was now ruined. He felt so angry now that he knew it could not possibly be the right time. No, it would have to wait again, as it had so many times before. And all for nothing. Even if that dirtbag had been innocent this time, Edward was sure he was guilty of other crimes. Shapeshifters always were.

"Edward?" she repeated.

"I'm fine," he said, blinking away his tears. "I'm just disappointed that they didn't catch the guy, that's all. And I ran out on our lunch date. I'm such an idiot."

Elsa reached across the table and stroked his clean-shaven cheek. He liked the way her cool smooth hand felt on his skin, and he nuzzled his face into her palm. He inhaled heavily, tantalized by the faint scent of her perfume. "You were just trying to do the right thing. You never give yourself enough credit," she cooed reassuringly.

"Yeah..." Edward forced a half-smile. Because he knew that while his intentions had begun purely enough, as soon as he'd seen Talbot's face and known who – what – he was, it had no longer been about catching a thief; it had been about taking out a monster. He wished more than anything that he could have put that monster behind bars since he had missed his chance to pop the question for the time being. Then at least he would have gotten something out of it.

"Come on, let's go home." Elsa stood, removing her hand from his face and interlocking her fingers with his.

"All right." He smiled for real in spite of himself and kissed her on the mouth.

As they walked away hand in hand, someone wearing gloves grabbed Edward's spoon out of his chilled soup.

# Chapter 2

Kurt Farkas sat up in bed, rubbing his face and eyes. He stretched, his toned arms flexing, his shirt being pulled taut over his thick chest. He threw the covers off and flung his legs over the side of the bed, the hardwood floor cold under his bare feet. He walked into his bathroom and flipped on the light.

The man he saw in the mirror's brown eyes looked groggy, still distant and not ready for the day ahead of him. He had a severe case of bed head; his hair was not necessarily long, but he had just enough so that he had to tuck it behind his ears and it rested on the collar of his jacket. He had a somewhat boyish face, clean-shaven with a rounded jaw but defined cheekbones, his ears framed by sideburns.

He ran his fingers through his hair in an attempt to flatten it, finally giving up and grabbing his comb. Once his hair was halfway presentable, he splashed water on his face and dabbed it dry with a towel.

He went back into his room and looked at the calendar. Only a few days until the next full moon. Kurt always hated that time of the month. He knew there were institutions for his kind: corridor after corridor of high security cells they could stay in from sunset until sunrise. Kurt utilized them whenever necessary. But he still hated the uncertainty, the chance of him or someone else breaking out.

Ever since the day he was born, Kurt Farkas had been a werewolf. He did not have a dramatic story like many he had met at the institution, about being attacked and barely escaping with their lives. He had always been like this, an unfortunate trait that his mother had passed down to him.

He had spent a good number of the twenty-seven years of his life trying to find a way to rid himself of his curse. While he typically was locked safely away during the full moon, there were a few times in his teen years when he had killed. They had never traced the maulings back to him, but they still weighed on his conscience every day.

He just wanted to live a normal life. A life without fear of losing control and hurting someone. A life without having to be locked up in a cell for three to five nights every month.

Kurt actually lived a very lonely life for fear that he would grow too close to someone and become careless. He had heard many stories of such tragedies, and he did not want to be responsible for the death of someone he cared for; the deaths of those he did not know that he had been responsible for were enough to keep him awake at night.

He worked as a sales associate at Home Depot: lugging around lumber, rolling dollies of appliances out to cars, stocking the shelves with heavy home and lawn equipment. The work kept him busy and in shape, as well as put food on the table.

Kurt grabbed a towel from the hallway shelf and went back into his bathroom, turning on the shower to allow the water to warm up. He began to shed his clothes, looking at himself in the mirror. For a man who turned into a wolf every month, he had much less body hair than one would expect.

He climbed into the shower, the hot water hitting his body refreshingly. He finally began to feel like he was actually waking up. Showers usually did the trick. That or a nice hot cup of coffee.

# Chapter 3

Carmichael Wilhelm III sat in the dim waiting room in a cushy faux leather chair. He bounced his foot rhythmically, his sweaty palms resting on his knees. Even in the dim light, his blue eyes glowed slightly, shadows emphasizing his sunken cheeks and pronounced cheekbones. He looked up at the clock, nervously running his hand through his short blonde hair.

He almost had not come. Yet here he was, nervously waiting in the otherwise empty waiting room of psychiatrist Dr. Brook Hydecker's office. After all, he had been putting something like this off for centuries.

A door opened, and a man with cropped dark brown hair stuck his head out. His hair appeared to be growing out from a crew cut, a thin mustache and goatee accenting thin lips, his olive eyes hidden behind round wire-framed glasses. "Carmichael?" he said, looking at the lone man sitting in the waiting room.

"Guess that's my cue," Carmichael muttered under his breath, standing and picking up his scarf which was balled up next to him in the chair. The man – whom Carmichael assumed was Dr. Hydecker – held the door open for him, and Carmichael entered an office as dimly lit as the waiting area. Not that it bothered him, he could see just fine.

The man walked over to a rolling chair and sat down in it, a clipboard and pen in his hand. A desk stood to the side of the chair.

"Please, have a seat," he looked at Carmichael, motioning toward a leather couch positioned so that it was facing the chair. Carmichael plopped down on the sofa, setting his scarf down beside him. "I suppose we should start with introductions. I am Dr. Brook Hydecker."

"Carmichael Wilhelm III," Carmichael said flatly. This whole affair seemed forced to him; they already knew each other's names.

"Nice to meet you, Carmichael. All right, now tell me a little bit about yourself. Why you wanted to start seeing me." Brook shifted in his chair, causing it to creak. "I usually don't take evening appointments, but my secretary said you were quite insistent, and I like to be accommodating when I can."

"Well," Carmichael stared at Dr. Hydecker, not breaking eye contact, his eyes maintaining that slight glow, "I suppose the first thing you should know about me is that I am a vampire."

Brook's eyes widened. "Well, that is a first for me." He jotted something down on his clipboard.

"Yes, my kind seem to be few and far between these days," Carmichael remarked. "Other things about me... I have wooed many women. Possibly fathered several children. Held almost any job imaginable - that interested me anyway. I have seen and done it all – and yet here I am. Alone and on the brink of suicide. I would have tried, you know," he leaned forward, his eyes glowing a little brighter, "but it's too complicated for me." He leaned back, turning away from Brook, his voice softening. "Immortality isn't all it's cracked up to be... I have just lost interest in life – in existing."

Brook had been jotting down notes on his clipboard, but now lifted his pen from the paper, looking at Carmichael. "I can see where you are coming from. But seeing the world change, all of the technological and cultural advances, it must be fascinating to some extent."

Carmichael stifled a scoff. He tightened his jaw, staring at Brook. "Remember black and white TV? Remember *no* TV? Now they have electronic streaming from the Internet right to your color flat screen high def television. It just ceases to amaze me anymore." Carmichael licked his lips. "It's enough to make anyone want to blow their brains out." Brook winced. "But then again, that wouldn't do anything to me." Carmichael realized he was stalling. "But I digress," he said quietly, "point is, I've been putting something like this off for a long time. I want to enjoy living again… to find something worth living for. A spark."

"Well I'm glad you sought out help instead of turning to suicide. I want to start seeing you on a regular basis. I will do everything in my power to help you regain your zest for living again." Dr. Hydecker stood, extending his hand to Carmichael.

"*There are much stronger powers than your patronizing words,*" Carmichael thought, but stopped himself from saying it out loud. "We'll see." He shook Dr. Hydecker's hand and exited the office. The night was cool, the road glistening in the streetlights from the rain earlier that evening.

# Chapter 4

A man stood shrouded in the shadows of the dark alley, his face hidden in the blackness. The hour was late, the moon hidden by hazy clouds. A dim purple neon sign buzzed at the far end of the alley. It was nothing special, just a violet triangle with a W in the middle, and it looked like it might go out at any moment. The mystery man lit a cigarette, the tip glowing orange as he blew streams of smoke out through his nostrils. He looked up at the soft glow of the moon barely visible through the clouds, trying to ignore the irritating buzzing of the sign.

A small door beneath the neon sign swung open. An old woman's voice rasped, "You wanted to see me?"

"Yes." The man took a long drag on his cigarette.

There was a moment of pause. "Put on your real face before entering. Then we can talk business."

The man coughed, taken aback by the hag's perception. His face slowly morphed in the dim purple light to reveal him as Lawrence Talbot. He walked toward the door, and his eyes beheld the form of a stooped old woman leaning on a crooked cane, her shoulders covered by a thin spider web shawl. "Do you mind?" he asked, indicating his half-smoked cigarette.

"Not at all." He saw a smile spread across her aged face as he followed her into the small room. The door slammed shut behind them on its own, and Lawrence thought he heard it lock. "So what is it that you want, Mr. Talbot?" She sat down at the far end of a round table; Lawrence remained standing. The table was covered in a magenta cloth, the only source of illumination a crystal ball at its center. It cast harsh shadows upwards across her and Lawrence's faces, and he could now see that one of her eyes was milky white while the other was black as pitch.

"To put someone in their place." He clenched his hands into fists by his sides. "For too long he has slandered our kind! Monsters. I nearly went to jail today because of him, because of his false accusations. Thankfully I was able to prove my innocence; I am an undercover journalist after all, I have to be able to get myself out of sticky situations. But not everyone will be so lucky. This has to stop. It's time to teach this man a lesson."

"And of whom are you speaking?" she asked, amused.

"His name is Edward Jekyll." Lawrence noticed her tense a little at the name. "You've heard of him?"

"Once or twice. Crime writer or some nonsense. What exactly do you want me to do?" the witch asked, licking her lips.

"Simple. Turn him into what he hates the most. Turn him into a monster." He reached into his pocket carefully. "I know you'll need something personal. His fingerprints should be on this." He handed her a small item rolled up in a dish towel. She unwrapped it to reveal a used soup spoon.

She examined it a moment with her black eye and her smile widened, revealing the few yellowed teeth that she had left. Lawrence could have sworn the crystal glowed a little brighter. "Yes, this will do quite nicely. Please, wait outside; I cannot work with people watching. I shan't be long."

# Chapter 5

Edward sat in bed, leaning against his propped up pillow. The cool fabric of the pillow case felt good on his bare back. He had been researching Lawrence Talbot on his tablet, trying to find some kind of dirt on him. Just the way the guy acted... even if he had not been a monster, there was just something not right about him. He had found out that Lawrence being an undercover reporter for *The Southern Bell* had made many people and companies uncomfortable that he could take on the appearance of someone different to get information for a story. As far as anything incriminating, he had come up empty-handed, and was now sitting on the bed staring at nothing, his legs hidden underneath a sizable comforter. His tablet had long since switched to its screensaver mode.

He looked up as Elsa walked into the room in her pajamas, her long hair down and flowing past her shoulders. "Hey handsome." She smiled at him and he smiled back.

"Hey."

She climbed on the bed next to him, resting her hand on his chest and nuzzling her face against his neck. The smell of her minty toothpaste tickled his nostrils. "Whatcha doin'?"

"I was just reading." He picked up his tablet from his lap, shutting it off and moving it to the bedside table.

"Hey, earlier, at the café, you wanted to tell me something. Then that guy robbed the store and once that fiasco was all said and done, you totally abandoned the subject. What did you want to talk about?" She looked up at him, scratching his chest gently.

He looked down at her. "It was nothing that important... I just wanted you to know that you mean the world to me." She smiled and kissed his jaw, humming contentedly. "I don't know what I ever did to deserve someone as special as you."

She grimaced, her eyes wandering to the foot of the bed. "What you said earlier, about wanting to be a good man," she said quietly, "you are a good man. You just have flaws and you make mistakes, everyone does. Nobody's perfect. Your hate is just... one of those flaws. But deep down you have a good heart, and I love you for it."

"You're perfect," he said, leaning his cheek against her forehead.

"No. I know that you think so, but I'm not." She tucked her legs under the covers. "But we have each other, and that's what's perfect..." Her voice trailed off as she began to drift off to sleep. In that moment, Edward had no doubt that he wanted to marry her. No fears to stop him from telling her, from asking her to be his forever. Just sleep, which had already taken her and was slowly creeping up on him.

# Chapter 6

"Will Dr. Alexei Frankenstein please come forward and address the board?" Chairman Lance Vapelli said loudly.

Alexei ran his long fingers through his grey pompadour and adjusted his white lab coat before walking to the front of the room. He was an older man with a scraggly grey beard and dim olive eyes, but he carried himself as if he were not a day over thirty.

"Good afternoon, gentlemen. I am Dr. Alexei Frankenstein, as most of you know. Today I want to show you an invention I have created for the sole purpose of producing light bulbs more efficiently than ever before, thus creating more profit. Productivity would be at a record high! Now, let me show you how it works."

He walked to the back of the room, gripping the handle of a covered palette cart and rolling it to the front of the room.

"Behold!" he shouted excitedly, pulling the tarp away that was covering the apparatus. "The Lux600 prototype!" The machine was approximately the size of a small car, with several moving parts and openings of varying sizes and shapes for completed bulbs to be extracted from. "Watch and be amazed."

As he flicked some switches and the machinery hummed to life, the chairman sighed and leaned over to his neighbor. "I hope this isn't another one of his illogical deathtraps. We have quite a bit of business to be attending to." His neighbor nodded in agreement; everyone in the room was all too familiar with Alexei Frankenstein and his reputation. Sure, he was the most intelligent man living in the modern age. While he had made several contributions to society as well as the scientific community, it was also no secret that the man was completely insane. Chairman Vapelli suspected that while it was his and several others' opinion that Frankenstein should be locked up in an asylum, that it was his contributions that kept him a free man.

"And... there!" The machine began whirring and let out a large belch of exhaust. Within a few minutes, Dr. Frankenstein reached into one of the openings and retrieved a light bulb. He screwed it into a nearby lamp and pulled the chain to click it on. The bulb lit up, then with a fizzle and a pop, went out. Alexei felt a pit forming in his stomach during the following silence.

Chairman Vapelli leaned forward slowly, folding his hands in front of him on the desk. He was a portly man, with a strip of brown hair that wrapped around the back of his head, the top of his cranium shiny and bare. He wore round glasses that rested on his pug nose, obscuring his blue eyes. "Dr. Frankenstein, I must ask – respectfully of course – if you tested your latest invention before coming here?"

34

"Of course I tested it! It must have been a bad filament, that can happen with any bulb. I can-"

"I'm not just referring to the bulb." Chairman Vapelli took a deep breath, peering over his glasses at Alexei. "That billow of exhaust was just ghastly. The planet is in enough trouble as it is, what now with the 'Go Green' campaigns to save it. If we had your machines implanted in factories, it would only add to the pollution problem. *Immensely*. And how much would it cost to produce a Lux600?"

"It is not as noticeable in larger spaces – it is not as much exhaust as it seemed. I would say that it took... about..." Alexei's voice trailed off as he searched for a dollar amount to give the chairman.

Several members began taking notes and murmuring among themselves. Finally Chairman Vapelli sat up straight, facing Alexei once more, a small sneer visible on his lips. "After a short evaluation, we have decided to turn down your proposal."

"What!?" Alexei said loudly, his voice echoing around the room.

"Listen, Dr. Frankenstein, we would be more than happy to review your proposal again at a later date. *If* you make some changes. Use a cleaner fuel, for instance – something to make the operation more eco-friendly. And give us an actual estimate of the

cost. Perhaps next time a 'faulty filament' won't sabotage you."
He gathered up his papers, preparing for the next presenter.

"I know a thing or two about electricity," Alexei said emphatically, refusing to budge from the show floor.

Chairman Vapelli did not look up. "Yes, we've heard about your... zombie child." Alexei clenched his fist, tightening his jaw in a hateful glare. "How is he doing, by the way? Still alive and well, I presume." He looked up at the disgruntled doctor.

"He's not a child!" Alexei shouted, his eyes burning into Chairman Vapelli's.

Chairman Vapelli chuckled, dropping Alexei's gaze. "Well, whatever he is, I hope he exceeds the performance of your 'Faulty Bulb and Pollution Producer.'"

Alexei lunged forward, and the chairman fixed his gaze on him again as the security guard rested his hand on his baton.

"Alexei, please just leave. Make the changes to the machine. I wouldn't want to have you arrested. Especially after all the *good* work you have done for us over the years."

Alexei glanced over at the guard, then back at Chairman Vapelli. "That's 'Doctor' to you," he said, fluffing his jacket. "You're all idiots... utter dimwits!" He turned on his heels, promptly exiting the room, smirking at the security guard as he passed.

36

"Dimwits. Fools," Alexei muttered as he made his way to his car. He opened the driver door of his clunky grey Oldsmobile and plopped into the torn leather seat, slamming the door closed behind him. He took a few deep breaths and then jammed his key into the ignition and twisted it, speeding out of the parking lot. They could keep the damn prototype, not that any of them would know what to do with it.

Alexei drove through town until he was driving down a street with several empty storefronts. He parked along the curb in front of a brick building with a large white and red 'For Lease' sign in the front window. He climbed out of his car and manually locked it, walking down the sidewalk with his hands buried in his pockets. He walked with his shoulders hunched and a scowl on his face, cursing crossly to himself as he went.

Suddenly he stopped, ducking between two buildings and making his way to a set of locked storm cellar doors. He twirled his keyring around his finger before inserting a small silver key into the lock and pulling open the doors to reveal a dark tunnel descending deep under the street and buildings. Alexei stepped onto the stairway leading down, lowering the door over him. He fished in his pocket, pulling out a small flashlight and clicking it on as he continued down.

To some the walk would have seemed long and arduous, but he had taken this trek so many times that he could likely traverse the stairs in the dark; however, he was too old to risk a fall like that. He reached the bottom and pushed open the heavy metal door in front of him.

He walked through the doorway into his lab. He had to keep a low profile and the location of his lab a secret. There were several other scientists and business tycoons chomping at the bit to steal his secrets. Once, long ago, he'd had a lab broken into. It had only taken that one time for him to decide he needed to work in secrecy, emerging only when he had something to show the world. Although, there were several projects that never left the lab.

Alexei slumped into a metal chair, resting his elbows on the table and sighing heavily. He stared at the chemistry set in front on him: flasks, test tubes, Bunsen burners… all fairly simple things, but when he took them in his hands and let his mind run free, he could make extraordinary things. Only to have dolts like Chairman Vapelli tell him to make changes.

Chairman Lance Vapelli had had it out for Dr. Alexei Frankenstein for years. Anyone who was anyone knew that. He had not liked Alexei from the first time they'd met: some thought he envied Alexei's heightened intellect, while others thought there was something about their personalities that just did not click,

38

while yet others thought that Vapelli thought it was an injustice that Dr. Alexei Frankenstein was free to do as he pleased instead of locked up in an asylum. The first time that Chairman Vapelli was given a reason to dislike the man was when he had rejected a serum Alexei had developed. He had gone into a blind rage, tearing up the show room, yelling that Vapelli was an idiot. Vapelli had pushed to have him locked up, but the government always sided with Frankenstein, if for no other reason than having his brain to pick and use against their rivals.

"How'd it go?" a gentle male voice said from behind him, a pallid green hand resting on his shoulder.

"Terrible, Jesse," Alexei rasped back. "Please… I'd like to be left alone," he suddenly sat up straighter, tugging at his lapels, "there are revisions to be made! Work to be done!"

# Chapter 7

"Benson, I want you to cover the new Langston Bakery opening down on Central Avenue." Harley Dauber, the editor in chief of *The Metzen Gazette* leaned back in his chair, a toothpick clenched in his teeth. Harley was a thickly built man, typically wearing a white polo shirt with black suspenders attached to khaki pants. He wore thick rimmed square glasses that slightly distorted his dark eyes and always seemed to be sliding down his bulbous nose. His hair – what was left of it anyway – was a deep shade of auburn, a few strands combed across the top of his quickly balding head.

Matilda Benson rolled her brown eyes, the light causing them to appear violet when it hit them just right. She tossed back her shoulder-length black hair and looked across the table at him. "Come on, Harley, nobody really wants to read about that. I want a good story, something people will actually want to read. I want stories like Lawrence Talbot over at *The Southern Bell*, but I want to get them the ethical way. By going out there and finding a good story that the other papers aren't writing about." She sighed, readjusting her brown suede jacket.

"Look, Benson, we've been over this a thousand times," Harley pushed his glasses up on his nose, "we're on a tight schedule here, I can't afford for you to go around hoping that you find a good story. Talbot may be a slime ball, but he gets good stories that way. You can't change your face into anybody or anything you want. So please, take the bakery story." Harley impatiently pushed a manila folder across the desk, picking up a stack of papers by his keyboard and shuffling through them.

"Fine, I'll write the boring story. But mark my words, Harley. I am going to come in here with a news story that will knock your socks right off." She shook the folder, turning to exit his office.

"I can't wait," he retorted nonchalantly.

Matilda stepped out into the hall, fuming. She had become a journalist to write fascinating stories, to talk to people. Instead she got stuck covering the opening of some shop everyone was raving about. Harley always stuck her with these kinds of stories – sometimes, she thought, on purpose. Whether he thought he had more experienced writers to cover the big stories or he thought he was protecting her from the harsh world, she did not care. She knew she was fully capable of handling herself. And she was going to show Harley Dauber. She was going to show all of them when she found a really intriguing story.

# Chapter 8

Matilda wandered through the bar, her notepad in her hand. She was not quite sure how she had ended up here of all places. Maybe she had seen an interesting looking fellow on the street and attempted to follow him, ending up in the boozy nightlife scene. At least the bar was not one of those kinds that was falling apart at the seams. It had a fairly nice pool table, a vintage jukebox giving off a neon glow, and several small tables dispersed around the bar which actually had vinyl cushions on the stools.

Kurt sat at the bar sipping a whiskey sour. It had been a long day at work. One of the forklift operators had barely misjudged as he was backing and took out the side of a lumber shelf. Kurt had spent most of his day helping a few of his co-workers try to stabilize the shelf and then loading the lumber had begun. Of course people wanting to buy wood for new decks or God knows what had complained about the inconvenience. Kurt just smiled and gave them what they needed; he had found that was the best way to treat angry customers.

Matilda made her way through the crowd to the bar and climbed up on a stool by Kurt. She set down her notepad, resting her elbow on the edge of the bar and leaning her head forward so that it rested in her hand, rubbing her temples in frustration. Maybe Harley had been right, maybe she should stick to boring articles that just wrote themselves.

Kurt noticed her next to him. "Rough day?" he asked, finishing what was left of his drink.

"You don't know the half of it," Matilda glanced at him from under her hand.

"Buy you a drink?" he offered, taking note of the way she was dressed: her suede jacket, buttoned black vest with a gold chain over a white camisole, knee-length brown skirt, and black pumps. She was not attired as most people he saw in this bar – classier.

Matilda blew her breath, but appreciated the gesture. "Sure." What could it hurt? It was not like he could drug it with the bartender right there where he could hand the drink right to her. "Thanks," she added in a softer tone.

"What'll you have?" He smiled, turning so that he was facing her.

"Oh hell, I don't know. I usually just drink wine at home... a cosmo I guess."

"Another one for me and a cosmo please," Kurt tapped the counter with his glass. He turned back to Matilda. "So what brings you into this neck of the woods? I'm Kurt, by the way. Kurt Farkas." He extended his hand.

44

"Matilda Benson, I write for *The Metzen Gazette*. I came here to get a good story, but I guess I overestimated my abilities." She shook his hand.

"I think I've read one or two of your articles. They aren't half bad."

The bartender set down their drinks.

"Ha, yeah, if you consider bakery reviews and business specials 'news.' I want to write something worth reading. I want a *real* story about *real* people." She took a sip of her cosmo. "Tangy," she commented. She looked apologetically at Kurt. "I'm sorry, I should probably go-"

"No, wait," Kurt reached out but did not grab her arm; he did not want to come off as brusque, which he certainly was not. "You said you want a real story? About real people? I'm a man with a story." His eyes darted to her empty notepad, then back to her face. He took a deep breath, "I'm a werewolf," he said quietly.

At this, Matilda seemed to grow more interested. "Really?" She relaxed on the stool, no longer wanting to leave. "That must be one hell of a story. Do you still have the scar?"

"The scar?"

"From being bitten."

"Oh," Kurt chuckled, "er, no. I wasn't bitten. I've always been this way. I was born with it."

"Oh jeez, that was super insensitive of me to ask. Why do you even want to share your story with me? All I've done is bicker and complain."

Kurt shrugged, sipping his drink. "Maybe I had a rough day too." Matilda smiled. "I figure just sitting here talking might be a way to unwind. And maybe you'll get that real life story."

"It just seems a little personal to share with someone you just met."

Once again, he shrugged. "You haven't even heard it yet."

"Almost all monsters' stories are sad." Matilda took a sip of her drink.

"I'll drink to that." Kurt took another drink, the headlines about a dead high school girl found torn to shreds flashing through his mind.

Matilda noted the sudden change in the tone of his voice. She decided to steer things in a slightly different direction for the time being. "What if we start with you telling me a little about yourself? Like… what you do for a living? How you ended up in this city? What kind of music you like? How old you are?"

He side-glanced at her, smiling and messing with the stirrer in his whiskey sour. "Well… I work at Home Depot. I do most of the heavy lifting parts of the job, you know, hauling lumber etcetera. I lived in the suburbs most of my youth, never went away

46

to college, so ended up in an apartment in downtown. I actually really like indie music. And I am twenty-seven." Matilda began scribbling things on her notepad. He liked seeing words on the previously blank paper for some reason. For a brief moment he questioned why he was telling her all of this. He shrugged it off. Maybe it was the booze talking – even though he did not even feel buzzed yet - or just how desperate she was for a story. Or maybe he just wanted someone to talk to.

Matilda paused her writing and looked up at him. He was now staring down into his drink. "Kurt?"

"Are you sure you want to hear this story?" he said quietly, his tone suddenly serious. "You were right, you know. Most monsters' stories are sad."

Matilda felt the urge to rest her hand on his arm to comfort him, but resisted. "I'll listen if you want to tell it. Like I said, I want real stories from real people."

Kurt smiled slightly, then pursed his lips. "I guess it all started when I was born. My mother, she was a werewolf. I'm not exactly sure how that happened: if she was also born that way or if she was attacked or… The point is, she passed that trait on to me. At first, it seemed… 'normal.' The heightened senses, going to the cell block a few nights each month with my mother. It was when I started going to school and playing with other kids that I began to notice I was really different.

"For one, I was a lot faster and stronger than they were. For another, none of them had to stay in the cells. That didn't really start to bother me until I was about eight years old. Then I didn't want to be different. There were other werewolves out there, just not my age. I told my mother that I didn't want to go to the cell block anymore. She, of course, said that was silly and that we had to. But I rebelled. I hid from her as she searched for me. That was when the lost time began to scare me.

"In the cell blocks, I had always just gone to sleep. I knew what happened on those nights – the transformation - my mother had carefully explained it to me so that I wouldn't be afraid. But when I was out and free… I didn't wake up in my own bed. I woke up on a stranger's lawn with no recollection of how I had gotten there. I finally found my way home. I had never been more thankful for my heightened sense of smell. When I got there, my mother was in dire straits. She swatted me good for hiding from her, but only after she had hugged me close, crying and saying she had feared what I would do. Or what people would do to me if I were caught. Even at that young age, I feared what I had done when I had lost the time. I had never transformed outside the institution before; I had always been confined to my cell.

48

"I never hid from her again after that. I grew, began to go through puberty… I discovered girls." Kurt winced, taking a drink. "I should have known better… I should have been paying closer attention. I got wrapped up in hanging out with my friends, and the girl I liked at the time was with them. By the time I got headed to the institution, the moon was already too high in the sky… I finally had to pull over to avoid wrecking the car. I transformed, free to roam again. And this time, I was nearly a fully mature wolf." He clenched his jaw, taking another drink and then staring into the little bit left in the bottom of his glass. "… A girl died that night."

Matilda looked up from her writing. Kurt glanced over at her. He could not tell if the look on her face was fear, disgust, or concern. He suddenly felt ashamed, like maybe he should not have told her. After all, she was some girl he had just met, she might think he was some kind of killer. And he was letting her write down his confession.

"That was a long time ago though…" he said in a hushed tone, continuing to stare down into his drink.

This time Matilda did not stop herself, she reached over and touched his arm. He glanced over at her. "Why are you willing to tell me all this?"

"I guess I just needed someone to talk to. You wanted a story and… it gets lonely, this existence." He hunched his shoulders a bit. "After the girl, I tried to be less careless." He sighed. "The teen years are hard enough on their own; trying to find yourself, without having a… a monster living inside you. Even though I swore to be more careful, there was one more time… a friend of mine got hurt. After that, I became distant. Keeping people at arm's length would prevent them from getting hurt. And I wouldn't be distracted. My mother fell ill not too long after that, and she passed away only a few years after I graduated high school.

"It was actually after the girl when I decided that I needed to find a way to free myself from this… this 'curse.' But-"

"Last call!" the bartender shouted, turning down the music. The last few stragglers in the bar murmured to themselves, setting down pool cues, grabbing a last beer or shot for the road, putting the last of their change in the jukebox.

Kurt checked his watch. It was well after midnight. "I'm sorry for keeping you out so late," he said apologetically, climbing off the bar stool.

"Hey," Matilda flipped her notepad closed, sticking her pen absently in her pocket, "you never got to finish."

Kurt turned back, a sad smile spreading across his lips. "It doesn't have a happy ending."

"I still want to hear it." She lifted her eyebrows.

He hesitated. It was against his life policy - his better judgement - to allow someone in. But for some reason, he trusted her. He *wanted* her to know the full story.

"Fine." He internally cussed himself for giving in, but he had put himself in this situation. "Meet me here tomorrow night, same time. And I'll tell you the rest of my story."

# Chapter 9

Carmichael stood on the grass, his face pressed between two of the cold metal slats of the fence enclosing the property. A large mansion stood in the distance at the end of a long winding driveway, illuminated by the waxing moon. The fountain stood as it had, but no water aside from rain had run over its surface in many years. No one aside from vandals and partiers had inhabited those walls for just about as long.

Screams echoed in Carmichael's mind as he looked at the darkened windows, the aged brick walls, the ruined and neglected roof. He clamped his eyes closed, trying to shut out the sound and unpleasant memory. Tears formed along the rims of his eyes, and he looked back at the house, pulling back and hitting his forehead against the cold metal fence.

The house had seen its fair share of pain and sorrow, yet it stood steadfast for all these years. And who knew how long the house had been there before Carmichael Wilhelm III had ever set foot in those tortured walls?

Carmichael turned to the front gate, chained and padlocked shut. A 'Condemned' sign hung across it. It would seem no matter how steadfast, eventually everything came to an end. Everything, that is, but him.

He gritted his teeth, one of the tears that had formed in his eyes falling down his cheek. "Condemned," he said out loud, gripping the gate in his hands, swaying back and forth.

He had an appointment with Dr. Hydecker soon. An appointment he wasn't sure he would keep. But then again, what better things did he have to do with his time but talk to a sympathetic ear about his feelings, under the pretense that he could somehow help him get his shit together? A lovely sentiment, but also a fantasy.

Carmichael released the gate, giving the house one last look before walking down the sidewalk toward Hydecker's office. He wiped away his tears with the back of his hand. He did not want Hydecker to know what he'd been thinking. That he had considered trying to impale himself on the spires of the fence around his old home. Of course, it wouldn't have hurt him; he would have been stuck there in unspeakable pain until someone came along and found him.

Not that the idea of the pain bothered him; he would welcome that. But the idea of being found hanging there, having to have someone remove him. He did not like that idea. Not one bit.

If there was one thing Carmichael hated more than his immortality, it was feeling like he was not in control. Hell, his immortality made him feel like he was not in control; he could not die even though he damn well wanted to.

The sign to Hydecker's office came into view, and Carmichael pushed all of those thoughts from his mind. No matter how much he viewed Dr. Brook Hydecker's ability to help as a fantasy, he had made a promise to himself to at least try. The money was no issue, especially with how cheaply he lived these days. He wiped his eyes once more, hoping the dim lighting would hide the redness of them.

Carmichael was not even seated in the waiting area when the door to Dr. Hydecker's office opened. "Was starting to wonder if you were going to show," Brook said with relief. Carmichael looked up at the clock. It was about five minutes after his scheduled session time.

"Got distracted," Carmichael replied flatly, walking into Dr. Hydecker's office and taking his respective spot on the leather sofa.

"How are you tonight, Carmichael?" Brook asked as he sat down in his chair.

"I'm... fine," Carmichael replied monotonously. "I'm here, aren't I?"

"Yes, Carmichael, you're here, no matter how late..." Carmichael thought he maybe heard a slight edge to Brook's voice, but it was hidden underneath his shrink's tone. "But I suppose we should really get started with your session. You mentioned previously that you'd seen and done it all. I'm curious, where all have you travelled to?" Brook said, jotting something down on his clipboard. Carmichael harrumphed and Brook looked up at him. "Given all of your... 'life experience' and jobs you've held, I would assume you have gone to many places. I want to explore that with you."

Carmichael rolled his eyes, propping his arm up on the armrest and leaning his head against his hand. "All right, I'll bite," he grinned mischievously at his pun. "My roots are in England, but I have spent most of my time on this earth stateside. I did bounce around some from time to time. I saw the Eifel Tower once, when it was practically new. But other than that," he raised his eyebrows, "nothing noteworthy."

"So, if you're from England," Brook said, scribbling away on his clipboard, "when did you first come to America?"

"1617. Back then it was The New World. Then there was a war and times changed. Same old, same old."

"I guess one could put it that way. But change is necessary, for life to move onward and upward."

"For most things, yes." Carmichael let that statement hang in the air a moment. "I want to tell you a story, Dr. Brook Hydecker. Like I said, I bounced around some in my early years, but I returned to England in the late 1920s. I stayed there for a few decades – I was there when World War II started.

"The year was 1941, and I was in some nightclub – I don't even remember the name anymore. I frequented them a lot, drinking my woes away and just listening to the music, sometimes losing myself in dance with a partner.

"But on this particular night, in this particular club, I met a woman. She was a singer, a dancer... really talented, and real pretty too. I was quickly enamored, as I often was back in those days. Drunk and lonely, women like her seemed to hold all the answers, even if for a fleeting moment."

Carmichael smiled to himself as he remembered the jazz band playing: the long notes of the saxophones, the beat of the drums. The dancers with their cocktails. Drunken lovers unable to keep their hands off each other even in the public eye. "Oh we danced, and we sang. My hand worked its way down her back, another cocktail made its way down my throat."

Then his expression darkened. "But as I said, it was England in 1941, and the Germans were bombing the city. And on that particular night, that particular nightclub was bombed." He lifted his head from his hand, playing with his perfectly manicured nails and staring at Brook.

"I was the only survivor." He let the pause that followed drag on. "… I saw her body there in the rubble: burned in places, shrapnel embedded in her skin, her limbs turned in ways they shouldn't be able to turn. I saw the lovers still in embrace, some with the men lying over their partners in an attempt to protect them – a gesture which still ended in two corpses.

"As I stood there among all the death and destruction, I was reminded of something. I was reminded of just how lonely eternity is and that life isn't fair. I didn't even know her name, but she had that spark I've coveted for myself for so long. And it was snuffed out, just like that." Carmichael snapped his fingers, tears balancing precariously on his lower lids.

Brook had stopped scribbling on his clipboard and was looking intently at Carmichael. Neither man spoke for what seemed like a eons. Brook pushed his glasses up on his nose. "What made you decide to tell me that story?" he finally asked.

"Perspective," Carmichael replied flatly.

"Perspective for me, or for you?" Brook asked seriously.

Carmichael exhaled heavily. "To put things in perspective for you. So that you could understand where I'm at now. Where I'm coming from. Why I want to die." His voice softened, but maintained some edge. "Why I wanted to die then. Just how lonely it was to be the only one alive amidst all of that death. Wanting what no one ever thinks they will – wanting to join them."

Brook stroked his mustache, then scratched his goatee. "That is a very normal – very human – reaction, actually. It's what we call Survivor's Guilt, a syndrome sole survivors of any traumatic event often feel. They feel guilty for surviving when everyone else died, like they should have died too or could have done something to prevent it, when in reality-"

Carmichael slammed his fist down on the arm of the sofa, gritting his teeth and shouting, "I *know* what Survivor's Guilt is; I have lived with it for centuries! You're just telling me what I already know and doing *nothing* to help me! I knew these sessions would be a waste of time!" He stood, heading for the door.

"Carmichael, wait. You have to be patient, these things – healing – takes time."

"I've got all the time in the world," Carmichael remarked bitterly, slamming the office door behind him.

Brook sat in the echo of the crash, thinking about Carmichael's story. It had been moving, tragic. It had touched Brook more than he liked to be by his patients. Staying detached was what helped him stay levelheaded and able to assess what action needed to be taken. And of all people, it had been an annoyingly bitter vampire that had gotten under his skin. Then again, maybe he had just made the story up to gain Brook's pity.

# Chapter 10

**A few years ago…**

Alexei brought the last of the plastic-wrapped bundles from his walk-in freezer. Finally, he had what he needed – the last piece of the puzzle. Who would've known how hard it would be to get your hands on a brain, especially with the black market for organs these days?

He began to carefully unwrap the plastic bundles, pulling out preserved arms, legs, feet, a slender midsection, a head with full black hair, numerous organs – until he had all of the makings of a complete human male. Several bags of blood labeled 'O-' sat on the operating table along with the dismembered parts. While Alexei had been lucky enough to procure cadaver parts not yet pumped full of formaldehyde, they had still been drained of blood.

He put on his thick-rimmed glasses and began precisely trying to thread a large needle with surgical thread. There was quite a storm brewing, and he needed the body in one piece by the time it hit. He had been collecting all of the parts for quite some time, and who knew when an awful storm this glorious would strike again?

While Alexei certainly knew his anatomy, the pieces could not be stitched together to sheer perfection: impossibility. He pulled his hair in frustration; no matter how small the flaws were, they were still there. After stepping back for a moment, however, Alexei had to admit that he had done an admirable job. Despite being from several different bodies, the parts appeared to go together, and the head he had gotten bore a well-preserved handsome face: defined cheekbones, a button nose, and thin lips. He had shoulder length jet black hair that had been parted slightly off-center and combed neatly. He was nearly perfect, aside from the large scar across his forehead where Alexei had had to insert the fresh brain.

Alexei took one more moment to admire his handiwork before moving on to the next step. He slit each of the blood bags carefully and poured them all into a transfusion machine. He wrapped a tourniquet around the cadaver's left arm above the elbow and found the largest vein. He jabbed in the needle and switched on the machine. As the body filled with blood, the skin took on a slightly rosier shade, but maintained most of its pallid green hue.

A crash of thunder caught Alexei's attention. The storm was nearly upon them. While the machine continued to pump blood – all one-point-three gallons - into the body, Alexei retrieved two large metal bolts from his desk drawer. He pressed the end of the first bolt into the right side of the neck and screwed it deep into the flesh and muscle tissue. He did the same on the left side.

62

The transfusion machine stopped whirring; the body was full. Alexei removed the needle and pressed a cotton ball over the prick point to stop the bleeding. He clamped metal restraints built into the operating table that were coated in rubber over the body's wrists and ankles. He brought one large leather strap around the waist. He pulled open the mouth, inserting a rubber mouth guard, and closed it once more. After checking that all the restraints were secure, he rolled the table over to a large machine set into the wall. The machine was dotted with several dials, toggles, and switches.

Alexei stepped to the side of the machine, scrutinizing equations scrawled on a chalkboard. By all rights, it *should* work. He had done everything down to a tee. The machine was attached to cables that ran up to several lightning rods on the roof. All of the electrical energy from lightning striking the rods would be channeled directly into the machine. If this storm proved to be as intense as it was supposed to be, he should succeed in bringing the dead back to life.

Alexei walked back over to the body, covering the chest in electrode gel and then stuck the AED pads to the torso in the proper places, their wires attached to the machine. He connected two more cables to the bolts inserted in the neck and two more with finger clamps onto the index fingers of each hand. The first flash of lightning lit the skylights as Alexei flipped the first toggle on his machine.

Another flash followed shortly after, and sparks flew from the machine, the body beginning to convulse as electricity coursed through it, every black hair standing on end. Thunder crashed and more lightning struck, the body convulsing more violently, pulling at the restraints. Alexei thought that he could smell something beginning to burn, and he quickly switched off the machine.

Steam rose from the flesh of the body, the skin letting off a soft sizzling sound, the hair still sticking out all around the head. "Dammit," Alexei growled under his breath, slumping into a chair and holding his head in his hands.

*"Nnnngghhhh."*

A throaty groan issued from the operating table. Alexei slowly turned to look at the cadaver. The fingers began to twitch, then move more definitely as if they were trying to form a fist. Another groan escaped his lips as his eyes moved under the lids. His eyelids began to flutter as he attempted to open his eyes, his head rocking slightly from side to side; he began wiggling his toes.

Alexei stood shakily, approaching the table. The young man's eyes opened, revealing grey irises. His pupils fluctuated in size as he tried to focus. Alexei leaned over him, staring at him, awestruck.

64

"You... you're alive?" Alexei said breathlessly.

His eyes finally focused on Alexei's face, and he tried to mumble something. Alexei suddenly remembered the mouth guard and yanked it from his mouth. All that followed were a series of troubled utterances, but he was clearly trying to speak.

"You're alive," Alexei said, realization washing over him. "*You're alive!*" he shouted, jumping up in the air and shaking his fist. "They said it couldn't be done! But I showed them! *I showed* them!"

The man wet his lips and uttered, "oo am I?"

Alexei stopped guffawing and stared at the man. "What did you say?"

"Who... am... I?" He repeated slowly, but more clearly.

"You don't remember?" The man slowly shook his head. "Interesting..." Alexei said, running over to the chalkboard and scribbling a note at the bottom.

He returned to the tableside, undoing the belt around the man's waist. He carefully undid the clamps holding down his wrists; while he seemed frail, Alexei knew that the only predictable thing about how a reanimated corpse would act was his unpredictability. He decided to leave his ankles restrained for the time being. He felt in his pocket for the syringe of sedative; it was still there and ready. He reached out and put his arm around the man's back, taking his right hand, and gently helping him sit up.

The man let out a cry as his torso bent, dark crimson blood flying from his mouth and running down his chin. "I'm sorry," Alexei said once the man was upright, pulling a handkerchief from his pocket and dabbing the side of his mouth. "It's due to the stitched impurities I'm afraid. If my calculations are correct, you should be fine, just experiencing a bit of discomfort."

"Are you a doctor?" he sputtered, tears running from his sunken eyes.

"Yes. My name is Dr. Alexei Frankenstein. You know what a doctor is? What else do you remember?"

"Thirsty..."

"Oh yes, of course! I will get you a glass of water." Alexei hurried to the sink and brought him a tall glass full of water. The man gulped it down, choking slightly as he tried to make his throat function. "Now," Alexei said, "what else do you remember?"

"I... can't remember much. I do know it's 2011, or at least it was the last time I read the paper." He rattled off several more basic facts.

"Interesting, interesting," Alexei jotted down more notes on the chalkboard and continued to ask him questions to ascertain just how much he knew. One thing he determined very quickly was

66

that his creation was no mindless lug; he was a very soft-spoken individual with a seemingly kind disposition and a fair amount of smarts.

"Who am I?" the young man finally asked again, waving the glass to indicate that he needed more water.

Alexei grimaced, taking the glass and refilling it. He handed it to the man, carefully thinking of how to answer his question. "Who are you? Well, as I stated before, *I* am Dr. Alexei Frankenstein. I am considered the most intelligent man of the modern age. Many doubted that I could bring the dead back to life – reanimate a corpse, as it were. I cannot honestly answer your question, for the parts I received did not come with any names attached. But you are my latest creation, my supposedly impossible success. What I am trying to say is, you were dead, and now you are alive."

The man stared at him a moment, processing what he had just been told. "But… you are saying all the parts aren't mine?" He turned his free hand over, staring down at it.

"Yes. Well, they weren't. They are yours now, every last one of them."

"So all that blood I coughed up earlier?"

"Science isn't perfect." They sat in silence for a moment, and then Alexei spoke. "I suppose you do need a name." He stroked his scraggly beard. "I shall name you Jesse James – a memorable name. A name that went down in history, just like you will my boy!" He clapped his hands together enthusiastically and Jesse smiled. "Oh but you must be exhausted. I have a room ready for you, if you can stand." He undid the clamps around Jesse's ankles. "Be careful, too much jostling could result in coughing up more blood and discomfort, and neither of us wants that."

Jesse eased himself carefully off the edge of the table until his feet touched the floor, and Alexei held out a hand to steady him as he wobbly stood. Jesse took his first few steps with uncertainty and nearly fell, but caught Alexei's shoulder. By the time they reached the doorway to his room, he was almost walking by himself.

"You're a quick learner," Alexei beamed. "There are clothes in the room. Put them on and get some rest." He turned and began to walk away.

"Thank you," Jesse said quietly. Alexei stopped but did not turn around. "This is quite a peculiar situation to find myself in, but you have been more than kind."

Alexei did not know why this simple gesture moved him so as he found his eyes welling up with tears. He realized how long it had been since anyone had had anything nice to say to him.

"You're welcome," he said tersely, walking back to his lab as Jesse entered his new room. The mood did not last long; Alexei was still far too elated by his success.

# Chapter II

Edward stopped typing and leaned back in his computer chair, rubbing his eyes. He glanced out the window and saw that it was now dark outside. How long had he been typing? He felt like it was just minutes ago that the man in the cubicle next to his had said, "goodnight," as he was leaving. It had still been daylight then. He looked at his watch. It was after eight.

"Time to go," he muttered to himself, saving his article and closing the file window. Edward shut down his computer and pulled on his coat, draping his scarf around his neck. He gathered his things that were scattered all over his desk and unsystematically put them in his messenger bag before slinging it over his shoulder. He bent and picked up a piece of wadded up paper from the floor and squeezed it tightly in his hand. When he reached the door, he threw it over his shoulder and it landed in a nearby wastebasket. Edward congratulated himself, and then flipped off the lights before exiting the floor.

He climbed into the elevator and hit the button for the parking garage level. The elevator doors closed and he checked his watch again. Nearly eight-thirty. He would send Elsa a text message once he got in his car so that she would not get worried.

The elevator dinged and the doors opened. Edward stepped out of the elevator into the cool, dark parking garage. Except for his and the night janitors' cars, the garage was empty. His footsteps echoed as he made his way to his car. He pulled his keys out of his pocket and pressed the button to pop his trunk.

He shrugged his messenger bag off his shoulder and leaned into his trunk to put it in. He heard a shuffle of feet to his left and someone slammed the trunk door down on Edward's head and shoulders.

"Ow! Fuck!" Edward cried out, stumbling backwards in a slight daze. Two hands grabbed him gruffly by the shoulders, and his attacker kneed him in the stomach. His assailant then threw him down on the pavement, the side of Edward's face hitting the ground hard. He winced, wanting to cry out in pain, but all of the air was knocked out of him. He tasted coppery blood in his mouth as he tried to squint up at his mugger, but his vision was becoming cloudy. His face ached – as a matter of fact, everything ached.

Edward began to pass out as he felt his attacker pull him up into a sitting position. His head lolled forward until the mugger propped it back, Edward's mouth coming limply open.

The last thing he was aware of was a fluid being poured down his throat. He began to choke on it, but his assailant pinched his nose closed, forcing him to swallow. It tasted putrid, like paint smells. His assaulter pushed him back to the ground, Edward coughing on the last few drops of the substance. Then everything went black.

~

Edward's eyes fluttered open. Even the dim lights in the parking garage were blinding to him, causing him to squint.

"Well look who decided to join the living," a familiar voice stated. Edward jumped, looking around frantically. Lawrence Talbot sat on the ground a few yards away, his back against Edward's car, smoking a cigarette.

"It was you?" Edward sniffed, wiping his nose with the back of his hand. He pulled it back to see powdery dried blood dusting his skin.

"Who else?" Lawrence said superciliously, raising his arms in the air unenthusiastically.

"But w-" Edward was cut short as a lightning bolt of pain shot through his body, causing him to let out a scream, his voice echoing off the walls of the sparsely populated parking garage. All of his muscles tensed, his face constricting in pain. He began writhing on the ground, spittle mixing with the blood dripping down the side of his mouth.

He finally regained some control of his body, balling his hands into fists and trying to suppress the involuntary spasms. "What the hell did you do to me!?" Edward shouted angrily at Lawrence.

Lawrence stood, flicking his cigarette butt out of his hand, blowing out a final stream of smoke. He deftly walked over to where Edward lay. "I made you like me." He smiled, kneeling beside Edward, who was quivering and perspiring from effort. "I made you a monster. But when you change, when you take on your other form, you won't take on someone else's face like me; you won't sprout hair or long claws. You will be the worst version of yourself." Edward looked at him in horror, slowly shaking his head, his eyes wild. Lawrence pulled a small mirror from his inner jacket pocket. "Edward Jekyll," he said his name snidely, "say hello to Mr. Hyde."

He held up the mirror so that Edward could see his reflection. At first Edward did not notice any changes, but as he looked closer, he saw them. They were subtle, but they were there. His brow was pronounced, furrowed cruelly. His eyes were dark and sunken as if he had not slept in weeks, his green irises appearing to glow a radioactive green. His previously neatly combed hair was now sticking out in every direction, each strand standing on end. But worst of all was the evil sneer on his lips.

"It's amazing what seventy-five dollars and a fingerprint can get you, when taken to the right person," Lawrence snickered, placing the mirror back in his pocket and revealing a small glass vial. A little bit of chartreuse residue was collected in the convex bottom of the vessel.

Edward groaned as he felt his brow relax and the wicked sneer leave his lips. His hair was still a mess, but the strands had relaxed.

"Hyde will come out from time to time. Who knows when? Just know this," Lawrence brought his face so close to Edward's that he could smell his smoker's breath, "You can't keep him from coming out, from taking control. The harder you try to suppress him, the more often he'll take over. That's how this little spell works." Lawrence stood, pocketing the vial, and began to walk away.

"I knew you were a scumbag from the moment I met you! You're a *monster!*" Edward shouted after him.

Lawrence stopped, the curve of a small smile visible at the edges of his lips. "So are you," he replied without looking back, and then exited the garage.

Edward sat on the pavement a moment longer before shakily climbing to his feet, the convulsions having subsided. His trunk was still open, so he started by closing it firmly. He noticed he was not as sore as he had been before his episode. He climbed into the driver seat and examined his face in the mirror on the back side of his sun visor. His face was not bruised or scratched. There would have been no evidence that he had been mugged if it were not for the dried blood collected around his nostril and lips. He assumed that accelerated healing must be a side effect of the potion.

He put his key in the ignition and turned it, looking at the glowing numbers of his car clock. It was nine-fifteen. He knew he needed to get home; Elsa was probably already worried sick. He pulled his phone out of his pocket. He sat there a moment, wondering what to text her, but came up blank. Edward returned his phone to his pocket, sighing.

He sat in the car a moment longer, still a little in shock from his ordeal, before shifting into 'Reverse' and backing out of his parking spot. He was halfway out of the parking garage before he realized he had forgotten to turn on his headlights.

# Chapter 12

Edward turned into the driveway of his and Elsa's house.
They lived in the suburbs, in a small but very nice house. It was
very modern contemporary, built in streamlined rectangles, roof
flat across the top instead of forming a triangle like most traditional
houses. There was a wall on the second floor that was completely
glass, overlooking the city skyline.

Edward sat in his car, shifting into 'Park' but not bothering to
shut off the engine. He had let what Lawrence said really sink in
on the quiet drive home. He was a monster now. He was what he
hated most in the world. And as it turned out – ironically enough –
it was his hate that was now his curse.

The living room light was on, drawing Edward's attention to
the window. The curtains were parted and he could see Elsa
slumped over on the couch, sleeping, colored lights coming from
the television screen dancing across her serene face. She had likely
fallen asleep waiting for him to come home.

Edward clenched his jaw, trying to fight the tears he felt
coming on. He could feel his heart breaking. He knew that being a
monster - especially the kind that he had become - could be
dangerous. It could be dangerous for Elsa to even be around him.

Hyde's appearances would be unpredictable and spontaneous, Lawrence had promised him that much.

He thought back to the previous night, lying in bed with Elsa. She had told him that deep down he was a good man. While he had always strived to be good in spite of his tattered past, he had his dark moments. And if – *when* – that darkness manifested into an actual being, Edward feared what he would be capable of.

In the miasma of his despair, he knew one thing for certain. He did not want to hurt Elsa. He could not ask her to marry him, at least not until he had found a way to cure himself of his affliction.

He still did not know what he was going to say to Elsa. How he was going to tell her what had happened, that he was going to have to leave her, at least for a while. He did not want to break her heart.

He needed more time to think this over. A lot had happened over the past couple hours, a lot that his brain still needed to process. Edward tried desperately to ignore his aching heart and think logically, but he was tired and still in shock from being mugged. He shifted into 'Reverse' and slowly backed down the driveway, hoping Elsa would not hear the car. He would come back in the morning and tell her that he had pulled an all-nighter at the office. He would be better equipped to say what he needed to say after some rest and time to reflect on it.

# Chapter 13

Kurt stopped outside the bar. He considered turning around and just going home. Sticking to himself like he had for several years. Keeping anyone else from getting hurt. What was it about this woman – Matilda - that had made him come back to the bar?

He took a deep breath and walked through the door. There she was, sitting at the counter in the same spot as the night before. She was dressed just as sharply. Kurt slowly approached her. She turned and saw him, waving.

"Was starting to think maybe you forgot about me," she teased him as he sat next to her.

"*How could anyone forget about you?*" he thought, once again shocked by his own thoughts. "Traffic was a bit crazy," he lied, forcing a smile. He ordered himself a drink and took a sip. "Where was I?"

"You said your mother had passed away, and after what happened to the girl and your friend you began looking for a way to break your curse."

"Oh." He took a slightly bigger drink. "Well, after my mother died, I knew that I didn't want to live the rest of my life like that. I didn't want to live in fear, having to lock myself away to protect the world. I just wanted to live a normal life. So I began searching. I haven't really been too successful. I have met several other people like me at the institution – werewolves – and no one seems to know of a cure. But I know there has to be a way."

He looked at Matilda, hope glimmering in his eyes. She felt her heart flutter. He really was handsome, in an innocent sort of way. She liked that.

The glimmer disappeared from his eyes. "But after dead end after dead end, I've started to wonder if there is a way…" His voice trailed off. He looked up at her. "So that's how it ends, Matilda. Just a lonely monster at a bar who's lost hope of a normal life, a life where he doesn't have to live in fear."

Matilda set down her pen and reached over, grabbing his hand. "That doesn't have to be the end of the story."

Kurt felt the urge to pull his hand back, but he resisted. Her hand was smooth and cool against his, comforting. His eyes met hers. She smiled at him. "I know you mean well. But maybe that's just the way life is." He stood, sliding his hand out from under hers. "This was a bad idea, I need to go."

"Kurt. No, Kurt, wait!" Matilda dropped a few dollar bills on the counter and snatched up her notepad, placing it in her bag and following him out.

It had begun pouring rain outside and Kurt shoved his hands into his pants pockets, leaning into the wind as he headed in the direction of his apartment. Matilda stepped out into the rain, looking both ways and spotting Kurt walking down the desolate street.

"Kurt!" she shouted, starting after him. He continued walking; she was not sure if he did not hear her or was ignoring her. She began running, water splashing up on her shins as she did so. "Kurt!" She touched his arm, and he stopped, turning back to her. They were both soaking wet from head to foot, water dripping off the tip of Kurt's nose. "That doesn't have to be the end," she had to yell over the pounding rain. "There has to be some way. I... I want to help you."

Kurt looked at her sympathetically. "People around me – my kind – just tend to get hurt. I know you mean well, but... it's dangerous. And you barely even know me."

"I know. But there's just, something about you... I want to help. I don't just want to write about you... I want to be a part of your story."

The two stood there a moment in the pouring rain, staring at each other. Matilda suddenly grabbed him and pulled him toward her, kissing him. He let out a startled sound, so disconcerted that he made no move to resist. The kiss lasted no more than a couple of seconds, but the feeling of her lips lingered on his even after she released him.

"Oh God…" Matilda put her hand to her mouth, staring wide-eyed at Kurt. "I, uh, I'm so sorry."

"For what?" Kurt asked, wrapping his arm around her so that his hand rested in the small of her back, and he pulled her closer to him, kissing her again. As he pulled away, he breathed, "There's something about you too. I don't know what it is, but ever since we met, I haven't been able to stop thinking about you. I almost believe you when you say we can change my story's ending."

Matilda attempted to look up at him, the raindrops stinging her eyes. "Maybe it's time you let someone in. Let me help you."

Kurt looked deep into her eyes, which seemed to have an odd violet sheen in the reflection of the streetlight. "Okay."

# Chapter 14

Jesse walked through the door of his favorite diner. He had discovered the little hole-in-the-wall place when he had first begun exploring the world through fresh eyes. It was a mere few miles away from the hidden lab, bordering the unfortunately abandoned district. The place was dimly lit, making it a comfortable environment for him. He could hide in plain sight and interact with people. Despite the world being a cruel place, Jesse had an insatiable impulse to be a part of it.

He made his way to the bar and carefully seated himself upon a stool. Jim Bailey – the head bartender – approached him, smiling broadly. "Jesse James! What'll it be today?"

"A burger, all dressed up, and a pint of Miller please," Jesse said, smiling.

"Sure, coming right up." Bailey scribbled down the order and passed the paper through the window to the cook. He poured Jesse's beer into a frosted mug and slid it in front of him. Bailey was a hulking man, standing at about six foot five inches tall. He had a full head of brown hair that fell down over his ears and blue eyes that gleamed when he spoke. Jesse took a sip, letting the astringent flavor tickle his tongue and slide down his throat. Even after four years, certain sensations still fascinated him. The taste of alcohol was one of those things.

As Bailey brought Jesse his burger, a young woman walked in and sat at the bar. She shrugged off her stole, revealing bare slender shoulders. The way she sat at the bar accentuated her curves, as she pursed her red lips and perused the menu with striking dark eyes. Her dark hair was pulled up tightly in an updo, exposing the nape of her long neck.

Jesse felt his heart fluctuate in his chest, and he tried to focus on his food. He picked up his burger, taking a large bite, cheese dripping out from between the buns. The woman continued to distract him; she was sitting directly in his line of vision. Bailey walked over to take her order, and she smiled lopsidedly at him as she spoke, a dimple indenting into her cheek.

Attraction was a complicated thing for Jesse. Just like the taste of alcohol, it was a sensation that fascinated him. It also terrified him. The circumstance of his resurrection was an unavoidable topic; while talking with anyone, there were just certain tells about his appearance. Even getting drinks with his baby face and no ID had proved difficult just about anywhere but here. And then there was the prospect of sex. Given his physical condition, Jesse honestly wondered if sex was even possible for him. To be fair, he had never gotten close enough to a woman romantically to find out.

But as he looked down the bar at this particular woman, he thought to himself, *"What the hell?"* After all, he would be happy with just a nice chat. And in the dim light, maybe she would not even notice his discolored skin. And the large scar across his forehead could have a simple explanation.

He finished eating and motioned for Bailey to come over. "Would you mind giving that young woman another of what she is drinking, with my regards?" He slid Bailey a ten dollar bill.

Bailey raised his eyebrows and walked over to the drink counter, mixing a bright green martini and sliding it in front of the woman. She looked confused, but then he leaned toward her and murmured a few words, indicating Jesse. The woman looked at him, then picked up her stole and walked over to where Jesse sat, sliding the martini glass across the counter's surface as she went.

"I hear this one was on you?" she said in a sultry voice as smooth as silk.

Jesse suddenly felt very self-conscious under her gaze in his slightly-too-big untucked button-down shirt, his hair wild despite his attempts to comb it. "I, uh, couldn't help but notice you across the bar. Drinking alone is no fun." He extended his hand. "I'm Jesse. Jesse James."

"Interesting name," she smiled, taking the stool next to him and shaking his hand. "And I'm Eva Braun." She chuckled.

He smiled back at her. "So, what brings you out tonight?"

"Off work for the weekend. That alone merits a drink." She pulled out a cigarette case and lighter. "You don't mind if I smoke, do you?"

"Of course not. So what is it that you do that you are so glad to get away from for the weekend?"

'Eva' put a cigarette to her lips, flicking the lighter a few times before the flame sprang to life and the tip glowed orange. She blew out a stream of smoke, replacing the cigarette case and lighter in her handbag. "Accounting. Lots of numbers. Sometimes you just have to get a little high for the numbers to not just blur all together." She looked at him, tilting her head and picking up the martini glass. "What about you, Mr. James?"

A chill ran down his spine. This was one of the questions he dreaded, and he just didn't have it in him to lie. "I... am a lab assistant. I work with one of the top scientists in the country."

"Ooo, intriguing." 'Eva' took a sip of her drink, swirling it around.

Jesse shifted slightly on the stool, but his hip popped out of alignment and he almost fell. He gripped the side of the bar to catch himself. He felt the stitches in his side pull and a stabbing pain shoot through his midsection. He tried to suppress a cough as he felt thick blood working its way up his esophagus, but he could

86

not. He hacked up a glob of dark crimson blood, the fluid splattering on the floor at the base of 'Eva's' stool. She let out a scream, spilling what was left of her martini all over the bar, snatching up her handbag to avoid it getting wet. Her cigarette fell from her gaping mouth, spraying ash and orange cinders as it hit the floor.

"What the fuck!?" she finally managed to articulately scream, snatching up her stole in the hand opposite her purse.

"Wait, let me explain," Jesse wiped his mouth with a napkin from the bar. "It's all right, I-"

He saw her eyes straying to his neck, and widen. He realized his collar had shifted, revealing the bolts in his neck.

"What the hell kind of monster are you!?"

"I can explain. Remember when I said I worked with one of the top scientists in the country? I work with Dr. Alexei Frankenstein. I'm a-"

"Oh my God, Dr. Frankenstein! What, has he been... experimenting on you? Good lord, who knows what I've-" she cut her statement short. "I have to get out of here!" She turned and ran for the door, not taking her eyes off Jesse until she was outside, draping her stole over her shoulders.

Jesse watched her through the windows until she was out of sight, sighing heavily enough to make his lungs rattle. He grabbed more napkins, kneeling carefully and mopping up the blood from the floor, disposing of them in a nearby trashcan. He sloshed down the rest of his beer and slapped a one dollar bill on the counter.

"Sorry Bailey. Do you need me to mop or anything?" he said, standing.

"No, it's all right, I've got it."

"Thanks," he said, readjusting his shirt collar to hide the bolts in his neck before leaving. He began the trek back to the lab. This was by no means the first time something like this had happened. For starters, he had not gotten the reception Alexei had expected when he revealed him to the scientific community. Some had been sure it was a trick. Others had been sure that the negative repercussions must outweigh the discovery. And yet others had shunned him for playing God, saying he had gone too far. To the general populace, he was something to be feared, heavily misunderstood.

Being a reanimated corpse made trying to live a normal life – what Jesse really wanted – all but impossible. Even in this world of monsters, he was an anomaly. As he reached the lab door, he opened it, descending the stairs. Once he reached the lit room, he found Alexei bent over a collection of flasks, scribbling away in a notebook, muttering to himself. Jesse wasn't sure if he had even realized he was there.

# Chapter 15

The glare from the computer screen reflected on the lenses of Brook's glasses. He typed '1941 British club bombing' into the search engine's dialog box. Several results came up, and he began scrolling through them, looking for something that might jump out at him. Finally, a headline grabbed his attention. 'Horrific Photos of the Aftermath of Civilian Bombings – WWII Edition.'

Brook clicked the article and waited for the page to load. He began scrolling through the old monochromatic photos, some still black and white and others stained sepia with age. The headline had not lied, the photos were horrific: ruined city blocks, bodies lying under or near rubble, pieces of those deceased's belongings lying in the streets. Brook tried to fight off the nausea he felt coming on. Suddenly, he stopped scrolling, going back a few photographs. He leaned in close to the monitor.

The picture showed a mostly ruined building, its sign broken and hanging onto part of the remaining structure by one corner. Several people dug through the rubble, while bystanders gathered to stare and grieve. And among them was a man who looked unmistakably like Carmichael. The caption read 'bombed night club, England, 1941.'

"You really were there, you devil," Brook said to himself. "You weren't just trying to garner pity." In spite of himself, Brook felt guilty for considering that Carmichael had made it up. Looking at the photos was enough. He could not imagine actually having been there in the middle of it. He found himself able to understand, even if only partially, why Carmichael had lost his excitement over immortality. When he closed his eyes, he had to remember things like that bombed club.

For a man who seemed so put out with living, Carmichael also struck Brook as being very self-centered. These two things seemed to contradict each other. Brook had seen contradictory traits in patients before. Now the vampirism, that one was new to him. He decided that at their next session he would try a different approach. If Carmichael came back, that was.

# Chapter 16

Edward parked his car behind Elsa's and stepped out into the early morning light. He had stayed at a hotel for the night, trying to get some sleep, which had evaded him despite how tired he was. The bad thoughts, the fear of what now currently lay dormant inside him, had kept him awake. However, his insomnia had allowed him to think of how to approach Elsa about the whole affair.

There had been one point where he had thought that it would be best if he just disappeared into the night. But he knew that would not only be difficult for him to do, it could potentially destroy Elsa. He wanted to think he would only have to be gone a short time, long enough to hunt down a witch or warlock that could undo the curse upon his head. But what if he never found one? What if they could not, or *would* not, help him? What if he *never* ridded himself of his evil alter ego? Would Elsa wait forever, waiting for him to come back or his body to be found? No, just leaving was not the proper tactic.

Edward had tried to rehearse what he would say to her, trying to pick the best words and least hurtful way to leave. But much like his failed proposal attempt, he had finally come to terms with the fact that no matter how much he rehearsed it, chances were that it would not come out right.

So he had finally decided to just tell her the truth - everything that had occurred after he had left his office at eight-thirty - and see what happened. The hard part would come after, the part where he would have to leave her. It was not merely the thought of leaving her that gave him pause. It was the thought of how long he would have to be away from her.

He had then managed to get a few hours of sleep before collecting the few belongings he had with him and heading back home to face the music. He walked up onto the front porch and began to put his key in the lock, but before he had even gotten a chance to turn it, the door flew open and Elsa threw herself at him, wrapping her arms around his neck in a tight embrace.

"Edward!" she exclaimed, sighing heavily, tears welling up in her eyes. "Where were you? I have been so worried. I tried to call, but you didn't pick up." She continued to hold him close to her, as if she were afraid to let go. He was speechless, taken aback and touched by her outburst. But what else had he expected? It was unlike him to stay out all night, at least without so much as a text message or phone call.

"I-" his voice caught in his throat, "Elsa... we, uh, we need to talk. I have to tell you something."

Elsa slowly pulled away from him and looked at his face. His eyes were forlorn, his mouth turned down in a weak frown. She frowned, her own eyes now filled with concern. "What is it, Edward?"

"Can we go inside?" He started to reach for her hand, but restrained himself. He did not want to be within striking distance if Hyde decided to rear his ugly head.

"S-sure," she stammered, walking in ahead of him. He set his messenger bag on the table and then followed her into the kitchen where she was finishing cleaning up from breakfast. "What is it?" she asked, scouring the skillet.

"You remember that guy from the other day? The one I thought robbed the store? Lawrence Talbot."

"Yeah. What about him?"

Edward set his jaw, exhaling heavily before speaking. "He... he uh, paid me a visit last night. I was walking to my car and he mugged me right there in the parking building."

Elsa looked up from the skillet, studying his face once more. "Oh my God, are you okay?"

"Yes, um no, just..." He began to get flustered and had to stop to collect his thoughts. "I'm not 'hurt' per say... but he put a curse on me, Elsa. I'm a... I'm a..." he began to cry as he knew he would have to confess to her what he was; he would have to say the words, "I'm a monster."

"Edward, what're you talking about? Why would he do something like that, hell, why did he want to mug you? Money? Because you falsely accused him of theft?" She had completely abandoned the skillet and taken a step toward him.

He took a step back from her. "Look, you have to keep your distance from me, I could be dangerous." He held his hands out in front of him, gesturing for her not to come closer. "He wanted revenge: partially because of my false accusation and partially because of my prejudice against monsters. He got a potion somewhere and he mugged me, forcing me to drink it." He swallowed, trying to stop his tears from flowing, but he knew that the worst had yet to come. "I… he turned me into a monster. The very thing I hate the most. Which is where my true downfall comes into play. When I change, I will become the worst version of myself. A man named Hyde; a man – *monster* – born of all my shortcomings and hatred. And my transformation isn't triggered by a full moon or the sun setting or my own will. He can come out at any time, and I will be powerless to stop him." He looked at Elsa painfully, taking another step back. "That is why you have to stay away from me."

He turned away from her. Now was the moment of truth, the moment he had dreaded the most, the moment that had kept him awake all night. "And that's why I have to leave." He let out a small sob, then continued, "I have to get rid of... *this*. I have to rid myself of this curse before we can be together again. I don't want to... I can't allow myself to hurt you. I don't know what this Hyde fellow is capable of, but if it's the worst of me, it can't be good." He saw Elsa putting her hand to her mouth, her eyes dropping to the floor, fresh tears forming and balancing precariously on her lower eyelids. "I love you," he said, and she clamped her eyes closed, causing the tears to fall, "I love you more than anything. And that's why I have to do this. I hope finding a cure won't take very long. Because I don't want to be away from you any longer than I have to be."

They stood there in silence, both fighting tears and failing miserably.

"You don't have to do it alone," she said quietly, not raising her eyes from the floor.

"What?"

"I said you don't have to do this alone." She looked at him, wiping away her tears with her hand. "I love you too, Edward. I want to help, I want to stand by you." She took a step toward him, reaching out for him.

"Stop, don't come closer to me." He tensed, real fear showing in his eyes.

"I know you would never hurt me." She continued toward him.

"I wouldn't," he said, watching her apprehensively, "but Hyde would."

"I will never leave your side. Monster or no monster. You're special," she smiled, new tears rolling down her face as she stroked his cheek, "and you're mine."

"Elsa, please," Edward said, wincing at her touch. "I have to do this alone, I've made up my mind."

"And I've made up mine. I will see this through with you 'til the very end." Her voice did not waver; it was filled with determination.

"Elsa, please, you don't understan-" Edward suddenly cried out, falling to his knees and grabbing his stomach.

"Edward! Edward, are you all right?" Elsa cried frantically.

Edward gulped in a few deep breaths before answering. "Fine… I'm just fine." Elsa did not notice his change in tone, his disheveled hair. As he grabbed the counter to help himself stand, he kept his face turned downward so that she would not see his furrowed brow and glowing eyes.

"Here, let me get you a glass of water." Elsa rushed over to the sink, grabbing a glass from the cabinet.

Hyde looked around while her back was to him, noticing the butcher block sitting only a few inches away from him on the kitchen counter. He slowly removed a boning knife from the block, gripping it tightly in his hand.

"Here," Elsa turned from the sink with the full glass of water, "this should help you feel bett-" Hyde thrust his arm forward, burying the knife in her stomach. She gasped, the sound barely audible.

The glass slipped from her fingers and fell to the floor, shattering into a million pieces. The water spread across the linoleum floor, making it slick. Red blood began to drip from around the blade, mixing with the water. She brought her hand up to the knife's handle, her mouth agape in shock as she decided whether or not to pull it out. She left it, pulling back her now-red hand and looking at Edward in shocked disbelief. Her disbelief turned to terror as she noticed his creased brow, his vibrant green eyes, his wild hair. But worst of all was the sneer he wore on his lips as he looked at his handiwork.

His expression changed, and he leaned against the counter, shaking his head as if he was suddenly dizzy and trying to get ahold of himself. When he looked up at Elsa, his eyes no longer glowed and his eyebrows were raised in confusion. He looked around for a moment, his eyes landing on her and widening.

"Oh God..." Jekyll breathed, gripping the counter tightly, "what have I done?"

"I'll be fine, honest. You'll see," Elsa tried to reassure him, gripping the knife handle and trying to dislodge it from her stomach. She stifled a scream, letting go and taking a few deep breaths. "It'll... be... fine..."

"Oh God, oh God," Edward gripped his hair, trying not to go into hysterics. He closed his eyes and tried hard to focus on something, anything to get ahold of himself. He began trying to recite the alphabet in Latin. *"Alpha, Beta, Gamma, Delta..."*

Elsa looked back at the knife jutting out of her gut. Now that she thought about it, it would likely be unwise to remove the knife just now. But she would need medical attention. She tried to take a step toward the phone, but the movement caused an awful pain to shoot through her abdomen. She tried to take another step and nearly slipped on the wet linoleum.

Edward looked up at her and started toward her, but stopped. He wanted to help her, but what if Hyde came out again to finish the job? He had blacked out for that brief moment when Hyde had taken over, but it was not hard to figure out what his intentions had been.

"Really, I'll be fine." She stumbled over to lean against the counter for support. "It wasn't you who stabbed me, it was Hyde."

Edward was stung by her words. He knew that in a sense, she was right. It had been Hyde that had stabbed her. But that did not mean that he - Edward Jekyll - had not. His worst fears had been realized; his dark side was capable of truly terrible things.

But he could not dwell on that. Elsa was seriously hurt; he needed to get her medical attention. The problem was coming up with a plausible story for how she had gotten hurt that did not put him behind bars. While he would have felt safer – everyone else would have been safer – he would not find a cure for his curse locked up in jail.

He wrestled his cell phone out of his pants pocket and typed in '911' but did not hit the call button. He looked back at Elsa, saw the blood still leaking out around the blade embedded in her gut. It was evident that she was trying to keep how much pain she was in from showing on her face. She was trying to spare Edward's feelings. That killed him. He hit the call button with his thumb and put the phone to his ear. He would come up with something when he spoke to the operator. But he had wasted enough time already, he had to just bite the bullet and make the call.

The phone rang a couple of times and then a woman's voice came over the line, "911, what's your emergency?"

"It's my girlfriend, she's had an accident! She slipped in the kitchen while she was carrying a knife and..." Edward hated lying, but what choice did he have?

"Sir, where is the injury? Is it a cut or puncture?"

"Her stomach. She stabbed herself in the stomach."

"Is she conscious?"

"Y-yes."

"I am going to need your address so that I can send someone over there to assist you."

Edward gave her his address. "Please hurry."

"They always do." The 911 operator hung up and the call ended.

Edward glared at her last comment. He knew that emergency personnel took their time getting anywhere in this city. Sometimes too much time. He had been writing about the crime beat for long enough to see several situations that could have been better-resolved or avoided if the police or paramedics had arrived just a little sooner.

He turned his attention back to Elsa. He did not think that the wound would be fatal, but he still hoped that they would hurry.

She took a long deep breath and swallowed before exhaling, trying to moisten her dry mouth. "We have to get your fingerprints off the handle," she stated, her voice strained. She gripped the knife's handle in her bloody hand, trying to rub its entire surface area to remove any evidence that Edward had ever touched it.

"Is there anything I can do?" Edward stood across the room awkwardly, clenching and unclenching his fists nervously.

"A glass of water would be great," she croaked.

He looked at her a moment longer, wishing there was something he could do to ease her pain. He broke out of his daze of self-pity and carefully walked across the wet floor to the cabinet where they stored their cups. He took down a small glass tumbler and walked over to the sink, turning on the faucet and filling the cup with cold water. He walked over to Elsa, handing it to her carefully.

"Thanks." She smiled weakly, taking a small sip.

"I'm so sorry Elsa," Edward said sadly as he reluctantly brought his hand up to touch her face, his eyes filled with remorse. "I'm so sorry." He fought fresh tears as he stroked her cheek. She tensed a little at his touch, more of a reflex than anything. This caused Edward more pain than anything had yet. The fact that in spite of herself, Elsa was at least a little fearful of him. He pulled his hand back.

Edward heard sirens outside, and he spun around, running for the front door and nearly slipping on the waterlogged floor. He threw the front door open, thankful to see the paramedics had arrived and the police were following from just down the street.

# Chapter 17

Kurt walked into the bar where he and Matilda had met. He had called her office number after their kiss in the rain, and the two had talked for a while – probably longer than they should have since she was at work. During this conversation, cell numbers had been exchanged. Kurt had discovered that Matilda actually had a lot in common with him during that talk. They had not been able to meet immediately following the kiss, but had made frequent phone calls, discussing anything from their day at work to the daily news to if they had found any leads to ridding Kurt of his curse.

Kurt sat at a table this time, seeing as it was midafternoon. He was supposed to meet Matilda for lunch, and he had thought the bar where they met would be fitting. She said she maybe had a few leads that could help him, but nothing concrete.

Matilda walked in, spotting him and walking over to his table. She sat next to him. "How are you?" She smiled.

"Better now." He smiled back. His tone grew serious. "What'd you find?"

"Well, I didn't want to have to tell you over the phone. I found out it was a bit of a red herring… the person I found is well-known for charms, spells, and curses. Unfortunately, as it turns out, she doesn't know jack shit about werewolves." She grimaced. "Sorry…"

Kurt tried to hide the disappointment in his voice. "It's all right. At least I get to see you again." He smiled. "I missed you."

"I missed you too." She grabbed his hand under the table. "You're good, Kurt. You have a good heart. I promise, I am going to help you find a way."

"You're sweet." Kurt squeezed her hand. "I just…" he did not know what to say.

"What?" She blushed, brushing a strand of hair behind her ear.

"I don't want you to get hurt. Magic, curses, *werewolves…* you're kind of playing with fire."

"I'm a reporter. I'm always playing with fire." She smiled mischievously at him. "I was just looking for a story and I got so much more than I bargained for: I found you."

"For better or for worse." He chuckled.

"You're no danger to anyone unless the moon's full. And you stay in one of those… institutions then, right?"

"Yeah."

"Then we have nothing to worry about. And besides, we are going to find a way to free you."

# Chapter 18

Edward Jekyll sat in the hospital waiting room, hoping that at any moment a nurse or doctor would come out and tell him that everything was fine. They had wheeled Elsa back into the emergency room as soon as they had arrived at the hospital, the knife still embedded in her abdomen. Edward had ridden in the ambulance with Elsa, almost scared to hold her hand, but she had insisted.

During the ambulance ride, he had been internally blaming Lawrence for everything that had happened. If Lawrence had not created Hyde, none of this ever would have happened. But one thing that Lawrence had said stuck out in Edward's mind: *"But when you change, when you take on your other form, you will be the worst version of yourself."*

And the cold, harsh truth was right there. As much as he wanted to say that Lawrence had created Hyde when he had turned him into a monster, that was not true. Hyde had been inside him all along, his darkness and hate biding its time, waiting for the chance to burst forward. No matter how hard he had wanted to be, no matter how hard he had tried to be a good man, there was always that voice in the back of his head. That voice that sometimes won.

That voice was Hyde before he had been able to take on a physical form. All Lawrence had done was given Hyde the chance to take control. Lawrence did not make Edward a monster; he always was.

The door to the emergency room came open and a doctor walked out. Edward looked up, hoping that he had news concerning Elsa.

"Mr. Jekyll?" The doctor looked in Edward's direction.

"Yes." Edward stood. "How is she?"

"It looks like she is going to be fine. She may need a couple of days of bedrest to recover, but thankfully the blade didn't hit anything vital."

"That's good to hear. Can I see her?" Edward asked anxiously.

"She's sleeping now, still out from the anesthesia, but we have her set up in a room if you want to wait there for her to wake up."

"I'd like that."

The doctor led Edward through a different set of doors and down a long hallway, stopping outside of the door to a patient room. "She's in there," he gestured to the door. "I'll give you two some privacy." He shook Edward's hand and continued down the hall.

Edward stood outside the door, resting his hand on the handle for a moment. He took a deep breath before opening it. Elsa lay in the bed, her eyes closed, sleeping calmly. One of her hands was hooked up to an IV. He could see the shape of a bandage causing her shirt to bulge upward. He walked over to the bed, looking down at her peaceful face. He stood there for a moment, just taking her in. Her bangs covering a fraction of her forehead, her long blonde hair down and splayed across the pillow. Her long and lovely eyelashes. Her soft pink lips. The definition of her cheekbones. The steady rise and fall of her chest as she breathed.

He gently touched her hand with the IV needle attached to it, tightening his jaw. He knew this was his chance; that this was what he had to do.

"I love you Elsa," he said softly, not wanting to disturb her rest. "I have to leave and you can't follow me. I hope we don't have to be apart for long... I don't know how long I will be able to stand it. But at least I'll know you're safe." He leaned over her, carefully brushing back her bangs and lightly kissing her forehead. "I'm sorry," he whispered, a single tear rolling down his cheek as he let go of her hand and quietly exited the room, pulling the door closed behind him.

# Chapter 19

Brook heard a knock at his office door. He checked his watch. He had about fifteen minutes until Carmichael's session; and after his exit the last time they'd met, he was not expecting him to be early, if he showed up at all.

"Who is it?" Brook asked reluctantly.

There was a moment of silence and then Carmichael's muffled voice came through the door. "It's me. If you aren't too busy, I wanted to talk."

Brook furrowed his brow, surprised, walking over to the door and opening it just a crack. "Sure Carmichael," he opened the door wider, "what's on your mind?"

Carmichael entered the office, plopping down on the couch. "I guess first off, I wanted to apologize for my outburst last time. I am generally a patient man, but I have my... moments of weakness."

"We all do." Brook smiled slyly. "How are you tonight, Carmichael?"

"Fine I suppose. Repentant." Carmichael leaned forward, stroking his bare chin. "But that's part of what I wanted to talk to you about. How are *you* doing?" Brook looked taken aback. "Cause I hate one-sided conversations."

Brook looked at him suspiciously, considering him, trying to analyze the root of the question. As a psychiatrist, he was naturally analytical. For the time being, he decided to humor him.

"I'm doing all right, Carmichael. I'm a little tired, have a little bit of back pain, but I'm doing all right."

Carmichael nodded and bit his lower lip, then his eyes shot back up to Brook. "Why do you sit here and listen to other people's problems? Are you really as good of a man as you want people to believe?"

Brook's jaw tightened. Carmichael smiled slightly to himself; he had struck a chord.

Brook stroked his goatee, taking a deep breath. "Honestly Carmichael, because the world we live in is shitty. When I was younger, my life was no cake walk. I was severely bullied, even before I started school. Or knew other kids. My father was no 'gem' to be around... he was an abusive drunk that my mother never had the courage to stand up to. Once I started school, the bullying and teasing started almost immediately; the *abuse* continued. When I thought I couldn't take anymore... I finally decided to seek help.

"At first I was bitter. Angry. I wanted to lash out at those who hurt me: the other kids, my father, even my passive mother who did nothing to stop the bastard. But when I found people who actually wanted to help, who cared," he paused, looking at his hands, then back at Carmichael, "things took a positive turn for me. I decided one way I could continue to feel better about myself – and possibly make the world a better place – was to help others. Those like me. The hopeless and the hurt.

"So while to get here, I had to bury my nose in books about the brain and psychology, that all stemmed from wanting to help people. So all in all I like to think that I am a generally good person, even if I do have some selfish motives."

Brook leaned back in his chair, folding his hands over his chest and looking at Carmichael. Carmichael bounced his leg up and down, then looked up at the ceiling. Brook had surprised him; he hadn't tried the whole shrink shtick. As a matter of fact, Carmichael was fairly certain that he had been completely candid with him. Sure, some of it seemed cliché. But not sugar-coated.

"I suppose that is a good enough answer." Carmichael scratched his knee. "After all, we all have selfish motives in the end. And the world we live in is shitty."

"You should understand that better than most." Brook sat up straighter. "What about you Carmichael? Do you consider yourself to be a good person?"

Carmichael stopped bouncing his leg. The tables had turned. His little game was over, at least for now. He turned to look out the window, the streetlight outside distorted by the plastic blinds. "No, not really," he said huskily. "Like I said, we all have selfish motives."

Brook smiled slightly, nodding. "Yes, that is true in most cases, I suppose. Do you think these motives are part of the cause of your depression?"

Carmichael glanced up at him. "I suppose… life's a very fragile thing, Hydecker."

Brook's expression grew troubled as he tried to think of how to best phrase his next question. "Have you ever been responsible for anyone's death, Carmichael?" The air grew tense between them and there was nothing but silence and the whir of the ceiling fan. "… Have you ever killed anyone?"

"Well, I'm a vampire aren't I?" He half-smiled. "They didn't always have the blood distribution centers, you know," he replied quietly. "That was a man named Edwyn Gwaed's idea in the late 1700s I think it was. Take the blood they drain from cadavers at the mortician's and package it up nicely for bastards like me.

112

"The 1880s into the 1920s, I was in a particularly low place. I had turned to smoking, alcohol, even drugs to give my life what it was lacking."

"Drugs?" Brook asked.

"Marijuana. Opium. Cocaine. All of it. I can get high as a kite without having to suffer any of the consequences. But the effects of those things were only temporary. In the end, I wasn't finding what I was looking for in an opium den or the bottom of a bottle." Carmichael looked gravely at Dr. Hydecker. "I'm sure you've heard of the infamous Jack the Ripper." Brook nodded. "I met him once, though he no longer went by that name – he went by the name of Herman Webster Mudgett, or H.H. Holmes. Interesting man, but more importantly, a man who *lived*. His murder castle was amazing. Inspiring.

"So, in the early 1920s I turned to a new pastime. I frequented speakeasies as it was, since the Prohibition was in full effect, and I needed my alcohol fix. I practically lived drunk or high in those days – mostly drunk.

"I was much more low profile than Jack, and the speakeasies provided the perfect hunting ground. If people went missing from them, either nobody noticed; or if someone did, nobody would report it. After all, just admitting to being there was incriminating. Over the years, I had accumulated quite an impressive sum of money. Invested some, held on to the rest. I had a rather sizable house – hell, a mansion, right here in this very city. And not to be too egotistical, but I am quite a good-looking fellow.

"So it wasn't really difficult to lure young women who were usually drunk out of the speakeasies and back to my residence. Their reactions were usually the same: 'Is all this really yours?' or just bedazzled eyes looking around the interior of the foyer. One of the things that hasn't changed over the centuries: women love a man with money.

"After that, things could go a number of ways. We typically ended up in the bedroom. Sometimes I would use tools – belts, canes, candlesticks, other objects that could inflict pain – and do a little beating. Other times, if they were into this sort of thing, I'd wait until they were tied to the bed. But often times, I was quick and to the point.

"Once in the bedroom, I would push them up against the wall and we would be kissing – hell, sometimes, they were already starting to undo the buttons of my shirt. I would slowly work my way down along the jaw to their necks. They'd let out little moans of pleasure, sometimes a titter of laughter. Then I'd sink my fangs into their throat, my mouth filling with their blood due to their heart racing from the fiery passion they were feeling, making it easy enough to-"

114

Carmichael noticed Brook's shoulders had tensed and he was gripping the arm of his chair with his free hand.

"It was thrilling, for a while. Like most things, the appeal wore off after some time. Not that it was a case of having to lay low; no one was ever after me. I disposed of the bodies in the furnace. But once the thrill was gone, I decided it was time to return home to England. That was in 1928." Brook shifted in his chair, clearing his throat. "Are you uncomfortable, Brook?" Carmichael sneered. "How would Mrs. Hydecker feel about this? Armchair talk with a murderer?"

Brook suddenly glared at him, his face turning red and his body growing tenser as he gripped the armrest white-knuckled. "Get out of here. Your time is up," he said crossly.

"Look, I don't do that anymor-" Carmichael was taken aback by this response.

"I said get out!" Brook rose from his chair a little, pointing at the door, his eyes ablaze.

Carmichael knew that he had really struck a chord this time and decided it would be best to leave before one of them did something they'd regret.

# Chapter 20

Edward sat down on the edge of the cheap motel bed. He set down his duffel bag, filled only with the essentials he would need for a short time. He had gone back to the house and gathered clothing for several days, basic toiletries, and made sure he had his license and debit card in his wallet. He had decided to start looking for the answer to his problem in his own city. While it made him uncomfortable being in the same city as Elsa, he also hoped that he would not have to travel far. The more distance between them meant more time apart and more heartache. Edward had heard rumors of several witches, warlocks, and other magic practitioners in the area. He had just never thought he would have to go to one for help. He honestly hated the idea.

He felt his guts twisting up into knots, and he wasn't sure if it was because of the fact that he had not eaten all day or if it was a sign that Hyde was lurking just below the surface. He personally hoped it was the prior, *that* problem he could fix.

His mind turned to Elsa. He hoped that she would not hate him for leaving her in her vulnerable state, but if he had not, she would have surely tried to follow him. And that would not do.

The churning in his stomach only grew worse, and he lay back on the bed, facing the ceiling. He put his hands over his face, letting out a mournful cry. And Edward Jekyll lost consciousness. He brought his hands down to reveal his cruel brow, unnaturally glowing and sunken eyes, and wicked sneer. He climbed off the bed and walked into the small bathroom, looking at himself in the mirror, roughing up his hair.

His smirk grew wider as he looked at his reflection and he snickered lightly to himself. "It's time to have a little fun."

# Chapter 21

Kurt walked along the sidewalk toward Wulfen Institution. The sun was just beginning to hang low in the sky, but it was better safe than sorry. Not better late than never; late was not an option. He jammed his hands into his jacket pockets, the wind tousling his hair. The yellow neon of Wulfen's sign glowed brightly against the darkening sky. As he drew nearer, a man stepped out from the shadow of the building.

"Hey, you Farkas?" His voice was gravelly.

"Yeah..." Kurt slowed his pace, wanting to keep his distance from the guy.

"Word around here was you're lookin' for a way to get rid of your, er, well ya know." He pointed his thumb over his shoulder at Wulfen. He was about mid-height, wearing all black including a black knit hat. His eyes were shadowed by a protruding brow, and salt and pepper stubble covered the lower half of his face.

"Yeah," Kurt stuck to his one word answers.

"Then you're in luck." Kurt stopped walking as the guy took a few steps toward him. "I know a guy who, uh, is interested in someone like you. He's a master really. There hasn't been a animal he hasn't been able to tame."

"What're you saying?" Kurt was still suspicious of the guy, but also curious.

"You ever heard of a guy 'round these parts? Calls 'imself the dog trainer. He's the guy you should be talkin' to, not all those witches and other magic mojo folk."

"Look, I'd love to chat with him, but the sun is setting and it's the first night of the cycle-" Kurt tried to walk past the guy, but he stepped in front of him.

"He wanted to meet with you and get started *tonight*." Something about his tone had changed; he apparently was no longer trying to win Kurt over, he was commanding him.

Kurt gritted his teeth. He could just push the guy out of the way and be done with it, locked away safe and sound. Or he could go with him and see if this 'dog trainer' could really do what he claimed. He may not get another chance...

"Okay. But we have to be quick about it. The moon will be rising soon."

"Knew you'd be smart about this. C'mon," the guy started through the parking lot of Wulfen, and Kurt followed, unsure of what he was getting himself into. He followed the guy across several streets until he took a sharp left and headed down a sidewalk, Kurt close on his heels. He stopped abruptly and Kurt almost ran into him. "Here." He pointed at what had once been an
120

athletic wear shop, the windows now boarded up and 'No Trespassing' signs plastered on the windows and door.

"This is the place?" Kurt said skeptically.

"Yeah. Guy has to operate a little more… under the radar, know what I mean?" The guy slapped his hand down on Kurt's shoulder. "C'mon, follow me." The guy walked up to the door, pulling a keyring from his pocket and looking at the keys in the dusky light before finally grunting and inserting one into the door's lock. He pushed the door partially open and motioned for Kurt to follow. Kurt considered his last moment to flee, but decided to follow. He was dying of curiosity, and if they tried to rob him, he was stronger than them anyway, and guns would not do much good against an angry wolf.

Much to his surprise, the inside of the old shop was dimly lit and smelled slightly of smoke. There was also the ever-so-faint scent of cologne.

"Miles?" the man hissed into the darkness.

"Just let him in and leave."

"Yessir." The guy turned and practically ran past Kurt.

Kurt squinted into the darkness, trying to see who the voice had come from. A man stepped forward, silhouetted against the light coming from the far end of the room. From what Kurt could see, he had slicked back short hair and a slender face. He appeared to be wearing a suit, the outline of a collar and jacket visible where his neck joined his shoulders. Wisps of smoke came up from a cigarillo held between his fingers.

"Kurt Farkas, I take it?" the same voice as before said. "I'm Miles."

"Yeah I'm Kurt. And if you are who he said, you know I am about to transform into a wolf in about twenty minutes or less."

"Yes, yes. I suppose you are right, no time for idle chit-chat. What *did* he tell you about me?" Miles took a puff of his cig, the smoke billowing around his head.

"Said you were some kind of dog trainer. That there wasn't an animal you couldn't tame."

"He was right about that." Miles walked to the far wall. "I have been a dog trainer for some time. Spent a few years in Berlin training circus animals: the wildest and baddest there were. Nobody had wanted them until I got ahold of them. So once I got back to the states, I decided that I wanted to try something new." He flipped a switch on the wall, and the whole room was illuminated by old fluorescent light fixtures. "I wanted a new challenge, and to help."

Miles was tall and slender, his hair jet black and parted on the side. He had an aquiline nose; he looked as if he had once been quite handsome, his face now lined by premature aging, probably

122

due to his line of work and smoking. Kurt guessed that he was not much over forty. He had narrow hazel eyes, his face set in a seemingly permanent serious expression. He wore a black suit with the jacket collar popped, the only contrast a white shirt. Even his tie was black.

"Why help me?" Kurt asked suspiciously.

"Because, I heard that you were looking for a way to lead a fairly normal life. And I have been working with wild and disobedient animals for so long, I want to shift my work to helping people." He put his cigarillo out in an ashtray on a nearby table. "If I can tame the wolf inside you, I could revolutionize living arrangements for werewolves all around this area - maybe even around the world." A small smile spread across his thin lips. "It's time your kind stopped having to hide."

Kurt looked out the door. The sky had grown darker; he knew he did not have much time before the transformation. "What are you proposing?"

"Come with me." Miles motioned to a back room and Kurt approached him. Miles stood next to him a moment, shoving his hand at Kurt. Kurt looked at him blankly. "Well shake it," Miles said, snickering, "we're business partners now."

Kurt smiled slightly and shook Miles' hand, following him into the back room. Miles flipped another switch, and a large steel-barred cage came into view.

"A cage?" Kurt felt his heart sink.

"Only until I can teach you certain commands. Heaven knows I wouldn't want to put either of us in any real danger until I see what kind of contro- how easy it is to tame you." Kurt looked at the cage uncertainly. "What have you got to lose?" Miles urged him.

Kurt knew he did not have much time to deliberate about it. "All right. I guess we can give it a shot."

"Excellent." Miles rubbed his hands together, opening the cage for Kurt to go inside. As Miles locked the door behind him, Kurt's whole body began to convulse. His skin began to ripple. He clenched and unclenched his fists as he bent over, the bones in his back beginning to shift position. "No!" he cried out, his cry turning into a growl as hair sprouted on his face and worked its way down his neck to his torso. Hair sprouted up on his arms and his nails grew into pointed claws. His face began to elongate and take on a canine look, his hair assimilating into the fur now covering his head as his ears became more pointed.

He stood in the center of the cage, breathing heavily. His now-black nose twitched, and he suddenly turned to face Miles through

124

the bars, his eyes no longer housing any humanity, now a bright yellow. Miles stood confidently, popping his knuckles. Kurt let out a loud roar and began to charge the bars.

"Down boy!" Miles yelled, holding his hand out in front of him authoritatively. Kurt pounded against the bars, sticking his arm out and swiping at Miles. Miles gritted his teeth and yelled with even more determination this time. "I said *down boy!*" Kurt paused, cocking his head and considering Miles. He pulled his arm back through the bars and stared at him, perplexed. "Now that's more like it." Miles stepped a little closer to the cage, but still kept a fair distance. Kurt snarled and snapped at his approach. "Now stop that right now!" Miles held his ground. Kurt did not seem to like being scolded and stopped growling, licking his chops. "Good dog." Miles decided to try a new command. "Sit," he demanded, pointing toward the ground. Kurt did not seem to understand what he wanted. Miles merely chuckled. Compared to some of those circus animals in Berlin, this was turning out to be easier than expected. "Sit," he commanded again, walking over to a small box on the table. He pulled out a red strip of meat. "Sit and I'll give you a treat."

Kurt seemed to understand what 'treat' meant and charged the bars again, reaching for the strip of meat. He began snarling when Miles kept it out of reach.

"Down boy! Sit!" Miles pointed impatiently at the ground again and Kurt retreated from the bars, still not seeming to fully comprehend what 'sit' meant in his wolf state. Miles slowly lowered himself to the ground, then waggled the meat at Kurt and repeated himself. "Sit."

Kurt snorted, seeming to analyze Miles and then slowly lowered himself into a strange sitting position somewhere between a human and canine.

"Good boy," Miles threw him the meat and Kurt snatched it up, his teeth tearing through it. It disappeared within a matter of seconds. Miles smiled to himself. "I think you and I are going to get along just fine."

~

Kurt opened his eyes, looking around him. He was suddenly disoriented, his surroundings foreign to him. Why wasn't he in his cell? Had he hurt anyone? Where was he?

"Good morning." Miles walked into the room, setting a plate of bacon and eggs by Kurt where he lay on the ground. Kurt looked around and spotted a large steel cage across the room.

"Wha-what happened?" he asked groggily, sitting up and taking the plate in his hands.

126

"We had a very successful first night. I was even able to let you out to stretch your legs." Kurt looked up at him, still confused. "You want proof? I have the whole place set up with surveillance cameras, let's have a look, shall we?"

Kurt slowly stood and followed Miles into a small office with several television monitors. One showed the room with the cage. Miles pressed a few buttons on the control panel below the screens and ran it back. Kurt watched in amazement as he watched himself charging the bars, Miles holding up his hand and yelling something – the recordings had no sound. He watched himself, as the wolf, back away from the bars. Miles fast-forwarded the tape, and Kurt watched as Miles unlocked the cage. He stepped out and walked around Miles, who continued to shout commands. Kurt watched his wolf-self sit, lay, rollover.

"But... how?" Kurt had yet to touch his food.

"I never found a dog I couldn't train. Any animal for that matter. I've just always had a way with them." Miles adjusted the cuff of his shirt as he spoke. Kurt continued to stand there in shocked silence. "Are you satisfied with the results?"

"I, uh, I guess so." Kurt took a bite of one of the pieces of bacon. "Will it last? I mean, will I continue to be non-aggressive without you shouting commands at me?"

"That remains to be seen. Would you like to return here tonight for more training? I think with a little more time, I could fully tame that beast inside of you. And then," he smiled, "you would never have to worry about hurting anyone again. You wouldn't have to lock yourself away. You'd be free."

Kurt felt hope wash over him. He had seen the results with his own eyes. For the first time since he was a wishful teen hitting up psychic after psychic, witch after warlock, he felt like he had a shot at a normal life. His mind then moved to Matilda Benson.

"Yes. Yes, I want to continue," Kurt nodded enthusiastically, a real smile spreading across his face.

"Good choice. I knew you'd make the right decision, Kurt."

# Chapter 22

Alexei sat stooped over his desk, his head resting on his propped up fist, glowering down at the mess of papers littering his desk. He wiggled a pen between his fingers, sighing heavily, his breath escaping his nostrils in puffs of steam due to the chilliness of the room. Jesse came out of his room, walking over to where Alexei sat. "What're you working on?"

Alexei gritted his teeth, throwing down his pen and slamming his fist onto the tabletop. "I'm bored, Jesse, bored! I want to do something else, something new!"

"What about the Lux600?"

"Light bulbs, phooey! Useless, stupid- it's been done before. Now I need some time to come up with something… a ham sandwich is what I need!"

Jesse chuckled. "Ham sandwich. Got it."

Alexei sat back down at his table as Jesse ascended the stairs. While Jesse was content spending time sitting and sipping a drink or throwing seeds to pigeons from a park bench, Alexei's mind worked differently. He had a mind that was always ticking; it could not stand still. He always had to be doing something, working on a new breakthrough. And then instead of sitting back to enjoy the fruits of his labor, he was on to the next thing, his previous accomplishment all but forgotten.

Except for Jesse.

Jesse was the one accomplishment that Alexei had not immediately put to the side to be used by others or collect dust. Jesse knew that he loved Alexei. Despite his insanity, Jesse loved him in the way one loves their senile old uncle. Jesse wasn't sure how Alexei felt about him. If nothing else, he could connect with Jesse in a world where he connected with no one. That, if nothing else, was the one thing they shared. They were both outcasts.

~

**A few years ago...**

Alexei looked up as the door to the lab flew open, and Jesse came stumbling through. His cheeks were streaked with tears. Dark blood stained his chin and the side of his shirt. Coming over the threshold, Jesse's ankle twisted, causing him to sprawl face-first onto the laboratory floor.

"Jesse, what happened?" Alexei exclaimed, kneeling to help him back to his feet.

Jesse sniffed back more tears, letting out a small sob as he held his side with his free hand. "Am I a monster?" he asked in between sobs, looking up at Alexei with tear-rimmed eyes, but avoiding eye contact.

Alexei frowned, a deep crease in his forehead. "No. No, you're not a monster." He rested his hand on Jesse's shoulder.

"W-why do people fear me? They call me a freak... and a monster."

"People are afraid of what is different, what they don't understand. You are different, truly one of a kind, even in this diverse world we live in. The term 'monster' is relative anyway." Alexei tried to meet Jesse's gaze, but he was now staring down at the floor. "What do you think a true monster is, Jesse?"

"... Bad," Jesse replied after a moment.

"And you are the farthest thing from." Alexei smiled reassuringly. "People are cruel – sometimes they are more a monster than any vampire, werewolf, or shapeshifter. I've been called a monster by some."

"But you're not bad," Jesse said, wiping away the last of his tears.

Alexei's smile turned morose. "I have to get back to work Jesse."

~

Jesse took the ham sandwich from the shop owner and began the walk back to the lab. He knew that Alexei certainly had his demons, despite how often he lived in a state of manic euphoria. While like all humans, his intentions were not all pure, Jesse did not think that he was bad. In the short time Jesse had spent among Alexei's peers, he knew there were many who believed him to be so intelligent and logical that he could not feel. But Jesse knew that underneath his nearly constant ecstatic state, that Alexei was capable of caring. And that he felt a certain level of self-loathing. Jesse did not know why, but he did see it there sometimes, behind the brilliant olive hue of his eyes. Different than loneliness, darker… sadder even. But then again, maybe Jesse was overthinking things.

# Chapter 23

Matilda sat at the table, tapping her fingers on the tabletop.
Kurt had texted her that he had good news. But then why couldn't
she shake the anxious feeling in her gut?

Kurt walked into the bar, and headed for the table she was
sitting at. She opened her mouth to speak, but he kissed her
passionately before she could get any words out. He pulled back,
beaming at her. He sat down adjacent to her, resting his hands on
hers, causing her tapping to cease.

"Well you're in a good mood," Matilda said to him, still in a
slight daze over his jubilant entrance.

Kurt looked into her eyes, his smile widening. "Matilda, I
found a solution to all of my problems. Or I guess I should say that
it found me. I found a way to tame the wolf inside, for the time
being at least. Until I can find a more permanent solution."

Matilda smiled weakly; she could still not shake the feeling
that something was amiss. "How?" she queried.

"This man, he's like a dog trainer. His name is Miles. He's
amazing. It... what he said he could do, it actually worked. I saw
it, right there on the surveillance tape. He was getting through to
me – it."

Matilda stiffened, dropping her gaze to the floor. Something about his description of Miles hit a familiar chord with her that she just could not place.

Kurt noticed how pensive she had become. He squeezed her hand gently. "Don't you know what this means? There's a chance that I won't have to hide anymore. I could finally have a shot at a normal life. Everything I've always wanted; no more fear of hurting anyone."

Matilda smiled a little more genuinely at him. That glimmer of hope had returned to his eyes. She did not want to be the one to extinguish it. Maybe she was just being paranoid. "I hope so." She flipped her hand over to hold his.

"What's wrong?" Kurt searched her eyes, but she avoided his gaze.

"I just... I don't want to see you get hurt. I mean, how much do you even know about this guy? A better question is how did he know so much about *you*?"

Kurt shrugged. "I mean, he supposedly trained the biggest and baddest circus animals in Berlin. After what I saw on that tape, I would be hard pressed not to believe him. He said he wants to move on to helping people with his gift – he's always had a way with animals. He wants to revolutionize the werewolf's lifestyle."

"But how did he know about you?"

134

"I assume he must have seen me going to Wulfen. Or one of his, uh… assistants. Miles sent a guy to wait for me outside Wulfen and talk to me about seeking 'treatment' with him."

Matilda pursed her lips, then smiled at him. She scooted her chair closer to him. "All I want is for you to be happy. And if you think this man – Miles – is what can do that, I guess I want you to give it a shot." She reached up with her other hand and caressed Kurt's cheek. "But just remember this. I love *you*, Kurt. That wolf inside, it doesn't define you. It doesn't control you."

Kurt turned his head and kissed her palm, closing his eyes. He reached up and stroked the back of her hand and then looked back at her. "I love you Matilda. And that is part of why I have to go through with this. I want a better – a normal – life for us. One where I don't have to worry about hurting you. If I did that-" he stopped short. "This is the only thing I've found that's ever even halfway worked. I have to try."

"Then do that. I will support you no matter what choice you make. I just want you to… be careful."

"I know," he leaned forward and kissed her forehead.

# Chapter 24

Edward tossed the few things that he had used during his stay at the motel into his duffel. It was time to move on to a different living space. He had probably stayed here too long, the police could show up at his door at any minute looking for Hyde. And if they arrested Hyde, they arrested Jekyll.

*"They won't catch us, I was extra careful not to leave a trail,"* Hyde's voice said inside his head.

"Us!? No, *you* did this!" Jekyll snapped back.

*"Oh please,"* Hyde scoffed, *"I'm just a facet to the gem that you call your life."*

Jekyll winced. He could not remember what Hyde had made him do; when Hyde took control, Jekyll was pushed to the side, made unaware of what terrible acts he was carrying out. But he knew it was bad, just a feeling in his gut told him that much.

"What did you do?" Jekyll slumped down onto the bed with his head down, his eyes to the floor.

*"Just went out for a little fun,"* Hyde teased.

"I don't think you and I have the same idea of 'fun.'"

*"Well... I guess I could let you remember just a tad of the other night."* Hyde chuckled and Jekyll began to regain some of his

memories, but they were distant, as if he was looking through a slowly clearing mist.

In his mind's eye, he saw himself walking down the hall of his floor of the motel. Hyde was trying to find something to do for fun, he was terribly bored. He wanted to do something *bad*. And that was when the elevator doors opened and a middle-aged woman stepped out. She was laden with bags and struggling to get them and herself through the elevator doorway.

Hyde saw his chance. "Let me help you with those." He said as pleasantly as a being born of pure evil could.

"Oh, you really don't have to." She blushed.

"I insist." Hyde smiled, his face taking on a wicked glow. But she did not seem to notice.

"Well thank you." She handed him a bulging bag and led him down the hallway. She got out her keycard and unlocked Room 304. "You can set it down just inside the door." She walked over to her bed, setting the bags on it and reaching for the lamp. Hyde set the bag lightly on the floor, quietly kicking the door closed behind him. He reached into his coat and brought out the boning knife – Jekyll recognized it as the one from his own kitchen. "Thanks again." She switched on the lamp and turned to see him looming behind her, his arm raised with the knife in his hand. She began to scream and everything went black for Jekyll.

Hyde decided to let him see just a bit more, but some time was lost in between. He saw himself washing dark crimson blood off of his hands and the knife. Miraculously, none had gotten on his coat, but there was a thin splatter across his forehead.

"Oh my God, you killed her." Jekyll buried his face in his hands. "How did you get the knife?"

"*I took over for a brief moment while you were packing. Wanted to make sure something of use found its way into your luggage.*"

Jekyll was suddenly overcome with rage, clenching his hand into a fist. "I never wanted to kill anyone!" he growled through gritted teeth. He thought of Elsa, and his voice softened. "And I definitely didn't want to hurt Elsa."

Hyde was silent. It would appear he had gone, for the time being at least. He decided to seize the moment and leave the motel while there was no chance of Hyde taking over. Or a slim chance, anyway. He slung the duffel strap over his shoulder, giving the room another once-over to make sure that he was not forgetting anything. He walked out the door of his motel room, bumping into someone walking down the hall.

"Oh, I'm sorry, I wasn't looking where I-"

"Edward?" The sound of Elsa's voice cut him off, and he looked up to see that she was the person that he had bumped into.

His eyes widened. "Elsa! What are you doing here?"

"When I woke up at the hospital and you weren't there, I knew you had probably tried to leave when I couldn't follow. That was confirmed when I got home and you weren't there. This was the least likely place you'd go," she motioned around at the motel hallway, "which made it the most likely place to find you."

Edward just stood there a moment, dumbfounded. He admired her, how smart she was, the fact she had known to find him here. He also felt stupid for making it so easy for her.

"I'm not going to let you face this alone." She reached out and took his hand in hers. "You need someone by your side, someone who can help. I know you'd do the same for me."

A slight smile tugged at the corners of his mouth in spite of himself. It shrank as he looked deep into her eyes. "You know this is dangerous. I would never hurt you, but he would."

She looked back at him seriously. "I love you; all of you, the good and the bad."

"You would risk that? You would risk your life for me?" He brought his free hand up to her stomach and gently rested it where he could see the swelling of the bandage through her clothing.

"Of course I would. I love you."

"I think that deep down I know I can't stop you," he said, his voice strained. "That's part of what I love about you... I love

140

everything about you." His voice caught in his throat, that same fear bubbling in his gut as the day at the café. But he needed to say this now, no matter what happened. "You're the one, Elsa." He felt his eyes getting wet as he looked at her, refusing to break eye contact. "I love you more than anything and if… if anything terrible," his eyes strayed to her stomach, then back up to her face, "*more* terrible happened to you, I don't know what I'd do. I… I, uh, I was going to propose that day at the café. But then the robbery happened and I just didn't feel that the time was right." He began to cry, sniffing in an attempt to keep his nose from running. "And then all this Hyde business happened and I knew that I couldn't propose, not while he could hurt you. But being away from you, it kills me Elsa. I want to spend the rest of my life with you." He closed his eyes, turning away from her and breaking into light sobs.

Elsa took his face in her hands, turning his head so that he was looking at her again. Tears glistened in her eyes as she looked at him. She brought his face down to hers, kissing him passionately. He gradually brought his hands up along her back in an embrace, pulling her close to him, savoring the feeling of her lips against his. She ran her fingers through his hair, running her other hand down his back. In that moment, Edward Jekyll felt like he could face anything. He just feared that Hyde had other plans for him.

# Chapter 25

Kurt made his way to the abandoned athletic wear shop. Miles had said he would leave the door unlocked for him, and sure enough, it was unlocked when Kurt arrived. He slipped inside as the sky shone a deep pink with streaks of orange.

"Glad to see you kept your word." Miles sat in a swivel chair, smoking and reading a magazine. "I think we can start you outside the cage tonight."

"Oh really? So soon? It's only the second night," Kurt said, a little taken aback.

"You saw the tape. I am making fantastic progress with you, Kurt. But let's go in the back room for security, shall we?" He put out his cigarillo in the ashtray and set down his magazine before standing and leading Kurt into the back. Kurt took deep breaths; he was suddenly tense, his hands balled into fists. "What are you so nervous about?" Miles flipped the light switch.

"I guess I'm just… still getting used to the idea of not being locked up during the change."

"Well, you won't have to be locked up anymore, if things keep going the way they are."

Kurt felt his body begin to quiver. He bent over, grunting. The transformation was always a little painful, considering that his body was literally twisting and changing shape. His grunts and sighs turned into a long howl as he threw his head back, his face lengthening into a snout. He turned to look at Miles almost immediately.

Miles smirked, standing up a little straighter. "Stay," he commanded and while Kurt looked as if he wanted to lunge forward, he stayed rooted to the spot. Miles twirled his index finger in a circle. "Now turn around." Kurt walked around in a circle. Miles' smirk widened, and his face took on a certain type of menacing glow. Miles took a step toward Kurt. He stepped even closer. The wolf watched him closely, but made no move to swipe at him. Miles loved this feeling, the feeling of having control over something so powerful. He reached out to touch Kurt. Kurt tensed, but made no move to bite or swipe at him. Miles let his fingers run through a patch of the brown fur now covering Kurt's back. He removed his hand and took a few steps back. "Now, I am going to teach you a new command." He crossed his arms, his expression now downright malevolent. "Kill."

# Chapter 26

Alexei looked at himself in the men's restroom mirror as he washed his hands. He looked exhausted, dark bags ringing his eyes, his cheeks even more gaunt than usual. A toilet flushed, and the stall door opened. Chairman Vapelli walked out.

"Ah, Alexei. Didn't know you were at the office today," Vapelli said, turning on the faucet and running his hands under the water. "You look tired."

"I'm fine, Chairman," Alexei replied flatly, turning off the water and grabbing a couple of paper towels.

"That's good, I suppose." Vapelli also turned off his sink, drying his hands. "Enjoy it while you can. You may not be free to walk the streets doing whatever you want for much longer."

Alexei smirked, balling up his saturated paper towels. "Please Chairman, save your empty threats."

"Oh, but that's just it, Alexei Frankenstein. They're not as empty as you think. You see, there happen to be a considerable amount of people who agree with me about you. And the rumor is, we will be coming under some new leadership soon. Leadership that hasn't been here to reap the benefits you bring. Leadership that may see you for just what you are: dangerous."

Alexei threw down his paper towels and lunged at Vapelli, gripping him by the throat one-handedly and pushing his back up against the wall. Vapelli's eyes bulged and he tried to yell, but all that came out was a choked gag.

"Dangerous am I?" Alexei said, staring into Vapelli's startled face, squeezing a little tighter. He stood at least a foot taller than the wheezing man. Vapelli winced, his tongue lolling out of his mouth, sweat beading his bald forehead. "You like to talk big," Alexei squeezed even tighter, bringing his face closer to Vapelli's, "but without security guards at your beck and call, you're nothing but a scared, fat little man." Tears began to form in the corners of Vapelli's eyes as he struggled to breathe. "Until you get some bite to go with that bark, I'd keep it to yourself." He released Vapelli, letting him fall to the floor. Before he could regain his ability to speak, Alexei exited the restroom and started down the hall.

Vapelli sat on the floor, holding his neck and coughing. He struggled to stand, the tiled floor slick under the soles of his shoes. He wiped the tears from his face as he pushed open the door, leaning on it for support. He could see Alexei further down the hall and yelled after him. "I'm going to see you put away! I won't rest until I see your crazy ass behind bars, or better yet, in a padded room!"

146

# Chapter 27

Carmichael could see the dimly glowing violet W at the end of the alley. He kicked a rock across the pavement. Did he actually want to go down that alley and deal with the witch at the end? Not really, but it was worth a shot.

He clenched both of his hands into fists and shook out his shoulders, closing his eyes and drawing in a deep breath. When he opened his eyes, he let the breath out and extended his fingers, his eyes set on the W as he started down the alley.

As he reached the door and raised his hand to knock, a voice spoke from behind him. "I've been waiting for you to come around."

Carmichael froze, shaking his head slowly as he lowered his fist. "I'm sure you have," he replied, turning to face the old woman behind him, "W."

She smiled as she looked at him, the wrinkles in her aged face becoming more pronounced. "Don't call me that… we've known each other too long… you're just as handsome as the day I met you." Tears glistened in her mix-matched eyes as she slowly reached a hand out toward his face, veiny and quivering. His face remained emotionless as he took a step back from her. She took her hand back, rubbing her fingers against her palm. "I still care for you, but I'm an old woman now. Time takes its toll on some people."

Carmichael harrumphed, smirking slightly. "Time takes its toll on everyone, it's just more noticeable for some."

"Why are you being so cold to me? You know that I've never done anything but love you. And they say time heals all wounds." He chuckled derisively. "Why did you come to see me then?"

His smirk widened and he lifted one eyebrow. "I'm so glad you asked. I want you to undo the spell." He leaned toward her. "I want to be able to die."

W smiled, her white eye seeming to glow slightly. She pulled her spider web shawl tighter around herself. "Magic doesn't work like that. It doesn't have an undo button like the fancy technology they have nowadays. You should know that." Her smile shrunk a little. "And even if I could lift the spell, you know I wouldn't."

Carmichael clenched his jaw, his eyes seeming to glow brighter. "Please stop. We both know you don't really care about me. It was all a power game to you, that's all it ever was." He glided past her.

She closed her eyes, tears sliding down her age-spotted cheeks. She spun around, crying after him, saliva flying from her mostly toothless mouth. "It was never a game! Not with you! There are days – no, specific moments – when I truly miss you. Since you, I have lived a loveless existence. But I always knew you were around somewhere and I prayed that someday you would find your way back to me!"

He continued walking down the alley and turned onto the sidewalk. Then he was out of sight.

# Chapter 28

"This is stupid, most of these people are probably fakes," Edward huffed, leaning back in his desk chair, sifting through the classified ads for anyone claiming to be a witch, warlock, psychic, or some other practitioner of magic.

"We have to start somewhere," Elsa replied, sitting on the floor and also sifting through papers.

Edward had taken up residence at a much nicer hotel, getting himself a suite with most of the conveniences of home. He had made Elsa promise to stay at the house at night and even given her his keys so that Hyde could not come and go from the house as he pleased.

"I know," he sighed, "I just feel like the 'real deal' people would not be posting their services in the classifieds. You would likely have to know the right person, work the channels. A lot like crime journalism." That reminded Edward he had not been to work in several days. While he wanted to be upset about it, being fired seemed to be the least of his worries at the moment. He would worry about getting his job back or trying to get hired at another paper once all of this Hyde business was behind him. He knew one thing: *The Southern Bell* was already ruled out.

"So, when Hyde takes over, can you see what is happening and just not stop it? Or does everything go black?" Elsa asked. They had also agreed that the more she knew about Hyde, the better.

"I completely black out. It's like… I fall unconscious, but Hyde takes control of my body. So there is some form of consciousness… but I am not aware of it. Unless he decides to show me after the fact. I think that most of the time, I would be glad to be kept in the dark. I'd rather not watch him use my body as his puppet to perform heinous acts if I am powerless to stop him." Edward gave Elsa a sideways glance, a look of guilt flashing in his eyes.

"It's healing well," she assured him, touching his hand.

"I know. And I'm glad." He forced a smile, turning back to the paper in his hand. He tried not to, but his mind wandered to the woman Hyde had murdered at the motel. Her name had been Giselle Michaels. He had seen her picture plastered on the front page of one of the papers. Her killer was still at large. It had almost been easier for Edward to deal with before he could put a name to the face. One thing that gave him some miniscule amount of comfort was that she was not married and had no children; he had not murdered a wife or mother.

"It wasn't your fault." Edward was not sure if she was referring to what he had done to her or Giselle Michaels' murder;

he had told her what Hyde was capable of. He had wanted her to understand exactly what she was getting herself into.

He sat in silence, trying desperately to focus on the ads in front of his face. But he could not seem to focus, his mind wandering here and there. His lack of mental control made him worry that Hyde might be lurking just beneath the surface, waiting to pounce.

He looked at where Elsa sat on the floor. She was between him and the door to the hotel room. If she had warning, she could run out the door before him if she needed to. He really hoped she would not have to. But it was a possibility that needed to be taken into account.

Something else that also bothered him was that he could not account for the boning knife, which Hyde seemed to have taken a sick liking to. As far as he knew, Hyde had not taken control over the past couple of days, but what if he was taking control of Jekyll while he slept, going about his business undetected? Edward shuddered. He needed to stop overthinking it. If he did not, he would lose his mind, and he felt like he was quickly on his way to losing it as it was.

He grunted, his head beginning to feel woozy. "Elsa," he struggled to say, feeling the impending darkness closing in.

She looked up at him, saw him about to fall out of the chair. Her first impulse was to help him, but she restrained herself. She knew what this meant, Hyde was about to take over. She thought back to her last encounter with him and stood, her eyes wandering over to the door. She could make it out into the hall if she tried, but she did not want to make any sudden movements. She did not want to attract more attention to herself than necessary.

"Looking for magicians in the paper huh? Wow, he must be desperate," Hyde's voice mocked as he looked around the room littered with newspapers. Elsa made a move for the door. "Oh no you don't!" Hyde suddenly leapt up, bounding toward her.

She tried to run for the door, but he was there, blocking her path. She turned, instinctively running for the bathroom. In her peripheral vision she saw Hyde retreat to the bed, but decided not to risk going for the door again. The bathroom door had a lock, and she could wait until he had turned back into Jekyll - the Edward that she knew. As she turned to pull the bathroom door closed behind her, Hyde reached under the mattress and something glinted in his hand. Elsa shuddered: the boning knife. She felt a phantom pain in her stomach, and Hyde turned with the knife in his hand, looking directly at her. She pulled the door closed, locking it.

He began pounding on the door. "Elsa! Elsa, let me in!"

She remained silent, retreating to the bathtub and sitting down in it. She hoped that the door would hold. But she was sure that

154

Hyde would not destroy the door; too much noise would attract attention and - as evil as he was - he was not stupid.

She tried to change her course of thought. Hyde could not be truly evil. If he were, that meant that Edward – Jekyll – had some evil in him. And she refused to believe that. Some darkness, sure, everyone had even a little bit of darkness in them. But not evil.

"Elsa..." he hissed from the other side of the door, "don't make this harder on yourself. Just open the door." She heard him try the knob again, letting out an angry sound as he found it to still be locked.

She continued to sit in the tub, hoping that this would not last long. Then another thought crossed her mind: what if he got bored waiting for her to come out and left the room? What if he hurt someone else? She could not allow that. One poor soul had already fallen victim to Hyde, and she wanted to keep that number from growing.

She quietly climbed out of the tub and tiptoed across the bathroom to the door. She rested her fingertips on the doorknob. She knew Edward would not approve of what she was about to do; but then again, he would not approve of anything that could put her in danger. She could not really blame him. But this was something she knew she had to do, to keep others safe from Hyde. If she just remained calm, this plan would work.

She gripped the knob firmly, trying not to make a sound. She wanted to catch Hyde completely off guard. A thought caused her to pause. What if he was standing right on the other side of the door, waiting for her to give in and come out? Or what if he had already left the hotel room? No, that could not have happened, she would have heard the door. She twisted the knob and flung the door open.

Hyde had been sitting in the desk chair, facing the bathroom, playing with the knife. He jumped at her sudden outburst, but was quickly on his feet, the knife in his hand. Elsa watched his every move carefully. If she wanted to disarm him, she would have to get the timing just right. She desperately tried to remember the tips from the self-defense seminar she had attended in college, but was coming up blank. Something about gripping the wrist...

He was getting closer. He put his weight on his back leg, pulling his arm back to slash at her face and neck. As he swung his arm, she ducked under his arm, narrowly missing the business end of the knife. She silently apologized to Edward as she kicked Hyde in the back of the knee. He let out a cry, falling. She lunged forward, gripping the wrist of his hand that held the knife and squeezing. The knife fell to the carpeted floor with a soft thump. She quickly bent to grab it and retreated to the desk.

Hyde stood, brushing off his jeans. He turned toward Elsa, and she held the knife up in front of her defensively. He chuckled hoarsely. "You going to stab me? You stab me, you stab your lover boy." She started to lower the knife, but stopped, continuing to hold it in front of her. If he thought she was serious, perhaps he would keep his distance. His sneer wavered a moment. Her hand began to shake. He chuckled again. "You don't have it in you to kill anybody. Or non-fatally stab them, for that matter." He took a step toward her, his hands both appearing like claws, his fingers outstretched as if he intended to grab her. "Now give me back my knife so I can slit your pretty little throat."

"No," Elsa struggled to steady her voice and her hand. "You're crazy if you think that I am going to just hand you the knife." Despite his harsh words, she noticed something – a change in the tone of his voice. She was not sure what it meant – what he was plotting, but he definitely had sounded different. She took a few breaths, watching him carefully. She decided to attempt to reason with him. "Do you know who you are?"

"I'm Edward Hyde. Why do you ask?" He seemed suspicious, like he thought she had something up her sleeve. Maybe she did, but she just was not sure what yet.

"W-why do you always do bad things?"

Hyde opened his mouth to answer, but stopped, pondering her question. He finally looked at her, cocking his head to the side. "I *enjoy* it. It's who I am. But you know that." His eyes narrowed. "You know that I am not a person all on my own; that I am Edward Jekyll's dark side." He looked at her a moment, cocking his head to the other side. "I can't do anything but bad. That's what I am."

"If you are self-aware, as you appear to be, then why don't you stop? Change your fate. Life is made up of choices." She felt her arm begin to relax and readjusted her grip on the knife.

"It doesn't work like that. I am all of Jekyll's potential bad choices." He smiled, his eyes flashing wickedly. "But I get the feeling that this is all you stalling. Waiting for Jekyll to regain control. I may not always be present, but I do know some of what you two talk about. And I know he has told you that I am all bad. 'The worst version of himself' as that shapeshifter called me." He took a step forward. "So enough small talk; give me the knife."

Once again, Elsa noticed that his voice was not as aggressive as it had been before. Was he putting on a façade, trying to trick her? Or had she started to get through to him? She could not be sure, which meant only one thing was certain: she had better hold onto that knife.

He ran his hand through his untamed hair, licking his lips as he looked at her, his glowing eyes burning into her. He popped his jaw, letting out a distressed huff and seemed to be fighting the urge to vomit when his eyes ceased to glow and the curve of his brow softened. He looked lost for a moment, his eyes surveying the room until they rested on Elsa holding the knife.

"Edward?" she said hesitantly, beginning to lower the knife.

"Elsa… what happened? Did he-"

"No. No, he didn't hurt me."

Edward let out a sigh of relief, walking over to her as she dropped the knife to the floor, and he hugged her tightly. Her hair tickled his face. He breathed in the scent of her, and it comforted him. She hugged him back.

"Why didn't you run?" he asked, not making a move to let go of her any time soon.

"I did. He was too fast. Then I locked myself in the bathroom. But then I thought… what if he decided to go after someone else? I knew if I was careful that I could get the knife from him."

"That was dumb." The words just came out of his mouth. What Elsa had done was noble, and he admired that. She was brave. What he did not like was that she had intentionally put herself in harm's way.

"If trying to make sure others were safe is dumb, then I'll accept that I'm dumb." She kissed his jaw.

"You're not dumb… *that* was just dumb." He snickered softly. "Dumb or not… you did the right thing. I just don't want you to get hurt." He looked down at her face. "But it seems you can take care of yourself." He smiled fondly at her.

They stood there in silence a moment. "I'm starving," Elsa said, "want to grab a bite to eat?"

"Yeah, sure." He leaned back, continuing to smile at her. Until she had said something, he had not realized that he was quite ravenous himself.

# Chapter 29

Kurt lifted some lumber up onto his shoulder, walking down the long aisle of shelves. He passed a couple of his co-workers standing around, all looking at the paper and talking among themselves. They looked up as he walked by, but quickly returned to what they were reading.

Kurt hoisted the wood up onto its proper place on the shelf and brushed wood shavings off his work vest and shirt before heading back toward the storage room. As he neared the group with the paper, one of them called out to him.

"Hey Farkas, you hear about that guy that was murdered not too far from here?" Kurt shook his head, walking toward them. "They're thinking it was an animal attack of some sort. Guy was ripped to shreds. Took them a couple of days to identify him. Look." His co-worker - whose name he was fairly certain was Fred - handed him the paper.

He began to skim the story. A man in his late thirties by the name of Alec Greerson had been found a few days ago at the intersection of Main and Fifteenth. He was torn up beyond recognition, seemingly by some kind of animal, so they'd had to check his dental records. They discovered he was actually in the criminal database. They had a picture of one of his mugshots accompanying the article. Kurt squinted at the low-quality photo, then suddenly gasped. He recognized this man! It was the man who had led him to Miles.

"I need to go," Kurt shoved the paper back at the man whose name he thought was Fred. He suddenly felt hot all over. He found it to be a startling coincidence that the very man that had led him to Miles had been mangled by some kind of animal during one of the nights of the lunar cycle. Images of the girl dead in the streets flashed through his mind. He tried to make them go away as he headed into the staff lounge. Maybe he was jumping to conclusions. He had, after all, woken up in the back room of Miles' center of operations. So why did he suddenly feel so guilty?

He walked into the employee bathroom, locking the door behind him. He needed time to clear his head, to think this through. He needed to talk to Miles, to make sure that he had indeed not left the abandoned shop. He turned to look at himself in the mirror, trying to regulate his breathing. He ran his fingers through his hair, causing some to fall into his eyes. His thoughts suddenly jumped to Matilda. If he had gotten out... he knew her scent...

"No!" Kurt shouted at himself, forcing himself not to jump to conclusions. He did not have a way to call Miles. He would just have to go by his abandoned shop and hope he was there.

~

Kurt pulled his green jacket tighter around himself as he walked down the street toward the abandoned athletic wear store. He hoped that Miles would be able to put his mind at ease, to assure him that he had not hurt – murdered – anyone. That Alec Greerson's death had simply been a coincidence.

Kurt tried the door. It was locked. He tried to look through the windows or door to see inside, but the boards made it impossible to see. He pounded on the door frame with his fist. He hoped that Miles was in, that he would hear him knocking. He knocked again just to make extra sure.

Only silence for a moment. And then he heard something crash to the floor. Kurt pressed his ear against the door in an attempt to hear better; had he not been a werewolf, he probably would not have heard the sound at all. A dull thump followed, and then the scuffle of shoes. Someone closed a door inside the abandoned shop and footsteps made their way toward the front door. Kurt sniffed the air and caught the scent of Miles' cologne, accompanied by the soft but acrid scent of cigarillo smoke.

Kurt pulled his ear away from the door, standing upright. He could hear Miles struggling with the key in the lock and then the door opened just a crack. Miles peered out, his eyebrow furled suspiciously over his dark eye. Once he recognized who was standing on the other side, he lifted his eyebrow and opened the door wider.

"Kurt," he said, surprised but happily, "you have perfect timing; you were just the person I wanted to see."

Kurt chuckled, slightly taken aback. "What a coincidence, you are just the person I wanted to see."

"Well let's hope we can help each other out then." Miles ushered Kurt inside, sticking his head out the door and looking along both sides of the street before pulling the door closed and locking it. He walked partway into the room and then turned to Kurt, pulling the box of cigarillos from his pocket and smacking them against his palm. "So, what did you want to see me about?"

"Uh, an article I saw in the paper." Kurt suddenly turned to stare at the door leading to the back room; he could have sworn he heard something move just beyond the door.

"An article?" Miles had stopped smacking the box and returned it to his pocket without taking out a cig. Kurt remained motionless, trying to listen for additional sounds in the back room. "Kurt?"

Kurt slowly turned to him. "Sorry, I thought I heard something. It was an article about an animal attack." Miles stiffened slightly, but reached up to scratch the back of his neck nonchalantly. "The man killed was Alec Greerson... when I saw his picture, I realized that he was the same man who brought me here." Kurt took a deep breath. "I want to take away any doubt in my mind. I was here all night, right? I didn't get out? I couldn't have, you know... hurt anyone?"

Miles looked down at the floor, a small smile spreading across his face. "What makes you think that you would have had anything to do with it?" He looked up at Kurt, raising an eyebrow. In the dark room, his dark and pointed features caused him to look quite sinister.

"I just thought it was an odd coincidence." Kurt took a few steps back from Miles. He thought he heard another sound from the back room, a movement accompanied by a muffled whimper. He shifted his gaze to the door, but did not turn his back on Miles. "Is there something back there?"

Miles continued to smile. "Come on, Kurt. Let's see if you can help me with my little problem, shall we?" He headed for the door to the back room, and Kurt followed him at a wary distance. Miles opened the door and flipped on the light.

A man sat tied to a stainless steel chair just to the side of the cage Kurt had been trained in, a red necktie wrapped around his mouth serving as a gag. He began making a series of grunting and whimpering sounds, his eyes widening. Kurt guessed he was in his early thirties, with short ruffled blonde hair and terrified wide blue eyes. He watched both men, his eyes shifting between them, but resting primarily on Miles. He pulled at his restraints desperately.

Miles turned to Kurt. "You see this man right here?" He pointed at his prisoner. "He owes me a lot of money. Now I have given him several reprieves, but he has still failed to pay me even a percentage of what he owes." He turned to look at the man right in the eyes. "Alec Greerson had the same problem." Kurt's eyes widened as Miles walked over to his desk and opened the drawer, pulling out an automatic pistol. He walked over to Kurt, not taking his eyes off of the man in the chair. He took the gun by the barrel, extending the grip toward Kurt. "I want you to kill him."

"Wait, what, no!" Kurt put his hands up, backing away from Miles.

The smile shrunk from Miles' face and he glowered seriously at Kurt. "Kill him," he said firmly. Kurt wanted nothing to do with it, but he felt his body trying to move toward Miles of its own

166

accord. He fought the urge to reach out for the gun, but Miles continued to stare at him unwaveringly. "Do it," Miles continued to glare at Kurt, then raised his voice, "*kill him!*"

"No!" Kurt lurched forward, grasping the gun. "*What the hell is going on?*" he thought to himself. His body was moving against his will. He turned to look at Miles, who now had his hands pressed together as if in prayer and was smiling in delight. "You made me kill Alec Greerson, didn't you?" Kurt struggled to keep the gun down by his side.

"Smart boy," Miles said condescendingly. "Now kill him."

Kurt let out a small, involuntary 'woof.' He lifted the gun in terror as he realized what was happening. He looked at the man, who was leaning back in the chair as far as he could, trying to back away from the gun now pointed in his face. His eyes were wide in fright, tears gathering along his lower eyelids. Kurt closed his eyes, wincing in regret. He sighed, and it oddly resembled a slight snarl. He reopened his eyes and looked at the man. "I'm so sorry." The gun sounded two times, and Kurt's arm fell limply by his side.

The chair clattered loudly as it fell backwards, being toppled by the force of the two shots. The man was dead, blood now flowing from two bullet holes in his skull.

Kurt threw the gun down, turning on Miles. "Why – how – did you make me do that? I'm not a murderer. I just... I..." He broke down into tears, kneeling on the ground and burying his face in his hands.

Miles knelt beside him. "You did wonderful, Kurt. Better than I would have even expected." He patted Kurt's shoulder and Kurt slapped his hand away.

"Don't touch me."

"Making you kill Alec Greerson was nothing. But controlling you when you are not in wolf form… it worked out better than I had ever hoped for." He smiled at Kurt evilly.

Kurt stood, starting for the door. "No. I won't kill for you. That isn't what I signed up for."

"Stop!" Miles stomped his foot and Kurt froze. "You came here and willingly let me train you. *You* allowed *me* to control you. So you are *my* guard dog now. Now, *you* work for *me*."

Kurt spun around to face him, rage taking control. "You sought me out. You sent Alec after me, had him bring me here. Why?"

"Oh, so you want an explanation?" Miles smirked. "I suppose, considering that you can't do anything to stop me, that I could tell you a little. I have been working with animals almost my entire life. And so one day, it occurred to me, that if I controlled the wolf, then I controlled the person. After all, they are essentially one." Kurt continued to stare at him in bewilderment. "Of course,
168

I would need a willing test subject. I sent Alec around Wulfen to get the scoop on your kind. And your name kept coming up: how you talked to the others about wanting a free life and how much you hated the institution." Miles' smile widened. "And I know just about everything about you, Kurt Farkas. I had you followed. I know you work a shit job at Home Depot, that you are always alone, that your mother died a wolf." Kurt wanted to punch him in the face, but knew that would likely not do any good. "And I know about your reporter friend." Kurt felt his whole body go numb. He had not even thought about Matilda until that very moment. "But back to my original point… I deal with a lot of… 'interesting' people. And I was tired of getting my hands dirty. I wanted protection. So I determined I would need a guard dog – a guard dog that was also nearly impossible to kill. Real dogs, they drop too easy. So I found myself a werewolf." He walked over to Kurt so that they were staring into each other's eyes. "And so, I repeat myself: you are mine now."

Kurt felt hopelessness take hold. He had thought that he was meant to meet Miles, that he was the man that could finally help him – that Miles had wanted to help him. But instead it had become a kick in the crotch, another one of life's cruel jokes. The worst part was that Kurt knew Miles was right. With the wolf living inside him, there was no way that he could ever hope to fight back.

"I see I have made myself clear." Miles walked across the room and knelt to pick up the gun. "I want you to dispose of the body. Dump it in the river or something where no one will find it. Then, for now, you are free to do as you please. But when I need you – and believe me, I will need you – I will call. And you will answer."

# Chapter 30

Elsa pulled into her driveway, her headlights reflecting off of the dark windows. She turned off her engine and gathered her things, shoving the few newspaper clippings she had thought might be of some help into her purse. She put the strap on her shoulder and climbed out of the car, locking it. She heard a sound near the corner of the house – the scuffle of shoes. She tried to see who or what had made the sound, but saw only darkness.

She held her car key in her hand like a tiny knife, walking slowly toward the house. A man came from behind the house, still hidden by the shadow. "Who's there?" she said, trying to keep her voice steady.

The figure jumped at the sound of her voice, then slowly began toward her, his face becoming visible as he stepped into the illumination from the streetlight.

"You," Elsa glowered at Lawrence, "you're the one who did this to him."

"The one and only." Lawrence did a small bow before lighting a cigarette, the end glowing orange. "I did have a little help." He took a long drag, putting his arm down by his side, the cigarette perched between two of his fingers. He walked around Elsa, looking her up and down. "You seem like a nice girl. Wanting to help your boyfriend. But you should get far far away from him, if you know what's good for you."

"Is that a threat?"

"No. A warning."

"I won't leave him to do this alone. And what do you care? You're the one that made him like this."

"That may be true, but that evil was inside him all along. I just let it out." Lawrence raised his eyebrows, pointing at Elsa and flicking some ashes from the tip of his cigarette.

"He could never be evil. I've begun to get through to him."

"Good luck dealing with that." Lawrence shook his head. "You're gonna end up getting yourself killed."

Elsa just glared back at him. "What were you doing lurking around my house?"

"Well, I did come around to see how my handiwork was paying off." He leaned in close to her, blowing smoke in her face. "The fact of the matter is, I wanted to make his life Hell. To turn him into what he hated more than anything."

Elsa stared back at him, her eyes red-rimmed, both irritated from the smoke and from emotion. "Who helped you?"

"First things first: did I succeed?"

Elsa's voice caught in her throat. "Y-yes, you succeeded in releasing his inner darkness. In turning him into a 'monster' as you would say." She hated calling Edward a monster.

"Then why let the fun end there?" Lawrence smirked.

"Fun? You think this is fun? Someone has died, he nearly-" she stopped short.

"Yes, fun. Edward Jekyll has been a thorn in the monster community's side for years. I'm just the one who finally put him in his place." He blew smoke streams out of his nostrils. "You really should have a better taste in men."

"He isn't all bad. He's good deep down."

"Yeah, you keep telling yourself that sweetheart." Lawrence dropped his cigarette butt, stomping it out on the pavement.

He put another cigarette in his mouth, pulling out his lighter when there was a rustle in the bushes and someone emerged from the nearby hedge. Whoever it was stepped out into the light from the streetlight and they both recognized him as Hyde.

"Well I'll be damned," Lawrence said, lowering the lighter and letting the unlit cigarette balance limply between his lips.

"You lay a hand on her, and I'll end you!" Hyde growled, pulling the knife from inside his jacket, pointing it menacingly at Lawrence.

"Hey now, is that any way to talk to your liberator? Show some gratitude." Lawrence put his hands up defensively. "It's because of me that you can walk around freely like this."

Hyde stepped between Elsa and Lawrence, his back to Elsa, the sharp tip of the boning knife inches from Lawrence's chest. "I said, 'don't touch her.'" His eyes glowed atomic green as he glared at Lawrence.

"*I* wasn't going to. I'm not the danger to her." Lawrence looked back at him confidently. He looked around Hyde at Elsa. "W. That's all you'll get from me. Do with it what you will." He raised his lighter back to the end of his cigarette, lighting it as he looked back at Hyde. He brought the lighter down, returning it to his pocket. "I'll see you around." He blew smoke in Hyde's face before turning and walking down the driveway toward the street.

Hyde watched him go, not taking his eyes off of him until he was out of sight in the darkness. Hyde slowly lowered the knife, turning to look at Elsa over his shoulder. She stood there frozen, staring back at him. What was that look in his eyes? She did not recognize it, for it was not filled with mockery or contempt. It almost looked like... relief?

The glow dimmed in his eyes, and he closed them, shaking his head and putting his empty hand to his temple. When he opened his eyes, he was Edward Jekyll. He looked around the dark driveway for a moment before looking at Elsa. "How did I get here?" He looked down at the knife in his hand, thankful to see that it was not covered in blood.

Elsa stood silently in a mild state of shock. Had Hyde just protected her? She needed time to think about what had just happened before talking to Edward about it. "Hyde... he, uh, he came here. But I guess it was a brief spell, since you've already regained control."

Edward looked concerned, walking over to Elsa and placing the handle of the knife in her hands, holding them between his for a moment. "Take this. I don't want it where he can get to it. Be extra sure that you lock all of the doors tonight." He kissed her forehead.

"I will," she said in a hushed tone, leaning against his chest, taking the knife and allowing her arm to rest by her side.

"I should go." Edward took a step back and away from her.

She grabbed his hand before he was out of reach and he looked at her. "I love you," she said, smiling at him. "I just wanted to remind you before you left."

He smiled back at her. "I know. I love you too." He started to pull his hand away from her, but then turned back to her, running to her and kissing her. Then he released her hand and disappeared into the night before she could say anything else.

She looked after him, her heart both full and aching. She looked down at the knife in her hand and headed for the front door. As she unlocked it, she pondered what Lawrence had said. What could the letter W possibly mean?

Once inside, she locked the door behind her and walked around the house to check the other doors. She placed the knife in the dishwasher before walking upstairs and into their room. She changed into her pajamas and lay down, pulling the covers up around her shoulders. She looked over at the vacant pillow beside her and rested her hand on its cool surface. She spotted Edward's tablet sitting on the bedside table to his side of the bed. She stretched her arm out to grab it and brought it across the bed to her. She powered it on and the screen lit up, illuminating her face. Too much had happened for her to sleep. She was going to see if she could dig up anything on W, whatever that meant. Whether it was a person, place, thing, or nonsense, she was determined to find out.

# Chapter 31

Kurt walked along the aisle, taking inventory of the different sizes of lumber. The sounds of buzz saws and forklift engines were almost deafening. A customer turned down the aisle, and Kurt turned to greet them and ask what he could do to help when he recognized her. It was Matilda, clad as usual in her suede jacket and knee-length skirt, sporting black pumps even at the home improvement store.

"Kurt!" she shouted over the large machinery. Even over the smell of woodchips, her scent flooded his nostrils as she quickened her pace to approach him. "Where have you been? You've been really scarce the past few days."

Kurt ran his fingers through his hair, scrunching up his face. He looked into her inquisitive face and smiled in spite of himself. "You're right," he said loudly, "we need to talk. But not here… meet me out back in about five minutes." She crossed her arms, standing her ground. "Five minutes, I promise," he said, taking her in his arms.

She looked at him a moment longer and finally nodded. "Okay. Five minutes."

She walked out of the aisle, and he made his way back to the employee lounge. He sat down at the table, sighing heavily. He did not know how to tell her about Miles. He did not want to scare her off. Or worse, ignite a fire and have her putting herself in certain danger. But she deserved an explanation for his distance over the past few days, for the unreturned calls and ignored text messages. He looked up at the clock. He knew that he had better go out back and talk with her. He stood and walked outside.

She was there waiting of course, a few of Kurt's co-workers out on smoke break admiring her from afar, making the occasional catcall. All that stopped when they saw Kurt approaching her.

From the moment Matilda had seen him in the aisle, she had known something was wrong. She could always tell by his eyes, which had been filled with a combination of surprise and deep sorrow. "What's up? What's on your mind, Kurt?"

"It's Miles, he-" he blurted, not really thinking before he spoke, "-he has control over me. Not just when I'm the wolf, like I thought, but even when I'm like this. The wolf inside... it's stronger than I ever knew. It's more of a part of me than I think I or even my mother realized. Matilda..." He reached for her hand, taking it in his. "I don't have any control over myself anymore. I was so naïve. I wanted to believe so badly that he wanted to help me - that he *could* help me - that I was blinded to who he truly was. I'm so stupid." He stared at the ground, still gripping her hand.

"You're not stupid." Matilda stepped closer to him, feeling the heat radiate off his body. "You were just... desperate. You wanted to believe, to have hope. There's nothing wrong with that." She stroked his cheek, and he nuzzled his face into her hand.

"But now I have no control over the wolf. At least before I was safe at Wulfen, and the wolf only came a few nights every month. Now it could happen anytime and anywhere."

Matilda suddenly grew serious, the aching in her heart for Kurt becoming unbearable. She gripped his chin so that he was looking at her and looked him in the eyes. When she spoke, she spoke firmly. "Listen to me, Kurt. Remember what I said before. That wolf inside you, it doesn't define you. You're a good man and... you're stronger than that."

"But it does control me, Matilda." Kurt said sadly. "When Miles commands it to do something, it takes control of my body and uses me like a puppet."

"Then there's only one thing to do," Matilda said seriously. "We have to find a way to break your curse. To get rid of the wolf. Forever."

"How do you propose we do that?" Kurt asked.

"I don't know yet. But I know that we will find a way. Because if there's no wolf, I have a feeling that Miles will have no hold on you anymore."

# Chapter 32

"Dammit!" Alexei cried, slamming his fists down on his desk. His pens rattled and a glass of water toppled off the edge, spilling onto the floor. "Weeks, and nothing! What is wrong with me? I can't think. I can't work. I just want to disa-" he looked down at the spilled water on the floor, his voice trailing off, "-ppear..."

He knelt, the crease in his forehead deepening as he continued to stare at the small puddle. He stretched out his hand, laying it flat in the water, a splashy sound issuing as he wet his palm and fingers. He lifted his hand, staring at his fingers and rubbing them together, droplets of water falling to the floor.

"Disappear... that's it!" He stood, grabbing a piece of paper; it stuck to his wet hand in his haste as he began to scrawl down notes and equations.

After a while, Jesse peeked into the lab and saw Alexei hard at work at his desk. "What're you working on?" he asked, approaching.

"It has been in front of me this entire time," Alexei said, holding up a glass of water to Jesse. "Transparency... invisibility. I am going to develop the first serum to turn oneself invisible."

"Invisible? How do you intend to do that?"

"I'm not sure yet, but the answer must lie here," he pointed to the glass of water, "and somewhere in here," he turned back to the paper of scribbles.

"Good luck," Jesse chuckled, heading back to the door.

"Laugh if you want, but this is just another puzzle. I unlocked the secret of life, after all, so how hard can it be?"

"You have a point," Jesse smiled, ascending the stairs.

~

"So what is old Alex up to these days?" Bailey asked as he handed Jesse a cream soda.

Jesse took a drink, sighing slightly. "He wants to turn himself invisible."

"Invisible? Jeez, that old guy just gets crazier and crazier, huh?"

Jesse harrumphed. "I suppose you could say that."

"Oh, I didn't mean nothing by it. You turned out all right," Bailey said apologetically.

"No offense taken. He is insane of course, everyone knows that. He's just different."

"That's true. We're all different. Just look at you and me. The zombie and Old One-Ear," Bailey said, lifting his hair to reveal the missing top half of his right ear, an ancient scar etched into his scalp where it once had been.

"Yeah," Jesse said, looking across the diner at a group of friends laughing together. *Different.* Between the two of them, Jesse was sure he and Alexei could count their friends combined on one hand. Sure Jesse had Bailey, the few other people he had managed to have reasonable conversations with. Even he fared better than Alexei, who would only be able to speak of one: Jesse James.

"What about you?" Bailey's voice broke through his thoughts. "What are you up to these days?"

The questions caught Jesse off guard and for a moment, he was frozen, his voice caught in his throat. "… not much, Bailey." He turned, staring into the fizzling bubbles of his drink. "Not much…"

# Chapter 33

Elsa was stuck in traffic. She had been up all night, trying to find out what she could about what W meant and thinking about Hyde's strange appearance, so she had not gotten much sleep. She knew she should have left the house to get to the hotel before the lunch rush, but she had just been too tired.

She had not been able to find anything concerning the letter W that stuck out as important, but she had not given up hope. All she had been able to find were conspiracy theories about a witch, but nothing concrete. She decided to ask the magicians they hunted down if they knew of any significance of the letter. A piece of her wondered if Lawrence had sent her on a wild goose chase. Another part of her felt like he had decided to give her one clue; after all, he hated Edward, not her.

And what of Hyde's sudden appearance? Any other time Elsa had encountered him, he'd had his mind set on one thing: killing her. But when he had appeared that time, he had threatened Lawrence, even tried to protect her from him. When he had looked at her with those glowing green eyes, as sunken as they were under his crude brow, they had not been filled with malicious intent. They had been filled with relief, as if he were glad that Lawrence had gone and she was okay.

But such an emotion should not be possible for Hyde, given his nature and what he was: the manifestation of all of the darkness within Edward Jekyll. So what did his actions mean? Had Elsa actually begun to get through to him? And did that mean that he was more human than she and Edward were giving him credit for?

There were still so many questions, Elsa was not sure if she should tell him what had happened at the house. As far as she could tell, he did not remember Lawrence Talbot being there at all. Would it do more bad than good to tell him that Lawrence had come to gloat?

Elsa could finally see the hotel's sign. She took out her cell phone and dialed Edward. It rang once before he picked up.

"Hey. Where are you?"

"Not far from the hotel. I got caught in lunch hour traffic." It made her happy to hear his voice. Sleeping in their bed alone made her miss him even more.

"Okay... did you check any of the leads yet?"

"No, not yet," Elsa replied guiltily. "I was too tired last night," she lied. She did not want to bring up the letter W to Edward yet; just in case it was nothing, she did not want to get his hopes up. "I was planning to once I got to the hotel."

"Okay. See you in a few?"

"I sure hope so," she laughed nervously.

"Sounds good. Love you." Edward hung up.

"Love you too," she said, even though she knew that the call had already ended.

She pulled into the hotel's parking lot, walking inside. She climbed into the elevator and punched the button for Edward's floor. As she rode up, she decided that she would hold off on telling Edward that Lawrence had been prowling around the property. They needed to focus on finding someone who could reverse his curse.

She pulled the clippings out of her purse. Most of them looked like bullshit, but there were a few that stood out. There was a man who went by the name of Zeleni Malakai. While his ad was showy – he had had it printed in color – there was something about it that grabbed Elsa's attention. Maybe it was the fact that he did not list himself as a warlock or psychic, his title simply stated 'Zeleni Malakai: Soul Doctor.' Sure, it was cheesy, but at the moment, a soul doctor sounded just like what Edward needed.

The other two that stood out to Elsa were female psychics, although she did not know how much help psychics would be with what ailed him. But she had said herself, they had to start somewhere. The elevator dinged, and Elsa stepped off, slipping the newspaper clippings back into her purse. She began down the hall, and then knocked on Edward's door.

He opened it slightly, peeking out at her. "Finally," he opened it wider, "I was getting worried."

"I'm fine." Elsa set her purse on the counter. "You – Hyde – didn't come back last night."

"I don't like that he was there *at all*," Edward crossed his arms.

"We both knew there was a chance of that happening." Elsa bit her lower lip, Hyde's irregular behavior replaying in her mind. "I got a chance to look closer at a few of the ads while I was in the elevator. I saw a few that could be promising." Elsa decided to steer the conversation in a different direction.

"And?" Edward looked at her hopefully.

"This should probably be our first call." Elsa pulled the ad for Zeleni Malakai out of her purse.

Edward took it and read it. "'Soul Doctor,' really?" He looked at her skeptically.

"Of all the stuff here, it's the one that looks the least…" Elsa tried to choose her words carefully, "like BS." Edward sighed. "It's either that or a couple of psychics. And I don't know how much help psychics will be, given your condition." Edward tensed at the word 'condition' and Elsa quickly regretted saying it; at least she had not called him a monster.

He ran his hand through his hair, then handed her back the ad. "I guess you could call him, if you really feel like he's our best bet." Edward looked at her seriously, half-smiling. "I trust you."

Guilt washed over her as she thought of the secrets that she was keeping from him. She quickly tried to push those guilty feelings to the side. She had to keep telling herself that she was doing the right thing by not telling him, for the time being at least. She picked up her cell phone and began dialing the number on the ad. Edward paced to and fro as she hit the call button and put the phone to her ear. It rang. Once. Twice. A third time. Elsa was about to hang up when she heard someone pick up on the other end.

"Hello?" A man's voice came through the receiver, laden with a heavy Middle-Eastern accent.

"Hello, is this Zeleni Malakai?" Elsa asked sheepishly.

"Yes, it is I, Zeleni Malakai: Soul Doctor! Might I ask who I am speaking with? Your voice... it is beautiful, but weighed down by the pain of some terrible burden."

Edward had stopped pacing and was now looking in Elsa's direction, listening carefully.

"My name is Elsa McIntire. My boyfriend, Edward," Elsa left out his last name, knowing his infamy among the supernatural community, "has been cursed... It is a lot to explain over the phone. Do you think we could make an appointment with you? Today, maybe?"

She heard him mutter something under his breath and a grating sound, like fingernails scratching facial hair. "It would appear that I do not have anything else on my schedule, Miss McIntire. What time would you two be arriving?"

Elsa looked at Edward as she spoke. "We could be there in half an hour. I know it's a bit of a drive from where we are staying... make it forty-five minutes tops!"

There was silence for a moment and Elsa assumed he was writing something down. "Very well. I will see you and this Edward in forty-five minutes."

"Yes. Thank you for seeing us on such short notice."

"That is what I do. I am the soul doctor after all. Until we meet again, Miss McIntire." And the man known as Zeleni Malakai hung up.

Edward looked at her, then he moved to grab her purse without any words being exchanged. She told him she would drive, much to his chagrin; he wanted to go in separate cars in case Hyde decided to rear his ugly head, but Elsa insisted and assured him that everything would be fine.

"I can handle Hyde," she said, gripping his hand and smiling at him. She saw his eyes drift down to her stomach, and she did her

190

best to ignore it. A part of her feared that even once all of this was done – if it ever was – that he would never forgive himself for having stabbed her.

As she maneuvered the car down the busy streets toward their city's version of Chinatown, her mind wandered back to Lawrence's clue. There was not a single W in Zeleni Malakai's name, but maybe that did not mean anything at all. Elsa knew that Lawrence made his living on deceit and lies. But there had been something in his voice... She was overthinking it again. She needed to focus on their meeting with Zeleni Malakai.

She pulled up in front of a strip of old oriental-styled buildings all pressed together to form a city block. The slot that was Zeleni's was nothing special. His name was printed in violet and silver letters across a glass door with a wooden frame. A beaded curtain hung directly inside the door obscured the view inside. The windows were old - one terribly cracked – and also shrouded with beaded curtains. The building had once been red, but was now a faded red-orange with the paint peeling off to reveal the aged drywall underneath. All in all, it looked like a dump, pieces of the words even scraped away from wear, but still legible.

The two stepped out of the car, and Edward took Elsa's hand. "You sure about this?"

"*No,*" she thought to herself, but her mouth said differently, "Let's go." They crossed the street together and as Edward opened the door for Elsa, a little bell jingled.

The inside was not much different from the outside. It looked as if no one had renovated it in years. The smell of incense stung their nostrils, a light haze of smoke hanging in the air. Besides the small and scantily decorated room they stood in, one doorway – also filled with a beaded curtain – led further into the shop.

At the sound of the bell, a man walked through the beaded curtain from the back room, letting the strings glide through his fingers. He was a sight to behold. He was tall, with olive-toned skin. He wore strange exotic-looking clothing: a silky purple vest with golden embroidery and no shirt underneath, a maroon scarf slung around his neck with a matching belt around the waistband of his brown gauchos, and black boots on his feet. His arms, wrists, and fingers bore many gold rings and bracelets. He had short black hair slicked to the side, but it seemed to have a mind of its own even when saturated in hair gel, a few strands sticking up. He had a black horseshoe mustache underneath a long and bulbous nose. His eyes rested under heavy black brows, seeming to have a lavender sheen to them. His arms and exposed chest were covered in tattoos of strange runes.

Elsa could sense Edward's immediate dislike of the man. It was not until that moment that Elsa really thought about what a stretch this was for Edward. He had always hated monsters and those who dabbled in the supernatural. Elsa knew it had something to do with an event that had occurred when he was only a boy, but he never wanted to elaborate further. Walking into the shop of a 'soul doctor' and asking for help was probably one of the last things he had ever seen himself doing.

"Welcome!" Zeleni proclaimed exuberantly. "It is I, Zeleni Malakai. Miss McIntire?"

"Please, just call me Elsa." She took a step forward, extending her hand to shake his. He shook it, taking a small bow as he did so and kissing the back of her hand before releasing it.

He turned to Edward. "And you must be the boyfriend, Edward..." He let his voice drift off, as if waiting for someone to finish his sentence.

Edward took a deep breath, his face turning red; he was obviously flustered. "My name is Edward Jekyll." He looked at Zeleni and saw a look of repulsion flash in his lavender eyes, even if it was only for a brief moment.

"What could you possibly have come here for?" Zeleni asked, his tone suddenly more guarded.

Elsa weighed in before Edward would say something he regretted. "We were hoping you could help him – us." She smiled sweetly at Zeleni. "He's been cursed, you see. Cursed to be a..." she glanced at Edward apologetically before continuing, "monster. When he changes, he becomes the worst version of himself. He doesn't want to be a danger to others... please. Please help us."

Zeleni's expression softened. It would appear that Elsa had appealed to his better nature. "Please, come into the back and tell me more. The more details I have, the better chance I have of being able to help."

The couple followed Zeleni into the back room, Edward giving Elsa a grateful look. The room they walked into was draped in a combination of animal skins and velvet curtains. A table sat at the center, low to the floor, several plush cushions surrounding it. Zeleni sat down on one of the cushions, crossing his legs. Edward and Elsa did the same.

"Give me your hands," Zeleni said, looking sternly at Edward. He did as he was told, extending his hands toward Zeleni. Zeleni grabbed his wrists, turning Edward's palms to face the ceiling. He closed his eyes, breathing deeply. "Tell me... how long ago were you cursed?"

"About a week ago, give or take," Edward answered calmly, not really liking the way that Zeleni was gripping his wrists.

194

"And how did the cursing take place? Incantation? Potion? Runic drawing?"

"Potion."

"Was it thrown on you or ingested?"

"Ingested." Edward clenched his jaw.

"Who cursed you? Do you know, or can you remember, or..."

"A ma- shapeshifter by the name of Lawrence Talbot. But he didn't do it alone, he got that potion somewhere."

Zeleni sat in silence a moment, continuing to regulate his breathing. His face constricted in a slight frown. "Miss McIntire – Elsa – mentioned that when you turn, you become the worst version of yourself? Does this... this 'side' of yourself have a name? What does it call itself?"

"Hyde," Edward said with distaste, "Mr. Hyde."

Zeleni's eyes suddenly flew open and he released Edward's hands as if they had burned him, pulling away from him, his lilac eyes wide. "There really is a great darkness in you. I saw him – well, more *felt* him – for just a brief moment. And this is... powerful magic. Something much beyond what I am capable of, I am almost certain of that." He looked frightened, as if he had not expected such an intense encounter. His expression turned sorrowful as he looked between the two of them. "I fear that I am not magician enough to counter such a dark curse."

Edward stood, suddenly angry. He glared down at Zeleni, his eyes on fire. Elsa sat where she was, frozen, afraid of what he might do. She was actually more afraid of what Hyde might do; if Zeleni had felt him, then he was not buried all too deep at the moment. Edward clenched his jaw, shooting a glance in Elsa's direction and muttering, "I knew he couldn't help us," before turning and walking through the beaded curtain. Elsa heard the bell ting and knew that he had left the shop.

She turned to Zeleni. "I am sorry about that. He can be a little... hot-headed at times."

"You get that a lot in this business." Zeleni smiled warmly at her.

"Well thank you for trying to help us. How much do I owe you for the appointment?"

"You owe me nothing. I was not able to, uh, heal him. So there is nothing to pay me for."

Elsa sat there nervously for a moment. Now was her chance; Edward was outside the shop, and she really believed that Zeleni was not a faker, there had been true fear in his eyes when he had dropped Edward's hands.

"Can I ask you something before I go?"

"Of course."

"Does the letter W mean anything to you?"

196

Zeleni's face darkened, and when he spoke, his voice was low. "There was talk of a witch that went by that name a long time ago. Why do you ask?"

"A man – the man that cursed Edward – mentioned something about it. Could this W person still be somewhere around here?"

"I have heard some rumors of her still lurking around in the darkness, but she would have to be over a century old or just an alias taken on by several predecessors. Here, give me a moment." He stood and walked to small cabinet, pulling open a drawer and retrieving a piece of paper and a purple colored pencil. He sat back down at the table, carefully drawing an equilateral triangle with a W at its center. "This," he began, "is supposedly the symbol she used. A purple triangle and then simply the letter W." He set down the pencil, looking seriously at Elsa. He delicately took her hands in his own. "That is all I can tell you." He looked deep into her eyes. "But I must warn you, that if W is still out there, and if she is the one responsible for cursing your beloved, I must urge you to proceed with caution. She is one of the most powerful practitioners of magic to have ever lived. If they wanted him cursed… then there is a good chance that he may never be restored to his former self."

Elsa felt tears welling up in her eyes, but forced them back down. She removed her hands from Zeleni's, picking up the piece of paper and folding it, placing it in her purse. "Thank you." She stood and walked for the beaded curtain. Before she walked through, she stopped and looked over her shoulder at Zeleni. "Why are you trying to help us? You know who he is. How he treated you."

Zeleni merely smiled kindly back at her. "Because of your voice. It is pure; what you do, you do out of pure love. You are both courageous and kind. You can tell a lot about a person by their voice. And a voice like yours only comes around once in a blue moon."

She stared at him in shocked appreciation. "You really do know magic, don't you?"

Zeleni's smile widened and he waved his hands. The beaded curtain before Elsa parted so she could pass through unhindered. She chuckled softly, walking through. When she had almost reached the door, she heard Zeleni say "Good luck, Elsa McIntire," as the curtain closed behind her.

As Elsa walked out into the late afternoon sun, she saw Edward leaning against her car. He uncrossed his arms and stood a little taller as she crossed the street.

"What took you so long in there? I've been out here waiting."

"I was trying to see if Zeleni could point us in the right direction. Even if he can't help us, he might know someone who can."

Edward scoffed. "You actually believed that guy? I think the whole thing was an act. How much money did he try to squeeze out of you?"

"None," Elsa said matter-of-factly. "He didn't want any money." She knew that now would not be the time to tell him about W and what she had found out. He would not want to hear anything Zeleni Malakai had said, at least not at the moment.

"Let me get you back to the hotel." She climbed behind the wheel of the car, Edward climbing in shotgun.

# Chapter 34

Brook sat in his office, staring at the screen of his laptop. He had lost his cool with Carmichael. Lost control. He was normally able to keep it together, but that damn Carmichael had a way of getting under his skin. Sure, the talk of murder had made him squirm a little. But why had the little prick had to mention his wife: 'Mrs. Hydecker'?

There had never been any Mrs. Hydecker. Nor would there ever be. Brook's father's hatred for his son had not come without reason. The late Mr. Hydecker could not handle that his son was a homosexual. When his wife had become pregnant, he had prayed for a son to work on trucks and throw a ball around with - a real man's man. Instead, he had ended up with what he called 'a sensitive Nancy boy.' Mr. Hydecker had always treated his soft-spoken son as less than a man, taunting him about not being masculine enough. His suspicions about him were only confirmed when he found Men's Health magazines hidden under twelve-year-old Brook's mattress. It was after that that the abuse severely worsened.

Brook had a very vivid memory of when his father had tried to take him out shooting the first time. Brook had been nine or ten at the time, and his dad decided to start him small, with a 9mm pistol. Brook held up the handgun and started to take aim at the grain sack target his father had rigged up. He glanced up at his old man, who was staring out at the target, waiting to see where the first bullet would strike. Brook honestly thought about blowing the old man's head off right then. The safety was deactivated and he felt like aiming wouldn't be too hard.

But he just couldn't bring himself to do it and had broken down crying. His dad had thought he was crying at the thought of shooting a gun and called him a pansy, driving them both home in his old diesel truck in a huff.

The fact that he lacked a wife was still a very sensitive subject for Brook, and 'his wife' was a topic that most people – especially his patients – tended to avoid. It was not even so much the fact that he did not have a wife that bothered him, it was the memories it brought back of his father. It almost made him feel as if the man were resurrected for a moment.

Suddenly Carmichael burst through the door of his office, red-faced and wobbling, an almost-empty bottle of Southern Comfort gripped in his hand. "Well, here I am!" Carmichael shouted, his words all slurring together. "Not that I want to be, but here I am." He took a swig of what remained in the bottle and practically fell onto the sofa. Then he broke into tears.

Brook was still startled by the sudden entrance, and sat there staring at the crying vampire on his sofa. Just a few moments ago he had been thinking about what a downright prick Carmichael was. Now he didn't know what to think, and was angry at himself for kind of wanting to comfort him.

As Brook opened his mouth to ask what was the matter, Carmichael spoke again. "I tried again, you know. To end it. But it didn't work... my only chance to be free of this shit show and it didn't work. That was my last chance..." He returned to incoherent drunken sobs.

Brook knelt by the arm of the couch. "Carmichael, I don't understand-"

Carmichael looked up at him, spit flying from his mouth as he cried, "Let me tell you a story about a boy. A boy who had hopes and dreams for the future. He didn't know what he was asking for then. The last day I spent on this earth as a mortal human was in the year 1516, in England. It was the reign of King Henry VIII, and he was suspicious of all of the families of nobility wanting to take the throne from him. He even sent a few particularly threatening parties to the Tower for execution.

"I was a young nobleman in my prime: smart, wealthy, young, and handsome. While my family was of no real threat to King Henry, death seemed to be lurking in the grim shadow of the

Tower; with suspicion running rampant and the risk of plague, death was a very real threat to even someone in my position.

"I was betrothed to a young duchess, but I would be lying if I said my eye did not stray at social gatherings such as balls and banquets. After all, I received a lot of attention from the ladies of the court. I wanted to stay young and desirable forever, to never have to face death, a thing I feared very much at that point. My life was perfect, and I just wanted to freeze time and stay in that promiscuous lap of luxury until the end of time.

"I finally managed to find a man who claimed he could offer me such things. Looking back now, he was a shady bastard who only told me what I wanted to hear. Even in a world full of monsters, back then vampires were still believed to associate with the Devil and feast on the corpses of plague victims. He convinced me that this was all folly, that I would remain a dashing young noble forever. His only warning was to avoid the sunlight.

"What he did not warn me about was that the tales of bloodlust were quite true. Or the way that my perception of time would be altered. I allowed him to change me, and not being able to go out in the light of day quickly revealed what I had become. I was ostracized by the Tudor society. Not that I cared. I had escaped a loveless betrothal, and still had my good looks and fortune. I had forever, and I could not wait to explore the world, free from the fear of death.

"Due to my bloodlust – and the lack of blood distribution centers at the time – I had to bounce around a lot. But the first one hundred years were bliss. I saw and did so much, went on so many adventures. I worked a few jobs that tickled my fancy. Courted many charming women – as well as solicited a few 'ladies of the night.' Perhaps I even sired a child or few along the way. By the time 1617 rolled around, I had seen and done everything I wanted to in England, and I booked passage on a ship to America: the New World.

"I continued to live like this, enjoying all life had to offer, until the fall of 1733 when I met her. Emily Harker. She was beautiful, but that wasn't all. She was smart. She enjoyed the simple things. And for once, I didn't just want her body; I wanted *her*.

"I left my overzealous life for her. She was never one for fame and riches. I became a woodsman and built us a cabin to live in, away from the city. And before I knew it, she was Mrs. Wilhelm and we had a daughter on the way. I was happy. We were happy. Of course, I had to keep it from her when I went out to feed. She believed I was living off creatures in the surrounding forest. The blood distribution center industry would not start for another few decades.

"But then came the winter of 1765... and my dear Emily came down with scarlet fever. She was dead before I could even get a grip on what was happening. And that was the first time it really hit me – that the immortality I had wished for was a curse.

"Well, shortly after that, the Revolutionary War began, and I went into a 'hibernation,' if you will. I no longer cared about such things. When I awoke in 1809, I found out that Washington had won the war, and America was now its own country. I began this fruitless journey of mine – the journey to find some meaning in this life again. Sure, there were incredible things to be witnessed. But... I just no longer had the childlike wonder about the world that I had back in 1516 when I had thought I wanted to live forever."

Carmichael squinted his eyes closed, pinching the bridge of his nose. "When I met Emily, I believed that she was the reason I had been granted the 'gift' of immortality. So that we could meet. Because we were like kindred spirits. Sure, after she was gone, I considered suicide. That was why the hibernation occurred: I just refused to feed. But I just never followed through... I tried to return to my extravagant lifestyle, tried to fill the hole she had left with other women. But I eventually gave up..."

Carmichael opened his eyes, looking at Brook, who had retreated to his chair. "It's time I came clean with you, Brook. It's not that suicide is particularly difficult for my kind. Just for me."

"What do you mean?" Brook asked, still trying to take in and process everything Carmichael had already said.

"I'll tell you," he replied, surprisingly sober for how drunk he had been a few minutes ago. Brook assumed it was a vampire thing. "The year was 1882 and I had taken to the cowboy lifestyle, calling no town my home – just riding from one place to the next, with never one set destination in mind..."

# Chapter 35

**1882, Arizona**


Carmichael rode into town on a cool desert night. All lights were out save for the tavern and inn. That was good. After riding from twilight into the wee hours, Carmichael wanted nothing more than a drink and warm bed. Preferably with a curtained window. He tethered his horse outside and walked in through the saloon doors. The tavern was mostly empty except for the barkeep, a few men who seemed to be just a couple of drinks shy of passing out on the spot, and a woman sitting on the piano bench.

Carmichael walked over to the bar and rapped his knuckles on the countertop. The barkeep, a balding man in a white apron, approached him. "I need a room and a nice tall glass of whiskey," Carmichael said, hints of his British accent still ingrained in his voice.

"How many nights'll you be staying with us?" the barkeep asked, leaning on the counter.

"Not sure. A few days… probably at least to the end of the week."

"All right. I'll get you that whiskey." He walked over to the drink station and grabbed the bottle and a glass.

The woman walked over to him, leaning against a barstool. "I don't think whiskey is the drink for you." She had straight shoulder-length strawberry blonde hair and dark brown – almost black – eyes. She had a pretty face, but was obviously a little older - probably about forty. She wore a white button-up top with sleeves rolled up to the elbow, and a blue bandana loosely around her neck, the top few buttons of her shirt undone. This was accompanied by blue jeans and brown riding boots.

"And what do you think I'd rather drink then?" Carmichael turned to her, raising his eyebrow. "Think I seem like more of a beer man?"

She chuckled and looked down at the floor, then back at him. "No... let's try human blood."

Carmichael frowned, caught off guard, a chill running down his spine. "What makes you say that?" he asked tersely.

Her smile widened. "Don't play dumb with me. You're a vampire," she stated matter-of-factly.

The barkeep slid the glass of whiskey in front of him and Carmichael stared down into the amber fluid. "How do you know that?" he asked in a hushed tone.

"I'm intuitive." She took a step toward him. "Also a handsome stranger shows up in town in the dead of night. You'd have to be either a crook or a vampire. And then there's your eyes." Her tone changed and she extended her right hand out to him. "I'm Winona."

Carmichael stared down into his whiskey a moment longer and then shook her hand. "Carmichael." He smiled slightly.

"She was a sharp one," Carmichael paused, turning away from Brook to look out the window. "I liked her for that. And she was pretty, in a different kind of way. But meeting her was just the beginning."

"Can I buy you a drink?" Carmichael asked, climbing up on the stool beside Winona's.

"Sure." She cocked her head to the side. "So why drink the whiskey?"

"A vampire can still like to drink." He tapped the countertop. "Bartender, a drink for the lady."

The barkeep walked down to them. "What'll you have?"

"The usual, Jenkins," Winona nodded to the barkeep. She turned back to Carmichael. "Fair enough. So what brings you to this little town?"

"The fact that it is little. Out of the way. I need a second to catch my breath."

"Been around the block a few times, huh?" Jenkins brought her a gin and tonic.

"More than a few." Carmichael downed the rest of his drink and stood. "Well, the journey was a long one. I think I'll retire to my room. Good night, Winona." He started toward Jenkins to request his room key.

"Good night. I'm sure I'll be seeing you, Carmichael." Winona smiled, stirring her drink.

"Perhaps." Carmichael smiled to himself and went up to his room. It was small, but had a bed, wash basin, and curtains. It would suit him well.

He pulled back the curtains and looked out the window. He could see the first rays of sunrise on the horizon. It was time for him to sleep.

When Carmichael awoke, there was no sun leaking in under the drapes, and he could hear voices and laughter coming from beneath him, accompanied by music. It must have been time for the evening rush. Carmichael stood and stretched his legs and back. He figured he might as well go downstairs and join the fun. There were drinks to be had, at the very least.

Once he was dressed, he strapped his six-shooter to his hip and walked down the stairs. The tavern was full, a mixture of cowboys and farm hands, all the tables adorned with pint glasses, bottles, and cowboy hats. They were all facing the piano, which was being played by Winona.

Her fingers danced over the keys, her voice harmonizing beautifully with the notes of the ivories. Many of the men clapped or patted their thighs along to the music. A few whooped from time to time when she hit an especially difficult note.

Carmichael walked over to the bar where Jenkins was dreamily watching Winona play and sing. "Whiskey," he said, tapping the counter where Jenkins' elbow was resting.

"Oh, of course Mr. Wilhelm." Jenkins snapped out of his trance and went to pour his drink. "Your drink, sir." Jenkins slid the glass across the counter.

"Thanks," Carmichael dropped a coin on the counter and walked toward the group of men clustered around the piano, sipping his whiskey. Winona's eyes darted up from the piano as he approached, and he saw the smile she already wore widening. A couple of men had accompanied her with fiddles, adding to the music.

*"Lost my partner, skip to my Lou, Lost my partner, skip to my Lou, Lost my partner, skip to my Lou, Skip to my Lou, my darling."* The fiddles continued into a solo, and Winona let out a happy shout and rose from the piano bench, dancing into the crowd. All the men cheered, clapping as she made her way through the crowd, shaking her hips to the music. She swayed her way over to Carmichael and wrapped her arms around his neck, pulling him close to her and kissing him.

The other men let out a cacophony of sounds: several 'oooo's, sighs of disappointment, and yet more whoops and hollers. Her kiss burned Carmichael's lips the way whiskey burned his throat. He put his arm around her waist, resting his hand in the small of her back.

"Skip to my Lou, my darling," she said softly enough so that only he would hear. "You like that, Carmichael?" He nodded. "There's more where that came from."

The group danced and sang and drank late into the night. Eventually, many of the farm hands began the stumbling trek home, while most of the cowboys either passed out lying across tables or retired to their rooms. Carmichael's mind was long gone by the time Winona took his hand and discreetly led him up to his room. She laid him down on his back on his bed, undoing the buttons of his shirt. He sobered up quickly enough, as vampires are wont to do – something to do with their body chemistry.

"You really want to do this?" he asked. After all, she knew what he was and - more particularly - what he ate. His kind were often viewed as murderous scum.

"I sure do. There is something about you that drives me crazy." Winona bent and removed her boots.

"It wouldn't happen to be that I'm a handsome stranger?" Carmichael raised one eyebrow.

Winona laughed, a sultry sound deep in her throat, as she climbed on top of him. "You are a handsome devil. But that isn't all. You have a very… *lonely* charm about you." She ran her fingers through his hair. "Like you've seen much tragedy, but you weathered the storm."

"I know a fair deal about tragedy." Carmichael grew sullen, sitting up, his unbuttoned shirt hanging open as he turned his back to her.

She scooted closer to him, rubbing his back. He continued to stare at the floor. "What happened, if you don't mind my asking?"

"Life happened," he said quietly. "Let's just say, eternity isn't what I thought it would be."

"What did you expect it to be?"

"I guess I expected it to be perfect, like my life before. Good looks, riches, and fame. I didn't expect to be burying the love of my life... or to fall in love at all, I suppose. My life began in a loveless betrothal and what I felt for women was lust. That is, until Emily..."

Winona sat a moment, then rested her hand against his shoulder. "Why didn't you change her?"

"I considered it... but it was only for selfish reasons. When I truly thought about it, I didn't want a genuinely kind soul like her to have to live with the bloodlust. Or scum like me... And this world we live in is a truly despicable place... I didn't want her caught up in it forever. Then the fever got ahold of her, and she was gone before I could make any decision about what to do."

"It wasn't selfish to want to keep love alive," Winona nuzzled him and he looked over at her.

"We all have selfish motives in the end. Like I said, it's a despicable world we live in," Carmichael said decidedly.

"It isn't all ugly." Winona searched his face with her eyes. "Turn around. I want to show you something."

He rolled his eyes and sighed, but turned to face her all the same. She was holding her hand out in front of her, her palm facing the ceiling. She stared at her hand in deep concentration as she began to swirl her other hand over it in a circular motion. A yellow light began to issue from her palm. As the light grew, it began to turn orange toward the center until it spread and solidified into a floating red rose.

"So you know magic?" he said, a little surprised, but nothing he hadn't seen before.

"Yeah. I'm teaching myself... learning pretty fast, but... still just learning. My point is, look at this flower. It shouldn't exist; it came from nothing. Yet here it is, alive and beautiful. Much like you." He smiled slightly. "And there's something else," she set the rose on the pillow, crawling nearer to him. "Not all selfish motives are bad." His smile widened, and they laughed together, proceeding to make love.

She stayed until sunrise, then left him sleeping undisturbed in bed. She pulled on her clothes and snuck out the back way. When evening rolled around, she returned to the tavern, hoping to see Carmichael amongst the crowd. She did, and once again they danced, and once the crowd had thinned, they snuck up to his room.

"When do you think you're going to leave?" Winona asked him out of the blue one night while practicing her magic.

"Not sure," he replied. "Depends, I suppose."

"I wish you wouldn't go at all."

"You understand better than most why I can't spend forever in one place."

She stopped weaving magic and bit her lower lip. "Let me come with you then," she said, sitting down next to him on the edge of the bed.

He laughed exasperatedly. Then they sat together in awkward silence, abandoning the subject altogether.

On the fifth day of Carmichael's stay, a frequent customer of the tavern, a man named Royce Slade, had had a little too much to drink and started a fight with Carmichael. Royce was short, but wore tall boots to compensate. He had small beady eyes and short black hair, a handlebar mustache dominating his face, with a scar running down his left cheek.

Carmichael was sitting at the bar, Royce at a table, and Winona was playing piano. "And as for you!" Royce shouted drunkenly, pointing at Carmichael. "I think you've more than overstayed your welcome. Skulking around the bar at night, moonin' over the piano girl. Never showin' your face once durin' the light of day. Makes one think you must be a bandit, or some other kinda criminal."

Carmichael turned from the bar to face him. "Are you talking to me?"

"Yes I am, Mr…" his voice trailed off.

218

"Wilhelm." Carmichael stared at him, his blue eyes piercing.

"Mr. Wilhelm!" Royce stood, approaching the bar. "Listen to me and listen good. I want you outta town. Right now. Finish your drink, and get!" He leaned on the bar, his face so close Carmichael could smell the beer on his breath.

Carmichael stared into his eyes, not breaking his gaze. He saw Royce's hand gravitating toward his hip, and Carmichael rested his hand on his own revolver. Winona stopped playing, her eyes wide. Carmichael looked ready to kill a man, and she knew he was perfectly capable of doing so. But so was Royce Slade.

"Now boys," Jenkins said steadily, his eyes darting between the two men, "I'm not lookin' to have anyone killed in my bar tonight."

The whole tavern had fallen silent. The two continued to stare at each other. Royce finally spoke. "Sunrise. Out in front of the stables. We'll settle this then." He removed his hand from his hip.

"I'll see you there," Carmichael replied.

Royce smiled to himself and turned away. Before walking out the doors, he looked at Winona. "He's a dead man," he chuckled, then exited the tavern.

Carmichael knocked back the rest of his drink and climbed off his barstool, heading up the stairs to his room. Winona sat for a moment, then stood, running up the stairs after him. The door to

Carmichael's room was ajar, and she pushed it open to find him packing his things.

"You're getting the hell outta town?" she asked.

"No. Not yet at least. But I do want to get my things in order."

"You'd ought to leave. Royce Slade is about the best damn shot in this whole county!"

Carmichael smiled snidely. "You underestimating me, darling? You haven't seen me shoot."

"That is true, but you can't meet him at sunrise. You'll die, even if he misses you."

Carmichael turned to her. "I am no coward, Winona. I have never run from a fight before. I am not going to start now."

"So that's it then?" She was on the verge of tears.

"I reckon so."

She attempted to sniff back her tears, then ran from his room, leaving the door wide open. He shoved his tongue in his cheek, then shut the door behind her and sat down on the edge of his bed.

Ever since Emily died, he'd had thoughts of suicide, but had never relished the idea of wedging a stake between his ribs or burning alive in the sun. This way he would be able to die, and someone else could feel like they'd done the world a favor. And so what if he burned a little bit? He hadn't felt the sun on his skin in over 300 years. This was his chance to go out with a bang.

As the sun rose, Carmichael exited the tavern and stood in the shade of the awning. A crowd had begun to gather to watch the shootout. He did not see Winona among them. Good. It was probably better that she didn't see. Royce Slade appeared, leaning against one of the stable posts.

"You ready to die, Mr. Wilhelm?" he shouted across the street to Carmichael. Carmichael merely smiled and walked to the edge of the shade.

By the time Carmichael had stepped into the sunlight and pulled his gun, Royce had already drawn and shot. The bullet pierced Carmichael's chest – it was definitely a heart shot. The pain shot through him, but nothing happened. The warm sun shined on his skin, but it did not burn.

"*What the hell is happening?*" he thought, looking at the bleeding hole in his chest and squinting into the overly bright sun. Everyone else was staring as well.

Royce's eye twitched. Then he fired another shot, catching Carmichael in the shoulder. Once again, Carmichael felt pain, but was not weakened in the slightest. Still confused, he looked at Royce Slade and was suddenly filled with an immense rage. Royce started shooting frantically, emptying all of his bullets into

Carmichael. Desperate, he reached to his belt for more bullets. As he fumbled with the ammunition, Carmichael raised his gun and fired. The bullet caught Royce right between the eyes. His face had a few seconds to register pain, and then he fell to the ground like a sack of potatoes.

No one spoke. No one made a sound, not even a gasp. Carmichael lowered his gun, just as shocked if not more than the surrounding spectators. He needed a drink. He holstered his gun and stumbled back toward the tavern. Despite it not harming him, it felt good to be back in the shade and out of the sunlight.

The bar was mostly empty when Carmichael walked through the front doors – not many men needed a drink this early in the day. As he approached the bar, he was dragging his feet and practically fell onto the barstool. "Whiskey. Leave the bottle," he said in a daze. Jenkins stared at him a moment, his eyes wide. Carmichael suddenly remembered he had been shot six times. He looked down at himself, his white shirt now red with bullet holes torn into the fabric, stained with blood. He would have to pick the bullets out at some point.

As Jenkins passed him a glass and the bottle, the doors flew open, followed by Winona's voice. "You're okay!" she exclaimed, rushing over to Carmichael's side. "It worked!"

Carmichael knocked back his first glass of whiskey, then turned to face her. "It worked? What worked?" he said, still dazed.

"The spell, to protect you. I saw Royce Slade's body. And, well..." Her eyes drifted to the bloodied hole in his shirt over his heart.

"Y-you did this?" His voice rose in pitch. He seemed to return to reality, and his eyes locked on her face. He grabbed her gruffly by her shoulders, rising from the stool and shaking her. "*You* couldn't have done this. Who'd you hire to do this for you? W?"

Carmichael leaned back on the couch. "Even then, W was a well-known name."

"W?" Brook asked, quizzed.

Carmichael smirked. "One of the most powerful witches to have ever lived."

Winona hunched her shoulders, startled by his sudden outburst. "No, Carmichael. I did this – I saved you. I wasn't sure it would work, but it did."

He gritted his teeth, looking down at the floor, squeezing her arms tighter. "I... I was ready. I was ready to die. I wanted to!" He shook her again, screaming in her face.

Her expression changed, hurt visible in her eyes. "I thought... we... us... You really want to die?"

"Yes, Winona. I want to die. I'm done. I'm finally ready to rest."

"But I love you. I thought you loved me too..." She closed her eyes, a tear rolling down her cheek.

"Winona, I need this spell reversed. I need whoever did this to lift the spell."

"I already told you, I cast it! *I'm W!*" His eyes widened. "And no, I won't lift the spell."

"Y-you lied to me. Said you were still learning... wait... was this a power play? That first night that you approached me, knowing I was a vampire. It was all part of a plan. You put Royce Slade up to challenging me... it was all part of a plan." He released her in disgust.

"I was going to tell you, the timing just didn't feel right..."

The same rage as when Royce had been shooting him took hold of Carmichael. He gripped the whiskey bottle by the neck and smashed it against the bar, glass and booze flying everywhere. He gripped the collar of Winona's shirt, pushing her back up against the counter and holding the jagged end of the broken bottle against her throat.

"Whoa, Mr. Wilhelm, please-" Jenkins started.

"Don't test me!" Carmichael growled back, applying more pressure to the broken bottle, causing Winona to gasp. "Now," he turned his attention back to her, "lift the spell."

"I can't," she choked out, breathing heavily, "and even if I could, I wouldn't. Because I've fallen in love with you." He laughed wickedly. "Don't I mean anything to you?"

"No. Unlike you, I won't pretend. It was just a fling for the moment. Because that's all any of this would be for me: a moment. Then it's gone. You knew that." He glared, pressing the glass harder against her neck, a small dribble of blood appearing along its edge. "But now, this is a moment I will remember. The moment I cut your throat and watched you choke to death on your own blood."

"But it wouldn't have to just be a moment, Carmichael. Don't you see, it's different with me. I won't die, at least not for a long while."

Carmichael snickered nastily. "That's where you're wrong. You're going to die right here. Today. I've already killed one person today." He paused. "Why aren't you trying to stop me and save yourself?"

"Because I don't want to hurt you," she replied evenly.

"No," Carmichael smiled evilly, "because you can't. You've tied your own noose."

"If you're going to kill me, why not drink my blood instead of wasting it?"

"I don't want your blood, let it go to waste." Carmichael drew the jagged glass across her throat. Blood splattered across his face and shirt, running down the glass onto his fingers. She sputtered as he released her and dropped the bottle fragment to the floor, wiping his hand on his vest. She stood upright, putting her hand to her neck and spitting out blood.

"Oh Carmichael, you think in my line of work I wouldn't have a protection spell of my own?" She removed her hand from her neck, the slash gone, just a blood stain as proof that it had ever been there.

Carmichael cried out in frustration, baring his fangs. Jenkins stood behind the counter with his back up against the wall, mortified.

"Carmichael, I understand why you're upset. I shouldn't have lied to you. But I meant what I said – time works differently for me. We could get at least a good century together." She reached out her hand to him.

"Don't touch me!" Carmichael concealed his fangs once more. "I may not be able to kill you, but I can make you hurt." He turned for the staircase. "I'm taking your advice and getting the hell outta town. And - God willing - you'll *never* see me again." Winona waved her hand and he felt his insides shift. He looked over his shoulder to see her holding six blood-stained bullets in her hand. "Stop with the parlor tricks. I'm not impressed. W." He said the name with contempt, dropping money for the whiskey on the counter and going up the stairs.

She dropped the bullets, clenching both of her hands into fists by her sides. "Don't call me that!" All of the bottles behind the counter exploded as she cried out. "I never wanted to be W to you!" She let out a defeated sob. She suddenly remembered Jenkins standing behind the counter and turned to face him, her tone deadly. "You tell anyone what you saw here today, and I will end you."

Jenkins nodded, wide-eyed. "Yes ma'am." After a few moments had passed, Winona ran up the stairs and opened the door to Carmichael's room. "Carmichael, I-" she stopped short. He was gone.

"And that, Dr. Brook Hydecker, is why I can't commit suicide. I'm impervious to fatal harm of any kind. And I went to see her the other night in hopes she'd changed her mind…"

"Wait," Brook held up his hand, "she's still alive? That was, what, 133 years ago!"

"Yeah. Time works different for her, like she said." Brook lifted his eyebrows. "Do you have any more questions?" Carmichael asked, now completely sober.

"Just one. If you're immune to the sun, why did you insist on booking evening sessions?"

"Just because it can't hurt me doesn't mean I like it. I'm a creature of the darkness."

"Fair enough."

Carmichael looked at the clock. It was well after 1:00 A.M. "I should go. I've kept you late enough. You should get home to your wife." Carmichael stood. "Thank you… for listening to an old man wallowing in self-pity."

"It's my job," Brook lied. Sure, it was his job. But it was more than that. He *actually* cared for once. "And Carmichael," he said, Carmichael stopping on the threshold, "I don't have a wife. So no worries there."

Carmichael nodded absently and walked off into the night.

# Chapter 36

**Several years ago**...


Miles walked into the small oriental-themed shop, the smell of incense barely fazing him as he walked through the thin streams of smoke. A bell dinged as he entered and the door closed behind him. He was a handsome man, his long and thin features accented perfectly by his dark hair and eyes, although his face was already becoming lined prematurely with age. His short black hair was slicked back flawlessly, causing him to look very sharp in his black suit.

Miles fanned away the smoke as he waited for someone to come and assist him. A tall young man with olive-toned skin and a black horseshoe mustache poked his head out from behind a beaded curtain, his lavender eyes catching the light oddly as he looked at his new customer. He wore strange exotic clothes, tattoos of runes visible on his exposed arms and chest. His short black hair stuck out in every direction despite being saturated in hair gel.

"Can I help you?" he asked in a foreign accent, sizing up the tall, handsome young man that had just entered his shop.

"Yes, as a matter of fact I think you can." A small smile spread across Miles' thin lips. "Word had it that you were the man to see about magic. If you are Zeleni Malakai, that is."

"Yes, I am Zeleni Malakai: soul doctor! Come." Zeleni motioned into the back room and held the beaded curtain for Miles to pass through. The room was dingy and sparsely decorated with a few tiger and bear skins, a few velvet curtains draped over particularly ugly areas of the wall. A wooden coffee table with a marred surface sat at the center of the room, mix-matched cushions surrounding it. "Please, sit." Zeleni motioned to the cushions, and he and Miles sat across from each other, leaning their elbows on the table. "Now tell me, what is it that you want to know?"

Miles scratched the back of his scalp before speaking. "I know that this is going to sound odd... but I guess you are used to weird." He chuckled huskily. "But ever since I was very young, I have had this... *way* with animals. As a boy, dogs always seemed to flock to me. I used these talents as I grew to become a dog trainer, and I was a damn good one. But I also discovered that my talents were not limited to dogs. I actually just only recently got back from a *großartig Zirkus* – grand circus, if you will – in Berlin. They had heard about my expertise – like I said, I was a damn good dog trainer – and wrote to me asking me to come and attempt to tame their wildest and most disobedient recruits. No circus wanted them. Men had even died trying to break them. So I went.

"While I was there, I discovered much more about my gift. I was able to tame, well, any creature I tried my hand at. Lions. Tigers. Elephants. Even a Kodiak bear. No matter how terrifying or terrible they had been, I had them ready to perform within a matter of days." Miles cleared his throat, beginning to cough.

"Maybe you should stop smoking. Bad for your lungs," Zeleni said quietly as Miles tried to recover from his coughing fit.

"Maybe you should burn less incense," Miles rasped back as a retort.

Zeleni shrugged nonchalantly. "Fair enough."

Miles shook out his shoulders and sat up straight, still quietly clearing his throat. "So that is why I am here. I want to know about this gift, to understand where it came from. You see, I never knew my real parents… so I guess this is a way to learn more about them as well, through learning more about myself. If you can deliver, that is."

"We shall see." Zeleni hid his smirk under his mustache at how Miles seemed to underestimate him. Sure, the shop was slightly showy, but Zeleni had sensed a power emanating from the man the moment he had entered the shop; he knew what he was doing. "Give me your hands." Miles extended his arms across the table, and Zeleni took them in his, turning his palms toward the ceiling. He stared off into space, his eyes seeming to roll back in his head. His breathing became long drawn out deep breaths, and his grip tightened on Miles' hands. "I see a young boy... you, playing with a dog. A cocker spaniel... it's a girl. She never tried to snap at you and would always play and let you pet her whenever you wanted-"

"Please," Miles cut him short, "about my gift... and my parents."

Zeleni harrumphed, peeved by Miles' demands. Magic was not pulling a rabbit out of a hat; sometimes you got a lizard or a severed hand instead. Nevertheless, he dug deeper.

"I sense... a power. Not magic like mine, mind you, very specific. Yes, you are an animal whisperer; a rare gift these days. I am sensing a woman... perhaps this means that you got this gift from your mother." His breathing became more labored as he tried to see through the ethereal haze shrouding Miles' roots. The full moon was visible in the distance accompanied by a distant howl, overshadowed by a great darkness. And then, only darkness...

"Ah!" Zeleni threw down Miles' hands, his eyes becoming visible again, wide with fright.

"What? What did you see?" Miles asked excitedly.

"Please, go," Zeleni begged, the evil he had touched when he had reached Miles' heart still causing him to quiver. He had the exterior of a clean-cut, perfect, golden boy. But underneath, he had nothing but ill will. And he was plotting something. How soon it would come to fruition, Zeleni did not know, but he just wanted the evil man out of his shop - and life - forever.

"What did you see?" Miles demanded, his voice rising in pitch.

"Your mother, your mother is who gave you your gift. Now go!"

"Is she still alive? Who is she?" Miles leaned across the table, shouting in Zeleni's face, the smell of his smoker's breath invading Zeleni's nostrils.

"I don't know. I did not see that. Please just leave." Zeleni stood and retreated a few steps from the table, cowering from Miles.

Miles stood as well, smiling unpleasantly. He liked the way Zeleni cowered, liked the feeling of having power over a person. He had never had the same control over people he had over animals, and he hated that. He had hoped there was some way, that he had just not tapped into that power yet. As angry as he was at Zeleni for revealing it to him, at least now he knew that his powers were strictly limited to animals.

In the back of his mind, he wondered what Zeleni Malakai had seen that made him pull away from him with such insistence. He wanted to prod him for more information, to force him to tell him more about his mother. But maybe the guy really could not see anything else. Who was Miles to decide? He hardly knew anything about magic; he was an animal trainer by trade. And for the time being, his thirst for power had been sated.

"You really know nothing else?" Miles said mockingly, skeptically.

Zeleni peered at him sheepishly, slowly shaking his head. *"Lying through his teeth,"* Miles thought to himself, but when he spoke he said, "Well that's disappointing. I really had hoped you could help me." He turned and walked through the beaded curtain without paying.

# Chapter 37

Elsa opened her eyes, looking around drearily. She was in Edward's hotel room, sitting on the bed, papers surrounding her. She sat up a little straighter; the pillow she had propped up behind her back had slid down while she slept. She could not believe that she had dozed off while in Edward's hotel room, and even more so surprised that he had allowed it. He had a very strict policy about her letting her guard down around him. Surprisingly enough, Elsa did not feel all that apprehensive about having fallen asleep in Edward's presence. She was not sure if that was a good thing, but ever since Hyde had threatened Lawrence, Elsa's fear of Hyde had begun to dwindle.

Speaking of Edward, where was he? Elsa's eyes searched the room. He was not sitting at the desk as he had been before she had drifted off to sleep. The bathroom door was open, the light off, so he was not in there. For the first time since she had awoken, fear gripped her. What if Hyde had taken control and left the room?

She threw her legs over the side of the bed, suddenly frantic. As she gathered the papers on the bed, trying to pile them into a neat stack, she wondered how on earth she would track him down. She went over to the kitchen counter to grab her purse, when she noticed a movement in the dark bathroom out of the corner of her eye. She turned, edging her way toward the bathroom doorway. "Edward?" As she drew nearer she could see the shape of his legs and lower back. He appeared to be leaning on the sink. She continued walking toward the door, and her eyes began to focus on him in the dark.

The sleeves of his button-up shirt were rolled up past the elbow, his top two buttons undone and his tie loosened, dangling limply from around his neck. His shirt was, however, still tucked into his jeans, and he was wearing his shoes. He was staring at his reflection in the mirror, the glow from his eyes reflecting slightly off the polished glass. He was gripping the sides of the sink tightly, his knuckles white. He reached up and ran his hand through his disheveled hair. He did not appear to have heard Elsa say his name.

"Edward?" she said a little louder, standing just outside the doorway. "Hyde?"

He slowly turned to look at her, his face a mix of emotions. While his brow and tense jaw gave him the look of someone dangerous who was up to no good, his eyes had a certain sadness – almost remorse – about them. His mouth was set in a tight, straight line which was impossible to read. Had it not been for the protrusion of his brow and the glow of his eyes, he almost looked like Edward Jekyll.

"I'm conflicted," he stated, the malicious edge to his voice almost completely hidden. He took a few steps toward Elsa, letting the light from the main room fall over him as he exited the bathroom. Elsa instinctively took a few steps back; she found comfort in this, she at least still had a certain air of caution while in Hyde's presence. His eyes narrowed, but still maintained their almost Jekyll emotion. "I know that I am bad. Really, really bad. Not all too long ago, I would have murdered you without so much as a second thought." He loomed in the bathroom doorway, letting his words hang in the air for a moment. "But now… now I don't know what I want. There is a part of me that wants to hurt you – not kill, just hurt – and then there is the part of me that doesn't want to hurt you. I can't explain it… I don't know how. But I do know that I no longer want to kill… well, you anyway." A sneer flashed across his face, but was quickly gone. "I guess what I am trying to say, Elsa," he said her name for the first time, "is that I am conscious of what I am. But maybe, at least sometimes, I don't *want* to be that."

He looked at her a moment longer, then took a few steps toward her and leaned in seemingly for a kiss, closing his eyes and tilting his head to the right as he drew nearer.

Elsa put her hand up against his chest, pushing him back, and he opened his eyes, looking at her, obviously hurt. She stared back at him for a moment, and then dropped his gaze. "Not like this," she said in a hushed whisper. She let her hand continue to rest on his chest, keeping him at bay.

He looked stunned a moment longer, then finally spoke quietly. Almost tenderly, if Hyde was capable of being tender. "I'm still Edward… same person, same body, same heart beating in this chest. A heart that I am learning beats for you."

Elsa looked up into his eyes as he finished speaking. For a moment, she was moved. She thought back to the night with Lawrence on their driveway, Hyde standing between them with a knife pointed in Lawrence's face. Protecting her. But then she thought back to the stab wound in her abdomen and poor Giselle Michaels.

"No," she slowly shook her head, "you're not the same person."

"But I am!" Hyde's voice rose and he pressed against Elsa's hand, but she locked her elbow, holding him back. "I'm just a part of him! And you know that!" His eyes glowed brighter as he glared at her. He looked down at the floor, pulling back from her. His voice softened. "I know you feel it too. I've seen it, when you

look at me. The fear, it's still there. But there's something else."
He placed his hand over hers that rested on his chest.

She stood there a moment, deciding whether or not to pull her hand back. She decided to leave it where it was for the time being. "When I look at you," she began, feeling her voice grow thick as she fought back tears, "I am looking into the face of the man I love. A man that is flawed, just like anyone else, but he is a good man. When I look at you, I can see him inside. Behind all that darkness, I see the man that I love, a man that is also capable of love. A man named Edward Jekyll; not Hyde." She did not break his gaze, staring directly into his eyes.

She could feel his heart pounding in his chest, the rise and fall of his chest under her hand as he breathed heavily. For the first time, she saw tears forming in Hyde's eyes, the glow from his irises refracting off their wet surface. "Elsa, I love you," he said, his voice scratchy as if his throat were dry.

Elsa let out a startled sound, not knowing what to say to the man that stood before her. He was by definition only the bad within Edward Jekyll. And if that were true, how could he be capable of love, the purest of emotions? The answer, of course, was staring her right in the face. Literally.

Hyde was but one facet of Edward Jekyll, but a facet nonetheless. Edward Jekyll was deeply in love with her. Could his love be so strong that it even influenced his deepest darkest side?

Hyde suddenly glared, his face taking on an all too familiar guise of malignity. "I should have killed you when I had the chance. It would have saved me from all this torment!" he snarled, spit flying from his mouth as the first tears Hyde had ever cried finally fell from his eyes. "I would have never had to doubt who and what I am! I would never-" he stopped short, his voice catching in his throat. He let out a choked sound and turned his face away from Elsa, his heart rate picking up rapidly. After a few seconds, it began to slow back to normal.

Edward Jekyll turned to face Elsa, wiping his eyes with the backs of his hands. "Why am I crying?" he asked, half-dazed.

Elsa looked at his face for a moment, taking him in, the Edward that she knew and loved. She removed her hand from his chest, wrapping her arms around his neck and pulling him close to her. "It was Hyde," she said softly in his ear, "he... he said he loved me."

Edward pulled away suddenly, putting his hands on Elsa's waist. "He said what?"

"He said that he loved me. That he knows that he's bad, and while a part of him still wants to hurt me, another part of him
242

doesn't." She bit her lower lip, "Edward, I haven't been completely honest with you about the night Hyde showed up on our driveway."

"What do you mean?" Edward asked, frowning blankly at her.

"He came there for a reason." Elsa wanted to approach this situation delicately, so she chose her words carefully. "Lawrence Talbot was there." She saw Edward cringe when she said the name. "He had come to see if your life had turned into the living Hell that he wanted it to be, but he ran into me instead. Hyde followed me home to... to protect me." Edward's expression grew even more perplexed. "At first, I was scared to see him, but then he told Lawrence not to lay a hand on me and pointed that knife in his face until he had vacated the premises. Then he turned to look at me, right before you regained control, but the look in his eyes was... different.

"I didn't tell you then because I needed time to process what had happened. But after what just happened tonight, I have no doubts; Hyde is very much a part of you, even more than either of us thought. If he can love," she stroked Edward's cheek, feeling the prickles of his yet-to-be-shaved face, "that's just proof that your love is stronger than your darkness. It's influencing him." She decided to leave out the bit about W since she did not even know if she was still alive.

Edward smiled at her, his eyes pained. "Hyde killed someone," were the only words he spoke.

"He is very much a part of you. But he isn't all of you." Elsa ran her fingers up through his hair along his scalp, causing chills to run down his spine.

He looked at her in admiration for a moment. He removed his hands from her waist, caressing her face. "Loving a monster isn't easy," he started, taking a moment to collect his thoughts before continuing, "but you. You never hesitated, not for a moment. When I came to you, told you what I was, you didn't draw back. You didn't abandon me. The only option that you saw was standing with me, even if the monster that now lived inside me was the worst version of myself, all of my darkness and hate coming out. No matter what has happened, you have not wavered. You hunted me down in a dingy motel after he stabbed you, and even when he killed someone, you stood by me because of the goodness you believe I still have inside. Not only are you beautiful and kind and trustworthy, but you are the bravest woman – person – that I have ever met. I admire you Elsa. And my God, I'm in love with you."

He had barely finished speaking before Elsa had pressed her lips against his, holding him close in an intimate embrace before beginning to unbutton the rest of the buttons of his shirt. She pulled off his tie and pulled his shirt off around his shoulders, and reached for the snap to his pants when he pulled away for a moment. "I don't want him to hurt you."

"He won't," Elsa stated, pulling his mouth to hers and proceeding to make out with him as she pulled him toward the bed and wrestled with his pants.

He began pulling at her shirt, and they parted lips just long enough for him to pull it off over her head. The backs of Elsa's knees hit the edge of the bed, and she fell over backwards onto the plush bedspread, Edward on top of her. He undid her bra as she finally managed to pull his pants down to his knees.

As they finished removing each other's clothes, Edward realized just how much he had been missing the closeness he and Elsa had shared, now, lying in the same bed with his bare arms caressing her smooth back. He had allowed Hyde to come between them, to push them apart. He vowed to never let that happen again.

As Elsa lay there in Edward's embrace, she felt safe and warm and happy. She was sure that in the back of Edward's mind somewhere, Hyde was jealous. And she frankly, in that moment, did not care what Hyde thought.

# Chapter 38

Kurt sat at his outdated computer in his cramped apartment, trying to dig up anything about werewolf cures that he could online. He had come up empty-handed, which was what he had expected. No real cure for such a curse would be available via Google search on the Internet; if that were the case, places like Wulfen would be out of business.

He looked at his cell phone, sitting silently on the desk next to the computer monitor. He wondered what Matilda was doing. He secretly hoped that she was not doing anything dangerous on his account. He considered texting her, but shook his head. He trusted her; he had trusted her from the moment they had met. But he also knew that she would stop at nothing until they had found a cure. A cure which Kurt feared – had feared for many years – did not exist.

Meanwhile, Matilda sidled up to the front of the abandoned athletic wear shop. She had done a little digging on Miles, which was difficult to do since she did not know his last name. Surprisingly enough she had found help in her scumbag competition, Lawrence Talbot. While trying to sniff out a story, he had noticed an abnormal amount of activity in the supposedly abandoned shop. He had gone undercover, but immediately felt like he was in over his head and abandoned ship. He had been sure to emphasize to Matilda how glad he was that Miles did not know his true name or face.

The shop looked abandoned enough, but Matilda stood on tiptoe, trying to peer into the windows. It was no good; the boards made it nearly impossible to catch a glimpse, and it was completely dark inside. She sighed before pulling a lock picking device from her purse. She had always been serious about gathering her information ethically. But this wasn't for *The Metzen Gazette*. This was for Kurt.

"You won't find much in there," a man's voice said, causing Matilda to jump, and she quickly slipped the lock pick in her jacket pocket. She had not heard anyone approaching. She looked up into the face of a tall dark-haired man, smiling jovially at her, his hands shoved into the pockets of his black pea coat.

"Y-yeah," Matilda tried to play it cool; this was not the first time she'd had to talk her way out of a sticky situation – despite what Harley thought. "I was actually looking for another shop, but I guess my map app took me the wrong way…"

"A simple mistake. Might I direct you to where you were headed? What's the name of the shop?" Miles asked in a syrupy sweet tone.

"Um, well that's the problem, I don't actually know the name. My friend just told me about this athletic shop where she buys her running shoes." Matilda noticed Miles eyeing her black pumps. "I like to jog on my days off."

"I see. Well, I am sorry I can't be of more help, but I don't know of any athletic stores currently operating in the area. Perhaps you should ask your friend for the name and try again."

"Yeah," Matilda nodded, forcing a smile and biting her lower lip, "I'll do that. Thanks anyway." She turned to leave.

"Any time." Miles smiled and reached into his coat pocket, pulling out a fresh box of cigarillos and slapping it against his palm. "Care for a smoke?"

"Oh, no thanks. I don't smoke." She walked away down the street. Once she was out of sight, his expression turned to a deadly serious frown. He did not like Matilda Benson snooping around his headquarters one bit.

# Chapter 39

Elsa had left several hours ago. Edward stood in front the bathroom mirror in nothing but his underwear, drenched in sweat and shaking all over. His eyes had long since adjusted to the darkness, and he was scrutinizing his own reflection. He wondered if Hyde ever looked in the mirror. He did not have any recollection of it, but the only memories he had of being Hyde at all were when he had been 'born' and when he had murdered Giselle Michaels.

Edward had been in a state of euphoria after he and Elsa had made love; it had been somehow different, more special. Meaningful. Then after she had left, he had laid there in the bed alone, looking up at the dark high ceiling of the suite. Hyde had been born from his hate of monsters, a hatred that had roots over twenty years old. Edward had not thought about the event that had caused his hatred of monsters all those years ago in a very long time. Most people knew Edward Jekyll - the crime journalist - simply as the man who voiced strong negative opinions about monsters in his column and articles. Very few knew the true reason that Edward Jekyll hated monsters more than anything.

These memories brought back old feelings as well: the fear he had felt as a child, the hate that came with adolescence and new understanding. Now he stood, looking at himself in the mirror. In essence, *he* was that thing that had terrorized that seven-year-old boy. And for that, he hated himself.

"*Wallowing in self-pity after the day you had?*" Hyde's voice mocked him inside his head.

"Shut up!" Jekyll spat, clenching his eyes closed and smacking the side of his head with the palm of his hand, as if he had water in his ear.

"*That was quite the speech you gave her.*"

"That is none of your business," Jekyll huffed.

"*Everything you do is my business,*" Hyde said nonchalantly. "*Like I know you went to see that magic man, or 'soul doctor,' whatever he calls himself. Zeleni Malakai.*"

"Yeah. So what? It wasn't like he could help." Jekyll scowled with distaste. He walked out of the bathroom to the kitchen counter where he turned on the sink and filled a small glass with water. He gulped it down, smacking the cup down on the countertop and walking back over to the bed. "Now please, go away. I would like to get some sleep."

"*You can't get rid of me, Jekyll. No matter how hard you try, you'll never get rid of me.*"

Jekyll sat down on the edge of the bed, lying down and pulling the comforter over his bare legs and chest. "Watch me," he said to Hyde, closing his eyes.

*"I bet you'll have some unpleasant dreams tonight."* Hyde snickered, retreating into the recesses of Edward Jekyll's mind.

Meanwhile, Elsa sat on her and Edward's bed in their house, the glow of his tablet's screen illuminating her face. She had tried refining her searches for W, entering 'W purple,' 'W purple triangle,' and 'W purple triangle magic' into the search bar. She was still coming up mostly empty-handed, and she threw the tablet down on her lap, yelling in frustration.

After taking a few moments to collect herself, she picked up the tablet once more, powering it off. She lay back on the bed, staring at the ceiling and thinking. She thought about Edward, his rough but gentle hands rubbing her back, the taste of his warm lips, the feeling of his hair between her fingers. She wished that he were here now, or that he had let her stay at the hotel. But he had still insisted that she not sleep in the same place as him; despite Hyde's supposed feelings for her, Edward feared that he was still unpredictable. And Elsa felt that he was probably right to.

Her mind then wandered to Zeleni Malakai. He was the first and only call that they had made so far in search of a cure for Edward's curse. Edward had been so turned off by his showiness and inability to help that they had just not gotten around to calling anyone else yet. Elsa thought of the two other ads she kept with Zeleni's at the top of the pile, two female psychics: one named Blanche Grimwald and the other's name escaped her at the moment. Maybe one of them could be of more help in the search for W. Elsa unfortunately doubted that psychics would do much good when it came to curing Edward of his curse. But perhaps if shown the symbol Zeleni had drawn for her, they would be able to 'see' something of use. Or maybe they would even know something about the elusive witch who went simply by W.

Elsa felt her eyelids begin to grow heavy and as much as she fought it, sleep eventually overtook her.

# Chapter 40

Jesse sat in his room, his brow furrowed pensively in thought. He had been sitting there like that for hours. Finally he stood, exiting his bedroom. Jesse entered the lab to find Alexei. He did not know why he was nervous to bring up this topic, but his guts were roiling and his palms were sweating. Jesse did not see Alexei anywhere. This only made him more apprehensive, since Alexei very rarely left the lab without an appointment. The sound of someone clearing their throat caused him to jump. He looked around the lab again and noticed Alexei's grey hair sticking up from behind a microscope. He was standing as still as a statue, very intent on what he was examining. Jesse wiped his sweaty hands on his pants and began walking toward Alexei. He did not look up as Jesse approached, not even when he was right beside him.

"Alexei," Jesse said quietly, his voice faltering.

Alexei's head snapped up, his pupils fluctuating in size as they adjusted from staring into the microscope. "Jesse," he said after a moment, "you startled me. What is it?"

"I've just been thinking… and I want to try something new. I mean, I got given a second chance at life and… I want to do something with it. I'm not really sure what, but, I want to get a job. I just don't know where to start. I was hoping you could help me."

Alexei just stared at him. After a few moments of silence, Jesse wondered if he had understood what he'd said. Alexei exhaled heavily, bugging out his eyes. He ran his hand through his hair and scratched his beard.

"I never really thought of that..." he said, continuing to scratch his beard. "That you might want to leave here or get a job. Most of what I work with isn't really normally alive." Alexei's face had gone completely blank. "You don't have a birth certificate... social security... any valid form of ID. As far as the world is concerned, you don't exist."

"You truly have no record of who I - *any* of the people I was - were?"

"No..." Alexei shook his head. "Not much info was given with the parts. Especially not the ones I acquired illegally," he chuckled.

"So... there's no way that I could really go out on my own?" Jesse said, dejection creeping into his tone.

"I'm afraid so..." Jesse hung his head. "For now," Alexei added, trying to force a smile.

Jesse smiled weakly. "Thanks anyway... I'll let you get back to what you were working on."

As he walked away, Alexei peered back into the microscope. To the untrained eye, the slide would have looked empty. But very fine red streaks marred the surface of the sample. Red was undoubtedly the hardest pigment to eradicate, the red blood cells the only thing visible in the sample of human flesh.

Alexei looked around the table and picked up what appeared to be a holographic cherry. 'Holographic' translucence would not do; he needed to find a way to achieve one hundred percent transparency.

Alexei walked over to a cabinet and opened it, retrieving a tray of test tubes, each full of a red liquid, slightly ranging in hues. He had collected a series of red dyes, including that of cochineal bugs and hemoglobin. More tests would be needed. That was all right; as much as Alexei hated failure, he had all the time in the world for tests.

# Chapter 41

Kurt's phone vibrated. He pulled it out of his pocket and looked at the caller ID. The call was coming from a number he did not recognize. He hesitated a moment before answering. It could be a telemarketer. Or worse: it could be Miles.

He took a deep breath and then answered. "Hello?"

"Kurt," Miles' dry voice came through the receiver, causing Kurt to sit up a little straighter; he hated that.

"What do you want? How did you get this number?" Kurt said in a low and menacing tone.

Miles chuckled hoarsely on the other end, and then grew serious again. "Don't take that tone. We both know you can't do a thing to hurt me." Kurt hated to admit it, but he was right. "And I have several ways of getting what I want. You should know that. And now, I need you. Come to the shop, pronto." Kurt could hear him snap his fingers impatiently several times.

"No," Kurt said tersely.

"You don't get to say no, Kurt. Come here *now*." Kurt stood reflexively. He grunted and let out a soft whimper. "That's a good boy," Miles taunted. "See you within the hour." He hung up and the call dropped.

Kurt hung up the phone and went to the closet to grab his jacket. His body moved on its own, automatically, the wolf inside heeding to Miles' commands. Kurt had always hated the wolf. For a few years in his adolescence he had hated his mother – blamed her for making him this way. He had finally come to terms with the fact that she had not had a choice in the matter, same as him, but by then she had already fallen prey to the cancer.

Once he stepped outside into the brisk night, the wolf took control almost completely, his legs running as if someone had wound him up and set him loose in the streets. He ran fast, faster than most humans. He wondered to himself why he did not run more often – the feeling of the wind in his hair was exhilarating, the feeling of power in his legs - but the answer was obvious: he did not like to draw attention to himself.

He began to get short of breath after he had run several blocks – possibly even miles. He spoke aloud to himself, "Slow down. I can't even breathe." His legs resisted, trying to keep up the quick pace, but finally they began to ache and he slowed to a steady jog. He breathed in a lungful of air, the coolness stinging his nostrils and throat pleasantly.

He knew he was not far from the athletic store. For one, he knew and recognized the area. For another, he could smell just the faintest hint of Miles' cologne. His body finally allowed him to walk, knowing that he was close and could not turn back.

He jammed his hands into his jacket pockets as he walked along the sidewalk, regulating his breathing. He wondered what terrible task Miles had in store for him this time. He wished that he had never gotten caught up in this mess. If he had just gone to Wulfen instead of going along with Alec Greerson – a complete stranger – all of this could have been avoided. He should not have been so naïve, allowed hope to cloud his better judgement.

On the other hand, Matilda Benson had once been a complete stranger. He had trusted her with his darkest secrets - even told her that he had killed - and yet she had not seen him as a monster. She had seen the man – a man who had let the beast inside make him want to hide from the world. She had rekindled something in him, his urge to be free, to live life. To fall in love.

He sighed. Unfortunately his heightened wolf senses did not include a heightened judgement of character. He was at the abandoned shop and when he tried the door, it was open. Miles was sitting in the back room, twirling a pen between his fingers like a miniature baton. Waiting.

"I see you decided to show up finally," he said brusquely, his back still turned to Kurt, but he stopped twirling the pen, gripping it in his hand.

"I didn't have much of a choice," Kurt said through gritted teeth.

"Any choice." Miles stood, setting the pen on the desk and turning to face Kurt. His expression was grave. "I saw your reporter friend snooping around here the other day."

Kurt stiffened but hoped Miles did not notice. "She's a reporter. That's what they do." He strained to keep an even tone.

Miles laughed, coughing slightly. He cleared his throat and grew serious again. "Nevertheless, I don't like her prying into my business."

"I'll talk with her." Kurt's heart rate quickened. If Miles caught on that Matilda was trying to find a way to free him, she could become his next target. Maybe she already was.

"Just be careful what you say," Miles urged, an ominous edge to his voice. Kurt nodded. "Now, on to why I actually called you here. I need someone else… 'taken care of.' He has been a thorn in my side for a long time. I also know that he lied to me, right to my face. I can't do anything to touch him, but now that I have you, you can. Because you aren't merely human." Kurt glared at him, clenching his jaw. "This is his scent," Miles held up a piece of cloth. Kurt unwillingly took a whiff. It smelled of incense and a hint of man sweat. Miles pocketed the cloth and patted Kurt on the shoulder. Kurt wanted to slap his hand away, but knew that would
262

be both unwise and probably impossible. "Now you have the scent," Miles smiled eagerly, "now sic!"

Kurt practically leapt forward, the wolf inside hungry for blood. For being human, Miles seemed to have a fairly large appetite for blood himself. Kurt flung open the front door, sniffing the air, trying to catch the man's scent. He did not smell him nearby and took off running, continuing to sniff the air in hopes of catching the scent. While the wolf was frantically searching for the trail, Kurt hoped that he would not find it. He did not want to be responsible for anyone else's death. He was just thankful that Miles had not sent him after Matilda. While it broke his heart, he knew what he had to do. He would *make* her abandon her search for a way to break the curse, make her return to her life as a reporter covering bakeries and stores' grand openings. At least then she had been safe.

He suddenly stopped, taking a moment to really sniff the air around him. He had caught a slight whiff of the incense, but it had seemed to disappear. He spun in a circle, trying to figure out which way the smell had come from. He finally decided on his right and began bounding that way, trying to catch the scent again. He had no idea how far he had gone from Miles' headquarters, or even where he was; all that mattered was catching his prey.

These primal urges both fascinated and terrified him. More so terrified him. Until recently, he had never been conscious when the wolf was in control. He had always blacked out and awoken in his cell at Wulfen, or those few fateful nights in the street. But he had never known what it felt like to want to hunt. To kill. He did not like the way it felt.

He paused and took a moment to look around. From what he could see in the darkness, he was nearing Chinatown. The hairs on his neck suddenly stood on end. Was that... the incense? But more importantly, the scent of a human male along with it. The scent from the cloth!

Kurt let out a soft howl, the sound feeling strange in his mouth and throat, and began running in that direction. The smell grew stronger and stronger, and suddenly the glass door to a shop opened before him. A tall man with dark features, including an impressive mustache, closed the door behind him and turned to lock it when he noticed Kurt bounding toward him. He squinted, trying to get a good look at him. His eyes suddenly widened, but he held his ground. Kurt stopped a few yards from him, panting from having run so far.

"That man... Miles, he sent you, didn't he?" the man asked in a strange accent.

"Yes," Kurt replied, wanting to be completely frank with the guy – to at least give him the chance to run.

"I knew that this day would eventually come." Zeleni Malakai locked the door and then slipped the keys into his pocket, his legs braced to run if necessary. "I saw you in a vision, a long time ago. You're a werewolf, aren't you?"

"Yes," Kurt replied again, his legs already braced to spring forward when the time was right. "I'm sorry, I don't want to kill you. But I don't have a choice. He's too strong." He knew that the middle-aged man before him was not strong enough to fight him off.

"I knew from almost the moment he walked into my shop that he was trouble. Evil to the core, with a thirst for power that will never be satisfied. I am sorry you have fallen prey to him. But I also do not plan on letting you kill me tonight."

"Only if you're fast enough," Kurt said sadly. "I'm so sorry." He lunged forward.

"I only have to be fast enough to do this!" Zeleni reached into a small pouch strapped to his waist and pulled his hand out in a fist, lifting his hand to his mouth and opening his fist, blowing some strange powder in Kurt's face as he charged him. Kurt was immediately dazed, sneezing furiously as the powder entered his nasal passages. Zeleni turned, running down the sidewalk. Kurt fell to the ground, suddenly feeling terribly sleepy. The last thing he saw before he lost consciousness was the blurred image of the man he was supposed to kill disappearing into the night.

~

The sound of footsteps approaching caused Kurt to stir, but his eyelids were still heavy, so he just lay where he was and listened as the footsteps came up right next to him and stopped.

"Some guard dog you are," Miles' voice broke the silence, and Kurt heard his knee pop as he knelt. Suddenly he felt fingers in his hair and his head was pulled back, the cold blade of a knife pressed against his throat. The metal burned his skin; he knew that the knife must be silver. "What good are you if you won't carry out orders?"

Kurt took a few labored breaths, his flesh burning where the blade rested, and spoke breathlessly. "Just do it."

Miles chuckled, pulling Kurt's head back a little further so that his neck began to ache. "You'd like that wouldn't you?" He removed the blade and shoved Kurt's head forward, throwing him down hard on the pavement. Kurt coughed a couple of times, reaching up to rub the irritated spot on his neck. "That'd be too easy. I'm your master now. And you *will* listen to me."

266

"I tried to," Kurt spat, "but the guy was ready for me. He blew some kind of powder in my face that knocked me out. Said he saw me in a vision a long time ago. Knew you were rotten to the core."

Miles scowled, crossing his arms over his chest, the silver knife still gripped in his hand. Kurt looked up at him. If he could lunge quickly enough, he could shove the knife up into Miles' chest and then-

"Don't even think about it." Miles saw Kurt's eyes on the knife and quickly hid it from view in his coat. "Well I never suspected that he would see you coming. Me I knew he would anticipate. That really puts a damper on things." He stroked his chin thoughtfully. "I guess it is not imperative that he die. Not tonight, anyway, but eventually. Come on, get up," he said with authority.

Kurt groggily pushed himself up into a sitting position; his head was still spinning from whatever that man had blown into his face. "Who was that guy anyway?"

"That does not concern you. Come on, get up, I am sure it wasn't that potent. He was aiming to disarm, not injure or kill."

Kurt stood, loyally following Miles back to his parked car.

# Chapter 42

Carmichael sat at the bar, sipping a glass of his good old standby: whiskey. He was still mulling over W's refusal. He hated her for it; he had hated her for over a century. But in all truth, she had just confirmed what he already knew. That he could never die. For decades he had searched and hoped he would be able to find a way. But deep down, he had always known it was a doomed endeavor from the start.

But dying was not all that troubled him. Seeing W in her wretched aged state had not evoked much feeling in him, aside from a strong desire to break her frail bones in a way so that she would die slowly. But he had known that wouldn't work, same as the broken whiskey bottle had not worked 133 years ago. However, telling Brook the story of his curse had brought back feelings he had forgotten.

While it was true that he had never been in love with Winona, that did not mean that he had not cared for her. He had cared very much. When he had looked over the crowd gathering to watch him duel Royce Slade, he had truly been relieved when he did not see her among them. He had not wanted her to have to see him burn. He had kept her at arms' length when she had talked of them running away together because he knew it would only result in one or both of them getting hurt. Ironically, that ended up happening anyway. Bad luck had always been his fate.

He tapped his glass on the counter for a refill. Of all the things he hated about his vampirism, his heightened alcohol tolerance was pretty high up on the list. He just wanted to forget, more than anything. To forget all the bodies in the rubble of the club in 1941. To forget the screams and faces of all those women he'd murdered in that spacious house during the Roaring Twenties. To forget what it felt like when he and Winona made love: shallow and empty. To forget that he had been unable to kill her.

Maybe it wasn't his immortality he hated so much as remembering. To say he was not a good person would have been an understatement. Even in his first life he had been a scoundrel, only concerned with his wealth and handsome face. He had been willing to kill to keep that perfect face.

The only time in his life it could be said that he seemed to be headed down the path of redemption was in 1733 when he met and married Emily Harker. And even then, he had been a murderer behind her back.

To think he had been alive all this time – half a millennia – and his two greatest regrets were not changing Emily before she succumbed to the fever and failing to kill Winona. In this world, many people questioned what a true monster was. Carmichael knew: he was a true monster.

"Leave the bottle," he said to the bartender, removing the pour spout and knocking it back, the forgetting potion where no witch or magic was needed. The catch was that the effects were merely temporary.

~

"I've had an 'epiphany' of sorts," Carmichael said, leaning back on the couch in Brook's office. "I suppose I really haven't been fair to you Brook... or fair to myself. I haven't really tried to get better. I've wallowed and taunted you. But as I've stated before, I'm stuck on this earth forever and W only confirmed that." He looked directly at Brook. "And since that is the case, what kind of existence is a miserable one?" Carmichael noticed a look in Brook's eyes. Was it skepticism or relief? He couldn't make heads or tails of it. "The obsession with suicide - all the failed attempts - ends now. I'm done wasting time – especially since time, for you, is limited. I want to get better."

Brook sat in silence a moment, that same look in his eyes. He looked down at his clipboard propped up on his crossed leg, his right foot dangling limply above the floor. When he looked back at

Carmichael, the look was gone and replaced by a glimmer of hope. Brook's face broke into a smile. "That's great to hear, Carmichael," Brook said with such joyful enthusiasm that it made Carmichael feel worse for lying to his face. "As the saying goes: 'Where there is a will, there is a way.' I'm glad to see you coming to these realizations on your own. That is the first step to improvement."

"That isn't all," Carmichael shifted uncomfortably, "I don't really talk to many people besides bartenders these days. But I guess that it helps to know that there is someone rooting for me on the sidelines. Even after I've treated you like shit and wasted your time with self-indulgent stories, you have been nothing but genuine in your attempt to help me. And while a piece of me still thinks it may not be possible to pull myself out of this black hole I've fallen into... for the first time in a long while I feel like there is someone on the outside calling me back." Carmichael stared off into space, his voice trailing off, "It's a damn shame you'll die someday... even if forever is a curse."

The two sat in silence, the clock on the wall ticking away the seconds of their session.

"I suppose we should get on with the session," Carmichael finally said.

Brook pursed his lips, removing his clipboard from his lap and setting it on the desk. "Or we could just talk," he suggested, "man to man instead of doctor to patient. It's been a rather long day and I think a nice chat could do us both some good."

A smile crept across Carmichael's face. He chuckled, "All right... what do you want to talk about?"

# Chapter 43

A knock came at Chairman Vapelli's office door. "Come in," he said, not looking up from what he was reading.

Alexei entered his office, closing the door behind him and sitting down in a chair facing Vapelli's desk. Vapelli glanced up, then did a double take, dropping what he was reading. "What are you doing here? What do you want? I could call security with the push of a button in here, I-"

"I have a question for you, Chairman: what's scarier than a crazy man?" Alexei smiled threateningly at Vapelli. Vapelli glared at him, but gave no answer. "Well, to you Chairman, I can imagine fewer things are scarier. But the answer is: a crazy man that you can't see."

"What're you going on about?" Vapelli narrowed his eyes.

"Invisibility, Chairman. My latest work-in-progress."

"You're insane."

"Tell me something we don't both already know." Alexei chuckled. "Go on, I'm serious. I told you what I'm working on, so now it's your turn. Tell me something I don't already know."

Vapelli fumed, turning red in the face. He started to say something, but hesitated, then smiled with a sickly sweetness to his voice. "I am sure you will be happy to know that my new supervisor will be here soon. He wants a full review from all of his employees. And oh the review I will have for him on one Dr. Alexei Frankenstein!"

"You'll have to beat me then."

"What?" Vapelli looked completely taken aback.

"It's a race now, don't you see that? Which happens first: I turn myself invisible and you never see me again or you convince this new boss to have me locked away?"

"I'm fairly confident with my horse in this race," Vapelli smiled again, "because I'm not crazy."

"Last I checked, crazy had nothing to do with speed," Alexei stood, gripping the door knob. "You have a good day, Chairman."

# Chapter 44

Elsa walked down the busy sidewalk, navigating all of the other pedestrians and walking commuters. She had called Edward and told him that she had some errands to run, basic things she needed around the house. She still did not want to breach the W subject with him yet, not while it was still so flimsy. Despite his faith in her, he would likely shoot it down immediately, especially after how he had voiced his opinions about Zeleni Malakai. What Elsa was really doing was going to see this Blanche Grimwald to see if she could point her in the right direction to find W.

She stopped walking outside a nail and hair salon that's address matched the one on Grimwald's ad. The sign on the door read 'Nails, Hair, and More.' She assumed the 'More' was Grimwald's subtle word for 'Psychic Readings.' She took a deep breath. While Elsa did not share Edward's views about monsters and the supernatural, she had never been to see a psychic before. She did not know what to expect in comparison to Zeleni Malakai's shop, which was explicitly known as a magic den.

Once she opened the door, she was smacked in the face by the smell of turpentine, ammonia, and nail polish. Despite the strong smells, the shop appeared to be currently empty. All of the salon chairs sat vacant, their hoods propped back on their hinges. Little tables with nail polish, hand rests, and face masks were also unattended.

*Bing-Bong!* The door beeped to alert the clerk that someone had entered. A woman with curly platinum blonde hair stuck her head out from a back room. She appeared to be in her mid-forties, her wrinkles visible despite her attempts to hide them under foundation. Her dark brown eyes were accented by thick mascara-laden lashes and black cat-eye liner. She pulled a pair of mauve cat-eye framed glasses that hung on a beaded chain around her neck up to her eyes so that she could get a better look at her customer. She wore a lacy pale pink top, accompanied by pale capris and tall brown lace-up boots.

"How can I help you?" she said in a voice with a heavy Jersey accent.

"Are you Blanche Grimwald?" Elsa coughed as she spoke, the odors burning her nostrils and throat.

"Yes, I'm Blanche. Wanting to do something with that hair?"

Elsa suddenly became a little self-conscious of her messy ponytail and touched it absently. "Um, no, actually I'm here about your ad in the paper concerning your psychic services."

Blanche's expression changed and she stepped a little further out of the back room. She stared a little harder at Elsa. "What is it that ails you? Or I suppose the better question is: what ails he who is not here with you?"

"The man I love has been cursed," Elsa replied. "But that is not exactly why I am here. I need help finding someone."

"Come back here," Blanche motioned to Elsa with her hand, disappearing into the back room.

Elsa cautiously walked around the counter and through the doorway. This room was very different from the back room of Zeleni Malakai's. It had bare walls painted a heinous shade of pale banana yellow. A ceiling fan spun on 'Low' overhead, one of its four light bulbs burnt out. A few cardboard boxes were stacked in one corner. A table sat in the center of the room – one chair on one side, two on the other. A small filing cabinet sat next to the single chair. As Blanche walked across the dingy carpet toward the table, Elsa stood back in the doorway.

Blanche sat and noticed Elsa still lingering at the threshold. "Well come on! Sit," she said in exasperation, dropping her glasses back down so that they hung around her neck.

Elsa walked over to the table, sitting in one of the chairs and placing her purse on her lap. She reached inside and pulled out a folded piece of paper, which still slightly held the scent of incense. "What do you know about this?" Elsa asked, unfolding the paper and setting it on the table so that the drawing of the purple W in a triangle was visible. As Blanche's eyes fell on the paper, they widened.

She looked up at Elsa seriously. "Where did you get this?"

Elsa hesitated before answering; she was not sure if she could trust Blanche. "… From a friend."

Blanche looked at the symbol again, then back up at Elsa. "I know that I have not seen this symbol in a very long time. What do you want with it?"

Elsa took a deep breath. "I want you to help me locate the person who uses that symbol, if they are still alive."

Blanche's eyes bulged and she looked as if she had been punched in the gut. "Y-you want to find her!?"

"So she can be found?" Elsa said eagerly.

"Possibly," Blanche shook out her shoulders and fluffed her hair, trying to regain her composure, "she is one of the most powerful witches known to have ever lived. She is very dangerous."

Elsa refused to budge on the subject. "I have to find her if she is still alive."

Blanche sighed, reaching into the top drawer of the filing cabinet and pulling out a silver necklace with a moonstone pendant. "I will try to help you," she said as she hung the necklace around her neck, "but I cannot promise anything." She closed her eyes and began to breathe deeply and evenly, holding the pendant in her hand and stroking the moonstone with her index finger. She frowned in concentration, causing the wrinkles in her forehead to become more visible. She rested her hand that was not holding the pendant on the piece of paper with the symbol drawn on it.

After a moment her hand tensed, her palm rising from the paper, supported by the last digits of her fingers. She began to speak, her voice distant. "I see... a man. Not now, mind you – in the past. The symbol glows above him, ever so faintly." She paused, her eyes moving rapidly as if she were reading some text on the insides of her eyelids. "His face is not his own... a shapeshifter, he seems. She is not pleased with this nor fooled. He wants her help... there is a very odd buzzing sound." She shifted in the chair. "I can't see them anymore. Just the symbol, glowing... and that odd buzzing sound. I'm trying to pull back, to see..." She rubbed the moonstone more vigorously, relaxing her hand on the drawing, rubbing her palm over it. "I'm losing sight of it, the sound is dulling... an alley. A fire exit door is visible on one side, it says 'Bill's Crab Shack'......"

She paused for a long time. Then she opened her eyes and released the stone, pulling her hand away from the symbol. "Please, put that away where I do not have to look at it," Blanche practically pleaded, looking away from the table until Elsa had put

281

the paper back in her purse. "Did any of that mean anything to you?" she asked as she removed the moonstone necklace.

"Yes. It means that Lawrence Talbot did go to see W to help him get revenge on-" she stopped short.

Blanche's eyes widened once more. "Talbot sent you on this search?"

"Well, not exactly. It's... complicated. He is responsible for cursing, well... it's probably better if you didn't know who I was here to try and help."

"Edward Jekyll," Blanche stated bluntly.

Elsa sat a moment in shock and then chuckled softly. "I guess you can't keep many secrets from a psychic."

"You'd be surprised," Blanche said to herself, then turned back to Elsa. "He is all you have been thinking about since you walked in here except for that symbol." She fluffed her hair again. "Bill's Crab Shack, do you know where that is?"

"Yes, I do." Elsa stood.

Blanche grabbed her wrist. "As for Talbot... I've never met him personally, but I know that he cannot be trusted. If he told you to try and find her - especially if he went to her for help first - chances are he is steering you toward danger. If you really are going to do this, then please, be careful. W would not have lifted a finger to help Talbot if she herself had not wanted to harm Edward Jekyll."

Elsa felt a flicker of fear, but she pushed it away. "I have to do this. How much do I owe you?"

Blanche scrunched up her nose at the question. "Usually, I charge sixty... but forty for you, given the circumstances." Elsa set two twenties on the table and turned to leave. "Just remember this, Miss McIntire. There is a difference between bravery and foolishness."

Elsa slowed but continued out the door. She drew in a deep breath as she stepped outside, letting the fresh air fill her lungs. It was not until she was in her car, the scent of chemicals clinging to her hair and clothes, that she remembered she had never told Blanche Grimwald her name.

# Chapter 45

Kurt walked into the bar, his shoulders hunched. He had been dreading this moment since Miles had told him he had seen Matilda snooping around. His neck also still stung, he had put some lotion on it in hopes of calming the inflammation, but he still had a slight rash where the silver had rested on his skin for too long. He sat at their usual table and even though it was only the early afternoon, he ordered his usual whiskey sour; he really needed a drink. As he waited for his drink, he stared at the floor, bleakness and sorrow engulfing him.

Matilda walked into the bar and noticed him sitting at the table in his depressed stupor. She walked over to him, her face lined with worry. "Kurt. What's wrong?" she asked, and he looked up at her, seemingly surprised by her appearance. She noticed the red spot on his throat. "Oh my gosh, what happened to your neck?" She sat down, putting her hand over her open mouth.

"Don't worry about it, it's just an allergic reaction." The waiter came to set down his drink, and he fell silent until the man had walked out of earshot. "Miles saw you snooping around the other day. He knows who you are... more importantly, what you mean to me." Kurt took a large swig of his drink, wincing as the alcohol burned his mouth and throat. "You can't go around there anymore," he said distantly. He looked up at her, his eyes meeting hers. "You have to stop trying to help me Matilda. He could make me hurt you. I… I want you to go back to your life before you met me. Your safe life, covering 'boring' stories and griping about your boss to some guy at the bar."

"No, I refuse to believe that. You're a good man. You are stronger than that wolf. Our love is stronger than any hold Miles has on you." She gently caressed his face, staring deep into his eyes, her own swelling with tears. She smiled at him, taking in his handsome face, the genuine worry in his eyes. She knew they were not just words anymore; she truly loved him.

He smiled back at her, his eyes still filled with concern, reaching up to touch her wrist, cradling her hand in his. He knew that she was fully invested in him from the look on her face, the feeling of her touch. He tried to imagine if their places were swapped. He knew that no power on Earth would be able to make him abandon her, even if it was for his own safety. "I hope so… for your sake."

"I know so," Matilda pushed away that doubt in the back of her mind. She began to put the pieces together. Miles must have been the man who had spoken to her when she was about to break into the athletic store. That would explain why he had been so

286

syrupy sweet and urged her away from the store. She considered herself lucky that she had been able to walk away from him. But that may have only been because Kurt was not with him. The thought of that man manipulating Kurt just made her furious. And even more determined to get Kurt out from under Miles' control.

# Chapter 46

The sun had set, the moon now illuminating the sky. Elsa looked down at her phone, then up at the street signs. She was not far from Bill's Crab Shack. Her map app told her to turn left at the next intersection and then it would be on her left. It was late enough that only a few cars were still on the roads, most of the stores and restaurants in this district closed for the night.

Elsa turned left and saw the sign for Bill's glowing against the night sky. She closed the map app and locked her phone, placing it in her jacket pocket. She walked toward the sign, keeping her eyes peeled for an alley on either side of the building. Or the purple triangle with a W at its center.

Just before she reached the front of the crab shack, she saw a narrow alley branching off to her left. She looked down the alley for any sign of movement or purple light. She saw nothing but blackness. She felt a chill run down her spine as she looked into the expanse of darkness. She closed her eyes, trying to muster up the courage to leave the safety of the streetlights; she felt that even the moonlight would not do her much good once she entered the alley. Especially if the elusive W resided deep inside.

She opened her eyes, a look of determination on her face, and entered the alley. It was so dark that she could not even see her hand in front of her face. She began to consider turning back, but the thought of Edward kept her going. She would have gotten her phone out to use as a flashlight, but she did not want to draw too much attention to herself. Or at least, not yet.

The darkness around her began to take on a slight indigo hue. She looked ahead of her and a very dim violet light began to come into view. An odd electrical buzzing filled the air, barely audible, but definitely there. As she neared the violet glow, it became clearer: it was in the shape of a triangle, some kind of sigil at its center. Her pulse quickened; could she really have found W?

She finally realized where the buzzing was coming from as she drew ever closer to the glowing symbol. It was the buzzing of a neon sign, a neon sign that seemed to be in need of repair. The light was so dim that even once Elsa had nearly reached it the alley did not lighten. She squinted around below the sign. Where she would have thought a door should be, there was only a solid brick wall. She reached cautiously to touch it; but once her hand rested on it, it was just what it seemed: rough bricks. She tried feeling the wall for some sign of a door or passage for a little while longer. She finally stopped, sighing heavily and glaring up at the sign, which's buzzing was beginning to give her a headache.

She shook her head and crossed her arms, looking to either side of the alley for a door branching off to one side or the other.

290

Still nothing, just the walls of buildings that lined the alley. She sighed, out of both frustration and disappointment, before turning to head back out onto the street. A draft came from behind her, blowing her hair and the flaps of her jacket. Elsa turned around slowly to see an old metal door hanging open under the sign, the purple light reflecting faintly off its surface. But there had certainly not been a door there just a few moments ago; she had thoroughly examined the wall and all she had felt was bricks and mortar.

"You wanted to see me?" an old woman's voice croaked.

Elsa was frozen for a minute – by fear or awe she was not sure. She finally broke out of her stupor and spoke, stumbling over her words. "Are you... are you the one they call W?"

An aged cackle erupted from the old crone's throat. She stepped out from the dark doorway into the dull glow of the sign, the soft light falling over her stooped shoulders as she leaned on her cane. "I find it's easier if people don't know your name. Especially when you are in my line of business." She sighed, fanning herself with her hand as she began to cough from her laughing fit. "Come inside Miss McIntire, and then we can discuss business. You went to a lot of trouble to find me after all." She turned and shuffled into the darkness of the doorway.

Elsa tentatively followed her. Was she walking into the lion's den? Did it really matter, if there was even a chance that this could help Edward? As she crossed the threshold into the darkness, the door slammed closed behind her on its own. Elsa suddenly thought of Zeleni Malakai and Blanche Grimwald. If W – the witch – knew that Elsa had gone to a lot of trouble to find her, did that mean that they could be in danger? She tried to push those thoughts from her mind; she was here for Edward. Everything she had done leading up to this had been for him. She could not afford to back out on him now.

The room was suddenly bathed in light, revealing the inside of the witch's lair to be just that – a single room. The light seemed to be coming from a crystal ball sitting at the center of a large round table draped in a magenta cloth. The witch was seated at the far of end of the table, still coughing lightly into her gnarly old hand and leaning on her cane.

"So what is it that you want, Miss McIntire?" the witch asked. Elsa could now see that her eyes were different colors, one black and one white. "Please, take a seat. Or stand, if you'd rather." She smiled, revealing missing teeth. The light from the crystal ball cast shadows on her face that made her look deranged.

Elsa remained standing. "I know that Lawrence Talbot came to you for help... help cursing Edward Jekyll. I want you to reverse your curse on him."

The witch stared at her a moment, then started laughing all over again, hacking terribly. Once she got ahold of herself, she spoke between giggles. "Oh my dear... you went through all of this to... to ask me to reverse my own curse?" She finally stopped laughing, her tone turning dead serious. "No. I will not. Edward Jekyll got what was coming to him for a long time. Mr. Talbot wanted him cursed for a good reason." She smirked at Elsa, leaning forward and resting an elbow on the table. "Tell me, has he become a true monster?" The light reflected off of her black eye cruelly.

Elsa clenched her jaw, stopping herself from saying something she would regret. "He's not as bad as he could seem. Deep down, he is a good man. He's just flawed, like everyone."

"I don't think that's entirely true. What about your stomach?" The witch pointed at her. Elsa absently put her hand to her bandaged wound. "It would seem that your boyfriend has murderous urges deep inside, not a heart of gold."

Elsa fought tears, the look on Hyde's face when he had stabbed her resurfacing in her mind. She tried to push it away, to think of *her* Edward in there fighting for control. She suspected that the witch was trying to get inside her head and turn her against Edward. And that was not going to happen.

"I love him. More than anyone could ever understand. I love the good and the bad. Name your price," Elsa said firmly.

The witch's smirk became even more unpleasant. "I don't think you heard me the first time, dear. I said that I will not reverse my own curse. Especially not the one I made for Edward Jekyll." She examined her own long yellowed fingernails. "It was an extra special concoction I came up with just for him."

"Why?" Elsa asked, trying to abate the growing feeling of defeat that was bubbling up inside her.

"Because my dear. People like Edward Jekyll are why people like me have to live in the shadows. People like Edward Jekyll are the reason my brothers and sisters were hunted and killed in the past. People like Edward Jekyll are rotten. People like Edward Jekyll are the *real monsters*." Her mouth turned down in a hideous frown, a tear glistening on the edge of her white eye.

"I'm sorry about what happened to your kind in the past. But Edward never did anything like that. He just voiced his opinions in his articles and columns. Not that he was right, but, he wasn't burning witches at the stake."

Rage flashed in the old hag's eyes and she stood without using her cane, leaning across the table and pointing her gnarly finger in
294

Elsa's face. "He would have if he were given the chance! And you know this, and yet, you still stand by him." Tear streaks were visible on the woman's wrinkled cheeks, fresh tears running along the tract. Her legs suddenly grew weak and she retreated into her chair, her mix-matched eyes never leaving Elsa as she sank back into a sitting position. "No. That is my final answer. Edward Jekyll will just have to live with the consequences of his actions. Go now, unless you have something else to ask of me. And I would watch what you wish for. You have put me in a rather foul mood."

Elsa once again felt that flicker of fear, and the feeling of defeat consumed her fully. "I guess I'll be going then."

"I guess you shall." The door opened behind Elsa, the doorway lined in soft violet light.

She slowly turned, not wanting to let the witch out of her sight before the door was closed behind her. Once she was outside, she ran to the end of the alley. Once she had reached the road and the safety of the streetlights, she fell to her knees, crying, her tears a mixture of disappointment, fear, and heartbreak.

# Chapter 47

Kurt sat at the desk in the back room of the athletic store. Miles had called him there, but when he had arrived, Miles had been nowhere to be seen. He had almost turned to leave, but the wolf had not allowed it. So there he sat, tapping his fingers on the desk, waiting to see why Miles had called him with such urgency.

He leaned back in the chair so that he was looking up at the ceiling. He had never really looked closely at it, but now that he did, he noticed it had sustained quite a bit of water damage; bits of insulation were visible through the crumbling mineral foam ceiling tile. When Kurt stopped to think about it, the place really was a dump. But that was the point, nobody would think to look for a seemingly classy man like Miles in a place like this.

He heard the front door open and jumped at the sudden sound. He spun to face the door. For a split second he hoped that it was the police. He pushed that hope to the side; the police would have no reason to raid the store.

Miles appeared in the doorway. He looked frazzled, his usually slicked back hair ruffled and dark bags under his eyes. Kurt thought that he noticed a small scratch on Miles' right cheek.

His tie was also pulled slightly asunder, the top buttons of his pea coat undone so that it hung slightly open.

Miles gripped the sides of the doorway with his hands for support. "How'd you get in here?" he growled at Kurt.

"I came in the front door; you left it open. You called me to come." Kurt cringed a little in spite of himself due to Miles' harsh tone. *"Stupid wolf,"* he thought to himself.

Miles stared at him for a moment, his eyes wild, breathing heavily. He ran his hand through his hair to flatten and slick it back. He stood up straight and readjusted his tie. "Right," he said with more authority, though his voice still seemed distant, dazed.

Kurt just stared at him a moment, taking him in. He had never seen Miles like this. He knew that Miles was evil, but he had always had a certain calmness about him. An air of authority, like he was in control. But now he seemed to be distant and distracted, almost afraid, as if someone had roughed him up.

"You okay?" Kurt could not believe he was asking his manipulator how he was feeling, but the nature of Miles' entrance had really caught him off guard.

"I'm fine," Miles waved Kurt off, looking around the small room as if he were looking for something. He reached up, continuing to stroke his hair to flatten it to his normal look.

"You wanted me for something?..." Kurt was beginning to feel even more at unease than he usually did around Miles.

Miles suddenly spun to face him, shedding his pea coat and dropping it to the floor. His eyes narrowed and he pointed at Kurt. "You," he said accusingly, "yes, I wanted you to come here because we have some serious issues to discuss. I am going to have to keep a tighter leash on you, so to speak. I want you to stay – *live* – here, so that I have access to you *whenever* I need you." He was frowning seriously at Kurt, his gaze unwavering; whatever had distracted him before, he was completely focused on Kurt now.

"What!?" Kurt cried out, taken aback. "Wha-what about my job? My bills? My life?"

"Don't you understand yet!?" Miles shouted, pounding his fists down on the desk and leaning across it so that when he yelled, drops of saliva freckled Kurt's face. "You don't have a life anymore! You are mine; you belong to me now, Kurt Farkas! I am your master and you are my dog!" He gritted his teeth, his whole body shaking from rage. Kurt leaned back against the back of his chair. He knew that if he currently had a tail, it would be between his legs. Miles pulled away quickly, standing and reaching into his jacket pocket. "I need a smoke."

He finally dug out his box of cigarillos and a book of matches. He removed a cig from the box, holding it in place with his lips and trying to light a match. It took him several tries since his hands were shaking so badly; whether this was due to his anger or his ordeal before Kurt had arrived, he was not sure. The match finally sprang to life, and he lit the tip of the cig. He took a long drag and held it in his lungs for a moment, pulling the cigarillo from his lips and blowing a few smoky O's. He leaned against the desk, seeming to relax as he stood there in silence, almost as though he were meditating.

Kurt did not know what to do, but he knew that above all else he did not want to disturb this moment of peace; him or the wolf. After several long minutes of uncomfortable silence, Miles put out his cig in the ashtray on the desk, and began to reach into his pocket for another.

"What happened before you arrived back here?" Kurt asked sheepishly, curiosity getting the better of him.

"Don't worry about it, I took care of it." Kurt was now certain there was a small scratch across Miles' right cheek, as it was highlighted when he lit his second match. "Although now that you're my permanent resident, I won't be having to get my hands dirty anymore. That will be your job," he pointed at Kurt with the smoking tip of his cig.

Kurt sunk in his chair a little. He looked at the steel-barred cage and let out a small whimper. He hoped that this room was not

300

going to be his living space for the next however-long. Miles heard him snivel and let out a raspy chuckle. Kurt shot him a mean scowl.

"You probably want to kill me right now, don't you?" Miles said nonchalantly, taunting Kurt. He seemed to like taunting his underlings, reminding them of who was in control. "Too bad you can't so much as lift a finger to harm me." He shrugged, tapping some cinders into the ashtray. "For you, that is."

"What could have turned you so cold-blooded?" Kurt said through gritted teeth.

Miles laughed, causing a small coughing fit. When he finally recovered, he smiled unpleasantly at Kurt. "Nothing. I've always been this way. It's who I am. A man who craves power. And has power, most of the time." He put out his cig in the ashtray. "What made you come here that night, when I sent Alec Greerson to collect you?" He paused for Kurt to respond, and then lifted a finger, "And you can't lie."

Kurt clenched his jaw. He did not like this at all. Miles asking him questions was like giving a normal person truth serum. "I really thought that you could – that you wanted to – help me. I had hope."

"'Had.'" Miles grinned wickedly, looking at the floor as if remembering some distant memory. He scratched the back of his hand and then asked another question. "Have you lost all hope, Kurt Farkas?"

Kurt thought about the answer to that question. At the moment, trapped in the lair of a madman who had complete power over him, being toyed with like a cat plays with a mouse before finally killing it, he felt utterly hopeless. But there was Matilda, still fighting for him. Someone who loved him and that he loved in return. He wished for a moment that he had nothing to lose, but that was not true. He hoped Miles would not realize what a pressure point Matilda was for him.

"Not yet," he said firmly.

Miles' smile widened as he leaned down close to him, his smoker's breath stinging Kurt's sensitive nostrils. "Oh, but you will." He stood, walking over to an old locker left from the store's original décor and pulled out an old sleeping bag and a dingy looking pillow. He tossed them inside the cage and then looked at Kurt. The two looked at each other a moment before Miles motioned to the heap. "Your accommodations." He turned and walked out of the athletic shop before Kurt could protest, no matter how useless it would be.

# Chapter 48

Carmichael sat in his dark, one-bedroom apartment, smoking a cigarette, the only light from the streetlight outside his window. It had been years since his last cigarette, and the tobacco tasted wonderful, the nicotine tingling his senses. A knock came at the door. Carmichael leaned his head back, blowing smoke out his nostrils as he sighed heavily.

"Go away," he raised his voice slightly, turning toward the door. He did not hear footsteps disappear down the hall, but there also was not another knock. He turned back to staring up at the fairly barren ceiling, the fan blades sitting perfectly still, a thin layer of dust resting on the tops from lack of use.

He heard a rustle under his door and shot a sideways glance in that direction. An envelope had been pushed underneath, stark white against the charcoal grey floor. He smirked to himself, putting the cigarette out in his palm and tossing the butt into a nearby ashtray. He stood and walked over to the door. He never got any mail these days besides spam, and even then those usually accumulated in his PO Box downstairs. Maybe it was someone leaving political leaflets. Was it an election year? Carmichael didn't think so, he never could keep track.

He knelt and picked up the envelope. It was flap-side up, so he turned it over in his hand to read the sender address. When he flipped it over, the only writing on it was his name scrawled in shaky handwriting: 'Carmichael.' That sent a chill down his spine. He rented this apartment under a fake name; who knew it was him living here? He had even refused to disclose his address to Brook Hydecker when he had started his therapy sessions.

He stared at his name a moment longer. He was apprehensive about opening it. He didn't know why - Anthrax, a bomb, some other form of disease or bacteria, magic – none of it could hurt him. Maybe it was just the fear of discovering who had found him. He tore open the envelope and inside was a folded piece of stationery. Carmichael unfolded it to reveal a paragraph scrawled in the same shaky handwriting.

It read: *Carmichael. We need to talk. It concerns our history together. Most importantly, the spell I put on you. Please come. I would have come to you if I could... and you need to hear what I have to say. Even if you never loved me, this is important. To both of us. Please come. -Winona*

Carmichael gripped the paper in his hand tightly, causing it to crumple. She had found him. He should have known it was her. He closed his eyes, gritting his teeth. He set the now-crumpled letter on the kitchen counter and walked over to his closet to grab his jacket. As much as he did not want to see W, a piece of him was aching to know what she thought was so dire. Even more intriguing was why she had not showed up at his apartment since she clearly knew where he was hiding out.

He stepped out into the hall. He looked around the dark apartment before closing and locking the door behind him. It would be time to relocate soon. He didn't like staying anywhere too long, especially when he'd been sniffed out. The streetlight right outside the window had been starting to bother him anyway.

Carmichael shoved his hands in his coat pockets as he walked down the street. There it was again, that feeling he hated more than anything; that feeling that he was not in control. Not only had W found him, she had lured him out, right into her lair. Add to that that he had no idea what information she had for him; he was flying blind with a deceitful witch calling the shots.

He arrived at the alley that ran alongside Bill's Crab Shack. His nocturnal sight allowed him to see the dim purple glow at the end of the trek into darkness. As he neared, a triangle with a W at its center became visible within the purple light. Once he reached the weathered metal door, he raised his fist to knock, but turned to look over his shoulder. It wouldn't be the first time she'd snuck up behind him. But this time there was no one there.

He turned back to the door and knocked, his pounding on the metal cutting through the silence of the night and amplified by the shape of the alleyway. Nothing; no one answered. Carmichael knocked again, even louder this time. Still no one.

"Screw it," he said, gripping the knob. He was suddenly frozen, paralyzed as an energy coursed through his body. He should've known she would have the door rigged. While she may have been a bitch, she was not stupid. The paralysis soon subsided, as did the feeling of the energy, dying down to a dull tingling at the edge of his senses. The knob turned on its own in his hand, the door creaking as it clicked open.

"W?" he said, apprehensive after the blast of magic from the door. What fresh Hell did she have waiting in here for him? There was no answer, but his curiosity caused him to venture further into the dark room. He could see the magenta-clothed round table, a vacant crystal as its centerpiece. Another door was shrouded in shadow at the rear of the room, barely visible to even Carmichael's nocturnal eyes.

"W?" he repeated as he approached the hidden door. He heard a cough and then a barely audible voice that to him sounded like it said, "Who's there?" Carmichael hesitated before gripping the door knob. He did not want a repeat of what happened with the front door. He shook his head, laughing at himself; one would
306

think after all this time, he would have stopped hesitating for fear of harm. Some things are just hard-wired into humans. He gripped the knob and turned it, pushing the door open effortlessly and without incident.

This room was also dark, save for a dim torchiere lamp glowing to his left. It sat atop a wooden nightstand next to the bed. He could make out the lump of a human form lying under a dense afghan.

"Carmichael?" W's feeble voice rasped from the bed and the figure sat up slightly, revealing the elderly, lined face of the old hag.

"Nice stunt with the door. You have trouble with solicitors back here?" Carmichael said dryly, approaching the bed.

"Enchanted to let only you pass. I've made a lot of enemies over the years."

"Not the least of which is me." Carmichael gritted his teeth. He had thought W seemed frail the last time he had encountered her, but this was just downright pitiful: bedridden, bone-thin, barely able to talk between dry coughs.

"Yes, I know… that is why I called you here. I'm dying." Her breathing became more labored when she spoke.

Carmichael's expression softened slightly, but his brows remained furrowed, his jaw set. "About time."

W grimaced. "I would have given up the 150 years for a few decades with you."

"Sure, save it," he scowled, pitying her despite the hate he harbored for her.

"I mean it. Before you, there was only the power, that was all that mattered. But then... even the strongest spells fizzle out eventually."

Carmichael's cynicism increased. "One could only wish."

"Come closer," W motioned to him weakly. Carmichael hesitated. "No more tricks; I have something for you."

He slowly approached the bed and she stretched out her shaky arm to him; he could see something clasped in her liver-spotted hand. He held out his hand under hers, palm up. She dropped an amethyst crystal into his hand.

"When it glows and hums, my time will be nigh. Come back here... everything will be clear."

Still doubtful, Carmichael pocketed the gem. "Purple, how fitting." He scrunched up his face. "So this is it then? You dragged me out here for a purple rock?"

"For now. There will be more in time."

"In time! I've got all the time in the world!" He turned, storming out, slamming the front door behind him.

As he stepped out into the alley, the cold night air smacking him in the face, he inhaled deeply and broke into sobs. He was a storm of emotions inside, but mostly anger. Anger that W would soon experience the sweet release of death. Anger that he would not be the one to deal it out to her. Anger that she had dragged him out of hiding for this.

But also sorrow: Sorrow that he would remain, alone. It had been a long feud between him and his old flame, and as much as he hated her, there was a certain rivalry with her still alive. Sorrow that he would remain: once the mansion was gone, once the last normal vampire on Earth had succumbed, once Brook Hydecker was dead and buried.

And yet also relief that W would be out of his life forever, no longer able to torment him further. In truth, he felt so much that he did not know what he felt.

He buried his face in both of his hands and attempted to wipe the tears from his hot cheeks. He fluffed his jacket, trying to get a grip on himself. He sniffed, wiping his nose with the back of his hand as he started toward the mouth of the alley. Carmichael began to walk back to his apartment, his breaths exiting his mouth and nostrils as steamy puffs.

"Rough night for you too?" a female voice rang out from the bus stop's bench as he passed.

"Excuse me?" He slowed, turning to look back over his shoulder. A young woman sat on the bench, staring at him. She had dark brown hair pulled back into a messy bun and round blue eyes.

"Sorry to be presumptuous, you just look like you've seen better nights."

"… And you'd be right." Carmichael looked away from her for a moment, an odd expression crossing his face before he turned back to her. "Probably one of the worst nights I've had."

She bit her lower lip, standing and approaching him. "Well, it doesn't have to stay that way. We have the power in our hands to change the future."

The queer expression on Carmichael's face took on the form of a grin. "Just what are you proposing?"

"Whatever you're in for," she said seductively, smiling at him, walking her index and middle fingers up his chest.

"You know," Carmichael stood at least four inches taller than the girl, "it really isn't safe to talk to strangers. Especially in the city streets at night."

"Well how about I introduce myself to you, and you introduce yourself to me, and then we won't be strangers anymore." She raised her eyebrows, "Casey." She looked up at Carmichael expectantly, and he just smirked back at her. "Come on now, it's your turn."

"I never agreed to your little game." His eyes glowed strangely as he surveyed the street, catching the radiance from the streetlight. The road was desolate.

"That's fine, I like a challenge." Casey wrapped her arms around Carmichael inside his jacket; he could feel her cold hands through his shirt. "There's just something about you, I can't keep my hands off of you." She pushed his back up against the brick wall of the nearest building, pressing her lips against his.

He brought his hand up, tangling his fingers in her hair and deciding to return the kiss. He wrapped his other arm around her, resting his hand in the small of her back. She let out a soft moan of approval. Carmichael took a moment to savor the kiss. She was warm and alive and full of the ecstasy of passion. However, that was not enough to satisfy him.

He tightened his grip on her hair and pulled her head back so that she faced Heavenward, causing their lips to part. He brought his mouth down by her ear, his breath tickling her skin. "I warned you," he whispered, inhaling deeply to take in her scent; the aroma of fear and lust and maybe just a little bit of pot, "it *really* isn't safe to talk to strangers at night." He felt her tense up as he pulled her body up against his, allowing his fangs to elongate before sinking them into her exposed throat.

She went up on tiptoe, screaming as best she could with two fangs buried in her throat, blood and spittle escaping her lips. She punched his chest with tiny balled up fists, but he was locked in, sucking his prey dry of all life and passion: her very blood. Blood ran down the side of her neck, staining her blouse as her muscles began to slacken. The flow of blood slowed to a small pitter-patter as Carmichael continued to feed. She lost the energy to scream, to fight back, and he consumed the last of her essence. She was dead.

Blood ran down the side of his mouth as he pulled back from her, taking a deep breath of the night air and releasing her still-warm corpse, letting her fall to the ground. He wiped the blood from his mouth, noting a few drops on his shirt collar.

He felt a slight thrill, revitalized by the young woman's blood. One thing was for certain: once a killer, always a killer. It was just something in *his* blood.

# Chapter 49

Kurt lay on his side in the sleeping bag Miles had provided. It barely put any padding between him and the hard floor, causing his shoulder and hip to ache, but he had since grown stiff from lying on his back. Just a few nights spent in the poorly ventilated store had made him sore and achy all over. Not that Miles cared, the only decency he had shown was allowing Kurt to go home to collect some extra clothes and shower at a gym a few blocks over. As for the restrooms in the old shop, they still had running water, but were unsatisfactory.

His phone had long since died, but Miles did not want him to charge it. He wanted him cut off from the outside world. Kurt cursed him for likely making him lose his job. Not that he really needed money under his current living conditions, his housing and food were taken care of by Miles – if one could call what Miles fed him food. While it did not taste great, Miles did keep him properly nourished. He wanted to keep Kurt strong so that he could do his bidding when necessary.

Kurt heard a rattling at the door, the key being put into the lock. It would seem Miles had returned. Kurt wondered when the man slept, since he only ever seemed to visit the old shop at night.

As he lay there pondering this, he noticed that it was taking Miles a considerably long time to unlock the door. He hoped he was not having trouble due to being in a mood like the night he had pronounced Kurt his live-in slave. That had almost been worse than when he had made him murder that man tied to the chair. Almost. Kurt still felt guilty for never bothering to learn the man's name. But he had more pressing matters to worry about.

The door finally came open, and Kurt heard the quiet patter of feet, as if someone were attempting not to be heard. They were not doing a very good job, their shoes clomping fairly loudly on the hard floor – or at least 'loudly' to his wolf hearing. He sniffed the air. He did not smell cologne or cigarillo smoke. Instead it was another smell he recognized, like soft flowers.

"Matilda!" he hissed, sitting up as she walked into the room.

She held a finger to her lips, looking around nervously. "Yes, it's me. Is Miles here?"

"No," Kurt replied quietly, "but he could come back at any moment. You shouldn't be here."

"I knew something was wrong when you weren't returning my calls and," she shook her head, edging toward the cage, "I went by your work and said I was looking for you for some interview, and they told me you hadn't been in for days and they had failed to be able to contact you. Is he keeping you here?" She pulled at the cage door and it opened without much protest since it was not locked.

"Yes. But it's dangerous for you to be here." Kurt tried to untangle his legs from the sleeping bag.

Matilda grasped his hands. "I had to make sure you were all right. And I came to break you out. Come with me." She tried to pull him up, but he remained. She looked at him, hurt showing in her eyes.

He looked seriously at her. "I can't come with you, Matilda." He swallowed, fighting tears. "He'd just make me come back. And he could make me hurt you if we were together... As long as the wolf still resides in me, I can't fight him." He stood, pressing his forehead against hers, savoring the uncertainly brief time he would have with her. "I need you on the outside, looking for a way to break this curse. I love you. If he finds you here... I can't say what he'd do. But it would be bad."

Matilda closed her eyes, continuing to hold his hands, wanting nothing more than to kiss him with his face so close to hers. She opened her eyes, looking into his. She hated it, but she knew he was right. "This won't last forever. I promise, I will find a way-"

They both jumped as they heard the front door open. Matilda spun to face the doorway. Kurt released her hands, pushing her away from him, staring wide-eyed at the door. Miles appeared, an unpleasant smile on his thin lips.

"How touching," he said, looking between the two of them, putting his hand in his pants pocket, "but I'm afraid this ends here." His smile disappeared and he turned to look at Kurt. "Sic!" he commanded.

Kurt's body lurched forward and he grunted, all his muscles tensing as he fought against the command. His whole body began to shake and he gritted his teeth, struggling to look at Matilda. She was recoiling from him against the far wall. Miles walked over next to him, just outside the cage door.

"Matilda!" Kurt struggled to say. "Run! Run before I can't fight him anymore!" He took a labored step toward her.

She watched him, her heart breaking. She had never seen him like this, never seen him fighting so hard for control. She wanted to hurt Miles, to free Kurt from his grasp if only to relieve his suffering for the moment.

"You heard me, sic!" Miles said sternly. "Kill."

"No!" Kurt turned his face away from Matilda, letting out a small snarl. As he turned back to face her, his eyes flashed ochre for just a brief moment, the wolf struggling to take control.

Matilda finally got ahold of herself and turned for the door, running. She pushed the door open, letting it slam shut behind her, running down the street to where she had parked her car in a nearby alley.

"Get her!" Miles pointed after her, shouting now.

Kurt let out a cry, finally unable to fight against the urge to charge after her and took off bounding for the door, throwing it open and sniffing the air, but he heard her heels hitting the pavement as she ran and followed after her at incredible speed.

She could hear him behind her, but she could also see her car just a few yards ahead. She fumbled with her car keys in her jacket pocket and finally managed to hit the 'Unlock' button on her fob. Kurt was close behind, slamming against the brick wall of a building as he turned into the alley going a little too fast. He had spotted her as she pulled open the driver door of her sedan. He barreled toward her, letting out an inhuman growl as he crashed into the door mere seconds after she had pulled it closed.

She put the key in the ignition and turned it as he recovered from hitting the car so hard and began pounding on the window, letting out angry cries of defeat. She began to cry as she looked at him in this primal state, but knew she had to stay in her right mind and shifted the car into 'Drive,' speeding off.

As she drove off, she heard him let out a tortured howl. She began to let the tears fall freely. He was right. She had to find a way to free him from his curse. It was his – their – only hope.

# Chapter 50

Elsa stood outside the door to Edward's suite. She did not know how to tell Edward what she had found out. How the witch had refused to change him back. How she had been going about this whole 'mission' behind his back to avoid giving him false hope. But more than anything, she did not want to rip his hope away from him that he could be changed back. Because Elsa knew deep down that if the witch everyone called W would not reverse the curse, that it was likely no one else could.

She raised her hand, forming it into a fist, and knocked. She could hear him moving around inside the hotel room as he made his way to the door. He opened it and smiled instantly when he saw her face. She tried to smile back, but avoided his eyes.

"Hey beautiful," he said warmly, leaning in to kiss her. She brushed him off, walking past him into the hotel room. "What's wrong?" he asked, closing the door behind her.

She gritted her teeth, feeling the sobs building up inside her as she turned to face him. "I've been lying to you, Edward," she blurted. He stared back at her, appearing completely dumbfounded. "I've been lying to you and going behind your back. And it turns out it was all for nothing."

"What're you talking about?" Edward reached for her hand, but she turned away from him, trying to hide her tears.

"I... I've been conducting my own search for a cure on the side. When Lawrence came to the house, he gave me one clue as to how to help you."

Edward felt anger bubbling in his gut. "You trusted Lawrence?"

"Yes!" Elsa felt stupid for having trusted him, but she had. "I had to believe that there was a chance. He said that all he would say was the letter W. So I asked Zeleni Malakai for any information he had concerning that letter after you'd left. He knew of a practitioner of magic who once went by that name and their symbol. He drew it for me on a piece of paper and wished me luck, warning me to be careful. But I didn't care, I was going to do whatever it took to save you."

"Elsa-" Edward tried to interject.

"No, please, just listen. There's more... more lies and secrecy." She felt terrible, her insides churning as she confessed everything. "I still had no idea how to find this person, or if they were even still alive. So I... I went to see one of the psychics from the ads I saved. She was reluctant to tell me anything, but I was finally able to find out where this witch of lore that everyone called

W operated from. So I hunted her down and... and..." Elsa was consumed by her regret, sobbing and sitting on the edge of the bed.

Edward sat next to her and put his arm around her. "And? She didn't hurt you, did she?"

"No," Elsa sniffed, "no, she didn't hurt me. She refused to do anything to help us. She said..." Elsa winced, taking a breath before resuming her speech. "She said that you deserved what you got. That you were the kind of person that sent her kind into hiding. And... all kinds of terrible things about you. Things that aren't true, things she wouldn't say if she knew you." She looked up at Edward for the first time since she had started her confession, stroking his cheek. "She is one of the most powerful witches to have ever lived. If she won't reverse her own curse, then I fear... I fear... I fear no one can." She began sobbing again and Edward rubbed her shoulder tenderly. "I should never have lied to you. I just didn't want to give you false hope for it to all be a lie or worse - what happened - for her to refuse to change you back."

"Don't cry Elsa, please," Edward wiped the tears from her eyes, looking at her intensely. "I wish you had told me. You wouldn't have had to go there alone. I know you only had the best intentions," he pulled her close, hugging her, "but we are in this together. That was your decision, not mine."

She wrapped her arms around him, hugging him. "I just... I just don't know what we are going to do now."

He rubbed her arms, pulling back to look at her. "This psychic you saw, you trust her? You think she's the real deal?" Elsa nodded silently. "Then we will go back to her and see if she knows a way to cure me. Even if she can't do it herself, if she knows a way." He rested his hand on the side of Elsa's neck, smiling at her sadly. "I'll never stop trying to be a better man for you."

She reached up and held his hand, looking into his eyes. "I will never stop fighting for you. And I will never lie to you again."

His smiled widened and he leaned in to kiss her; she let him this time. "Let's go see that psychic then."

# Chapter 51

Alexei turned the revolving turret to the highest magnifying lens he had. He squinted his eyes so that they were nearly closed. Try as he might, he could not detect any red blood cells. He pulled away from the microscope, swishing the cloudy sky blue liquid in the beaker. Had he truly achieved it, the secret to invisibility? He knew there was only one way to find out.

He grabbed a nearby graduated cylinder, pouring the liquid into it carefully until it reached the topmost fill line. He turned to glance sideways into a mirror on one of the nearby cabinets. He took a deep breath, shaking out his shoulders and downed the concoction in one gulp. He grimaced at the bitter aftertaste, chalky silt settling on his tongue. He stood perfectly still. He felt a tingling in his fingers, and he looked down at his left hand. The veins in his hand began to stand out starkly against his rapidly paling blue skin.

# Chapter 52

Elsa and Edward stood outside the hair and nail salon, hand in hand. Elsa turned to Edward. "I'm going to warn you now, the place reeks. But she was able to help me before. Hopefully she can help me again."

"Yeah, hopefully." Edward squeezed her hand.

"You ready?"

"As ready as I'll ever be. This stuff is still... rather off-putting to me." He cringed slightly.

"I know." Elsa stood on tiptoe to give him a peck on the cheek and then led him into the salon. *Bing-Bong!* The door dinged. They were immediately hit by the acrid smells of the salon, and, based on the whirring sound, Elsa knew that they were not the only ones in the shop this time. She looked around and noticed a woman sitting in one of the salon chairs, the hood down over her head. She was reading an old issue of Vogue magazine.

Blanche Grimwald poked her head around from behind the chair, and her jaw dropped. She quickly pulled her glasses to her eyes from where they hung limply around her neck. "Why, Edward Jekyll, as I live and breathe!"

*"It's nearly impossible to breathe in here,"* Edward thought to himself.

"I heard that!" She pointed at him accusingly, then continued, "Why, I never thought I'd see you coming to a place like this for help, instead of just sending your charming girlfriend in your stead."

The woman getting her hair done looked up from her magazine, obviously confused about why a man like Edward was coming into a hair and nail salon for help, but decided not to judge too harshly and returned to her magazine.

"Whoa!" Edward was startled by her verbal response to his thought. "I, uh, I'm trying to change my ways," he struggled to say, even though he meant it.

Blanche squinted at him, staring, and then turned her attention to Elsa. "Well I see that you are still alive and kicking. Did you find W?"

Elsa's voice caught in her throat and after a moment she managed to choke out, "Yes, but she wasn't much help."

"You're lucky she didn't do you in. She is not one to be trifled with from what I've heard." She turned back to Edward. "You two wait over there while I finish up with Lucy over here. It shouldn't be much longer."

326

She pointed to some chairs in a waiting area near the door. They were terribly marred pink plastic chairs with metal frames, and Edward honestly wanted nothing to do with them. But Elsa led him over to the chairs, and he sat down beside her, trying to ignore the smells now penetrating his nasal passages. He began to bounce his leg up and down nervously. Elsa turned to look at him and smiled lopsidedly, resting her hand on his knee.

"It's going to be fine," she reassured him.

"I wish I was as sure as you." He glanced over at her. "I know I've done a lot to ruffle the feathers of the supernatural community around here. And what if Hyde decides to make an appearance?"

"I've told you; I can handle Hyde."

Edward looked at her seriously, but did not comment. They sat in silence while Blanche finished up with the woman named Lucy's hair and rang her up, receiving a pretty large tip.

She turned to the couple sitting in the waiting area. "Now, if you two will please follow me," she motioned toward the back room and dropped her glasses back down around her neck. Edward and Elsa stood in unison and followed her. Elsa observed Edward taking in the back room, and he actually seemed appreciative that it did not have the 'flair' that Zeleni Malakai's back room had. Elsa also noticed that Blanche had replaced the burned-out bulb in the ceiling fan.

Blanche took her seat at the table, waiting for Edward and Elsa to sit in the chairs opposite her. Her eyes burned into Edward as he sat. "Now," she said tersely, "what is it that you want? Why is it that you have come to me for help, Edward Jekyll?"

Edward took a deep breath, sitting uncomfortably in his chair. "It's true that Elsa did find this woman you call W. But she refused to help us... I want to know if there is any other way of beating my inner darkness. I-I know it's impossible to be a perfect person, but what I mean to say is: is there a way of destroying the dark side of me, known as Hyde, without W's help?"

Blanche rubbed her hands together slowly, her nails appearing to have been freshly done a garish shade of pink. "Give me your hand, Edward Jekyll," she demanded. Edward reluctantly stretched his arm across the table until she took his hand between her own. She closed her eyes, inhaling deeply and holding the breath. She let it out in small increments, rubbing Edward's hand with her thumbs. "Is this your dominate hand?" she asked.

Edward nodded, and then remembered that her eyes were closed. "Yes."

His mind began to wander, making his head swim. He wondered if it had to do with whatever Blanche was doing to him or if it was just the smells of the salon finally getting to him. He saw himself as a seven-year-old boy, walking home from T-ball practice. He heard a familiar voice in the park, and the sun was just setting, so he decided to check it out...

"Stop!" He pulled his hand back and held it close to his chest, out of Blanche's reach. "That... that's private."

"Honey, I'm a psychic, nothing's private from me."

Edward glared at her a moment, then asked, "Is there a way?"

Blanche pursed her lips, obviously irritated about Edward's outburst. "Perhaps." She glanced at Elsa, and her expression softened. "Yes, but it is not as easy as it sounds. First, you must face your deepest darkness, the root of your hate. From what I saw, I would say that you buried it very deep. But you never faced it. You allowed your fear to turn to hate and then let it control your life for the past several years. But anyway, here are the rules and what you must do... and even then I am not going to guarantee that this will work. It is very unpredictable and uncommon magic.

"Once you have truly faced and come to terms with the root of your hate, you must collect at least a few tears of remorse for those you have hurt because of your hate. Once you have those, keep them in a vial. This is where it gets tricky." She looked between the two of them. "You must get a drop of blood from the one who cursed you. That does not mean the one who made the curse, but

329

the one who actually carried it out. From what I can understand, that was Talbot, right?" Edward nodded. "Once you have done that…" She paused, Edward thought for dramatic effect. While her room was not as showy as Zeleni Malakai's, she was very showy in her own way. "You must allow a full moon to pass and then drink the solution. Sure, it will go down like Hell, but that solution *could* make it so that Hyde will 'die.' Kind of like weed killer for your spirit: kills the bad stuff, leaves the good."

Blanche sighed. "But as I said, I am not making promises. That is a spell that I once read about to vanquish a demon that was bound inside a person. I suppose one could compare Hyde to a demon, since he is an evil manifestation residing inside you." Elsa cringed at the word 'evil' being associated with Edward. Blanche did not seem to notice.

"And what makes you think that will work?" Edward asked, honestly trying not to be skeptical about drinking Lawrence's blood mixed with his own tears.

"Well, as for the demon anyway, when you face the root of your hate, it has a purifying factor. Purity meets demon – or evil manifestation – and boom! Dead. Gone. Or so I hope."

Edward took a deep breath, contemplating everything Blanche had just said to him. "… I guess it is worth a shot."

"You're damn right it is!" she exclaimed. "But it's all I can figure will work after sensing the other presence inside you. Oh, and the reading will cost you sixty." Her eyes narrowed as she looked at Edward. "I trust that will not be a problem."

"Not at all. Do you take debit?" he replied flatly.

"Of course." Blanche took his card and walked out of the back room to the cash register.

Edward turned to Elsa. "Do you really think it will work? This whole 'blood and tears' bit?"

"I hope so. It's a bit of a shot in the dark, but at least it's a shot." She smiled at him.

Blanche returned with his card and a receipt for him to sign. She turned to Elsa as Edward scrawled his name on the dotted line. "I would advise you to be careful for a while. W does not typically allow those that cross her to get away with it. And don't trust anything else that Talbot scoundrel says to you, he could have gotten you killed by sending you to search for her."

"Now *that* I can agree with," Edward stated, handing Blanche the receipt and her pen. Blanche bent to store the receipt in the lowest drawer of her filing cabinet. The two stood and Elsa headed for the door to leave, but stopped when she realized Edward was still standing by the table. He extended his right hand across the table and Blanche looked up from what she was doing in surprise.

"Thank you," he said quietly. Blanche stared at his hand a moment like she had never seen it before, and then shook it.

"Maybe you really are trying to turn a new leaf," she retorted with only minor skepticism before releasing his hand.

He half-smiled before turning and following Elsa out of the salon.

# Chapter 53

**1855, Manhattan**

Seven-year-old Winona Blanchette frolicked through the hallways of her family's house. It was not a mansion by any means, but also not a cabin; just a nice house with a few frills. The Blanchettes were a higher middle-class family, so they could afford some luxuries, such as a maid who doubled as a nanny for their little girl, Winona. Mr. Carter Blanchette was an accountant, an admirable job, but he often grumbled about wanting to move on to bigger and better things; he frequently mentioned the rail industry.

Winona continued to skip through the halls. She was bored. She was always bored. There was nothing to do in the house. Her parents were often out – her father always attending to business and her mother socializing. Her nanny, Nevaeh, had enough to keep her busy – between keeping Winona out of trouble and completing her other duties as the maid. Winona loved Nevaeh, but she often grew bored of her as well. Being an only child, finding a playmate was nearly impossible.

She arrived at the top of the staircase; going down could be fun, but one had to be careful not to lose their footing, or severe injuries could follow. She pranced down the stairs with the finesse of a veteran and continued down the hallway on the first floor.

As she passed the library, she noticed a flash of light escape from the doorway, the door slightly ajar. She ceased her skipping, curiosity gripping her. She took a few steps backward, tiptoeing over to the doorway and peering through the narrow crack.

There was Nevaeh, with her dark brown skin and black hair pulled back tight, her back to the door, her attention focused on something in the far corner of the library. Winona struggled to see what it was that had Nevaeh's attention. Another flash filled the room, coming from the thing in the corner. Winona's eyes widened as she realized what it was.

It was a book! But it was levitating, seemingly by itself. In spite of herself, she let out a gasp of amazement. The book fell with a large thump as Nevaeh whipped around to face the door, her brown eyes wide with fright.

"Winona!" she seemed to want to shout, but her voice came out as a hushed whisper.

"Nevaeh!" Winona cried out with excitement. "How'd you-" but Nevaeh was at the door, her hand clamped over Winona's mouth.

"Hush child!" she hissed, pulling Winona into the library and latching the door closed behind them. Nevaeh let go of Winona and knelt so that she was at her eye level. "Now Winona, just what did you see?"

"The book-" Winona shouted with excitement, but Nevaeh put a finger to her lips. "The book was floating," Winona said more quietly, "all by itself." Winona wrinkled her nose, whispering even quieter. "Do you know magic, Nevaeh?"

Nevaeh sighed heavily, and then spoke with a very even tone. "Winona, baby, what I am about to tell you, you cannot tell anyone. Not your friends, not the other help, not your mother… and definitely not your father." She took another deep breath, looking directly into Winona's little dark brown eyes. "Yes… I can do magic. Have my whole life. I was just practicing making the book float. I thought you were upstairs."

"I was, but I got bored." Her eyes lit up, an eager smile spreading across her lips. "Can I try?"

"Now Winona, I don't know-"

"Please, show me how and let me try. If you let me try, I won't tell Father."

Nevaeh pursed her lips. She could see that her hands were tied: if Winona told that she was practicing magic, she could very well lose her job as the Blanchettes' nanny and maid.

"All right. I will show you. But listen carefully," Nevaeh held up her finger, "magic doesn't work for everyone. Some people have the… 'spark' and others don't. So try not to get too disappointed if, well…" she nodded, thinking that Winona caught her drift; she was a smart young lady.

"Okay," Winona said, then smirked. "I'm sure I'll be able to do it."

Nevaeh chuckled at her enthusiasm. Magic was in her blood, her family had been practicing magic since before the Salem witch trials. As far as she knew, both of Winona's parents were as plain and *normal* as you could get. But Winona had asked her to show her how, and show her she would.

Nevaeh stood up, wiping her sweaty palms on her apron. "Now, it's not about a lot of mumbo-jumbo. It comes from in here," she pointed to her forehead, "but even more importantly, from in here," she pointed to her chest, indicating her heart. "You have to think of what you want, more than anything in the world. Let that be what powers you; passion is the strongest emotion we possess. Like this." Nevaeh took a deep breath and held her hand out in front of her, palm up. She stared intently at the book and as she lifted her hand toward the ceiling, the book rose with it.

Winona tried to focus on Nevaeh, to study her so that she could mimic her actions, but her eyes were drawn to the floating book. The cover flipped open and the pages turned rapidly, as if some invisible person was rifling through them in search of

336

something important. After a moment, the book closed once more and sank to its original position on the floor.

"Now it's your turn," Nevaeh stated, kneeling beside Winona. Winona looked at the book; she was now shaking all over with anticipation. She stretched her little arm out in front of her, tried to focus all of her attention on the book. It didn't move. She furrowed her brows, concentrating harder. Still the book remained unmoved, and she let out a grunt of frustration.

"Now baby, you have to find your focus-"

"I am focusing!" Winona snapped back, her face contorted into a full-blown scowl.

"Not just on the book, baby. What you want, more than anything. What your aim is. You have to know what it is that *you* want before *it* will do what you want."

Winona stopped and thought. What she wanted was for the damn book to float. No, what she really wanted was some excitement. To not be bored anymore. She wanted that spark that Nevaeh had mentioned.

She turned back to the book and held her hand out in front of her, palm to the ceiling, just like Nevaeh. She thought of her parents, always gone. She thought of the empty hallways, the echo of her feet as she skipped along. She thought of Nevaeh, working so hard that she was too tired to be much fun most of the time...

*THWACK!*

The book smacked hard against the ceiling, its binding splitting, sending pages fluttering all about the room.

"Good... God..." Nevaeh breathed, her eyes wide as she stared up at the ceiling, clutching her heart. She slowly stood up from her kneeling position.

Winona stood in the paper rain, staring at her hands, her mouth hanging slightly open.

"Winona, baby," Nevaeh said breathlessly, kneeling down beside her again, "you're a powerhouse."

Winona continued to stare at her hands, her breathing speeding up as she began to hyperventilate. Tears sat along the rims of her lower lids, waiting to spill over. "I-" she began to say, but her voice caught in her throat, "I did that?..."

"You sure did. You showered the room with Shakespeare's *The Tempest*. I have to say, I'm impressed. Astounded, really." Nevaeh put her arm around Winona's shoulders. She could still feel the energy from the magic burst coursing through Winona's tiny frame. "You have a gift, baby."

Winona looked around the room, the floor now littered with one of Shakespeare's finest works. "I made another mess for you to clean up..." she said absently, one of the tears spilling over and rolling down her cheek.

338

"Oh, that's fine baby." Nevaeh nodded, furrowing her brow assuredly. "You may just be the most powerful witch I've ever met. Or at least you have the potential to be." Nevaeh stroked her chin, thinking. "It'd be a shame to let all that power go to waste. And you need to learn to control it. How about this? You promise not a word about any of this to anyone, and I will teach you more about magic and how to control it?"

A small smile tugged at the corners of Winona's mouth. "Really?"

"Yes, really. You really surprised me today, baby. You really have a flair for this stuff." Nevaeh stood, grabbing the broom. "Now I've got to clean up in here. You run along for now. And remember," she said as Winona gripped the door handle, "not a word to anyone. Especially your father."

"Yes ma'am," Winona replied obediently, exiting the library and skipping on down the hall. She was so jubilant she felt like she was soaring. She could see her future, big and bright. No more boredom. Oh no, she was sure this adventure would be anything but boring.

## 1864, Manhattan

Winona sat in her room. She bounced her leg in anticipation. Nevaeh had said she had something important to show her. That meant magic; nine years later and Winona's favorite 'trick' was still making things levitate. However, she had also learned a lot in those nine years: healing potions, minor curses, making things disappear and then reappear. So of course she was anxious about if this was something good or bad that was so important.

She held her hand out in front of her, swirling her other hand over it. A small flash of light. A fizzle, then darkness. Winona sighed. She had still not mastered materializing a flower. It was too complex – too delicate – for someone with her amount of power, yet still so much lack of control. Nevaeh assured her that it was not for lack of trying, there was just a lot of power surging through her, more than anyone Nevaeh had ever met. And the more raw power someone had, the harder it was to control.

The door to Winona's room flew open, the crouched form of Nevaeh rushing in and kicking it closed behind her. She was bent over with her arms wrapped under her stomach, trying to conceal something under her apron.

Winona leapt from her bed, suddenly far too excited to feel anxious. "What is it!? What did you want to show me!?" Winona's voice grew higher as she tried to maintain a hushed tone.

"Oh, you're going to love this. I had to go all the way to the Lower East Side to get it. But I think it's time. I... I think you're ready." Nevaeh pulled the hidden object out from under her apron.

Winona stared at the large transparent orb in Nevaeh's hand. "Is that..." her voice trailed off as she reached out to touch it, but pulled her hand back.

"Yes. A crystal ball." Nevaeh also pulled out a small stand from under her apron and sat it and the ball on Winona's dresser. "Go on, baby, try it."

"Are you sure?" Winona looked at Nevaeh out of the corner of her eye, but the crystal ball now had her full attention.

"Yes, go on. Who knows, it may help you rein in some of that power."

"All right..." Winona focused her attention on the ball, slowly moving her hands toward it. A small white wisp appeared at its center, growing as she drew nearer. The wisp began to take on a purple hue.

"Winona!" her mother's voice sang out just as her fingers were about to touch the ball's surface. She drew back, startled. The orb became dormant once more. "Winona! Come downstairs, there's someone here to see you!"

Winona looked at Nevaeh disappointedly.

"Go on down. There will be time for this. We always find the time," Nevaeh assured her, taking the ball and concealing it under the bed.

"Yes, of course," Winona grimaced, checking her hair in the mirror before exiting her room to go downstairs.

"Winona, where are you?" her father yelled impatiently.

"Coming!" she replied, appearing at the top of the stairs. She could see three sets of feet in the foyer – her mother's, her father's, and those of the mystery visitor, who appeared to be male based on his polished black shoes.

"There you are." Her father walked over to her as she reached the bottom of the stairs. "Winona, this is Anthony Van Buren. He would very much like to make your acquaintance." He extended his arm to indicate a young man standing by the front door. He was dressed in a fine black suit, a bowler hat in his gloved hands. His short brown hair was combed to perfection and his blue eyes lit up when he caught sight of Winona. He was handsome, with a certain charm about him as he smiled. Winona thought he seemed terribly boring.

"Charmed," he said, bowing slightly and offering Winona his hand.

Winona shot her mother a look, which was not reciprocated. She turned her attention back to Anthony. "It's very nice to meet you, Mr. Van Buren." She accepted his hand, curtseying.

There was a moment of awkward silence. Mr. Blanchette cleared his throat, "Anthony came to call after a talk I had with his father. You became a topic of discussion, and he very much wanted to meet you."

"Well I'm flattered Mr. Van Buren," Winona gave what she thought seemed like the proper response.

"You are even more delightful than your father led me to believe. The honor is all mine, Miss Blanchette." His tone grew more serious. "I was wondering if I might interest you in a turn about your garden? What I could see as I walked up to your porch looked lovely. And it would give us a chance to get better acquainted."

Winona tried to hide her lack of enthusiasm with this whole affair. She stole a look up the stairs toward her room. She could feel the crystal ball calling to her...

"Er, but of course Mr. Van Buren. That would be lovely."

Anthony smiled, obviously pleased with her response. As he turned to offer her his arm, she shot her father a venomous look, which he ignored. She turned back to Anthony, smiling sweetly.

As they walked outside, Anthony placed his hat on top of his head, and they began their stroll through the flower garden kept on the Blanchettes' property.

"I take it our fathers work together," Winona started the conversation.

"Well yes, in a way. You see, my father works with steam, factories – he owns several throughout New York. And your father handles all of our accounts at the bank. So they do work rather closely together I suppose." His voice was strained, as if he were unsure that what he was saying was correct.

"Father meets all kinds of interesting people."

Anthony nodded in silent agreement. He stopped walking, turning to look at Winona. "What I'm really interested in is you." He blushed slightly. "What interests you, aside from your father's business affairs?"

Winona sighed. She could never tell someone like Anthony what truly interested her; practicing magic was not at all acceptable behavior for a young lady. "I like to read. I like how books can take you just about anywhere you want to go. And of course, like any woman," she paused to sniff a rose bush, looking at Anthony's face, "I love flowers."

Anthony stared at her a moment, captivated, then regained his composure. They resumed walking. "You like books you say. I cannot say that I am well-read, but the way you talk about travel, it sounds marvelous. We have an extensive library at my father's mansion-uh, house," he stumbled over his words. "Not that I often set foot inside that room. But you would be more than welcome to peruse the shelves some time, if you'd like." Anthony stopped walking again as they were nearing the edge of the property, and consequently, the garden. He looked into Winona's eyes, smiling nervously. "Miss Blanchette, I hope I am not being too forward, but my father is hosting a ball on the twenty-fourth, and I would like to invite you to come as my guest." He paused, taking a deep breath. "You are every bit as interesting as I had hoped and many times more beautiful than I imagined."

"Mr. Van Buren, you flatter me so," Winona said, trying to manage a blush. He was just as she had suspected he would be: boring and predictable.

"I take that as a yes?"

"Of course I will accept your invitation."

"Wonderful!" Anthony clasped both of her hands in his. "Then I will come for you on the night of the twenty-fourth. For now Miss Blanchette, I will walk you back to the house and bid you adieu. I look forward to getting to know you even better as time goes by." And with that, Anthony walked her to the front door, bid her and her mother farewell, and left in his carriage for home.

"What did he say?" her mother asked excitedly.

"That he thinks I am simply delightful, and he would like me to attend a ball at his father's estate on the twenty-fourth."

"Did you accept?"

"Well of course I accepted, how could I not." Winona rolled her eyes. "He's terribly boring."

"He was handsome and quite polite." Her mother swooned.

"Like I said, 'boring,'" Winona said under her breath, heading for the stairs. "I'm going back to my room. I must decide on what to wear to this all-important ball."

Of course, Winona had no intention of looking at her gowns. The entire time she had been with Anthony, the crystal ball had clouded her mind. She had to use it, see what secrets it held. Once in her room, she made sure that the door was latched behind her. She pulled the ball out from under her bed and sat it atop her dresser. She put each of her hands on either side of the ball as it came to life. Yes, given her secret life of magic and intrigue, Anthony was very boring.

# Chapter 54

**1864, Manhattan**

"Hurry Winona, Mr. Van Buren will be here any minute!" Mrs. Blanchette fussed through her bedroom door. "Your father left nearly an hour ago."

"Nearly done," Winona said with an annoyed edge to her voice. She and Nevaeh were almost finished with her hair. "It's fine, fine, I could probably go in rags and he would tell me just how delightful I am."

"Don't be like that, baby, Mr. Van Buren seems to have taken a real interest in you. Who knows, you might find out that you love him too."

Winona scoffed. "Love him; I don't even like him."

Nevaeh chuckled. "Well you look beautiful. Have fun tonight." Nevaeh hugged her. "And give Mr. Van Buren a chance at least."

Winona smiled sympathetically at Nevaeh as her mother yelled from the foyer. "Winona! Mr. Van Buren is here!"

Winona sighed, then composed herself and walked down the stairs. Anthony was dressed in a full tuxedo, his top hat clutched in his white-gloved hands, his black shoes shining. Winona did have to admit that he looked quite handsome. He also looked like someone she would typically never be caught dead with.

His eyes widened when he saw her. "Miss Blanchette, you look beautiful." He took her by the hand. "My carriage is outside. I'll have her home well before curfew, Mrs. Blanchette." He smiled charmingly.

The carriage ride to the Van Buren estate was uneventful, with Anthony asking the occasional question about her interests. As they pulled up before the house, she saw that he had not exaggerated: it was a mansion. The ballroom was full of people dancing and socializing. Anthony and Winona stood on the sidelines, waiting for the song to end. She spotted her father across the room, drinking a glass of wine and talking with several important-looking men.

The orchestra ceased playing, and as they began a new song, Anthony turned to Winona and held out his hand. "May I have this dance?"

"You may," Winona curtseyed and the two entered the dance floor. They spun and twirled; Anthony was quite the graceful dancer and Winona actually found herself having fun.

The song ended and Anthony kneeled before Winona. "Miss Blanchette, these past few days, you have not left my mind. You
348

are beautiful, intelligent, and the most intriguing woman I have ever met. And that is why I would like to ask you if you would marry me?"

"Oh," Winona was both taken aback and slightly appalled, "uh... no?"

The few people who had stopped to watch gasped. Winona spotted her father across the room. He was not pleased.

"I, uh, I should go. Th-thank you for a lovely evening."

Anthony still seemed too shocked to speak. Winona searched the room with her eyes and saw that her father was nowhere to be seen. Several people had stopped what they were doing and were now staring at the pair of them. Winona realized the scene she was making by rejecting the owner of the house's son. She wanted to vanish – hell, she probably could have if she wanted, but she had promised Nevaeh: this was their secret.

"I'll have a carriage take you home then," Anthony finally said, motioning to the butler.

The butler ushered her to a carriage waiting out in front of the mansion, a look of utter distaste on his face as he closed the door behind her. The ride home was quiet and bumpy. Winona thanked the carriage driver and began up to the front of the house. The door was open before she reached the porch, her mother standing there looking utterly irate.

"Winona, what did you do?" she asked through gritted teeth.

"Nothing," Winona pushed past her mother and practically ran up to her room. She stopped when she noticed that her door was ajar. She crept toward the door, pushing it open slowly. Her father stood by her bed, the crystal ball in his hand. She froze. Seeing all of that power in her father's useless hands made her both furious and terrified.

"I've tried to be patient," he said in an even tone, but she could tell he was close to the breaking point; there was a quivering undertone to the statement. "But enough is enough." He let the ball roll off his hand, and it hit the floor, shattering.

"No!" Winona shrieked, lunging for the shards.

"No! *You* listen to me! This is *my* house!" her father bellowed, holding up a stern finger. "Enough! You will apologize to Anthony." He paused, and when he spoke again, it was with the same low quivering tone as before. "Oh, and I've taken the liberty of firing Nevaeh. I know she's the one who put you up to this foolishness."

"She didn't do anything-"

"Oh stop it! I knew something was afoot, with you two's secret rendezvous; I just never imagined it was this," he pointed to the shattered crystal ball.

"But Father, I don't love Anthony. I… I love magic," Winona said, trying not to break down in tears.

Mr. Blanchette shook his head. "This childishness must end. You are a young lady, and you will act like one. You will apologize to Anthony and let him continue to court you. He's Vanderbilt's nephew; you *will* marry him. You will not ruin this for me. I've worked too hard for this."

Winona opened her mouth to speak, but no words came out. She began shaking all over, trying to control herself. She closed her eyes and tried to regulate her breathing. When she opened them again, she looked directly at her father. "I should've known you didn't want what's best for me. I'm just another business deal to you."

"Winona-"

"No, it's true!"

"Winona! This is my final word: you will apologize to Anthony. You will let him continue to court you. This magic nonsense ends tonight." He slid past her out of the room and started down the hall. He stopped, speaking over his shoulder. "And clean up the mess. I don't want the help learning about your deviant recreational activities."

Once her father was out of sight, Winona fell to her knees, sobbing. After a moment, she wiped away her tears, holding her hands out in front of her, the crystal shards floating and coming together to form an orb. It was imperfect, the broken edges still visible, its surface unsmooth.

"Too delicate..." Winona whispered, frowning, her face turning red as the crystal ball went up in flames.

~

Winona pulled her hooded cloak tightly around herself. Sneaking out at night was bad enough, but especially to this part of the city. It hadn't been hard to pry Nevaeh's address from the errand boy, he had walked her home on many late nights. Winona crept up to the door of the tiny bungalow and knocked. When no one answered, she summoned a tiny purple spark from her fingertips and sent it through the keyhole.

She could hear someone moving around inside, and the door creaked open just a crack. Only the white of Nevaeh's eye was visible in the darkness. "Winona? What're you doing out here so late?"

"I had to see you... I'm sure you're well aware, but my father... well he found out about us practicing magic. He shattered my crystal ball, forbade me from using magic anymore... But I also came to tell you that I never breathed a word to anyone. He found out all on his own. He is going to force me to marry Anthony Van Buren: just another business deal, it turns out he's Vanderbilt's nephew. You got fired and I can't even be who I am in my own home."

Nevaeh chuckled dryly. "I know you wouldn't tell; even if not for my best interests, for your own. We were foolish to think we could keep up this charade under his roof; I'm surprised it took him this long."

"I mean, he's never around." Winona groaned. "I can't do it Nevaeh. I can't go on without it, it's a part of me now. I can feel it singing in my bones. I'd never felt such rage as I did when he shattered that crystal ball."

"It has *always* been a part of you, baby. I've known that since that day in the library. You have a gift." She paused. "I probably shouldn't even be telling you this. But there may be a way you can placate your father and have what you want. There is a group of people - an 'underground' – of warlocks. People like you: the rich, people of middle-class society, even the sewer rats. They all come together and practice their craft, away from prying eyes under false names so that they can go about their daily lives unhindered."

"Where can I find this place?" Winona asked eagerly.

"There were whispers in the East Side, near the harbor. Something about a meeting place in the catacombs. Their leader -

Cobra as they call him - can be found in that area if the timing is right." Nevaeh's tone changed. "But Winona. Take care: they are not very open to the idea of a woman in their midst."

"I don't care what *they* like. I will show them what I can do. You know I can prove myself."

"Yes, I do. I just want you to be careful. And whatever you do, *do not* reveal your real name."

"I understand. If I hurry I can get there without anyone noticing that I am gone."

"No Winona! Don't go tonight; you are tempting fate as it is by being here."

"Nevaeh, I need this. They won't notice I'm gone."

"I ought not've told you."

"If you'd kept this from me-" Winona started, her face and tone taking on a certain darkness. She softened, "That's beside the point. I'm going tonight, and you can't stop me."

Fear flashed in Nevaeh's eyes, the same fear as when she and Winona had first begun their journey into magic together. The fear that would creep in when Winona lost control.

"Good-bye Nevaeh. And truly, I am sorry," Winona said over her shoulder before disappearing into the darkness. Nevaeh stared after her a moment. The feeling in her gut told her that directing

Winona to the underground had been a mistake; that there was no way this could end well.

~

Winona stood by an opening into the city sewers. Rumor had it that there was a network of catacombs somewhere inside. She held her hand out and blew, a flame rising from her hand and taking on the form of a cobra. She dropped it into the open sewer, letting it slither into the depths below.

"Is this yours?" a man's voice with a thick British accent said from behind her, startling her. She whirled around to see a tall man with pale olive skin holding her fire serpent by its tail. He had short black hair, a clean-shaven face, and striking narrow eyes. He wore all black – tall, dark, and handsome. Winona nodded. "Interesting way to call on someone." He snapped his fingers and it vanished. "I am Cobra. And you are..." He raised one dark eyebrow, looking at her.

"Wi-" Winona stopped herself from answering, "I go by W."

"W?"

"Yes... because I am *the* Witch."

He chuckled. "Is that so?"

Winona straightened her back, standing taller. "Yes," she said, trying to sound confident, "and I can prove it. I am not all talk."

Cobra smiled, his white teeth glinting in the moonlight. "You've got guts. Good, I like that in a young warlock." He held up his finger. "But a witch – even 'The Witch' – can't really hope to hold her own against a warlock. Am I right?"

"Why don't you tell me?" Winona stood her ground, offended by how he underestimated her. All of the doors in the alleyway began swinging on their hinges.

Cobra looked around. "Impressive. But how about this?" He reached inside his jacket and flung his hand toward her, several balls of golden energy soaring toward her.

The doors continued to swing as Winona lifted her hand in front of her. The balls turned to ice, falling to the ground in front of her. She turned her gaze to him and raised her hand. Cobra rose from the ground, held in the air by an invisible force.

"Are we going to keep playing games all night? Listen," Winona approached him, "I want in. I want to be a part of your so-called underground. Just like you, I'm sure, magic isn't acceptable in my walk of life. I need some place with people like me."

"I doubt there are many like you," he seemed to be in shock, but also impressed. "I'd like down, if you'd be so kind." Winona dropped her arm to her side and Cobra came tumbling down. "It

would seem I was wrong about you. I would love to have you."
He gave her a slight bow.

"Good."

"But it is late. Come back here tomorrow, drop me another one of your fire snakes, and I will welcome you into my world."

~

Winona knocked on the Van Buren mansion's front door; the new maid sat in the carriage, waiting. The Van Buren's butler came to the door. Winona couldn't help but notice the look of distaste that crossed his face when he saw that it was her.

"Good morning, Miss. How can I help you?"

"I'd like to speak with Mr. Van Buren... Anthony." She bit her lower lip. "I need to apologize for my behavior the other night."

He made no effort to hide his disgust anymore as he asked, "And who should I say is calling?"

"Miss Winona Blanchette."

"Just a moment." The butler pushed the door closed and Winona stood on the porch, waiting anxiously.

The butler returned to the door. "He will be down shortly; young Mr. Van Buren needs a moment to prepare himself. He was not expecting guests."

"Thank you," Winona replied. After a few minutes, Winona saw Anthony come running down the stairs. Once he reached the bottom, he straightened his jacket, ran his hand over his hair, and walked the rest of the way to the door.

"Hello Miss Blanchette," he said nervously, smiling as he took her hand and kissed it. The butler gave him a meaningful look before retreating into the manor. Anthony turned back to Winona. "Why did you want to speak with me?"

"I wanted to apologize. I was just, caught off guard by your proposal at the ball."

"Oh no, I fear I am to blame for that. I had not yet courted you properly and acted on a whim." He looked down at his feet, blushing. "Miss Blanchette, would you allow me a second chance at courting you properly?"

Winona thought of the underground that awaited her in the oncoming night – in all the nights to come – where she would be among her people. No matter what choices Winona Blanchette made, W – the Witch – would have what she truly wanted: power, freedom from the bore of the life she'd been dealt.

She smiled. "Of course Mr. Van Buren."

# Chapter 55

**1865, Manhattan**

Two men, one on each arm, dragged a third man through the abandoned carriage house. A large bruise was already swelling up on the right side of his face, causing him to look slightly disfigured. The man on his left kicked open the door in front of them, and they dragged him into a room lined with stalls, lit by several burning torches. At the far end of the room, someone sat in a chair, shrouded in shadow. As they passed through the door, another man closed and locked it behind them.

The two dragged their prisoner up in front of the chair and threw him to the ground. He tried to push himself up, but they kicked him so that he fell flat once more.

"Well, well, what do we have here?" a woman's voice came from the figure seated in the chair. Two unlit torches on either side of the chair sprang to life, revealing the seated person to be W.

The man's eyes widened. "No, no, please!" he screamed, trying to stand again, the man on his right burying his boot in his lower back to keep him down.

W chuckled, looking down for a moment, then looking up to meet the frightened man's gaze. "Jaws, isn't it?" He nodded, sniffing back tears, a small dribble of blood running out of the side of his mouth and down his chin. "They call you that for a reason, don't they? Because it's always flapping."

"No, wait, I can explain-"

"Explain!?" W shouted, all of the torches in the room flaring up. "You mean explain why the police have started asking questions; questions about a magic cult? I mean, Lark himself heard you getting friendly with an inspector at the tavern just a few nights ago. Telling him how you could do all sorts of magical feats, and so could your friends."

"I just... I'd had too much to drink. It didn't start like that, he probably thought I was lying anyway. It just... slipped out."

"Well whether he believed you or not, others did." W smiled, a truly wicked expression. "That's the thing about being part of a secret society, Jaws." She knelt, bringing her face close to his. "You can't let anything 'just slip out.'" W stood, looking at the men holding Jaws down. "What do you say boys? Should I silence the rat?" They both nodded, laughing.

"No, please-" Jaws was cut off, grasping his throat as W glared at him, her eyes glowing deep violet. She blinked and turned away. Jaws fell facedown on the ground, breathing heavily. After a moment, a mumble issued from his lips. He slowly sat up, trying to speak, a series of grunts and moans coming out instead.

W tossed her hair back. "Looks like a robbery to me. They beat him up pretty badly and took all his money." She looked up at the two men. "Take his wallet. Make sure there is some bruising or rope burns on his throat so no one questions his loss of voice. And throw him out in the streets for somebody to find."

The two grabbed him gruffly by his arms and dragged him out of the room.

"Ruthless as always I see, my little fire viper," Cobra cooed, appearing behind her.

"He deserved it."

"I said nothing to the contrary." He held out his hand, a spark of light appearing and solidifying into a bouquet of black roses. He extended them to her.

"Charming," W said, taking the flowers from him and dropping them into the chair.

Cobra looked down at his feet, undiscouraged, chuckling. "You're everything a man could hope for – beautiful, intelligent, intriguing," he licked his lips, "fiery." He wrapped his arm around her waist, pulling her up against him. "We would make quite the pair."

W laughed. "Oh, but we've talked about this before."

"Why won't you," Cobra asked, sighing, "marry me?"

"Because I am engaged. Remember," W said, holding up her left hand to show off a small golden ring set with a brilliant diamond.

"You don't love him," Cobra replied, smirking.

"No. I don't. But I don't love you either. That's because I don't fall in love." She pulled away from him.

"That may be so, but I also have what you do love," he looked at her, the smirk on his lips widening into a grin, "power."

"I guess that makes two of us," W said, pursing her lips.

Cobra rolled his neck, once again meeting her gaze. "Honestly though, why not marry me instead of some average dullard? Wouldn't you rather spend your life with someone like you?"

W grew serious, looking at the ground. Her expression turned to one of almost sadness. "In my other life, I don't have that luxury." She turned around and walked out of the room, leaving Cobra bewildered with the discarded bouquet.

"Fights are tonight," he finally said after her, and she paused, "are you ready?"

"Aren't I always?"

"Of course."

~

"I don't want to do it! You can't make me!" a small balding man shrieked, backing away from the few warlocks surrounding him. "I'll go up against anyone here. *Anyone! Just not her.*"

"You're not the only one who's scared of her, now get out there."

"No. I'll forfeit, I swear it! I am not fighting her. I remember what happened to Baal."

"Now we can't have that," Cobra appeared, looking troubled.

"Then put me against someone else. I have important business tomorrow. I cannot end up like Baal. What would I tell my associates?"

"I will take care of it. Don't worry. You won't be fighting W tonight."

Cobra disappeared, materializing where W waited to enter the arena. "Change of plans, my dear. Your opponent is too scared to fight you."

"Coward," she growled back.

Cobra stroked his chin, a sideways smile forming on his face. "You know… it could be fun if we were to face off in the ring. I know you have some aggression you want to take out on me."

W shot him a look, glaring. Then she nodded. The two entered the arena, standing on opposite sides and facing each other. "Don't go easy on me," she said mockingly.

"Oh, I know I won't have to with you." Cobra smirked, seemingly unaffected by her cold demeanor. He raised his hand, preparing to make the first attack at the drop of the hat.

"Stop!" a man's voice yelled from the main doorway. All of the magicians turned to see who had called out. It was none other than the chief of police. "All of you, stay where you are. You are hereby under arrest for practicing witchcraft as part of a secret society." Several officers poured into the room, followed by a few concerned relatives of potential members.

Several of the magicians began to run for the alternative exits or vanish as others were apprehended by the police. Among the relatives, W spotted her father's enraged face. "I thought I might find you here," he snarled, approaching her. "After Wenzel Thomas was found severely beaten, the police took his ramblings about a 'magical cult' more seriously. But what caught my attention was the talk of one woman who fancied herself a very powerful witch." Cobra turned to face him, standing between Mr. Blanchette and W. Mr. Blanchette shook his head, sighing in exasperation. "Winona, I thought we put this nonsense to rest. I should have known you were sneaking about when you were so compliant."

Cobra glared at him, extending a protective arm in front of Winona. "So this is your father," he took one menacing step toward him.

"Get away from my daughter, you filthy foreigner!" Her father tried to wave Cobra off, but he gripped Mr. Blanchette's arm.

"I'd have the mind to kill you for the way you treat her. She doesn't love that rich suitor you have her arranged to marry. She only started coming here to hide from you."

"Let go of me!" Mr. Blanchette smacked Cobra hard across the face with his free hand.

"Stop it!" Winona cried, but an officer was already upon Cobra, his baton raised. He brought it down on Cobra's head, and he released his grip on her father's arm as he fell to the ground.

"Listen to me, young man," he said, looking down at Cobra as the officer cuffed him, "she doesn't love you. She's using you at best. Because that's what she does."

"I learned from the best," Winona retorted defiantly.

Her father flared his nostrils angrily. "Come with me, Winona. I've cleared it with the chief. We're going home."

"You can't control her forever!" Cobra coughed as the police officer pulled him into a standing position. "She's stronger than you know."

"It's all a bunch of nonsense that she has no business with," her father replied. "It's just like I told the chief. Someone had been filling her head with notions of grandeur – nonsense." He turned to the officer, "Get him away from my daughter."

As the officer dragged Cobra to where the other captured members were being held, Mr. Blanchette gripped Winona's arm. "I *said* we're leaving." Outside several other members were being ushered into carriages by their families, trying to keep their faces hidden to hide the shame. "Get in," he pulled her toward their carriage and closed the door quickly behind them. They sat in silence for a while and the carriage began moving. Winona opened her mouth to speak, but her father held up his hand. "We have much to discuss with your mother. I have nothing to say to you now."

Winona was seething, rage boiling inside her, but she tried to maintain control. She had nearly killed a man in the underground - who went by Baal - once when she had let her anger take control.

"Whoa!" the carriage driver said to the horses, and the carriage rolled to a halt. Her father opened the door, allowing her to exit the carriage first. He followed her out and grabbed her arm again,

366

guiding her toward the house. He obviously thought she was a flight risk; he was not wrong.

Once inside, he pointed toward the dining room. Her mother sat at her typical spot at the table, her hands folded neatly in front of her. Winona took her own seat as her father entered the room, standing behind his chair at the head of the table. He gripped the chairback, breathing heavily, the only sound in the painfully silent room.

"Winona," he stated, in a voice so strained he seemed to be nearly at the breaking point; the calm before the storm. "We had an agreement. No more magic and you were to marry Anthony." He gripped the chair tighter, his knuckles turning white. He gritted his teeth, looking down at the grain of the table. "Were you fornicating with that foreigner?"

"That-" Winona started.

"Were you fornicating with him!?" her father shouted at her, his face red, veins sticking out on his forehead and neck. Her mother cringed.

"… No."

"A likely story, but I will accept it for now." Her father laughed unpleasantly. He looked toward the window for a moment, collecting himself. "Did you really think that I wouldn't catch you? That I wouldn't ferret you out; figure out your little game? This isn't the first time I caught you. You are *not* the sneak you seem to think you are." He leaned forward, resting his palms flat on the surface of the table.

"I shouldn't have to hide from you," Winona said quietly, looking down to avoid her father's gaze. "I should be free to let you know who I truly am. I don't love Anthony," she bit her lower lip, "so I won't marry him. I'm done hiding."

Rage flashed in her father's eyes, but he managed to maintain that even yet strained tone. "Whatever was going on in that place – with that man – is over now. You will learn to love Anthony Van Buren. You will marry him. This could be my one real chance to get into the rail industry. You and your childish games will not ruin that for me."

"I won't marry him," Winona said through gritted teeth, silent angry tears running down her cheeks.

"I am the man of this house – the head of the household. I have the final say-so, and I say that you *will* marry him!" He pounded his fist on the table, causing its contents to rattle and chime.

"No!" Winona stood, her chair scraping out behind her. She was shaking all over. "I refuse to live the life *you* plan for me. A life based on your own greed and hunger for personal gain. I am who I am. I will not hide anymore."

Her mother sat frozen, as rigid as a statue, her eyes wide and stunned, staring straight ahead of her, her hands still clasped together in front of her on the tabletop. Her father's eye twitched, and he slowly stood upright, hand prints formed from condensation remaining on the wooden surface. He suddenly gripped the chair, throwing it against the wall and letting out an angry unintelligible cry.

"Now you listen to me!" he bellowed, all his self-control gone. "I am your father! I have tried to be patient; time and time again, I have had to remind you that you must abide by the rules while you live here. And yet, you always forget." He slammed his fist on the tabletop again. "Defiance will not be tolerated. You are a young lady, and it's high time you learned to act as such." Her mother remained catatonic. He took a deep breath. "I'll arrange for you and your mother to take a trip to the country – perhaps Anthony could rent a house as well. I think some time away from the city would do you good. Especially after your latest shenanigan."

"No! I won't let you control me anymore!" Winona screamed.

Her father flew backwards, hitting the wall with a loud thud and crumpling to the floor. Winona froze, her eyes widening. Her mother finally snapped out of it, getting up and approaching her motionless husband.

She rested her hand on his shoulder, shaking him. "Carter?" she said quietly. Winona continued to stare as her mother rolled him over to look at his face. His eyes were open and glazed over, his mouth hanging slightly open. She looked up at Winona, her eyes rimmed with tears. "You... you killed him," her voice was barely audible. "You killed your own father."

"I-I'm sorry," fresh tears spilled down Winona's face as she took a few steps back, slowly shaking her head and staring at her parents. "I didn't mean to..."

Her mother turned back to him, rubbing his arm and beginning to sob. "Carter! Carter!"

"I didn't mean to..." Winona repeated, continuing to cry, turning and running out of the dining room. She had to distance herself from the house before her mother alerted the authorities; she was already in enough trouble with the police. She ran up the stairs, bursting into her room. She threw some clothing into a bag. She reached under the bed and pulled out the damaged crystal ball, wrapping it in an old skirt and throwing it in the bag as well. She ran back down the stairs, stealing one last glance into her dining room on her way out the door - one last glimpse of her mother.

Once she was several blocks away, she stopped running and looked back over her shoulder. She had her freedom, just not as she had planned. Her life as Winona Blanchette was over. Now she was just Winona, or the Witch: W.

~

Winona looked both ways before emerging from the brush and walking to the intersection of the crossroads. She was miles from Manhattan, but still cautious; one false move and her new life of freedom could be over.

She knelt and dug several inches into the soft dirt and laid a shard of the crystal ball in the hole. As she covered it, she looked around; there was still no one to be seen. She stood, brushing the dusty dirt from her skirt.

"Come on," she said under her breath, "show yourself."

"Ah, hello," a man's deep voice said from behind her. Winona whipped around to face a tall figure. His skin was as black as coal, his clothes – if he was wearing any – just as dark and blending into his flesh. He had matching jet black hair, parted neatly on the side. His teeth were as white as the whites of his eyes, a black pupil dotting the centers of radiant red irises. "I was wondering when you might call."

"I'm here to make a pact," she replied, standing her ground.

"Well, you came to the right place. I am sure you know how this works. What is it that you want from me?"

Winona took a deep breath as the Devil moved around her, seeming to melt into the darkness, nothing visible but his eyes and toothy smile. "I need time," she stated, "I need more time to master the art of magic. I want to live up to the title I gave myself: the Witch. I want 200 years to hone my skills; 200 years to make history."

"And in return?" The Devil materialized, extending his hand toward her.

"Oh, I've thought long and hard about this." Winona smirked, crossing her arms. "I won't be selling you my soul tonight. But," she could see she had his attention – and curiosity, "I would let you have the souls of those who wrong me – or harm my potential future clients. Any soul worthy of death by my axe will be yours."

He chuckled, his smile widening. His white teeth glinted as he spoke. "You drive a hard bargain, not selling your own soul." He put his arm around her shoulders, bringing his face close to her ear, inhaling deeply. "You are deliciously powerful." He glided away from her. "But clever. I like your spark. You know what you want and you take it. You love power." He chuckled once more. "You were even willing to murder your own father to hold onto that power." He paused and Winona realized just how silent the night had become: no crickets chirping, no tree frogs singing, not even a gust of wind. "But without your soul as part of the deal, I can only give you 150. 150 years of seeing your work would be a pleasure." He flicked his wrist and a piece of paper appeared in his hand. He passed her a quill. "Do we have a deal?" Winona hesitated, then nodded, taking the quill. "Then sign the contract." She wrote a single letter on the line: a capital W. "Pleasure doing business with you," he said, and vanished. The crickets promptly resumed their chirping.

**1874, Iowa**

Winona pulled her pea coat tightly around herself as she boarded the transcontinental train. If she could say one good thing about her father, it was that he had seen the smart investment of getting involved with the rail industry. Too bad she had never married Anthony Van Buren for him; or let him live past that fateful night in 1865.

No, it was definitely time for a change of scenery. She had made a name for herself along the East Coast and down into the southern bayou. Now everyone was moving out west, and as the witch to see, she would move with them.

She sat down in her seat by the window, looking out at the platform. Just as in the underground, an air of mystery and fear surrounded her. She loved that. She loved feeling – *being* – powerful. The notion of love was something she had abandoned several years ago. After all, what was the point? She still had over a century of life left. And she already had what she loved more than anything – that power.

The steam engine hissed as the train pulled away from the station, westbound.

**1882, Arizona**

Winona sat on the piano bench in Jenkins' bar. It had been quite the night, a few stragglers still lingering in the tavern.

The saloon doors swung open, and a tall blonde man walked in. He had a certain aura about him; Winona could sense it. He walked over to the bar, knocking on the counter. "I need a room and a nice tall glass of whiskey." The light caught his eyes, causing them to glow. That was it: he was a vampire. And ordering a whiskey no less. Winona snickered to herself. A vampire… now that could be interesting. She waited for Jenkins to go pour the whiskey.

Once he turned his back, she walked over to the stranger, leaning on the stool next to him. "I don't think whiskey is the drink for you," she said, a small smile creeping across her lips.

# Chapter 56

Matilda drove down the street toward the athletic store. She had tried calling Kurt, but she was sure Miles was not letting him take calls. Or at least not unmonitored calls. She was driving with her headlights off; she did not want Miles to be aware of her approach. It was risky enough going to his lair as it was. But she had to talk to Kurt. She had found something, a lead.

The full moon would soon be illuminating the sky, but that made it even more urgent that she find Kurt as soon as possible. She pulled over to the curb and stopped a few blocks from the abandoned shop. She stepped out of the parked car into the twilight, leaving it unlocked in case she had to make a quick getaway.

A slight breeze came up, and she pulled her jacket closer around herself as she approached the building. She could hear a rhythmic banging sound, seeming to rise and fall in frequency along with the wind. The storefront came into view and she realized that the sound was the door to the shop hanging ajar, being blown by the wind and slamming against the door frame when the wind slowed.

Panic suddenly gripped her. Why was the door hanging open in such a manner? Miles always kept the place under lock and key, especially since he had decided to imprison Kurt there. She had been anxious before, but now she was extremely worried. Had something terrible happened? She quickened her pace, no longer caring about making noise as she approached. She gripped the door to stop it from slamming and looked around the inside of the shop. It was dark and still and silent. Nothing stirred. Even the light in the back room was off.

She was about to take a cautious step inside when she heard a man cry out painfully from somewhere nearby. She spun around. It had sounded like Kurt! "Kurt?" Matilda said quietly, her voice shaking. She started in the direction she thought the voice had come from. She heard the scraping of a shoe against the pavement and another soft cry. She quickened her pace and looked down the alley that opened up just a few shops down from the athletic store.

The light from the nearby streetlamp illuminated the alley enough for Matilda to be able to see Kurt sitting on the ground, slumped against the far brick wall. "Kurt!" she cried out, rushing to his side and kneeling beside him. "What happened? The shop-"

"Get away from me Matilda!" He held up his arms as if he wanted to push her away, and a look of fear came across his face.

"I'm about to change and I don't want to hurt you." He winced, moaning as his body began to shake all over.

"Kurt, you have to hold on just a few moments longer. I found it, a way to release you from your curse." He looked up at her, his eyes wide and wet with tears. "We have to-"

A gun sounded and Matilda stopped speaking abruptly, her mouth hanging open, her eyebrows furrowing over eyes now filled with pain. She put her hand to her stomach as she sat frozen for a moment before falling against Kurt, letting out a delayed choked gasp. Kurt sat there a moment in shock, his eyes wide. Once Matilda had slumped over, he had a clear view of the alley. Miles stood at the entrance, his arm extended in front of him holding a pistol with a smoking tip pointed at where Matilda had been sitting a few moments prior. Kurt dropped his eyes to Matilda for a moment, who was now breathing in quick shallow breaths. He saw the hole in her jacket where the bullet had entered her back, now rimmed with blood that was beginning to spread and stain.

He looked back up at Miles. "You... you shot her," he said in disgusted disbelief, still in shock and denial. Miles lowered the gun, smirking and letting out a small harrumph before walking out of Kurt's line of vision.

Kurt sat there numbly for a moment longer, both rage and fear beginning to bubble in his gut. He wanted to run after Miles, to hurt him for what he had done. To *kill* him. But Matilda lay in his lap, her breathing becoming more labored by the second, blood now dripping off her jacket onto the pavement. She let out a small cough, her eyelids fluttering as she began to lose consciousness.

"Matilda," he reached for her face, holding her head so that she was looking at him. Her head began to loll, her eyes rolling back in her head, her jaw growing slack. "Matilda, no, stay with me." Kurt began to hyperventilate, feeling the first tears begin streaming down his cheeks. He stroked her cheek with his thumb, leaning his forehead against hers. "Stay with me. Please, don't do this. I need you." A violent spasm racked his whole body, and he looked up into the full moonlight, feeling his back ripple as the transformation began to occur. He looked at Matilda, now fully unconscious, barely breathing. "Oh God, please forgive me."

He let go of her face and her head fell forward. He gripped her hand in his, pulling up the sleeve of her jacket to reveal the flesh of her arm. He let out a slightly inhuman groan as he felt a few of his bones beginning to relocate themselves; he did not have much time. He took a deep breath and clamped his eyes shut before sinking his teeth into her arm. He felt her muscles tense slightly and she let out the tiniest of gasps.

After a moment he pulled back, wiping her blood from his lips and rolling her off of his legs, standing and running drunkenly from
380

the alley, trying to get as far away from her as he could before the full metamorphosis occurred. He could smell her blood, and he knew that he had to get far so that once the wolf took over he would not be able to find her. He continued to run, gradually growing faster, hairier, and more canid in shape.

~

Matilda's eyes fluttered open. She was lying on her back, staring up at a fluorescent light attached to a white ceiling. She could hear an occasional beeping somewhere nearby and gave her eyes a moment to adjust to the brightness of the room. She looked around and realized she was laying in a hospital bed, sunlight shining in from a window to her right. She turned her head to the left, the pillow feeling almost too fluffy underneath her head. She spotted Kurt sitting by her bed, watching her with concern.

A smile spread across her lips. "You."

He tried to return her smile, but his face was stricken with sorrow. "How are you feeling?" he asked quietly, standing.

"Okay, I guess. A little groggy..." She shifted, feeling an odd knot in her back. "Stiff... how long have I been here?"

"Just since last night. It's about 3:00 P.M. now." He looked down at the floor, biting his lower lip, and then looked back up at her. "How much do you remember? From last night?"

Matilda screwed up her face, thinking; her thoughts were still foggy from sleeping so hard. "I had come to the shop to find you. I became really worried when I found the door left open. Then I found you in the alley. I was about to tell you how to break the curse when I heard a gunshot and felt a terrible pain," the odd feeling in her back suddenly made sense as things came back to her, "in my back. After that it all gets a little fuzzy. Am I gonna be all right?"

His face constricted in pain, and he closed his eyes. She thought she saw the glimmer of tears under his eyelids through his lashes. "Miles shot you," he said, his voice scratchy as if his throat were suddenly dry. "I called the ambulance first thing in the morning when I changed back… Matilda, I'm so sorry. I've ruined everything." He began to cry softly, "I didn't have a choice, you were going to die. I had to save you."

Matilda was terribly confused. "Kurt, what are you talking about?"

He finally looked up at her, his eyes and nose red, his cheeks tear-streaked. "I turned you. So now you're cursed, just like me." As he finished speaking, Matilda felt a phantom pain her left

382

forearm. She lifted it to her face, looking at the very faint outline of teeth marks imprinted in her skin. Kurt sniffed, speaking again, his voice thick. "I'm so sorry…"

Matilda reached out shakily and gripped his hand with the tips of her fingers. He looked down at his hand, then back up at her face. "What're you sorry for? You saved my life."

"But I've cursed you." He sat back down in the chair, scooting it closer to the head of the bed.

Matilda smiled at him, running her fingers through his hair. "But you're forgetting something. I came to find you because I found out how to break the curse. How to free you – *us*."

Kurt thought of how optimistic he had been when he had met Miles. And look where he was now: in a hospital room with the love of his life. She had nearly died because of him, and he had now turned her into a monster.

"Are you sure about this?" he asked as she continued to play with his hair, massaging his scalp.

"I got the information from one of my contacts. I've known him for a little while. I trust him."

Kurt looked into her eyes, an involuntary smile tugging at the corners of his mouth. He bit his lips, rocking back and forth slightly, reaching up to brush a few strands of hair out of Matilda's eyes. "When I saw you lying there – when I saw the light begin to fade from your eyes, I knew... I knew that I didn't know what I would do without you." He paused, searching for the right words. "You brought me out of my isolation. You reminded me how it felt to feel close to someone, that it didn't always have to end in destruction. The idea of losing you, of losing that drive to have a life again... I couldn't bear it. I trust you. I love you Matilda."

"I love you too." Matilda propped herself up on her elbow, leaning to kiss him, continuing to grip his hair as she pulled him toward her.

They kissed, tears collecting at the corners of both their eyes as their lips met. He caressed her check, stroking her jaw, wanting to keep her close to him. In that moment, he felt strong enough to take on Miles, to take on anything. They parted lips, their faces remaining only inches apart. She gazed into his eyes, rubbing the backs of her fingers down his cheek. He leaned forward, kissing her again, more passionately this time. He gripped the back of her neck, never wanting to let her go.

# Chapter 57

Kurt held Matilda's hand, the other on her back, as they exited the hospital. Her back had fully healed as a result of her new werewolfism, so she had made a speedy recovery. There were some adjustments that still had to be made, however. She was not yet accustomed to her heightened sense of hearing and smell; and after being bedridden, her legs were shaky. The fact that she had very nearly died probably played some role in that as well.

"My car!" she exclaimed as she spotted it across the parking lot.

"Yeah. I went to retrieve it after they had you stabilized in the hospital. You're lucky no one broke into it or stole it, leaving it unlocked in that neighborhood for so long." He unlocked the car and then handed her the keys, opening the driver door for her. She climbed in and he closed the door behind her, running around the car and climbing in the passenger seat. He took a deep breath as she put the key in the ignition and started the car, the engine roaring to life and then letting out a steady purr.

He glanced over at her. "You're sure about this?"

"Yes. I've known this guy for a while. We can trust him." She reached over, touching Kurt's hand.

He looked up at her, smiling, but obviously uncomfortable. "Let's go then."

Matilda shifted into 'Reverse' and backed the car out of the parking spot. She pulled out of the hospital parking lot and followed the freeway for a considerable distance before exiting and driving down a road in an older part of town. She parallel parked in front of a diner, the windows filled with neon signs sponsoring beer and plastic clings featuring the daily deals.

Matilda shut off the car and turned to Kurt. "Let's go. He usually spends a lot of time here." She climbed out of the car, and he followed suit as she led the way into the small restaurant.

Soft country music played over the speakers of the dimly lit dining room. The tables either had old fashioned red booths or round-backed wooden chairs. A few people sat around, talking and nursing their food, a few others sitting at the bar sipping drinks. Matilda surveyed the room, then suddenly let out a little, "Aha," under her breath and grabbed Kurt's hand, leading him toward the bar.

"Jesse?" she said as they approached a slender young man sitting at the bar wearing a button up shirt that was a size too big for him, a red martini in his hand. He had shoulder-length black hair, and Kurt was not sure if it was just the lighting, but he seemed to have a slight green-grey hue to his skin. He turned on the stool

386

to face them, revealing a very slender, boyish face. His cheeks and pale grey eyes were sunken, but he smiled as he seemed to recognize Matilda. He smelled dead.

"Matilda," he said warmly and the two hugged gingerly. Kurt continued to try to determine what he could attribute the smell to, but kept coming up with 'corpse.' Upon closer physical examination, Kurt noticed a large scar on the right side of the man's forehead and as he brushed his hair behind his ear, a metal bolt was visible sticking out of the side of his neck.

"Jesse, this is Kurt Farkas. My boyfriend... the werewolf I was telling you about." She motioned to Kurt. "And Kurt, this is my friend Jesse James."

"A pleasure to meet you," Jesse extended his hand, shaking Kurt's.

"Is it true what you told me before? That the man who... 'created' you could break the werewolf's curse? Things have gotten a bit complicated since we last spoke... I'm a werewolf now too."

Jesse's eyes widened and he looked between the two of them before answering. "I can't make any promises. But there was a time he told me about a werewolf cure he was developing. I'm not sure if anything ever really came of it... but if anyone could come up with a cure, it'd be Alexei Frankenstein." He turned on the stool and suddenly began coughing violently, putting his hand up to his mouth. There was an awful wet sound, and when he pulled his hand back, a small puddle of blood was collected in his palm.

"Oh my God! Are you all right?" Kurt exclaimed.

"Oh, yeah, that happens sometimes. Alexei is a genius, but hey, nothing's perfect." He grabbed a cocktail napkin from the bar and wiped the palm of his hand with it.

Kurt still looked perplexed. Matilda turned to him. "I, uh, never really got a chance to tell you much about Jesse. He's different, kind of like you – us. You see, he was dead. He's, well…"

"I'm a lot of pieces stitched together," Jesse finished for her. "I don't actually even know what my real name used to be, since I am several parts of people… that's why Alexei named me Jesse James. Said it was a name that made history and I was going to make history." He sighed, sipping his drink, which now strangely resembled blood to Kurt.

"Jesse," Matilda's tone grew serious, "will you take us to him? To Dr. Frankenstein, so we can ask him for help? Word on the street was no one knows where to find him these days…"

Jesse knocked back the last of his drink and stood carefully so as to not displace his stitches. "Of course." Jesse grabbed a toothpick from the caddy on the bar and clenched it between his
388

teeth. "Shall we?" As the three exited the building, Matilda started for her car. "Oh, we won't be needing to drive," Jesse interjected. "The lab is within walking distance from here."

"Really?" Matilda said in confusion. As far as she knew there were only businesses and some apartments in this district. She reluctantly put her keys back in the pocket of Kurt's jacket that she was wearing. She already missed her suede one, but being shot had left it ruined.

Jesse led them down the relatively crowded sidewalk past several storefronts. Kurt noticed he had a slight limp, probably due to his flawed construction. For someone with so many ailments, Jesse seemed to be a fairly good-natured guy. Although since Miles, Kurt did not put much stock in his judge of character. He hoped the same could not be said for Matilda.

As they continued down the sidewalk, more and more of the storefronts had 'For Lease,' 'Out of Business,' and 'For Sale' signs in the windows. The crowd began to thin out, aside from those who had parked their cars along this sparse end of the street.

Jesse stopped abruptly, turning on his heels and heading down an alley between two of the currently vacant buildings. His hip popped as he turned and he grunted, trying not to slow his pace. The alley was littered with discarded newspapers and empty beer bottles, an unused dumpster sitting against one of the buildings.

Jesse pulled a keyring from his pants pocket and twirled it around on his index finger. He knelt before what appeared to be storm cellar doors set in the ground. He inserted a small key into the lock in the door and twisted it to the left, the lock clicking open as he did so.

Jesse turned to them seriously before opening the doors. "Before we go any further, you have to understand, Alexei – Dr. Frankenstein – is a little... *off.* Most people say he's crazy. And things have... changed recently. I guess what I am saying is I just want you to be ready for anything. You may see some things in there that are a little... odd."

"I've seen my fair share of weird," Kurt replied assuredly, squeezing Matilda's hand. She leaned her head against his shoulder.

Jesse looked between the two of them and then nodded. "Let's go then." He pulled open the doors. A long staircase led down into the subterranean darkness. Jesse began down them, his limp even more pronounced as he took each step one at a time. "Please close the doors behind you," he said over his shoulder.

Kurt and Matilda took the first step together, Kurt releasing her hand to close the doors. As the light dwindled down to a narrow line, Kurt interlocked his fingers with Matilda's in the suffocating darkness. The only way to go was down, following the sounds of Jesse's shambling footsteps.

# Chapter 58

The stairs took a slight curve to the left and a small square of light came into view. Jesse's silhouette blocked out the light for a moment, and the sound of heavy metal hinges screeching filled the air as a triangle of light came from the now slightly-opened door. The side of Jesse's face was illuminated as he looked up the stairs at them, causing his scar to stand out.

"Watch your step," he said as they reached the bottom.

When they were all on the same level, Matilda gently rested her hand on his shoulder. "Thank you, Jesse."

"Don't thank me yet," Jesse replied edgily. They stared at each other for a moment in the narrow sliver of light before Jesse opened the door wider and walked through.

They entered a large lab. Many beakers, graduated cylinders, and other chemistry equipment covered brushed chrome tabletops. Near the back of the room were what looked like a few operating tables sitting to the side of a desk, which was littered with papers. Filing cabinets lined the majority of the walls, several of their drawers hanging open, their contents covering the floor. There was a skylight above them, so overgrown with foliage that only a miniscule amount of green-filtered light leaked in. The room was predominantly lit by fluorescent lights hanging from the ceiling. As a matter of fact, the lab appeared to have been abandoned.

"Jesse?" Matilda said timidly, not wanting to break the eerie silence of the place. Kurt had hung back, but was looking around the room apprehensively.

Jesse's eyes surveyed the room. "Alexei!" he said loudly, his voice echoing around the desolate room. Nothing stirred, and he began further into the lab, looking around carefully.

"Maybe he's not here-" Matilda started.

"No, he's here," Jesse cut her off as he squinted in an attempt to see better, continuing to look around the lab.

Kurt sniffed the air as he took a few cautious steps forward. He caught the light scent of human perspiration and something else… paint? "Someone was here," he said, "I can smell them."

Matilda walked along one of the tables, looking down at its contents. She looked up and noticed something white floating in front of her. It took her eyes a moment to focus on what it was; but once she saw it, she let out a startled scream, accidently knocking one of the empty test tubes off the table. It crashed to the floor, shattering into a million pieces. For it was what appeared to be a human skull floating in front of her, a little above eye level.

Kurt and Jesse had both spun to face her at the sound of her scream and the shattering glass.

394

"You're lucky there was nothing in that, who knows, you could've blown us all to kingdom come!" the skull exclaimed. Upon closer examination, Matilda could see that it was not a real skull, it appeared to have been painted on.

"Alexei!" Jesse shouted in exasperation, running toward Matilda and the floating skull. Kurt was already by her side, the reason for the smell of paint now evident to him. Jesse reached them, bending over and resting his hands on his knees, trying to catch his breath. Once he had regulated his breathing, he spoke. "Matilda. Kurt. This is Dr. Alexei Frankenstein." He motioned toward the skull. "As you can see, he managed to turn himself invisible."

Alexei shook his head. "Jesse, you know not to overexert yourself." Jesse nodded silently, trying to keep his breathing regulated.

"Matilda Benson," she extended her hand out of habit, and then blushed as she realized that there was a naked man standing in front of her, "and this is Kurt Farkas."

"Charmed." Matilda felt him grip her hand and shake it. It was an odd sensation, and she had to stop herself from pulling her hand back. "So," he continued, a lab coat suddenly seeming to remove itself from the hook of a coat rack and draping itself over the form of shoulders and arms just below the painted skull. From the pockets he pulled out and donned a pair of leather gloves. "Why have you come to see me?"

"Well you see, Kurt – and I – are werewolves. Jesse told me that you were the only one who knew how to break a werewolf's curse." Matilda shifted nervously. "You're our only hope."

Jesse cut in. "I told them you had been developing a cure, but didn't know if you ever succeeded."

Dr. Frankenstein turned to look at Jesse, then turned back to Matilda. As she looked closer at him she could see the strands of his hair sprayed white and the contours of his whiskers covered by the white paint, his eyebrows faint under the thick black paint. The more she looked at him, the less he looked like a skull, the features of his face emerging. "I'm mad. Completely bonkers. But I also just so happen to be a genius, the smartest genius there is. Yes, I can help you."

"And it really works?" Kurt asked tentatively, not wanting to get his hopes up just yet.

"Yes, yes, it works. Tested it on a few willing guinea wolves, and they had no more trouble from the wolf. Got the idea from an old witch I met sometime back… Ah, well, her name escapes me at the moment, but interesting woman."

Kurt felt a swell of hope, but still had his reservations. He shot Matilda a sideways glance and guilt consumed him again for putting her in this predicament. "Will it be painful?"

"Terribly," Alexei replied without hesitation. Kurt looked mournfully at Matilda. "You are killing the wolf inside you, of course it will be painful, but it will be worth it. Right?"

Kurt turned to Matilda and took her hands in his. "I am so sorry. You wouldn't be in this mess if it weren't for me. I'm so sorry you have to go through this."

Matilda freed her hands from his and caressed his face, pulling it so that he was looking into her eyes. "You saved my life. What's a little pain for freedom from this curse?"

"So you were recently bitten?" Alexei indicated Matilda. She nodded. "Have you actually changed yet?"

"No, I haven't."

"Then it will not be *as* painful. The wolf within you is basically a newborn, much easier to snuff out." He turned his attention to Kurt. "And how long have you been a werewolf?"

"My whole life... my mother was."

"Oh, well you have a very excruciating process ahead of you," Alexei said with certainty. "Let's start with you, Miss Benson." Alexei walked over to a medicine cabinet and began perusing the shelves. He pulled out a glass bottle containing a thick burnt orange liquid. He swirled the contents before dipping the needle of a syringe into the liquid and filling it. "I am going to have to ask you to lie down on the table."

Dr. Frankenstein laid a fresh pillow on the metal operating table, and Matilda lay down on her back, facing the ceiling. She side-glanced at Kurt as he approached the table, gripping his hand and squeezing it. "Here we go," she said, her voice wavering a bit.

"I'll be here the whole time." Kurt forced a reassuring smile.

Dr. Frankenstein injected her with the serum. They were all still and silent as the first few minutes ticked by. Then Matilda let out a small whimper, her grip on Kurt's hand tightening, her whole body tensing. Her whimpers turned into light cries of distress. Kurt dropped his gaze to the floor; he could not stand to see Matilda in such pain. He gripped her hand, trying to block out the sound of her cries to no avail.

~

Jesse brought Matilda another glass of water. After a few hours of discomfort, she had fallen asleep. When she had awakened, she had felt very dehydrated and Alexei had run a few tests, such as seeing how she reacted to silver and a blood test to see if the serum had successfully cured her, and it had.

398

Now it was time for Kurt. He lay back on the operating table, exhaling, trying to prepare himself for the painful ordeal ahead of him.

Jesse brought Matilda a chair, setting it next to the operating table. "Thanks," she smiled at him and he smiled back at her, although he was unable to hide the concern in his eyes.

Alexei pulled a leather restraint around Kurt's waist and clamped down his ankles.

"What are those for?" Kurt asked, suddenly alarmed, beads of perspiration forming on his forehead.

"Trust me, you'll need them." Alexei finished strapping Kurt's wrists down and promptly injected him with the serum.

It was nothing like Matilda's experience. Kurt immediately felt like he had fire surging through his veins. He did not let out a whimper, he went straight into cries of agony as the serum reached his heart, now being pumped through his entire circulatory system. His body tensed, his back arching as he flailed against his restraints.

Matilda rested her hand on his arm, but it brought him little comfort. "I'm here," she said, biting her lower lip and fighting back tears.

The pain had now spread, giving him a severe headache, stomach discomfort, and muscle cramps in places he did not even know were possible. He had never felt any pain comparable to this, and was beginning to fear that it might kill him. Everything was blocked out by the pain: he could not hear, could not see, could not even feel Matilda's hand on his arm.

"Is he going to be all right?" Matilda asked as he pulled even harder at the restraints, crying out, tears rolling down his face.

"Fine. Fine," Alexei assured her. "Once the wolf is dead, that is."

"We've got a long road ahead of us," Jesse sighed, pulling up a chair for himself.

# Chapter 59

Edward stood outside the café. It was the same café that he and Elsa had eaten lunch at the day he had first met Lawrence Talbot. That was why it seemed only fitting that this was the place he had chosen to meet with Lawrence again. It was after closing, the sun setting and all of the café tables and chairs empty. He held a small pin in his right hand. He had worked out a plan to get a drop of Lawrence's blood, but it would only work if everything went according to his plan.

He had called Lawrence pretending to be Hyde. He said that he had a lead on the biggest story in the city for a dirt bag. Usually Lawrence would have been insulted, but since he knew Hyde could only be foul, he had immediately wanted to set up a time for the exchange of information. Edward walked over to one of the café tables and sat, a manila folder with pamphlets from the hotel lobby stuffed inside. All he needed was for Lawrence to trust him enough to shake his hand. Then he would have the drop of blood that he needed.

The hard part would be facing the root of his hate. Blanche Grimwald had been right: Edward had buried it deep and nearly forgotten all about it. After enough time had passed, he just knew the hate and chose to forget the story.

Then he thought of Elsa. All the work she had done behind his back. He could not bring himself to be mad at her for lying; after all, she had done it all for him. She had promised to never lie to him again. He knew he had to return the favor; he had to come clean to her about why he hated monsters so much. That was why he decided to get the blood first.

There was a movement in the hedge that ran along the side of the café. A blonde man stepped out from the bushes, a cigarette clenched between his teeth.

"Lawrence?" Edward broke the silence, causing the man to jump. Then he took the cigarette from his mouth, hunching his shoulders angrily and walking toward the café table. As he did, his face began to morph and his hair darkened.

"Dammit Hyde, you nearly gave me a heart attack-" Lawrence stopped short, looking at Edward. "Oh, it's you," he said in disappointment.

"I have what Hyde wanted to give you. Not that I like it, but I don't have much choice." Edward glared up at Lawrence. "We need to have a little chat first. Before the files."

Lawrence blew his breath, putting the cigarette back between his lips and falling into another chair at the table. "Fine. What do you want to talk about?"

"Elsa. You stay away from her. I know that you were prowling around the house that night. Hyde didn't like it; I don't either. I give you this, you stay away from her. Or I'll kill you myself. Hyde or no Hyde." Edward kept his hand pressed flat against the folder, staring intensely at Lawrence.

"Knew there'd be a catch." Lawrence blew smoke out of his nostrils. "Is that all? That's an easy one."

Edward stared at him seriously and then extended his right hand across the table. "Shake on it," he said flatly.

Lawrence rolled his eyes and reached across the table to shake Edward's hand. As they gripped each other's hands firmly, Lawrence suddenly let out a yelp, his cigarette falling from his mouth, and pulled his hand back, shaking it rapidly. "What the hell'd you do that for!?" Edward pulled a small glass vial from his pocket and put the bloody needle inside, sealing it tightly. Lawrence glared at him, holding his hand. "You tricked me," he seethed, his eyes ablaze.

"Nothing trickier than you would do." Edward pocketed the vial and walked off into the darkness.

Lawrence cried out in rage, stomping out his dropped cigarette and snatching the manila folder off the table. Edward suspected that he would be even angrier when he discovered its contents.

# Chapter 60

Kurt stirred, his head throbbing and his eyelids heavy.

"You're awake." He heard Matilda's voice, tired but relieved.

Kurt struggled to open his eyes and focus on her face. He tried to move his arms and discovered that his restraints had been removed. "How long was I out?" Kurt asked, his mouth and throat terribly dry. "Water... I need some water."

"I've got it," he heard Jesse speak and the creaking of a chair as he stood.

"You were in pain for several hours, then you fell into a deep sleep. You've been out for about twelve hours." She paused. "It worked."

He opened his eyes wider. "It... it worked?"

"You heard the girl. You're cured!" Alexei's voice rang out. A suit shrouded in a lab coat seemed to levitate around the room, the skull makeup removed.

"Dr. Frankenstein ran the tests while you slept and everything checked out. No reaction to silver and a clean blood test."

Jesse appeared with the glass of water, and Kurt sat up to drink it, still in a state of shock. As he gulped down the water, he felt surreal. He had always wanted this, but now that he had it... it felt like he was in a dream. His mind suddenly turned to Miles.

"Miles!" he said, looking frantically at Matilda. "He may not be able to control me anymore, but he is still a danger to those around him. I mean, he shot you. And there are more werewolves out there, many more..." He finished the water and tried to stand.

"Whoa whoa whoa, slow down!" Alexei rushed over to him. "Your body just underwent a terrible stress, you need to rest and recover before trying to save the world."

"He's right. As soon as you have regained some of your strength, we can go to the police," Matilda assured him.

Kurt reluctantly relaxed back onto the table. "I just don't want him to get the chance to hurt anyone else. The lunar cycle isn't over yet."

"I know, I feel the same way," Matilda agreed.

"But you also can't go out half-cocked and a nickel short," Alexei exclaimed.

"Here, have some more water," Jesse offered him a second glass.

"Thanks."

"By the way, what do we owe you for your services, Dr. Frankenstein?" Matilda asked.

"Owe me!?" Alexei seemed surprised by the question. "Hm…" He crossed his arms in such a way that Matilda assumed he was stroking his beard. "I created the serum to prove that I could. I guess it being able to help someone is a bonus…" He threw his arms up in the air. "You owe me nothing, lovely Miss Benson!" He turned to Kurt. "And handsome Mr. Farkas," he added as an afterthought. "All I ask is that you tell the world I was right. I did it! I cured the werewolf curse and I discovered the secret to invisibility! That'll show those doubting bastards! Tell everyone, everyone who will listen – hell, even those who won't!"

"I think I can do that," Kurt smiled, shaking Dr. Frankenstein's gloved hand.

# Chapter 61

Kurt opened the door to his apartment. It was dark and had taken on a slightly musty smell due to being closed up. As he flipped on the light, he noticed a thin layer of dust on everything.

"Well, make yourself comfortable I guess. Sorry about the dust, haven't been here since Miles forced me to live at the shop," Kurt said to Matilda.

"The mess is no problem. Especially considering the circumstances." Matilda looked around the room at a few pictures on the wall and the bookshelf as Kurt went into his room.

They had stopped at Matilda's place first for her to grab a shower and change of clothes. It occurred to him that he had not had anyone in the apartment for years, aside from the landlord. He grabbed clean clothes from his dresser and closet, then entered the bathroom and turned on the shower so the water could warm up. He looked at himself in the mirror. He looked terrible: his eyes had dark bags underneath, his cheeks were sunken, and his lips were chapped. He looked as if he had not slept in days. The serum, while curing him of his curse, had really taken its toll on him.

He climbed into the shower, the hot water feeling good against his body as he massaged shampoo into his hair. Once he was dry and dressed, he returned to the living room. Matilda was standing by the wall, looking at a hanging photo of a brunette woman.

"Who is that?" she asked curiously.

"My mother." Kurt walked up beside her, looking at the photo.

"She was beautiful."

"Yeah," Kurt said quietly. "I hated her for so long. Blamed her for making me what I was. I just..." he began to get choked up, "I just wish there had been a cure when she was still alive." Matilda grasped his hand, interlocking her fingers with his. They stood there a moment in silence. "Let's get to the police station."

The two exited the apartment and got into Matilda's car, driving to the police station.

The officer at the front desk looked up as they entered. "Hello, Miss Benson," he said dismissively, returning to what he was doing. He had short brown hair, was clean-shaven, and had a slightly heavier build.

Kurt walked up to the desk. "I need to see the chief. I have some information about a criminal who calls himself Miles." As the name left his lips the officer looked up, his brown eyes bulging. "I also have some information concerning the murder of Alec Greerson and another man's disappearance."

"J-just a moment," the officer put the phone to his ear, pressing a button and sitting in silence a moment. He began hissing into the phone. "… Yeah… Says he has information about Miles… Some murder and disappearance too… He came in here with Matilda Benson… All right, I will bring him back." The officer hung up the phone and stood. "Please sir, come with me. I am Officer Clifton by the way. You are?…"

"Kurt Farkas."

Matilda started to stand. "Miss Benson, I am going to have to ask you to wait out here," Officer Clifton said before leading Kurt back behind the front desk and down a hallway to a door labeled 'Chief Magluster.'

Officer Clifton opened the door. An older man with short greying hair and a handlebar mustache sat behind a desk, blue eyes peering out at Kurt from under thinning bushy eyebrows.

"Officer Clifton tells me you have some information about Miles?" the chief said seriously. "Chief Magluster, please, have a seat." He extended his hand to Kurt.

"Kurt Farkas." Kurt shook his hand before sitting in a chair facing Chief Magluster. "Where to begin… I guess it all started when Alec Greerson – I didn't know him at the time – came to Wulfen on account of Miles. He said that Miles could help me with my werewolf problem and he led me to a seemingly abandoned athletic shop, which turned out to be Miles' headquarters. He said he was a dog trainer, that he could tame any beast. He succeeded in taming the wolf inside me. But once he had control, he made me kill Alec Greerson and another man… I'm sorry, I never got his name." Kurt pinched the bridge of his nose. "There would have been a third victim, but I failed to make the hit. After that, Miles forced me to live at the shop so that he could keep a closer eye on me.

"Matilda Benson and I, we, uh, well… are romantically involved. Miles tried to make me kill her too when he caught her digging around at the shop, but she got away. She came back for me though, and that time he shot her. In order to save her life, I changed her into a werewolf. But we were able to find a cure to the curse, one created by a man named Dr. Alexei Frankenstein. We're both just human now… I would have come forward sooner, but Miles' control over the wolf wouldn't allow me to."

Magluster stared at him for a moment and then pulled open one of his desk drawers, bringing out several photos paper-clipped to 'Missing Person' files. "Do any of these look like the second man you say Miles made you kill?"

Kurt began to go through the photos. He had nearly reached the bottom of the stack when he saw him. "This is him!" He handed the photo to Magluster.

412

"Chaz Aldran…" Magluster said, stroking his mustache. "Well I'll be damned, you seem to know just about everyone on our watchlist: that crazy old Frankenstein, Greerson, Aldran, Miles… If what you're saying is true, you are the closest thing to an inside line we've had on Miles. We have numerous accounts of his criminal activity: fingerprints, even security footage and pictures. But we are always a few steps behind him." Chief Magluster turned to Officer Clifton. "Get a squad together. We are going to raid that athletic shop. *Tonight*." The chief stood, pulling on his hat and jacket as Officer Clifton left to gather the other officers. "Farkas, I want you riding in my patrol car. Come on."

"What about Matilda?"

Chief Magluster wrinkled his nose. "I, uh, want to keep the press away from this at the moment. I'm sure you understand. It may also put her at risk to go, you said he tried to kill her once before. Who knows what he will do when we have him cornered."

Kurt set his jaw, but nodded before following Magluster out the back door to his patrol car. Other officers were piling into three other cruisers as Kurt climbed into the passenger seat of Magluster's car. All four cars' red and blue lights lit up in unison, the screeching of sirens filling the air as Magluster pulled out onto the road, followed by the others.

Matilda heard the sirens and saw the cars speeding off in the direction of the abandoned athletic shop. Worry gripped her. What if Miles tried to hurt Kurt? It would be easier to do now that he was no longer a werewolf, especially in his weakened condition.

All four cars skidded to a stop in front of the abandoned shop, their red and blue lights illuminating the storefront in the sunset. All of the officers exited their cars, drawing their guns. A few ran up to the building, others hanging back with their guns aimed at the door or watching the alleys on either side.

"Hang back," Magluster commanded Kurt as he headed for the storefront.

One officer rammed the door a couple o times before it broke open, and they all streamed inside, their guns at the ready. The front room was dark and predominantly empty, the faint smell of smoke hanging in the air. As they moved to the back room, they discovered the large steel cage and a solitary desk. While Officer Clifton searched the desk drawers – which appeared to be empty – the rest filed into the security room. The monitors and control panel for the surveillance system appeared to have been used recently, but all of the footage was missing.

Kurt stood outside anxiously, listening for gunshots. It was odder than he had thought it would be without his heightened senses; having had them his whole life, he had never considered

414

what it would be like without them. Had he still been able to, he would have sniffed Miles out if he were around or been able to hear the officers' conversation within the shop.

Chief Magluster exited the building, approaching Kurt. Behind him, Kurt could see a few officers entering the shop with a forensics bag and another stringing 'Caution: Crime Scene' tape across the storefront.

"He must have known something was up. Hell, maybe he could sense he had lost his hold on you; I don't know how that paranormal shit works. Any footage and papers are gone. But it's obvious that *someone* was in there recently. And then there's the cage you told us about. I have my men dusting for prints now." He shook his head. "Always a few steps ahead," he muttered under his breath.

As Magluster walked back to the shop, Kurt pulled out his cell phone and dialed Matilda.

"Oh my gosh, Kurt! Are you all right?"

"Yeah, I'm fine." He sighed. "I'm at the abandoned athletic shop. But he must have known something was amiss. He and anything of importance are gone."

Matilda was silent for a moment. "Don't worry Kurt, they'll find him. You gave them an amazing lead. He can't have gone too far, and the police are hot on his tail now."

"I hope so." Kurt looked at the police bustling about the shop, his face flashing red and blue in the police lights.

# Chapter 62

Jesse sat down from cleaning the last of Kurt and Matilda's drinking glasses. The scar on his forehead itched and he scratched it absently. Alexei's footsteps echoed through the lab as he approached Jesse, pulling up a chair next to him. He had sprayed his hair grey, the strands matted where the spray had dried. He had also covered his face in makeup and put in blue contact lenses.

"I thought making myself visible would be less jarring. Jesse... I want to talk to you. You see this photo?" He held up an old Polaroid, handing it to Jesse. There were two people in the yellowed photo: a younger Alexei sporting jet black hair and matching whiskers and a young woman with blonde hair wearing a dress. The two looked happy.

"That was my wife, Madalynn," he said quietly, taking the photo back. "Not many people know about her. I knew her a very long time ago. She was my closest friend; the only one who never doubted me. She was intelligent, someone I could actually have long conversations with. She understood me... our banter was a wonderful thing. And after we had been married a couple of years, she became pregnant... and I thought I was going to be a father."

He stared off, the blue contacts on his clear eyes betraying his deep sorrow. He chuckled softly.

He pinched the bridge of his nose, coming back to reality. "I was at the institute, working, when I got called to the phone. It was the police…" He paused, clenching his jaw. "… Madalynn had been in an accident. She and my unborn son were dead." His mind strayed back to that day…

He felt his fingers go limp as the receiver fell from his hand, clattering to the floor. He walked out of the institute in a daze.

"Alexei!" His colleagues shouted after him, asked him what was the matter, but he could barely hear them. He walked until he stood at the end of the pier in the harbor, looking out over the ocean. The wind blew off the water, whipping his black hair all about and stinging his face. His jacket flapped violently, his nametag threatening to come unpinned and fall into the water below.

Alexei closed his eyes, breathing in the salty air deeply, trying to fight back the tears that were already rolling down his cheeks. He clenched his fists, his nails digging into his palms.

"*NOOOOO!*" he cried out into the harbor, his voice bouncing off the waves, unleashing all of the agony he felt inside, falling to his knees.

"Alexei?" Jesse said tentatively, touching his wrist.

Alexei started, turning to look at him as if he had just woken up. After another moment, he wet his lips and spoke. "Losing her was worse than just losing my lover... that day I lost my only friend. My one chance at a family. Something I'd never thought I was cut out for. I knew, even then... I don't love like other people. My brain just doesn't work like that. But she didn't mind that I couldn't love her the way she loved me. She just loved me anyway."

He took a deep breath and turned toward Jesse, sections of his makeup washing away with his tears. Jesse realized that he had never seen his creator cry before. "They are part of what sent me down this path of solitude. I even think their deaths may have contributed to my insanity. But all geniuses are a little kooky," he chuckled sadly. "After that day, I buried myself in my work. I developed anything from cures to helpful inventions to useless gadgets, even brought a man back from the dead just to prove that I could do it."

His tone changed slightly. "But you became more than just another achievement. You became a part of my life. A friend... something I had not had since my wife died. My insanity and my unmatched IQ make it nearly impossible for me to relate to other people. But you... we understand each other because of what we are. Unique. What some call monsters. You became the son I never got to have."

He leaned forward, beginning to cry into his hands. Jesse leaned against him, wrapping an arm around his back, hugging him. "I'm sorry."

"What are you sorry for?" Alexei sat up quickly, part of his face completely see-through again. "I named you Jesse James because it was a memorable name. Because I wanted you to go down in history... to be great... to do great things. I want you to go out and make something of yourself... something that isn't attached to me. You're a good man; you shouldn't go on living in my shadow. A shadow tainted by years of misunderstanding and contempt."

"But... where will I go? You said it yourself, I don't exist."

"Not yet you don't. I have some 'connections' in the seedier areas of the city. A false identity was nothing to get compared to

420

black market body parts." He furrowed what part of his brow still had makeup clinging to it. "It's time for both of us to leave this place." He looked around the lab. "I need you to do one last thing for me." He stood, reaching behind one of the rolling blackboards and brought out a briefcase. "Keep this safe. It is my most important work. Do right by Miss Benson and Mr. Farkas – make the cure available. Keep my work out of the wrong hands." He paused. "It has everything you'll need, including a considerable amount of money."

"I-I can't take this-" Alexei put a finger to Jesse's lips.

"You *will* take it. My fondest creation... my friend." He pulled Jesse into a close hug and held him there. When he spoke again, his voice was thick. "That should be enough to get you started. I already called my contact, Earl. He can help you make up any documentation you will need. But if you ever need anything... anything at all, I will always be there for you, as long as there is air in my lungs." He continued to hold Jesse close to him, as if he never wanted to let go.

"You've forgotten one thing," Jesse said, fighting back his own tears. "What about my imperfect stitching? I'm falling apart at the seams these days."

Alexei pulled back from him, looking him up and down. "Science made you what you are. Perhaps magic can fix those imperfections. There is a witch – she is very powerful – known only as 'W.' I am certain that she would be able to help you. You need only to look for her sigil. She keeps to the shadows these days, but that can guide you."

"But… what about you?" Jesse said finally. "How will I find you?"

Alexei smiled. "I'll be around."

Jesse returned the smile. He walked to his room and gathered the rest of his things; he had never had much. The two looked around the lab before ascending the stairs for the last time. At the top, Alexei extended his hand to Jesse, but was met instead with one last tearful hug before the men parted ways.

# Chapter 68

The phone began to ring and Elsa turned the food she was cooking down on 'Low' so she could answer without it burning. She grabbed the phone off of the wall and pressed the button, putting it to her ear. "Hello?"

"Elsa? It's Edward. Could you come by the hotel... we need to talk. It's about... Well, it's about my past."

"Sure, but um, Edward? I'm in the middle of cooking lunch, so it may be a little bit."

"All right," he laughed hoarsely, "just as soon as you can. I love you."

"Love you too," she said before hanging up and returning to the sizzling chicken on the stovetop. Once it was fully cooked, she had a quick bite to eat and got in her car to head to the hotel.

She was apprehensive about this meeting. She had always known that Edward had a past with monsters – that much he had been straightforward about from the start. But he had never been willing to explore the subject further than that. *"They're all bad, every last one of them. Look at them: they were clearly built to kill and strike fear into the hearts of others,"* he had said, and then changed the subject after that.

Elsa pulled into the parking lot and climbed out of the car, taking a deep breath and standing a little taller. She did not want Edward to see just how uncomfortable she was and want to call the whole thing off. She knew that he needed this and that it would already be hard enough to recount what had happened. Her mind wandered to his reaction when Blanche had begun to breach those memories. She climbed into the elevator and rode it up to Edward's floor. She walked to his door and knocked. He opened it immediately, and she wondered just how long he had been waiting there.

"Hey," he said, forcing a smile as she walked in. He walked over to the bed, sitting down and leaving enough room for Elsa to sit beside him. He turned to her as she sat, his eyes filled with worry. "After you went to see W, you said something to me, about not lying to me anymore. Elsa, I don't want secrets between us. And I... I think it's time I told you where my hate for monsters originated." He reached over and grabbed her hand. "I think that's the best way to truly face the root of my darkness."

She looked back at him, biting her lower lip. "Go ahead and tell me. You know that you can tell me anything."

He looked down, avoiding her eyes. "Yeah, I know. It's just... this isn't easy. Not at all. These are terrible memories, that's why I buried them so deep. It was Hyde that brought them out where Blanche could see them." He exhaled and then began his story. "When I was just a little boy - seven years old - I saw something terrible. I played T-ball back in those days. I eventually graduated into playing actual baseball, but those were the early years. I was walking home from practice one evening. I was going past the park when I heard a familiar voice. It was my elementary school teacher's voice. He was one of the nicest people I knew. He was a young man, passionate about making the lessons fun and including everyone. He was kind to all his students: well-behaved and not, straight-A students and flunkies.

"The sun was setting, so there was still enough light to see. I decided to step into the park to say, 'Hello.' But then I saw that he was talking to someone that I did not recognize. They seemed to be having an argument, so I stayed hidden in the bushes and listened. I did not really understand what they were talking about, but the other man's blue eyes seemed to glow a little as the sun sunk below the horizon. Finally, my teacher threw his arms up in the air, shouting at the other man that 'he just needed more time.' At this the man grew angrier and his eyes definitely lit up as he revealed hideous fangs. I gasped, quickly clamping my hand over my mouth. I had never seen a vampire before, but this one scared me because he was so aggressive.

"He grabbed my teacher by the shoulders – I really wish I could remember his name, but it escapes me at the moment – and shook him, yelling all kinds of profane words that I was not allowed to say. My teacher brought his arm up, socking the vampire in the jaw. He stumbled back in shock, and my teacher began to run. But the vampire was much too quick; he grabbed my teacher from behind and sunk his fangs into his neck." Edward swallowed, taking a break; the pitch of his voice had been rising as he remembered the horror he had witnessed. "There was blood everywhere… just shooting out of his neck. The vampire took multiple bites of his neck and face, shaking his head to tear away bits of his flesh and then spitting them into the grass. He only drank a little of the blood… I think he just wanted to maim and murder the man, not feed.

"A woman walking her dog spotted them and saw the blood spurting out of my teacher's neck, the flow slowing as he died there on the path, and she screamed. The vampire ran off into the darkness as people gathered around to see why the woman was screaming. I slipped away during all of the commotion as an ambulance arrived, a little too late. I ran home and kept what I had seen to myself.

"As I tried to sleep, the vampire's face burned in my mind. I thought of stories I had heard about people who turned into wolves
426

and lost control, killing those around them. Most lived in special institutions that locked them in when they would change, but the idea of a monster even scarier than the vampire I had witnessed terrified me. I couldn't sleep, and when I did, I had terrible nightmares. School was cancelled the next day due to the discovery of the body of one of their staff members. Everyone in town was touched by the death of the kindly schoolteacher who was loved by all his students. Until the truth came out." Edward paused, continuing to stare at the floor.

Elsa let him sit in silence for a moment. "What was that?" she asked softly.

"The vampire that killed him was finally IDed. He was the leader of a gang trafficking drugs all through the town and even to a few neighboring cities. The reason he and my teacher were in the park that night... was because my teacher was wrapped up in the gang. He was helping them sell drugs. Back then I was still too young to really understand that, and I just couldn't wrap my head around why anyone would want to hurt such a nice man. Especially in the gruesome manner I had witnessed. I held my mom's hand a little tighter when we saw monsters in public. I hid behind my father when one would politely wave at me. Every time I saw one, I would remember that vampire's face, all of the blood shooting out of my teacher's neck. It was horrible. I never told my parents that I had been there when it happened."

He took another deep breath. "And then, when I was eleven, our neighbors got robbed. It was a group of shapeshifters, and they morphed their faces into hideous mask-like forms. Not only did they take anything of value my neighbors had, the very sight of them had given the wife a heart attack, sending her to the hospital. She survived, thankfully. But they lost so much that night.

"In that time I knew very few monsters, and what I did know was that they hurt those around them. They were bad. Hell, you just had to look at them and know that they had been built for one purpose: to strike fear into the hearts of others. And to kill. So as I grew, my fear turned to hate and I eventually buried those memories as deep as I could. I had to do something to be able to sleep at night. I forgot my kindly teacher and the neighbor lady. I just wanted to save the world from the evil which was monsters."

He looked up at Elsa, his eyes filled with sorrow. "I allowed my hate to blind me. I pass people on the street every day. I pay cab drivers and give my order to waiters and waitresses. I go about my day and encounter all kinds of people, people that could be monsters and I don't even know it. Some of the most decent people I have ever known could have been monsters that just… didn't look 'different.' Even after all the times I bashed on

428

monsters in my column, all the accusations made solely on what they were and not who... Zeleni Malakai and Blanche Grimwald were still willing to help me. Good people with good hearts." Edward looked into Elsa's eyes, tears forming in his own. "Most of them have never hurt a soul. But Hyde... he killed that woman, Giselle Michaels. Just like that vampire killed my teacher. What W - the witch - said is true. I'm a real monster." He began to cry, and he completely forgot about the vial in his pocket.

Elsa put her arm around his shoulders as he cried, remembering the bottle and pulling it from his pocket, undoing the lid. She held it up to his face. "Here," she said soothingly. A few tears dripped into the vial, mixing with Lawrence Talbot's blood. The fluid began to change color, turning a deep shade of maroon. Edward wiped his eyes with the back of his hand and looked at Elsa. He put his hand up to the vial, holding it and her hand in his. He made no move to actually take it from her, just looked at her. "What?" She smiled, blushing.

"Just you," he said quietly, his eyes bloodshot from crying. "I tried to push you away to keep you safe. But I never would have gotten this far without you. You are amazing." He kissed her and took the vial, swirling its contents around in the bottom. "Now to let it sit under the moon."

# Chapter 64

Kurt and Matilda sat in Matilda's car parked outside of Wulfen. The fingerprints in the shop had matched what they had on record for the elusive Miles, so they thought he would be on the down-low for a while. Kurt, however, thought he would try to tame another wolf now that he had been successful.

Kurt looked up at the full moon lighting the night sky. He had never gotten the chance to just look at the moon. If he could see the full moon, it was already too late.

But he could not focus on the moon's aesthetic at the moment. He had to be watching Wulfen for any sign of Miles.

Miles walked close to the building, staying to the shadows. He would not – *could* not – risk getting caught. He was still angry about losing his hold on Kurt, a loss he was now certain of. If not, Kurt would have had no choice but to return to the athletic shop, tail between his legs. When a couple of days had gone by with no sign of his dog, Miles had packed up and relocated. Good thing too, he had found out the police raided the place a mere sixteen hours after he had fled. Probably due to Kurt rolling over on him. What Miles wouldn't give to kick that traitor's face in!

But soon, he would not have to. Soon, he would have not one, but *several* werewolves at his disposal. Because with an army like that, what would be the point of laying low anymore? He would be virtually unstoppable.

One of the side doors was hanging slightly ajar, a sliver of light visible. *"You would think a place housing several of the most dangerous monsters in the city would have better security,"* Miles thought to himself as he entered the door, although he was not complaining.

Kurt had noticed a movement along the side of the building. While it was hard to tell for certain, he was sure it was Miles he had seen slipping into the side door.

"Call Magluster. I am going in there to stop him before he does more damage." Kurt opened the car door to climb out, but Matilda pulled him back into the car, kissing him long and intensely.

"Be careful," she said, releasing her hold on him.

"I will," he said, still a bit taken aback. He closed the door behind him and ran toward the building. Matilda watched him with apprehension as she dialed the police station.

Miles squinted against the harsh fluorescent lights as he entered from the dark street. He could tell he was in some form of locker room. As he peered through the doorway into the next room, he saw a man at the front security desk, his back to him.

Miles looked around the locker room and spotted a bowling pin covered in Sharpie signatures sitting on the central table. He picked it up and gripped it in his hand, walking up quietly behind the guard. He swung the pin hard, hitting the guard where his skull met his neck. He let out a soft, "Oomph" and crumpled to the floor, falling out of his chair.

"There we go," Miles said, setting down the bowling pin. "Can't have you sounding an alarm." He searched the desk for a moment, finding a small map of the complex. After scrutinizing it for a moment, he headed in the direction of the main cell block.

Miles stepped through a closed door into a corridor lined with locked high security doors, the sounds of snarls, howls, and barks coming from behind each. Glimpses of brown fur, large yellow eyes, and sharp teeth were visible as they looked out and walked by their cell windows.

Miles smirked, running his hand through his slicked back hair and shaking out his shoulders. He stood up straighter, letting out a loud shrill whistle. All of the werewolves fell silent, snouts and yellow eyes all appearing at the windows to see who had called them to attention.

Miles' smile widened. "I could get used to this-" He was cut off as someone body-slammed him from the side, both of them falling to the floor.

Miles looked up to see Kurt. He drew his arm back to punch Miles in the face, but he threw Kurt off of him.

"Well, well," Miles stood, a few strands of his dark hair falling into his eyes. "I suppose telling you to stop wouldn't do much good now," he brushed off his jacket, glaring at Kurt, "traitor."

"Traitor?" Kurt said incredulously. "You're the one who promised to help me. You promised to tame the wolf inside and then you betrayed me."

"I didn't lie. I did tame the wolf," Miles sneered, "for myself."

Kurt glared at him. "I'm not gonna let you enslave anyone else." Kurt lunged at him, pulling a roll of duct tape from his jacket pocket. But this time Miles was ready for him, moving out of the way and grabbing ahold of Kurt's wrists.

434

"I may not be able to control you anymore, but at least now you're easier to kill." He twisted Kurt's arm, looking into his sunken eyes. "You look like Hell." He released Kurt's wrists and wrapped his hands around his neck, starting to strangle him.

"Yeah, well looks aren't everything," Kurt grunted, punching Miles in the eye, causing him to release his neck and stumble backwards.

As Miles put his hand to his face, Kurt kicked him in the gut, causing him to fall over backwards. With the air knocked out of Miles, Kurt saw his chance. He pulled out a long strip of tape, ripping it with his teeth and dropping the roll. As he brought it down around the sides of Miles' face, Miles cried out, grabbing the collar of Kurt's jacket. Kurt struggled with the tape as Miles wrestled with him, looking around the room. His eye was already darkening into a bruise. Kurt struggled to pull Miles' arms behind his back. Miles socked him in the jaw. He grabbed Kurt's shoulders, throwing him against the wall, his shoulder hitting it hard as he slid down the wall. Miles' eyes were ablaze with an insane fire as he spotted the 'Emergency Cell Door Release' switch on the wall.

"Miles, no!" Kurt reached toward him, wincing as he moved his shoulder. Kurt stood, grabbing him by the shoulders, but Miles shrugged him off, continuing for the switch. Kurt grabbed his arms, then in an act of desperation, pulled the tape around Miles' mouth, pulling it taut. Miles lunged forward, pulling the switch as the ends of the tape met in the back as Kurt pulled at his head.

Miles shoved Kurt, causing more pain in his shoulder, as a loud alarm sounded and red lights began to flash. Kurt looked on in terror as the cell doors all came open. "What have you done?" Kurt grabbed Miles' arm, trying to drag him out of the corridor, but Miles once again threw him off. He had his eyes on his prize, seeming to have forgotten the tape wrapped around his head, covering his mouth. He looked down the corridor, raising his arms in triumph over his kingdom.

As Kurt began backing out the door, he saw the first of the werewolves exiting their cells, sniffing the air and looking around, their ears twitching at the sound of the alarm.

Once Kurt was out the door to the cell block, he began running for the front entrance. As he passed the front desk, he heard a groan and slowed, looking over the desk to see a guard laying on the ground, holding his head. He recognized him from when he had been an inmate at Wulfen.

"Come on, we've got to get outta here!" Kurt ran around the desk and grabbed the guard's arm, trying to pull him to his feet.

"Wha-what happened?" the guard slurred, his head swimming.

"No time, Larry, he's pulled the cell release; we need to get out of here while we can!"

"Farkas?" The guard's eyes focused on Kurt's face. "What?... How?"

"I said no time! Once we're out of here, I'll explain everything."

As Kurt and Larry reached the front door, Larry keyed in an emergency code that would lock all of the facility's doors. "We have ten seconds before that door locks, go!" Larry pointed toward the street.

Meanwhile, the werewolves had noticed Miles. He tried to open his mouth to give his first command. But his voice came out muffled. Then he noticed - and remembered - the tape. His eyes widened as he began tugging at the tape, trying to remove it from his face, but it clung to his skin and the back of his hair. His lips stung as the adhesive held onto them.

The werewolves sensed his sudden sense of urgency and panic, saw him pulling at his face. Snarls began deep in the front wolves' throats, and Miles felt sweat collecting on his brow as he backed away from the growing pack.

He clawed frantically at the tape, his dull nails scraping the flesh of his cheeks. His back hit the door and he spun around, pulling the handle. The door did not budge.

*"No..."* he thought, a knot forming in his stomach. *"Kurt! That bastard must have locked the doors!"* He looked back over his shoulder at the quickly approaching pack. He let out a cry, a small sound escaping out his nose as he pulled at the tape again.

More of his hair fell into his face as he frantically tried to find a weak point in the tape, the edge beginning to pull up, wanting to cling to his skin and hair follicles. The pain brought tears to his eyes.

The first werewolf lunged forward, sinking its teeth into his arm. He let out a muffled cry, the veins in his neck standing out as he strained. Blood shot out around the wolf's jaws. They had drawn first blood. The others smelled it, signaling that the hunt was truly on. They all howled, charging Miles.

*"No! No! Not like this!"* Miles tried to scream, the tape obscuring his words, the adhesive loosening as he sweated even more profusely. More teeth and claws dug into his arms, legs, and torso. Blood began to pool on the floor, flesh and muscle tissue tearing off in their mouths. Miles slowly fell to the ground, screaming, being torn to shreds and eaten alive by the very creatures he had wished to enslave.

438

Kurt and Larry ran to Matilda's car, police sirens audible in the distance. Matilda stood outside the car, running to meet Kurt when she spotted him, embracing him.

"What happened? I heard the alarm and-" she stopped short, pulling back so that she could look at his face. "You're bleeding..."

"It's just a scratch. Better than Miles, I fear."

"What happened?"

"He pulled the emergency cell release... but only after I had gagged him. He won't be ordering them to stop - or do anything else for that matter."

Matilda put her hand to her mouth.

"Farkas," Larry clapped his hand on Kurt's shoulder, causing him to wince. He quickly removed his hand. "I'm glad you saved me and all, but... how are you still *you*? Not changed..."

"Well, I'm not a werewolf anymore." Larry's eyes widened. "I found it, the cure I've been looking for," he put his arm around Matilda, smiling at her, "and when the sun rises, I intend to tell the others."

The police arrived, and Kurt and Matilda explained everything. Larry of course backed them up, telling the police how Miles had knocked him out and Kurt had saved him. They were just going to have to wait until the sun rose to go inside, or risk losing more lives.

~

Once the sun rose, all of the werewolves – now in their human form – were gathered into a conference hall. The police found Miles – or at least what was left of him – in the cell block.

"We took the body for analysis, but I am almost positive everything will match what we have on record for Miles," Magluster said to Kurt. "Now, they're all in the conference hall. You say whatever it is you're needing to say, and then we will release them."

Kurt nodded, walking into the conference hall. All of the inmates turned to look at him as he entered and walked to the front of the room. Expressions of recognition spread across some of their faces. "Can I have everyone's attention please?" Kurt said loudly over the murmur of voices. The room fell mostly silent, a few people still whispering here and there. "My name is Kurt Farkas. I have been a werewolf my entire life. The man who came
440

here last night - the man who was killed - wanted to take control of you all, to turn the wolves inside you into his guard dogs. Like he did with me." Several members of the crowd gasped. "As many of you here who know me are aware of, I have spent a great deal of my life searching for a cure to this curse – *our* curse. I thought he could help me. I was wrong. But there is a light at the end of every tunnel. I did finally find a cure, one that truly works. I made a promise to the man who created it: I promised him to tell the world about it. I intend to make good on that, starting here.

"There is a man named Dr. Alexei Frankenstein. I am sure some of you have heard of him. He is a genius. He created a cure. I am no longer afraid. I no longer have to hide during the cycle of the moon and fear that by some sick twist of fate, I will not make it here in time. I am free. And safe from people like Miles who wanted to use me – *you* – for their own evil designs. I'm leaving the choice up to you. But for the first time, at least you have that choice." Tears glimmered in his eyes as he looked out over the crowd. "Thank you."

He turned and began to exit the room when someone started clapping. This was followed by a few others until the whole room was giving him one big round of applause.

# Chapter 65

Carmichael took another hit of the joint. Casey's face flashed into his mind. Not for remorse of killing her; life is fragile and she would have died eventually anyway. But for the thrill of the kill, the exhilaration of feeling her blood inside him, tasting her pure passion sliding down his throat. What he wouldn't give for that feeling to last.

But he didn't have it in him for another killing spree, at least not for a few more decades. The screams of his victims from the twenties sometimes still reverberated in his mind, causing him to feel a tinge of regret. All his time on this earth had all but desensitized him; but deep down, some of his humanity still remained.

He took another hit. His perception had already begun to become altered. Casey's face melted into blackness, the darkness of his heart surrounding him. This high was not doing what he'd hoped – what it usually did for him. Instead of feeling elated, with all of the walls he'd put up down, longing ate away at him. Not his typical flavor - not the desire to die, but the desire to be wrapped in Emily's embrace. To feel the warmth of her hands burning his back through the fabric of his shirt. To feel her soft lips against his, see the look of adoration he'd always relished in those emerald eyes. He had always questioned how someone so kind and beautiful could love someone – some*thing* – like him. If only she could see him now.

Shit. Maybe it was remorse he was feeling. Sure, he looked the same on the outside; but time had only continued to twist his insides, squeezing out any semblance of a decent human being and leaving a hideous monster in its place.

"Ow!" He dropped the end of the blunt as it burned down to his fingers. Now the drug was gone, and he was already coming down.

He tried to push Emily out of his mind. Still W's crystal remained dormant. Another trick. Another lie. Another way to torment him. How he wished he could kill her, bring her back, and kill her again.

Since the murder, he had spent more of his time high than not. He had kept this from Brook, of course. He had been so happy that Carmichael seemed to be showing signs of improvement – of abandoning his obsession with suicide – that Carmichael didn't have the heart to tell him otherwise. He would just let Brook believe his fairytale – that he was capable of helping him.

He actually liked Brook. Despite the rough start to their relationship, he was one of the handful of people Carmichael had ever liked, or trusted. Brook knew everything.

Well, not quite everything, but more than any other living soul could boast.

The thought of killing him because he knew too much had never crossed Carmichael's mind until that very moment. Still, he did not really consider it, seeing as he actually felt a fondness for him.

A dull hum, like a cell phone vibrating, suddenly caught his attention. He had no idea how long the buzzing had been going on, he had been so wrapped up in his own head that he had not really noticed anything going on around him externally.

He stood, beginning his search for the source of the sound in the small apartment. As his senses returned to him, he also heard the bustle of traffic outside, the smell of incense from the neighboring apartment, his nocturnal eyes adjusting quickly to see his sparse surroundings.

A movement caught his eye. A pulsing, like the rhythmic glow of a firefly's light. He froze, waiting for another pulse to help him try and detect the source. The light rose again, in cadence with the humming. It was slightly lavender. Then Carmichael realized it was the item in his jacket pocket: W's crystal.

He walked over to where his jacket hung on the handle of his closet and reached into the pocket, gripping the crystal in his hand. It vibrated more violently at his touch as he pulled it out. He knew what it meant. He put on his jacket and headed for the door. Ding dong, the wicked witch would die.

The sun shone brightly outside, causing him to squint and shield his eyes with his hand. Invulnerable he may be, but he still hated the sunlight. Natural instinct – a vestigial instinct, in his opinion. He began toward W's alley for what he knew would be the last time.

As he got closer, the crystal vibrated more intensely and glowed even brighter; no longer an undulation, but a constant light. He had arrived at the entrance to the alley, but something made him hesitate. W had promised when her time came - when he returned to her - that all would be clear. He hoped she had been telling the truth; he really did. But he had also learned that she was talented at trickery. Maybe she had just not wanted to die alone. Maybe she was still holding onto the hope that she could make him love her. To see her death, Carmichael would have bought front row tickets. But to make him love her was like trying to get blood from a stone.

He took his first step into the alley, then continued, one foot in front of the other in automatic succession, until he was at her door. He remembered the last time at the door, the moment of paralysis.

446

He gripped the knob all the same. There was a brief chill that ran up his arm and circulated through his body. The door opened.

Everything was coated in a layer of dust. The place looked abandoned, like no one had been inside for a long time. Now that he thought about it, the purple light outside had barely been lit. Was he too late? No, the crystal was still active. He ventured further into her lair.

He found her where he had before, lying in the bed in the farthest reaches of the place. She was practically reduced to a skeleton, her skin pulled tight across her bony frame, the wrinkles still visible – deeper, somehow. Her flesh itself had taken on an ashen hue, a blue and red network of veins visible underneath. Her eyes were partially sunken back in her skull, a few wisps of white hair still clinging to her mostly bald head.

"You came," she breathed, her voice like a piece of rusty machinery in dire need of oiling. She attempted to smile, but could only manage a minor cheek twitch.

"Yes," Carmichael said, standing in the doorway, looking at the somehow still-animated corpse.

"I… I wanted to see you one last time," her voice grated on, each word a struggle, "before the end."

"If anyone is going to see you go out, it'll be me… after all this time." He approached her, sitting in a chair conveniently placed by the bed.

"I-I don't have much time," she half-choked on her own spit due to her mouth producing too much saliva. "I told you that all would be clear. And I intend to keep that promise." She drew in a deep rattling breath. "Once I am dead, the spell I put on you will no longer be intact." His eyes widened, his rock-hard expression softening. "You will be a vampire, the same as any other." There was a tremor to her voice, a sadness. "My own life force… it is what has been powering the spell all this time."

Carmichael sat in silent shock, his jaw slack, a strange sensation starting in his gut and working its way up his throat but stopping at his heart. "Winona… is that true?" he finally asked, his voice distant.

She closed her eyes, a tear running down her aged cheek. "You… you haven't called me Winona in over a century." This time she managed a partial smile. She opened her eyes, looking over at him and reached out to him feebly.

Carmichael decided to indulge the old hag. These were her last moments and for him it was Christmas. He had come to see her die, but now he not only got that, he was repossessing his mortality. He embraced her, her narrow arms attempting to do the

448

same. Her hands were already cold enough for him to feel through his clothes, her stiff joints stabbing him in the ribs. She felt so frail, he found it hard to believe that this was the woman so many feared – the woman he had danced with and made love to over a hundred years ago.

She exhaled, going limp, his arms the only thing holding up her small amount of weight. He slowly laid her back down on the bed, releasing her. Her eyes were already closed, a small smile still on her lips.

He felt different, as if a veil had been lifted from him. For a brief moment, he felt that he was not alone in the room, that another person lurked in the shadows watching him. He shrugged it off.

He looked at her body one more time, then turned and left the room, shutting the door behind him. A shape shifted in the dark, white teeth and red eyes suddenly visible. An obsidian hand rested on Winona's. "Good show, old girl. Maybe I'll see you in Hell." Then the figure faded back into the darkness.

Carmichael exited the den, looking out at the sunny midafternoon street at the end of the alley. He licked his lips in anticipation. He longed to burn. But not yet. First he had some affairs to get in order.

# Chapter 66

Jesse walked down the alley, which seemed to shut out all sunlight the deeper he went. He had been able to get more information about W's whereabouts from Earl when he had met with him to create his new identity: Jesse James Hoover. He could see a burned-out purple neon sign at the far end of the alley. He was sure that was the sigil that Alexei had been referring to.

Underneath the burned-out neon W was a battered door, hanging slightly ajar. There was something off, Jesse could feel it in the air; it hung around him like a thick fog. He slowly pushed the door open, walking in. "Hello?" he called out, his voice echoing in the dark empty space. He stood for a moment, allowing his eyes to adjust to the blackness. At the center of the room sat a table with a crystal ball at its center, dusty from disuse. The place looked as if it had been abandoned for a long time.

"W?" he said loudly, walking further into the room. "Are you here? A friend of mine said you might be able to help me." He looked around again, spotting a piece of paper on the floor. He knelt to pick it up and squinted to read it. `Zeleni Malakai: Soul Doctor` read the cut-out newspaper ad. He shrugged, pocketing it. When he looked back up, he noticed another door. "W?" he said, walking through it.

The room was small, lit by a single lamp, casting a yellow hue around what appeared to be a bedroom. In the bed, he could make out the form of a body lying under the covers.

"W?" He approached the bed, reaching out to touch the gnarled old hand sticking out from underneath the large afghan. It was cold.

"You just missed her," a deep voice boomed from behind him. Jesse whipped around to see two bright red eyes peering out from what appeared to be a swirling black cloud. The cloud materialized into the form of a jet black man, from the hair on his head down to his toes. He stared at Jesse, taking a silent step forward. "I have never encountered a being like you before." He dematerialized, floating around Jesse, his eyes never disappearing from view. After a moment he regained his form. "What are you?"

"I'm, uh, reanimated," Jesse replied. He had never encountered a creature like the one questioning him before either. "What I mean to say is, I was dead and then I was brought back to life – by Dr. Alexei Frankenstein."

"Ah yes, Frankenstein. I've heard of him." He changed the subject, turning to the bed, "What could something like you have possibly wanted from her?"

452

"Just some help," Jesse tried to sound resolute and hide just how afraid he still was. "If you don't mind my asking, what kind of creature are you?"

The 'man' chuckled in response, a sound from deep in his chest that seemed to shake the entire room. "I go by many names. However, probably my most well-known title is the Devil."

Jesse felt a knot form in his stomach. "Then you should already know my next question: what could you have possibly wanted with a witch?"

The Devil smiled, revealing shimmering white teeth. "I came here to bid her farewell." His smile widened. "Miss Blanchette here and I go way back."

Jesse took a step toward the door. "Well, I'd best be going-"

"Nonsense!" the Devil swooped around behind him, placing a searing hot hand on his shoulder and blocking the exit. "You came here seeking help, and help I can provide."

"I don't think I want to pay the price for your kind of help."

"You want to be normal? I can do that," the Devil purred. Jesse knew he had gotten inside his head. He felt tingly all over and reached up to touch his neck, only to discover that the metal bolt was gone. He gripped his side, but could not feel the bulge of his imperfect stitches. His whole body felt different, somehow more whole. "Isn't this what you want?"

It was. But one thing still wore on Jesse's mind. Everyone knew what the Devil charged for his services. "But I would have to give you my soul…"

"Soul? Pah!" The Devil laughed, slapping Jesse on the back. "You haven't got one of those; they're all long gone."

"But then… what would you want from me?" Jesse's voice caught in his throat.

"We're both creative individuals. I'm sure we could think of something." The Devil's grin widened to Cheshire proportions.

"N-no," Jesse said, pulling away from the hot hand, the tingling sensation leaving his body.

The Devil narrowed his eyes. "But it's what you've always wanted. Why shouldn't you have it?"

"Yes," Jesse felt the familiar bolts in his neck, "but I don't want to get it like this. I'll find another way."

"Your decision is… final?"

"Yes."

"Suit yourself." Black lids closed over the brilliant red eyes and the presence was gone; Jesse felt completely alone in the room with the witch's cadaver.

He struggled to make his legs work, walking out of the small space. He pulled the newspaper clipping he had found out of his pocket.

454

"Soul Doctor?" he said quietly to himself, exiting the alley.

# Chapter 67

Elsa and Edward sat on the bed, staring at the vial gripped between Edward's fingers. He had left it on the sill overnight. But now there was the lingering doubt of whether it would work or not.

"Well, here goes nothing," Edward sighed, gripping the vial's stopper.

A knock came at the door.

"Who could that be?" Elsa thought out loud.

The knock came again, louder this time. "Room service!" a voice sang out from the other side.

"But I didn't order any room service..." Edward looked befuddled.

The hotel worker knocked again. "Room service!" he shouted impatiently.

"I'm going to go tell him he has the wrong room," Elsa walked across the room to the door, Edward standing with the vial still in his hand. Elsa pulled the door open to see a man standing on the other side in a hotel uniform. But he was not holding any tray. "I'm sorry, you have the wrong room."

"Oh, but I don't," the man said menacingly, reaching out and grabbing Elsa's arm gruffly, pulling it around behind her back, turning her to face the room, and pushing her inside, kicking the door closed behind him.

"Hey, what the hell are you doing!?" Edward shouted as the man sneered at him.

"Oh, just a moment," he said, and his face began to morph and change.

"Lawrence," Edward said through gritted teeth before he had even finished transforming.

"You got me!" he said, pulling Elsa's arm up farther behind her back, causing her to cry out.

"You let her go," Edward said sternly, taking a step toward them.

"Wouldn't do that if I were you," Lawrence said, pulling out a spring-loaded pocket knife and whipping out the blade. He put the knife to Elsa's throat. "Now give me that vial or I'll kill your girlfriend. I'm done with the theatrics."

Edward looked at the vial in his hand, then back at Lawrence. "How did you find me?"

"Oh you know, I just used my journalist tracking skills. And I know where you live. It wasn't hard to follow Elsa here." He pressed the knife against the flesh of her neck, causing her to flinch as the cold metal touched her. She let out a small whimper.

Edward adjusted his grip on the vial. "Take a sip of that, and I'll bleed the bitch right here and now."

"I give it to you, and you'll let her go?" Edward said, his eyes on the knife pressed against Elsa's neck.

"I guess you'll just have to find out," Lawrence smiled evilly at Edward.

Edward stood there a moment longer, placing the lid back on the vial. He took a step toward Lawrence, his arm outstretched. "I give you this and you let her go." He extended his other hand toward Elsa.

Lawrence readjusted how he had his arm around Elsa, the blade still held against her neck, and reached out for the vial. Edward took a deep breath, hoping for the best as he dropped the vial into Lawrence's hand; his heart was beating out of his chest. Lawrence closed his fingers around the vial and pulled the knife away from Elsa, shoving her at Edward.

He caught her in his arms, holding her close to him. "Are you all right?" he asked.

"I think so."

He loosened his grip on her and shifted his gaze to Lawrence. He was examining the fluid in the vial, ignoring the two of them completely. Anger bubbled up in Edward, and he felt Hyde taking control. For the first time, he welcomed the change.

"Get back," he said, taking a few steps away from Elsa and bending over, his fists clenched. He grunted and when he stood upright, his eyes glowed menacingly as he focused on Lawrence Talbot standing across the room from him. He suddenly charged him, grabbing him around the waist and pulling them both to the floor. Lawrence cried out, startled. The vial fell from his hand as he hit the floor, rolling across the carpet.

"He warned you to stay away from her!" Hyde snarled, punching Lawrence in the jaw.

"No! I will not give up! Not after what I went through for this!" Lawrence kicked Hyde and attempted to crawl after the vial.

Hyde grabbed him by his legs, dragging him backwards as he clawed at the carpet. He rolled around, swinging wildly at Hyde. While the two fought, Elsa made her way over to the vial, placing it in her jacket pocket.

"You really are the worst of him, aren't you?" Blood trickled out of Lawrence's nose as he threw Hyde off of him once more. He pushed himself up on his elbows and knees, taking a moment before trying to stand.

Hyde sat up behind him, gripping the sides of his head in his hands. "He promised that if you broke our deal, one of us would kill you." He jerked Lawrence's head sharply to the left, a sickening crack filling the air as he snapped his neck. Lawrence immediately stopped struggling and Hyde released him. He fell limply to the floor with a dull thud.

Hyde stood, breathing hard. He looked down at Lawrence and kicked the body. No response; he was dead. He turned to Elsa, his expression changing. "Elsa... please. Don't let him kill me." He walked over to her and dropped down on his knees, clasping his hands together, "Please."

Elsa looked down at him. She glanced at Lawrence's body laying on the floor of the kitchen and then back at Hyde. "I can't stop him. You've killed people, an innocent person. That woman - Giselle Michaels - she didn't deserve what you did to her." Elsa stepped back from Hyde. "You have to pay for what you've done... just like Lawrence."

"But I'm a part of him Elsa. You'd let him kill a part of himself? You said it yourself: you love the good and the bad."

"And when you're gone, *all* the darkness won't be. You just won't be able to hijack his mind anymore."

Hyde began to cry. "Elsa... please. I love you. I know you care about me too."

"I love Edward Jekyll," she said firmly and he gripped his face in his hands, crying out as he began to lose control.

Edward Jekyll looked around the room, uncovering his face and standing up shakily. He spotted Lawrence's body sprawled on the kitchen floor. "Is he...?" Elsa nodded. Edward lifted an eyebrow. "Well that's one thing he's done that I can agree with." He suddenly looked around the room, panicked. "Where is it!? Did it break?"

"I have it right here," Elsa pulled the vial out of her pocket.

Edward gripped it in his hand, pulling off the lid. He looked at Elsa before drinking it all down in one gulp. It tasted putrid, like salted sewer water. He suddenly felt a tight pain in his chest. He put his hand to his breast and cried out, his eyes bulging. And then he fainted, falling to the floor.

"Edward!" Elsa rushed to his side. He was still breathing. She lifted him and managed to get him up on the bed, propping his head up on a pillow.

# Chapter 68

Carmichael lugged the last box of his personal belongings down the stairs. There hadn't been much – about three boxfuls. He lifted the box up, heaving it into the dumpster, the sun setting in twilight. He wiped his forehead with the back of his hand; he wasn't sweating, it was more of an automatic gesture.

He walked back up the stairs and into the empty apartment. Were it not for the smell of cigarettes and marijuana that hung in the air, it would have seemed like nobody had resided there for ages. He picked up the cordless phone, but did not dial. This was the part he had been dreading. But he also knew he could not put it off any longer; he had waited over a one hundred years to be able to die. He didn't want to wait any longer than he had to. He punched in the number, putting the receiver to his ear. It rang a few times before someone picked up on the other end.

"Dr. Brook Hydecker speaking."

"Brook, it's Carmichael. We need to talk. Do you have time to spare?"

"My schedule's clear. Carmichael, what-" Brook's question died in his throat as he heard Carmichael hang up the phone. He hung up as well, returning the phone to its cradle and pacing around the room anxiously. He wondered – and worried – about what Carmichael could possibly want to talk about.

A knock finally came at the door, and Brook practically ran to answer it. Carmichael stood outside, an odd quality surrounding him; he seemed tired, almost haggard, but also elated. Brook tried to take the sense in stride as he stepped aside to let Carmichael in. Carmichael entered the office, but did not take his usual spot on the sofa.

"What did you want to talk about?" Brook asked, closing the door.

"It's W – Winona – the witch I told you about. She's dead."

"Oh," Brook said, unsure of what to say. "So... that's what you came here to talk about?"

"Yes... well, no," Carmichael scratched the back of his head. "It's... what happened after." Carmichael sighed. He could see that he was making Brook terribly anxious. "You know how I started seeing you to... work out my depression and find something worth living for in this inescapable existence?"

"Yes, of course I remember. That's my job."

Carmichael stared at the floor, searching for the right words. "When she died... the spell she put on me - the cause of my invulnerability - died with her." He looked up at Brook, meeting his gaze. Brook saw a look there, one he remembered from those first few sessions.

"No…" he said, stunned, his legs turning to jelly.

"Don't try and stop me Brook; it's futile. I have waited too long for this release. I just came here to bid you one final farewell… and to thank you for trying to help me – a lost cause." He extended his hand to shake Brook's. "You are one of the few people on this earth I have ever considered my friend."

Brook slowly shook his hand, dazed. He felt tears trying to bubble up inside him, but he suppressed them. Carmichael smiled at him tersely, turning to leave.

"Wait!" Brook suddenly exclaimed. "D-don't go… don't do this." He swallowed; his voice was quivering far more than he wanted it to. "I don't want you to die, to lose you… because… I think I am falling in love with you."

Carmichael halted, turning back to face Brook, taken aback by his sudden proclamation. He pitied him. He chuckled softly. "Don't fall in love with an immortal Brook. And a murderer at that. You should know better."

"That was a long time ago. You're better now, you've changed."

Carmichael chuckled again, more of a sad sound than a laugh. "Not as long ago as you think. I'm no good for anyone Brook. It's better that I walk out of your life now. You're a good person. Save those who can be. You deserve better than the monster I am." He turned back toward the door. "My decision is final… good-bye Brook." Carmichael exited Dr. Brook Hydecker's office for the last time, leaving him in heartbroken dismay. He had one more stop to make.

~

Carmichael made his way through the dark cemetery, his path lit only by the few stars twinkling in the sky, accompanied by the waning moon. He had done some digging into the public records and discovered the location of mean old Mr. Hydecker's grave. He wanted to pay his respects to the man who had broken Brook as a young boy, yet also molded him into the compassionate man that he was now.

It wasn't hard to find. The stone was barely a decade old, still shining with newness compared to its neighbors, the marbled red granite like a beacon amongst the varying shades of grey. Carmichael walked up to the stone, reading the embossed inscription upon it:

## Theo L. Hydecker
## May 15, 1946 – October 4, 2003

"Asshole," Carmichael muttered under his breath, unzipping his fly. He pissed on the grave, emptying the contents of his bladder. Once he was finished, he zipped up his pants and smiled sadistically. "I only wish you were alive so that I could have done that more directly." His smile shrank as he looked out over the city skyline. A small line of deep vermillion was visible along the horizon. The sun would be rising soon. It was almost time.

# Chapter 69

"These shenanigans have gone on for far too long. It is time to bring this madness to an end," Chairman Vapelli said down the long table of executives. "I've heard arguments before about all he has brought to the scientific community over the years. But the man is dangerous; he has been for a long time. We cannot continue to overlook what this could mean. If we allow this to go on until it's too late, we will have no one to blame but ourselves."

A disembodied lab coat seemed to levitate over an embellished granite gravestone. A few inches beneath the sleeve, a bouquet of calla lilies hung in midair.

"He is a man that is so logical and intelligent that I believe he is incapable of feelings," Vapelli continued.

"You never were a fan of roses," Alexei said softly, kneeling and setting the lilies on the freshly mowed grass in front of the stone. 'Madalynn Frankenstein' and 'Nicholas Frankenstein' were engraved into the face of the stone.

"And for a man in his position, that could easily turn deadly. He has no regard for other people's safety," Vapelli said with conviction.

"That day on the pier... when I found out you'd left me. I just wanted to disappear," Alexei sighed.

"I have to agree with Chairman Vapelli. Alexei's quickness to rage and refusal to recognize his own faults make him a very real liability."

"I've heard enough," said a very stern-looking man at the head of the table. "Vapelli, you said you have located his lab?"

"I do think so," Vapelli smiled with triumph, plopping a file down in front of his new superior. The man picked it up, opening the folder and examining the satellite image within. A red circle dotted the thought to be location of the lab.

"Send in the special team. Who knows what they'll find in there; it is *his* lab after all."

"But it turns out I still had a lot to do." Alexei looked out over the cemetery.

One of the special team members broke the lock on the storm doors, and the team filed down the stairs.

"Now I can finally disappear," Alexei smiled, removing his jacket, all trace of him vanishing.

471

"Dr. Alexei Frankenstein! Come out with your hands where we can see them!" the team leader shouted as the men fanned out around the lab, their guns ready. The tables were all barren, the cabinets emptied. A few members branched off into the adjoining rooms, shaking their heads upon exiting.

The leader approached the table at the far end of the room. A holographic-looking rotten cherry sat next to a note written in all capitals with black marker: **AND FOR MY NEXT TRICK, I WILL DISAPPEAR**.

"Commander, this is Squadron A Leader, do you copy?" he said into his radio.

"We read you A Leader, over."

"He's gone. We missed him." Vapelli clenched his fists, his knuckles white. "He did leave a clue. Switch your monitors to my cam, over." His view of the lab came up on the large monitor and A Leader held the cherry and the note up to the camera.

"That crazy bastard…" Vapelli said breathlessly, his cheeks flushed.

"What?" his superior asked, all eyes turning to Vapelli.

"He really did it. He managed to turn himself invisible." He slumped into a chair, dabbing his sweaty forehead with a handkerchief. "We waited too long… We'll never catch him now." Vapelli's horse had lost.

# Chapter 70

"And that's the whole story. So when I found your ad, I was hoping you might be able to help me," Jesse shifted on the cushion, looking up at Zeleni Malakai hopefully.

"Hm…" Zeleni stroked his mustache, furrowing his brow thoughtfully. "This is, eh, *new* to say the least. But I may be able to help you. It's a long shot, but… please go back out into the lobby and wait. This could take a while." Jesse stood and began out the doorway adorned with a beaded curtain. "Wait!" Zeleni suddenly cried, running over to him. "I nearly forgot. Spit." He held out a glass and plucked one of Jesse's hairs as he spit into the cup. Then he exited the room.

As he sat in the lobby waiting, he grew anxious, bouncing his leg nervously. He wanted it to work, but he did not want to get his hopes up too high; after all, Zeleni had said it was a long shot.

Finally Zeleni appeared in the doorway, wisps of incense smoke swirling around him. "Jesse. It's ready."

Jesse stood shakily and walked into the back room. The table was bare aside from a tall glass of iridescent green liquid. Jesse took a few deep breaths, then looked at Zeleni. "So… what is it?"

"It's for healing. Sometimes people come to me after intensive surgery because they have trouble recovering. In theory, it should heal what ails you. But as we also discussed, your case is truly unique." He motioned toward the glass. "Well go on. Drink it."

Jesse picked up the glass; it felt heavier than he'd expected and sloshed dangerously in his shaky hand. He drank it all within a couple of gulps. It didn't taste like anything and from the temperature in the room, it was surprisingly cold.

For a moment, nothing happened. Then, he felt tingly all over, like he had when the Devil had temporarily changed him. He looked at his hands, turning them over. They were pink, not pale and tinged with green. He pulled up his sleeve to reveal a perfect arm not adorned by stitches. He touched his bad side and felt nothing but his ribs.

"It… it worked," he said breathlessly, turning to the mirror that hung on Zeleni's wall. There were no bolts in his neck, no scar across his forehead, and his cheeks were rosy. He turned back to Zeleni, shaking his hand. "Thank you. This… this is all I've ever really wanted." He looked at his hands again in disbelief. "The chance to be a part of the world. Oh," he started, reaching into his pocket and taking out a small wad of bills, "I nearly forgot. I owe you this." He handed Zeleni the money.

Zeleni smiled, accepting the payment. "It was my pleasure. You are almost like my own Pinocchio, eh? Now you're a real boy." The two laughed, and Jesse thanked Zeleni again before exiting the shop.

# Chapter 71

Carmichael stood in the shadow of a tall office building, the sun beating down on the pavement mere feet in front of him. He had dreamed about - yearned for - this moment for centuries. It took him back to that early morning under the awning of Jenkins' tavern, waiting to duel Royce Slade. He had planned to let the sun take him before the expert shooter did. Instead he had been dealt over a century of misery.

He felt weightless, as if he might float away like a dandelion wisp and then eventually cease to exist. He pulled a small portrait out of his jacket pocket – the only personal belonging that had not gone into the dumpster aside from the clothes on his back – and clicked it open. He looked at the faded portrait of his beloved Emily. It brought tears to his eyes and he smiled down at it tenderly.

"I wish I could say I'd be seeing you soon… but I don't think there's any small chance of my getting into Heaven. And I know there is no way you're in Hell, my dear."

He clamped it shut, returning it to his pocket. He inhaled deeply and held the breath. A few seconds ticked away, and he exhaled, stretching his arms out by his sides and stepping out into the sunlight.

He craned his neck, looking Heavenward. He had to squint from the intensity of the sun, its rays warm on his skin. Too warm. He closed his eyes, grinning as he felt the first lick of flames around the collar of his shirt. His flesh began to flake away in grey ash, orange embers glowing underneath. Happy tears rolled down his cheeks, evaporating into steam as the flames grew, the embers glowing brighter, parts of his skull already visible, his hair falling away in fiery tufts. He felt his blood boiling, felt the last of his skin falling away as ashen dust.

His smile grew, mirrored by his skull's permanent grin. Unbeknownst to him, a crowd was gathering, staring at the vaguely humanoid shape of white heat. He was going out with a bang, in a glorious blaze of light. And he was finally free. ✍

# Chapter 72

Earl sat at the bus stop, the streetlight surrounded by an odd halo in the misty night. He was wet, cold, and miserable; he just wanted to take the bus home so he could call it a night. He rubbed his mouth with his dry cracked fingers, then reached into his coat pocket for his pack of smokes, peering inside. Only two left. He tapped the pack against his palm, then took one out and held it between his lips. He reached deeper into his pocket for his lighter, but could not find it.

"What the…?" he said to himself, patting his other pockets to see if he had just misplaced it.

"Looking for this?" a voice said from the darkness as a small flame sprang from seemingly nowhere. Earl jumped, crying out, the cigarette in his mouth falling to the ground. "Oh calm down, it's only me."

"Alexei?" Earl said after a moment, bending shakily to retrieve his cigarette. "Where are you? I can't see you."

"I'm right beside you. I've achieved the next great thing: invisibility!"

"Is that a fact?" Earl chuckled: half-skeptical, half-spooked.

"It is," Alexei flicked the lighter on again, and Earl could see that it was floating in midair. After a moment's hesitation, he took the light.

"Shit. Well I'll be damned." He took a long drag. "You know the police are looking for you?"

"Yes. And of course, they won't find me like this," Alexei laughed triumphantly. "But there is still so much to do! I will need someone to help me out, of course; someone I know will not try and turn me in. Someone to be my 'man on the street.' That's where you come in."

"Oh yeah. Well what do you want me to do? I already helped that Jesse James fella of yours out."

"Good. I do appreciate that, more than I can express."

"I'll take your word for it. But what else do you want me to do?"

"Being invisible – and now, wanted – has its perks as well as its downfalls. I will sometimes need supplies. Food. I'll tell you what I need when I need it. And I'm sure you won't argue, my payout rate remains the same."

Earl chuckled, "Well Dr. Frankenstein, it looks like you got yourself a partner in crime."

"Splendid!" Alexei placed the lighter in Earl's coat pocket. "You won't regret this. You are going to help me accomplish great great things, Earl Igor!" ◈

# Chapter 73

Edward and Elsa walked through the busy streets of the city, arm in arm. They were smiling and laughing, happy.

Edward had moved back home a few days after the ordeal with Lawrence. They had left his body at the bottom of the fire escape. When it was found, no one could figure out how he had gotten ahold of a hotel worker's uniform; although when they IDed him, they all commented that he was known to be a sneak. But they were sure he had fallen from the fire escape and broken his neck. Case closed.

They reached a small park, and Edward guided Elsa down the path to a bench that was not currently in use. The two sat next to each other and Edward hunched his shoulders against the brisk wind.

"There's been no sign of Hyde for almost a week now," Elsa said, also tensing in reaction to the wind.

"Yeah. I guess that potion worked." He jammed his hands into his coat pockets.

"It's nice having you back home."

"I agree," he smiled, leaning his head against hers, "I missed our bed."

"I missed you."

"That too." They sat there in silence a moment, joggers and dog walkers passing in front of the bench. Edward rubbed the small box in his pocket. He sat up straight, turning to Elsa. "A long time ago at a café, I said to you that I was going to try to do better. That there was no room for hate in a life filled with love." He chuckled before continuing, "I had no idea how right I was." He slid off the bench, kneeling on one knee in front of Elsa. "That day – hell, before that day – I knew that I wanted to spend my life with you. But after all of this that we've been through, there isn't a doubt in my mind." He pulled the ring box from his pocket, opening it. "Elsa McIntire, will you marry me?"

Elsa looked at the beautifully crafted gold ring, the brilliant diamond at its center. She looked past it into the eyes of her lover. "Yes, Edward. Of course I will."

He reached for the ring to remove it from the box and place it on her finger, but she gripped the collar of his coat and pulled him to her, kissing him like she had never kissed him before. He reveled in being able to let his guard down and savor the moment, not worrying that Hyde would come forth at any moment to wreak havoc.

Their lips parted and he plucked the ring from the box, sliding it onto her left ring finger. They both stood, interlocking their
486

fingers in one another's. He and Elsa walked back toward the street, ready to start their new life together. ∾

# Chapter 74

Jesse walked into the empty conference room. This would be his first meeting at his new job, and he did not want being late to be his first impression. Instead he was terribly early. He sat in one of the many empty chairs, running a hand through his thick hair. Adjusting to a 'normal' life had been weirder than he had expected. He had not realized how accustomed he had become to his ailments until they were gone.

He heard someone walk into the room and saw a woman who looked to be about his age with red hair and thick-framed glasses enter the room. She saw him looking and smiled at him, approaching him and taking the seat next to him.

"You're the new guy, right?" she asked, straightening her papers in front of her on the table.

"Yeah. I'm Jesse. Jesse Ja-" he stopped himself from saying his old name, "Jesse Hoover. It's nice to meet you. I don't really know many people here yet," he said, offering his hand.

"Shelly Winters." She shook his hand. "So how do you like it here so far?"

"It's good. I like working... I couldn't find work for a long time. So this is good." He smiled nervously, internally kicking himself for being repetitive.

"Yeah, it can be hard." A few other people began to wander into the conference room. "Well, I guess the meeting will be starting soon. I'd love to chat more though... Possibly over coffee?"

Jesse looked at her, surprised by the offer as she smiled hopefully at him. "Yeah... sure. That'd be great!" He returned her smile and the two laughed nervously. Jesse turned back to his papers, but quickly stole another glance of Shelly just to catch her still looking at him. Their eyes met and they did not speak, they just smiled at each other. ❧

# Chapter 75

Kurt sat at a table in the bar, waiting for Matilda to meet him for lunch. He had amazing news for her.

Matilda came through the door and saw him, walking over to him. He stood to greet her, wrapping his arm around her waist and kissing her. The two sat down.

"So, what did you want to tell me?" Matilda put her elbows on the table, anxiously leaning in close to Kurt.

"Magluster called. Everything matched up, including the DNA test. That was Miles, the 'criminal mastermind.' They were able to track down where he moved everything to before the police raided the athletic shop. Found the footage of him taming me. They were also able to confirm his connections to Alec Greerson and Chaz Aldran. He was even telling the truth about going to Berlin to tame circus animals. But he also left the country to fly under the radar until some things he was involved in stateside cooled down."

Matilda beamed at him, touching his hand. "You're a hero, Kurt. *You* stopped him."

Kurt smiled, blushing slightly. "It gets better. Magluster said you can have the story. A first look exclusive into 'The Mysterious

Criminal Mastermind: Miles' for *The Metzen Gazette*." He looked deep into her eyes. "Looks like you'll get your real story, about real people."

Matilda's eyes widened. She sat in silence a moment, not knowing what to say. The thought of the look on Harley's face when she walked in and put *that* story on his desk caused her heart to race. Then she looked at Kurt and everything seemed to slow down.

"I came to this place looking for a story," Matilda motioned around the bar. "I got so much more than that." She smiled, cocking her head to the side. "I got you."

Kurt looked down at the floor, chuckling huskily. Then he looked back at Matilda, his eyes and expression intense. "That wasn't all I wanted to tell you." He swallowed. "I love you Matilda Benson. And now... now that I have turned this corner in my life - now that I am free of my curse - I can finally see a future for myself. A future I-" his voice caught in his throat, "-can't imagine without you in it."

"I love you too, Kurt," Matilda said seriously.

Kurt smiled at her. "When I met you, you reignited a fire in me... hope. I hadn't had that for a long time. Without you, I'd still be a werewolf." His smile grew broader. "You're a hero too."

"I guess we're quite the power couple," Matilda raised one eyebrow, grinning alluringly at him.

"You could say that," Kurt laughed. They continued to talk, and the waiter came to take their order. ✺

# About the Author

Sarah J Dhue is a fiction author from Illinois and has been writing since she was in elementary school. She self-publishes her creative fiction and this is her fifth published book to date, with a sixth on the way. In addition to books she also writes poetry, short stories, and songs. She loves networking with other writers – and artists of other media – and runs a writing group that meets weekly at her local coffee shop.

Some of her other interests include coffee, photography, graphic design, social media, animals, art, travel, and music. Sarah currently resides with her family and cats in southern Illinois.

To learn more about Sarah, visit sarahjdhuephotos.com